BLIGHTCROSS

C. A. Lang

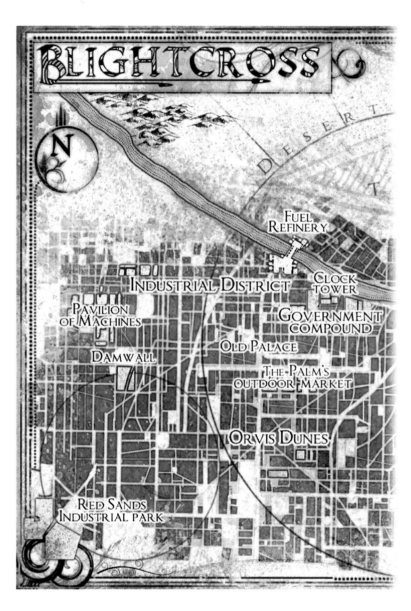

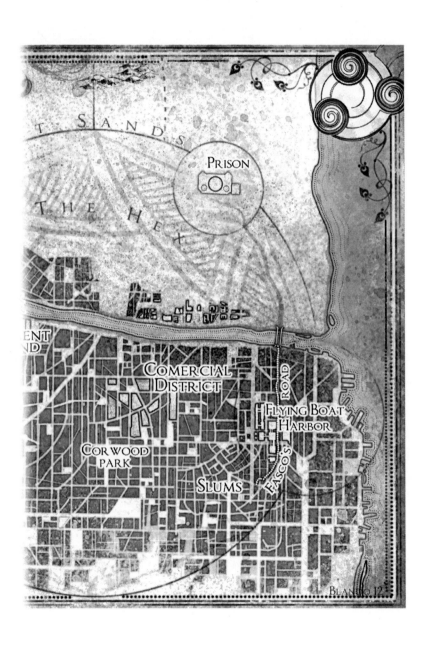

BLIGHTCROSS

C. A. Lang

TYCHE BOOKS LTD.

Blightcross: A Novel

Published by Tyche Books Ltd.
www.TycheBooks.com

Copyright © 2012 by C. A. Lang

Print ISBN: 978-0-9878248-2-0
Ebook ISBN: 978-0-9878248-3-7

Printed in the United States, United Kingdom and Australia
First Printing: 2012

Cover Art by Sarah Ellerton
Map by Jared Blando
Cover Layout by Lucia Starkey
Interior Layout by Tina Moreau
Editorial by M. L. D. Curelas

The publisher does not have any control over and does not assume any responsibility for author or third party websites or their content.

This story is a work of fiction. All of the characters, organizations and events portrayed herein are either products of the author's imagination or are used fictitiously.

For my mom and dad. ~ C. A. Lang

CHAPTER ONE

By now, the bumps, dips, and nauseating drops should have become commonplace. At least, that's what Capra had assumed. Four days aboard a flying boat ought to be more than enough time to grow accustomed to the strange sensations.

She had assumed wrong.

The green tint of the face frowning in the mirror told her so, if her roiling stomach wasn't enough. But a lady ought to keep herself composed, especially when she was pretending to be one. She plunged her hands into her purse, sifted through small tools and knives and other unladylike things, only to confirm her initial fear—she had forgotten makeup, and would have to settle with this unstylish shade of green. Yes, to any other woman, an arsenal of cosmetics would be second only to their wedding dress on such an occasion. But Capra had deeper concerns.

The bathroom mirror, all gilt and modern leaf designs, rattled against the wall. She steadied herself on the edge of the counter and swallowed hard. Wasn't there a pressure point in the wrists that could rid a person of seasickness? If, that is, being sick in the air was the same as being sick at sea.

A voice, deadened by the bathroom door, addressed her. "Darling, is everything all right?"

She bit her tongue and imagined herself standing on the dusty plains back home. Firmly planted. Firmly planted and not bobbing up and down and swaying and rolling...

"Everything's just fine, dear. I'll be right out." She turned around and craned to catch the back of her neck in the mirror, just to be sure that her collar still covered her tattoo. An army brand was the last thing she wanted to explain to the Baron.

She wrenched open the tap and plunged her hands into the trickle, splashed her face.

Baron Parnas, the old bastard. He just had to make it difficult. Why couldn't it have been a younger, more attractive man who had what she wanted?

No point in whining. It would be over soon enough. Just hold on long enough to do it all calmly and avoid being sloppy, and it would all fall into place. She straightened her back, adjusted the bejewelled clothes that Parnas had given to her. They were shapeless and boring, but apparently that was the style among these people.

Once she joined the Baron in their cabin, he frowned and said, "You're still looking a bit ill, Capra."

She made a vague gesture and began to pace. "Maybe we weren't meant to fly." All around her was the sound of creaking wood and a constant rush of the wind.

"Or maybe it's just that you Valoii have some catching up to do with the rest of us." He said this with a strange grin, and Capra wondered if revealing her nationality had been a mistake. "Unless your famed sheep herds have grown wings." He chuckled, but Capra couldn't see the humour in it. Some people evidently still thought it was acceptable to poke fun at a Valoii. But Parnas was old, and men of his generation might never pull abreast of the social progress that had burst like a fountainhead after the war. The Valoii were still backward in his mind, despite his romantic interest in Capra. That interest, she had figured out, was probably for the sake of novelty.

It wasn't all bad. She just found it hard to enjoy the intricate floral rugs, the stunning arrangements of diamonds and triangles in the wall parquetry, and the modern furniture under the circumstances. The peacock feather motifs and feminine figures reminded her of the sophisticated land she had just left, for which she already longed.

Parnas suggested they take a walk around the deck ringing the sides of the flying boat, and it was the best idea she'd heard from the Baron since she'd sent him that initial love letter. Fresh air—that's what she needed.

On through the corridors. Red carpet pillowed their feet like thick moss. Numerous times they met with the ship's servants, done up in their grey waistcoats and yellow sashes, and Capra flattened against the wall to let them through. She caught up with the Baron, who simply barrelled past oncoming traffic, outside.

Her balance took leave again, and the Baron caught her. She gave him a coy smirk and gripped the railing. Overhead, the flying boat's wings hung and flexed, and she caught a whiff of sulphur from the machine's many engines. "It's so different here. I didn't think Naartland was this barren."

"Much of it isn't, my lady. This is just the Blightcross Administrative District. The province to the north has fjords and rainforests, everything I told you about in our correspondence. You'll see once we get there."

The sky around the ship was a field of blazing orange, and the ground was more of the same. Sand, dunes, and a vein of dark water cutting into the heart of Blightcross proper. There hung a haze about the entire city, just enough to smooth over most of its details. She saw the basic outline—swaths of tall buildings, and at the far end, near the river, a monstrosity of what she guessed were pipes and conduits. At the centre of this stood the tallest structure in the city, and its immense height was about all she could glean from the smudged view.

She could only stare at the landscape below for thirty seconds before the rhythm of her stomach swirled and boiled again. She jammed shut her eyes and clutched the brass railing harder, tried to concentrate on calming her gut.

"You seemed somewhat more outgoing in our letters. I hope I have not disappointed you in some way," Parnas said.

A burst of cold air lashed her face, and she was thankful for the icy wind. Somewhere in the distance, thunder rocked the sky.

"Not at all, Baron." She cleared her throat. "I am sure once we clear this dreadful land, my mood will improve. I am somewhat sensitive to these things, you see."

"Ah, yes. Behind your fiery confidence, you are at heart a delicate lady."

She did a slight curtsy and smiled. Maybe it wasn't a lie after all—this odd place could be the reason for her illness. She had grown up in a desolate land, but she didn't remember it being like this place. There was an odd smell in the air, and each breath of it seemed to anchor the vertigo already plaguing her.

"But of course, Baron."

"Such manners for a Valoii. I still cannot quite believe what a wonderful find you are, my dear. It is simply exquisite."

She felt her cheeks flush. But Parnas wouldn't see the reaction through her olive skin, and besides, his flattery carried a cruel edge. Sure, many of her people were uneducated shepherds, but the times had changed, and she would wager that her education was far more extensive than the Baron's privileged upbringing.

On the other hand, he was treating her well. She could do far worse, and this was something she wanted to shove into the recesses of her conscience. She felt sick, and the last thing she needed was to feel sorry for Parnas.

"Baron, you'll spoil me with such flattery." The ship dropped for leagues, it seemed, and she felt the blood drain from her face as quickly as it had flushed.

"Perhaps we should see the ship's surgeon. It pains me to see you so uncomfortable. This should be a joyous trip, no?"

She nodded, then thought better of going back inside. At least the air out here was somewhat fresh. "It is joyous, Baron. I just need to get my bearings, that's all. I think if I gaze at the horizon for a few moments, my mind will right itself."

In the next while, she began to realize that Blightcross offered an attraction for the wealthy passengers. The deck soon filled with them—expensive frock coats and slim dresses, many of the men holding spyglasses and other devices even Capra could not identify, all with expectant looks and pointing at this or that feature.

Other than the peculiar monolith at the far edge of the city that appeared to grow out of the sand, and the strange odour endemic to the land, what could all the fuss be about?

For the first time since they had met in person, Parnas turned away and stared at someone other than Capra. She peered around him to find one of his business partners hurrying through the narrow deck. The man shoved one of the wealthy ladies aside, and when Parnas began to speak to his business partner, Capra at once felt invisible to them. She scanned the deck for a chair. There was one, right near Parnas' friend—

Just behind the man, she spotted him, and quite unexpectedly. Dannac, trying to mimic the look of ennui prevalent in the men around him but instead looking more like he was suffering from the same gastrointestinal upset Capra had just come to know.

She caught snippets from Parnas' conversation as she slowly angled around them to meet Dannac.

"I have a bad feeling, Parnas," Parnas' associate said.

"Come now. Your imagination is just getting the better of you. Perhaps it is this flying business. Are you new to it?"

"Baron, I am serious. That man has been following me. See? The one with the ridiculous jewel in his head?"

"I see nothing of the sort."

"I still think..."

Capra looked back to find the two men hunched close together. The bastard friend of Parnas' must be on to her scam. Parnas was trying to downplay it, but that little rat of a man with whom he did business with was clever. In all the dinners and parties she had attended with the Baron, that particular associate had never smiled nor kept his hands still and never failed to impress even Capra with his powers of observation and knowledge of every subject.

She found Dannac leaning over the railing like the others. "The rat man knows you're following him," she said.

Dannac kept his gaze on the city below. "I know. I will have to think of a way to calm his bloody nerves."

"Did you find it?"

He nodded.

"Then all we need to do is wait."

"If they keep it in the same locker. They might move it."

"I can't even imagine that right now, Dannac. Parnas is so not my type. This isn't the way I like to do business, either. I feel like..."

"Don't bother saying it."

She sighed. This was the last time, so maybe it was justified. But Capra knew what regrets could do to a person. They were not feelings she needed to renew.

The deck inclined, and Capra felt her feet slide towards the bow of the ship. A falling sensation ravaged her head.

"Are you okay?"

She held her hand in front of her and shut her eyes, while willing her stomach to behave. Deep breaths, calm, calm...

No use. She leaned over the railing, ready to concede. "Why won't it level?" she managed to say through gritted teeth.

"The flying boat is stopping in Blightcross. It is for a resupply or something like that."

It was coming—acid warmth crawling in her throat. But she suddenly realized that in the current social context, letting it go over the railing might betray her as the peasant she was.

So she slipped past Dannac and muscled through the crowd, hand held to her mouth. There was a public washroom just inside the aft exit...

All of this—flying, chronic lies, prostitution, for what? Mineral rights?

A clap of thunder shook the ship, and she reached the privy with a whole two seconds to spare. But while she vomited, she pictured handing the proceeds from her future mining operation to some corrupt Valoii official from her hometown in Mizkov.

*Blheeeeeeghhhhh here you are, General. *Burp* Call off your attack dogs. There's enough money here to outfit an entire aerial navy blehgghgouuug.*

She wiped her mouth, washed her hands under the pathetic trickle at the sink, and burst out the door feeling much more optimistic. Maybe if she had just allowed herself to throw up in the first place...

"Hello, Jorassian."

It was a male voice, and it spoke in Valoii.

She balled her hands into fists and would have rather vaulted over the rail outside than face the man. Not now. Not now, when she was so close...

"It's time to come back, Capra."

"I won't."

"Yes, you will."

Even though she knew this would eventually happen, she did not expect that Alim would be the man to bring her back to Mizkov. It must have been him—no one else spoke in that tone, specifically when stumbling over her family name. The way he stressed the first syllable... it had to be him.

"Alim?" Finally she faced him, all the while a ghost-image of the man burned in her mind's eye—average height, overworked biceps, and of course the blue eyes proven to be irresistible to Capra's friend from the battalion back home. The image blended with the man standing there, dagger in hand and beads of sweat along his hairline. "Tell them I'm dead. It's all you have to do. Everyone wins."

She expected him to at least show a flicker of recognition, but he kept his parade ground coldness.

"Deserters need to be brought to justice, Capra."

"They're just arbitrary rules, Alim. They don't protect anyone." She let out a nervous laugh. "They don't protect Mizkov."

He stepped forward, and for a moment, she swore that he showed subtle signs of agreeing with her, but the momentary softening of his face flashed back to its martial scowl. Was he brainwashed? There had to be something more to it.

"It's over, Jorassian." He waved the dagger. "Did you honestly think you could shrug away your service so easily? But that's something for the committee to deal with. Now, you can cooperate, or I can just kill you right here and we can all be assured that you won't be handing out secrets to our enemies just to spite us."

"No, that's not—"

He lunged forward. Capra, having been on edge since lifting off in this awful machine, dodged him and sprinted back towards the outer deck. She could find Dannac there, and there were enough people gazing at that awful city below to make it inconvenient for Alim to commit a field execution.

She glanced back to find two men trailing Alim, and they wore the same brown coats as Alim.

Of course he wouldn't have come alone.

During her dash through the crowd, the flying boat increased its descent. The passengers at the railing squealed at the sensation's novelty and clinked their glasses in that funny way westerners always did.

She collided with Dannac. "We have to go. Now."

"What?"

"Forget the claim. Forget the mine. We have to get away from here." She panted and glanced over her shoulder.

"And waste months of preparation? When we could have been doing real work, and now you want to just abandon it?"

She shoved him into an alcove. "The army. They've found me. They're here." She thought for a moment. "And this stop in Blightcross isn't for cargo or new passengers. Alim must have requested it so he can arrest me with the help of the local government."

"But—"

"Bloody Naartland, there's nothing they won't do to impress the big boys. They'll help anyone screaming about law and order and justice."

They could fight—two against three was not the worst situation they had dealt with, but now Alim probably had the ship's security under his command. Even though she was confident in their ability to escape, it was the last thing she wanted to do, other than die or face her superiors. Running would mean throwing away her ticket to freedom—barrels full of money, courtesy of the Baron's blasé mixing of business with his personal life.

She gestured to Dannac's forehead, which was covered by a stylish hat. "Can you see them?"

She watched Dannac, in particular the dead left eye. There were twitches of movement, but it was all random; it was the jewel buried beneath the hat on his forehead that gave him sight. Still, since the clear stone neither blinked nor moved in its socket, Capra associated Dannac's injured eye with his strange witch-sight.

"I see nobody coming that way. Maybe they went around the other side."

A large form swooped in to block the alcove, and the orange sunlight vanished like a snuffed candle. "I say, what is the meaning of this?"

She recognized the man's billowing blue cape, and the smell of clove cheroots had become a familiar stink during the past three days.

"Parnas," she said, affecting a girlish tone. "I..." They were no longer after the documents stashed with his business partners. She could just tell him to sod off and be done with the old bastard.

She looked to Dannac, but he just shrugged.

"Listen, Baron..."

"Yes? Have I done something to offend you? Something that makes you want to punish me with this... obvious display of discontent?"

"Well, actually—"

"I suppose I should have known that an exotic beauty such as yourself would be socially incapable of being my wife." Parnas sighed and dabbed his cheek with a handkerchief. "The barbarian women are impossible to train properly. I should have listened to their endless warnings! Oh, but it was just too tempting."

She opened her mouth to tell him that she wasn't lusting after another man, that she had aimed only to steal his business prospects, but stopped. There were soldiers from her homeland searching the ship for her, and each second she stood there like a stunned pig meant that the odds of escaping were significantly less, but she couldn't ravage the old bastard's fragile heart so callously. Not after hearing so much about the man's mother. Something about that kind of familiarity made her unwilling to deliberately hurt him.

"Parnas, I should have told you. I didn't think it would matter, but clearly it does." She glanced to Dannac. "Every Valoii girl is sold into marriage at the age of ten. I was promised to this man before the war. You see, the war had ruined marriage plans all over, and only just now did he find me. I am afraid that no matter how much I love you, I cannot break my parents' honour. I belong to this man."

Parnas leaned forward slightly. "Is that so? I had no idea." There was a hint of understanding in his voice. She half wondered if he thought it was interesting and romantic.

"Yes, and if I do not obey, he has the legal right to murder my family and take their land."

"Oh, I do see. Well, what if I just killed him?"

Dannac moved his head from side to side slow enough and frowned deeply enough that no living person could miss the signal of intimidation.

"But I will miss you, my dear."

"And I you."

She curtsied to him once more, and pulled Dannac out of the alcove. It felt as though she had cut the act short at the wrong time, but under the circumstances about all she had time for was a quick lie. Let Parnas wonder. It would keep him busy enough to stop his sobbing.

They jogged around the outer deck, towards the one of the propellers at the ship's tail. There was a vibration in her feet, and a clattering that sounded like a mechanical heartbeat.

Now the tall structure at the far end of the city stretched above them, and it appeared to reach farther into the sky than they had ever flown. The weak sun spilled across its polished surface, and some of the tower's details now showed through the haze. She bent backward to see the top, and found a gigantic clock face near the top. Below them flowed the dark river in which the flying boat would land.

"How far are we to the dock, do you think?" she asked Dannac. "The boat is practically in the water."

He grunted something and looked over the edge. "Too far for what you're thinking."

Behind them, the crowd began to part and jostle. Unless there was a sudden epidemic of what she had experienced a few minutes before and the impromptu party outside had become a battle royal for the privy, it had to be Alim.

"Are you sure?"

He looked over the edge once more, then towards the disrupted crowd. "Maybe not so much."

She scanned the layout below. There was a raised structure where the ship would moor, presumably after its already low speed dwindled to that of a proper boat and allowed it to turn around. On this stood three brass poles, on which flapped the flags of Naartland, Tamarck, and a rose emblem she had never seen before.

"We could still steal the deed, Capra."

"Are you insane? You of all people should know what Alim and his men are capable of."

"I think it's no more insane than your plan to jump off this ship. We can blend in with the passengers and disappear into the city once it lands."

"Alim won't allow that. He has the full cooperation of the government here. I know it. He wouldn't have revealed himself to me otherwise. I know how the Valoii military operates, Dannac. Did you forget about the tattoo around my neck?"

He gazed at the ground, which was slowly moving closer. "Either way, we're stuck in Blightcross." He growled.

"Come on, Dannac. At least this way we get a head start. There will be other jobs."

"But the point of this one was that it would be the last job either of us would need."

"There's money here. The Baron talked about it last night. Blightcross runs some kind of factory that produces... well, I'm not sure exactly what it was, but old Parnas was quite impressed with the place."

He snorted. "A factory?"

"Come on, there will be something for us here. There has to be. Forget about the mining scam."

She kicked off her uncomfortable shoes, and they tumbled across the deck only to disappear among scattering passengers. Without any of her previous hesitation, she hopped onto the railing, stayed there in a crouch, balanced on the thin bar of metal. "Well?"

"I still cannot fathom why your people allow women like you to fight as men would." Dannac tossed his hat over the edge and shrugged out of his frock coat. "Nor can I fathom why I continue to listen to you."

She grinned and stood, the brass comforting and cool against her bare feet.

"I say, clear the way, all of you." Alim brandished his Mizkov Defence Force issue stiletto at the crowd. Spoiled trash, the lot of them. All he found were confused stares, indignant ladies likely shocked that their luxury voyage had been tainted by such a display. Unfortunately, none of them seemed to recognize his weapon, or his tattoo. They had no idea that he was a soldier.

Where were the ship's guards? They could clear this deck in a heartbeat simply by showing up in their leather armour. Never mind that he had let Jorassian—

Or Capra, as he had known her in another life, before things had become complicated.

—bowl him over and escape. He had been hanging around outsiders too long, and their prejudices were creeping into him. A woman was just as deadly as a man, and he knew this because every Valoii knew this. Every Valoii knew this because after the war they had vowed never again to be caught off guard and victimized and slaughtered, and this included turning every healthy person into a soldier, regardless of their genitals.

Capra Jorassian - Specialist Armswoman, 2nd Class
#336 - 237 - 539.
Assignment: 5 Battalion, Veta's Swords
Status: Deserter.

That's all she was to him now. It's all she could be, and even that was generous considering that her unit had been all but destroyed during the border skirmish she had fled. That was the kind of dereliction one was taught to take personally.

He had to grit his teeth and push through the crowd, and concentrate equally as much to block out memories of Jorassian as an innocent school girl in her uniform, trading state-supplied rations at lunch and joking about the stupid fat literature instructor.

Status: Deserter.

He moved faster, and was relieved when he met with a squad of ship's guard, led by the sergeant-at-arms. Alim had spoken with the red-haired man on several occasions since he had arrived three days ago, and was glad to see him.

"They've gone aft," the sergeant said.

Alim clapped him on the shoulder and loped onward.

"There's nowhere for them to go, Valoii. Relax."

But he could not relax. His fingers wrapped around the stiletto vibrated with anticipation. He wanted a superior to reassure him, to say, "Yes, Alim, go ahead and kill one of Mizkov's precious daughters. She has proven irredeemable. Kill her. Kill her."

This kind of idle speculation would be the end of him. Anxiety wouldn't stop him from finishing this. He was fortunate to be given this special assignment, far from the disputed zones.

"Watch out for the Ehzeri," he said to his two men. "There is something different about him. Some new Ehzeri trick, I suppose." He flipped the stiletto in his hand.

"Magic," one of his men said. "Nothing new about that."

"But be aware anyway. Somehow I think that jewel in his head gives him more than what the average Ehzeri is capable of. Perhaps it gives him divine strength, or invulnerability."

They moved closer to the ship's engines, where a banging rumble shook deep inside his head, muddied his thoughts. There were no passengers outside down here, and no wonder. He could now see the stern, with its own engines placed on either side of a giant fin. Nobody there, but that didn't mean they weren't hiding behind a pipe or one of the crates stacked by the railing.

"Leave Jorassian to me."

The men mumbled their affirmatives.

When they reached the end of the wrap-around deck, Alim stood dumbfounded. He checked behind the crates—nobody there. Behind a pipe—nothing. After a moment of paralysis, he went to the railing and peered at the jetty below. The ground moved at a crawl underneath them, and there he glimpsed a black hat of the Tamarck fashion. Beside it was what looked like a ripped bottom half of a woman's dress.

The sergeant sauntered over, took position beside Alim. He looked at the jetty casually. "Well, I don't suppose you'll have to worry about them now. They couldn't have survived a jump, even if they had done it at this height. Probably they smacked the wharf and bounced into the river."

Alim's throat became dry and his face became hot. "I would not be so sure."

"Well, you tried your best."

Alim sneered at the sergeant. "How long will it take for this thing to dock?"

"Ten minutes and they'll lower the stairs, I imagine."

"Can you get a message to the authorities on the ground?"

"You see a signalman out there?"

Alim narrowed his eyes. It wasn't enough to swindle the transport company into cooperating with his orders. Now he would have to convince the law in this city to take Jorassian as a serious threat. Without help from the government here, she might disappear into the crowd again.

No. One thing he knew for sure—Jorassian would never again cross the Blightcross Administrative District's borders alive. She had always been stubborn and refused to concede, to the point of insisting they go into best-of-seven matches during their childhood. She made it difficult, but once someone beat her, she fell hard.

CHAPTER TWO

The now floating flying boat loomed over the city block, and Capra still felt uncomfortable with the huge bird-like shape. It seemed an affront to nature that such a thing could lumber into the air after a few minutes at sea.

She flexed her hands and rubbed them. They glowed red and there were bits of shredded skin, but otherwise the flagpole slide had gone better than she had anticipated.

Capra tore the shawl from her shoulders and dropped it to her side, where it settled among enough trash that the action must have been local custom. She rummaged in the satchel that now contained everything she owned and retrieved a red cravat. The thing ought to be enough to cover both the tattoo around her throat, as well as the burn scar across her shoulder.

It would do until she could find less daintier clothes. Hopefully she'd find something suitable here, but looking at the shapeless garb many of the richer citizens wore, she doubted it. There was no indication of the kind of fashion she had seen in the Little Nations, and this was perhaps the largest regret she had about meeting Dannac and entering the trade of thievery.

Dannac hurried behind. "So what do you plan on doing now? Besides drawing attention to yourself by wearing a man's garment."

"Leave this island, for one. Then it's back to the same old grind, I suppose." She dodged a trail of broken glass. In fact, the entire road glittered with shards of coloured glass, jagged metal, and empty cans. If only she had some decent shoes... "And I don't see how a cravat can only be worn by men." She

15

grinned and decided that she would wear this cravat at every opportunity.

She also expected that her torn dress, now barely covering her rear, might attract attention from the people they passed in the street. But these people, an odd mix of Ehzeri in their white cloaks, soot-smeared faces in tough blue clothing of a style Capra had never seen before, and men in proper evening dress, barely glanced at her. There was a whir of machines, like the flying boat's drone, all around. There were a few pack animals pulling carts, but not nearly as many as she would expect in a city of this size.

Her mouth went slack, as though she'd stepped into a dream. The smell of the place was not the banal stink of human waste, but something more peculiar that burned in her throat. And all the Ehzeri... what were they doing here? Perhaps Dannac would know, but for the moment all she could do was take in the tall structures, the clouds of smoke (and it was not coal smoke, but billowing white clouds of a size she thought impossible to be created by humans), and strange sounds.

The trance shattered when something hard knocked her aside. She fell onto a boardwalk, sprung upright, ready to kill, and found Dannac glaring at her. In the street, a carriage sped past, and there was that odd clattering-belching sound she kept hearing.

"Pay attention. The streets here are not for walking."

"Magic reigns here, then? There was nothing pulling that carriage... and all of the Ehzeri here..."

"No. *Vihs* was not at work there. I had heard that a lot of young people were giving up on joining the raids and coming to Naartland to work, but most of them were from depleted families. I think the Ehzeri here have nothing to offer but their labour. My people would not come to this place just to sell their birthright for a wage." He gazed to the horizon for a moment. "Sometimes I wish I could just go back and find out what is really going on with my people."

Dannac didn't wax wistful very often, and when he did, Capra's reaction was to pull him out of it as soon as possible. "Then what do you call all of this? It sure smacks of magic to me." She gestured at the wide road, strange contraptions bracing skeletons of towers in the distance, and noisy carriages.

"We should keep going. I don't want to be anywhere near that thing once it docks."

They were only a few blocks from the dock, and Dannac was right. A head start was something she didn't want to waste. It was just that the place was so unfamiliar, and not in the way that the Little Nations were. Her feelings here were a negative image of her travels on the continent. A bizarre reversal.

They hurried through an alley, wended through makeshift tents and ignored pleas for pocket change neither were in a position to give.

"So you know that soldier?" Dannac asked, once they came to a street with less traffic and beggars.

"Alim? Yes, unfortunately. Mizkov is small, and since we're all shoved into the service... well, everyone knows everyone. We have to rebuild Valoii unity, after all. I guess it works, in some ways."

"We ought to just kill him and get on with it."

She stopped. "No." And Dannac kept walking.

Over his shoulder, he said, "You've left your country, Capra. They mean nothing to you."

Was it true? Did she no longer care about everyone she knew, and the few Valoii that were left? Did she care about the new state they had been given by Tamarck, did she care for the bright new future promised to her and her descendants?

She broke into a jog to catch up with her Ehzeri friend. Her only friend, because friends like Alim only lasted as long as the correct national allegiances were reaffirmed with pledges and service to vague ideals and the oppression of the people their new state had displaced. Oh, how she wanted to do her part, to protect their borders the way she had been ordered. But some things were not worth giving up one's humanity.

"Look, Alim's just having fun on a paid-for trip around the known world just to track down deserters. We've dealt with worse before—like King Rotanour's Lancers. Or that time with the pirates. Pirates, Dannac. Alim's nothing."

He grumbled something.

She tried to affect a flippant tone, but wasn't sure if it worked. "We need to find work. Forget Alim."

"I work best when I can sleep without constantly watching the door."

"We haven't been able to do that since we met."

Dannac nodded slowly, then laughed. "Pirates."

By the Great Golden Ram, this man will not stop until he turns piss into ambrosia. Vasi held the object into the light and examined the intricate carvings. It was a diamond-shaped bauble, plated with etched copper. There had to be something else underneath the metal facade, since it was far too heavy. Lead, perhaps?

The stained glass arch across from her scattered sparkles of blue, red and orange along the artifact's surface. She shut her eyes and tried to feel out any potential *vihs* inherent in the object, but all she saw was the blackness and random sparkles of her own closed eyes, and sensed little more than cold weight inside the trinket.

Vasi set it on the table and made a note in her log. *Piece #0342: Koratian Ornament, circa 4560 U.E. Preliminary test: negative.*

No surprise, at least to her. It was too bad that Till Sevari ignored her warning that the artifact was nothing of importance. Another instance of Sevari cultivating too much hope before obtaining the appropriate information. Yet Vasi would not complain about living high in the clock tower to perform busywork for the chief administrator of Blightcross district. This was more than any Ehzeri could have dreamed of.

It might be a waste of her *vihs-draaf*, her work-skills, to aid Sevari in his occult curiosities. But the Ehzeri had to change with the times.

She gazed at the artifact with a satisfied grin. Things would improve for them all. The money she made here would stop the raids, break down barriers, save her family...

She stifled a cough and brought the ornament back to its shelf at the end of the chamber. Her footsteps sent clouds of dust into the spikes of coloured light from the stained glass.

She would have to call in the maintenance crew to give the place a quick cleaning. It was just that the maintenance crews were mostly Ehzeri from depleted families, and what could she say to them? Sorry for your misfortune, look at my huge paycheck and personal laboratory?

There was a knock at the door. Since part of the lab's security measures were that the doors were not equipped with handles, she willed the locks to unlatch and opened it with a quick discharge of her power. She scrambled across the lab where the refinery's mail clerk stood, holding a yellow envelope. His skin was grey and dull. She wondered if the man ever passed through the refinery's outer gates.

He held the envelope up to her. She instantly recognized her own writing. "I am sorry miss, but you forgot the postage."

She rolled her eyes. He couldn't have just taken care of it and billed her? "Oh, sorry. Sevari's got me working extra shifts up here. I don't know what I was thinking." She bit her lip, trying not to become angry at the fellow. "This month's ship... has it already gone?"

The clerk nodded. "Sorry, miss." He looked at his shoes and she knew that he understood how important the postal service was to most of the refinery's Ehzeri workers. There was no point in raising the issue and acting upset.

"Is there any way I could send it on one of the luxury ships?"

He scratched his head and peered inside. Vasi moved to block his view of the laboratory. "Afraid not. Those ships are already spoken for. Every last tenth of an ounce of weight."

She let out a deep breath. It was worth a try, anyway. After motioning for the clerk to stay where he was, Vasi hurried into the lab and found her satchel draped across the back of a chair. She sifted through copies of bank receipts, the few letters from home she'd saved, and jars of various remedies to find her bag of coins.

The clerk was gawking from his station in the hall, and it made her feel naked. Nobody had told her explicitly that mail clerks were forbidden from viewing her lab, but these days, who knew what people outside Sevari's research staff might think about the old *vihs* practices?

"There. That should cover it." She pressed a few coins into the clerk's hand.

He sifted through them once, and repeated the motion. "Look, it's uh... gone up."

"Gone up?"

"Postage to Mizkov."

"I know that, but why?"

"Just the way it goes." He wiped his forehead with the back of his hand. "You could always send it surface. Half the price..."

"And it still won't get there by the time next month's flying boat comes through." She went to get another coin.

"Smart move. I hear the seagoing ships don't get into Mizkov so easily these days. Something about—"

"I know," she said. "I know." It was just hard to hear a Naartlander's skewed version of her people's problems. They knew nothing of the situation, only the filtered bits that made it all the way across the ocean. Only the bits that served the Valoii, their foster parent state Tamarck, and Naartland.

And never mind the irony of her own people sinking the very ships used to carry the mail bags that carried hundreds, if not thousands, of bank notes sent by their own families meant to help them end the violence.

Once she paid the clerk, he leaned in close and looked about, eyes darting. "Now, I wasn't going to say anything..." He tried to see past her once more, but she edged the door closed enough to shut him out. "But I thought you should know."

"Know what?"

"They've found another body."

"Another body?"

"You haven't heard anything?"

She thought for a moment. "Well, no. I don't hear much news up here. This part of the tower is quiet, you see. And I have a lot of research... I mean work, to do for Sevari."

"Ah. Well, let's just say that they found another Ehzeri body in the refinery. I think you should be careful."

It didn't faze her at all; she had the second most secure room in the entire complex. "Thank you for the warning, sir."

He stepped closer. "But don't say anything. The staff are trying to keep it quiet, right? They can't have the workers panic. If they find out that I told you..."

"I have better things to do than gossip, you know."

"Good, good." He waved the envelope. "See you next month. And for the love of God, stay safe."

She uttered goodbye to him, and watched him scuttle towards the elevator.

Now, why hadn't Sevari warned her? The rules for research workers were totally different from the regular rules, and this should apply to sharing important information as well. Wouldn't Sevari want his precious Ehzeri minions to watch out for a potential killer? Ehzeri with enough skill to do what he wanted weren't nearly as common as the ones he employed in the refinery.

Paranoia, that's all. Sevari probably just didn't want to disrupt her concentration. Besides, he would have informed the security staff, and protecting the refinery was their job, after all, not hers.

The hall shuddered with the clank and rattle of the elevator. Out of the second one at the other end of the hall walked a boy in blue coveralls. She squinted and tried to figure out why there was a worker in this wing of the tower, before realizing who it was.

"Rovan?" She came into the hall, reaching out to the door with her mind to close it and secure the locks. There was a slam behind her, and a drum roll of lock-fastening.

"Ha ha, you missed the ship, eh?"

At once she remembered the clerk's warning and glanced around the dark, metallic corridor. "What are you doing up here alone? And yes, I did miss the mail this time. I hope you didn't."

"Oh no, my package went all right. Mom's going to have a new favourite, and it won't be you."

Vasi punched him in the shoulder. "You didn't answer me. What are you doing up here?"

He shrugged. "Just wanted to see how you were doing."

"And they allowed you to come here?"

He smirked. "Of course they did. I'm your brother. They wouldn't keep us apart, would they?" The kid knew of her privileged position, and she wondered if he meant that as a sarcastic remark. He didn't appear to have any *vihs-draaf* whatsoever, like many of his generation, and his labour was strictly manual. Vasi knew why, as everyone did, but nobody wanted to talk about it, especially the empowered ones working for Sevari. People like Vasi.

No, there was something cocky about the boy now, and it wasn't bitterness about the discrepancy between the two. Maybe he met a girl he liked. That usually turned a sixteen-year-old male into an ornery little bastard.

"You shouldn't be walking around this place alone."

Rovan rolled his eyes and scuffed his heavy boots along the floor. "What's going to happen in a stupid clock tower? Just a bunch of mouldy books and stupid things. At least the rest of the refinery has machines."

"There's a murderer around."

He made a noise. "Whatever."

"I am serious, Rovan. Someone is after people like us."

"Like us? You mean you or me?"

For a moment, her heart sank. "Like both of us. There's no difference between us, Rovan. I wish you could see that."

"Oh, sure." There was sarcasm, but no bitterness this time. "Look, I wouldn't want your job anyway. The door is always locked. I bet you couldn't leave even if you wanted to." He flashed his hand, and on his fingers gleamed a single copper ring, with a clump of blue glass set into it. "I'll be just fine without your old ways, sister. I'm going to get rich. Even if it kills me." He smirked and made a stupid gesture.

"Stop that."

"Just like Sevari. I heard he has a room full of women he owns, and that he also sells them on the side."

She slapped him lightly on the back of his head. "Rovan, shut up. He does not."

"He's rich. I'm going to be like that some day, and all without any of your *vihs* stupidness."

It was enough to make her stand there silent and blinking. Perhaps puberty was hitting Rovan just a year or two later than normal. She had to come to terms with the reality that she could no longer dictate his behaviour, and that the gulf between them might only widen.

"I think you should find a better role model."

"Sevari has lots of gold. Didn't you notice?"

She pressed her hand to her face. Had she been this bad at his age? Of course not. This attitude was new and specific to young Ehzeri males raised in the shanty surrounding the refinery. In fact, their obsession with gaudiness and wealth made it entirely possible that one of them was responsible for these murders the postal clerk mentioned. All the more reason for her brother to smarten up and keep near a guard whenever possible.

"Sevari has more than just gold, Rovan," she said with a grave tone.

"Oh yeah?"

"Mmhm. Now get out of here before I drop a message to your overseer." She held back a litany of comments, directives, and sage advice. She had to settle with the comfort of knowing that Rovan had escaped a life—likely very short—of cultivating hatred for the Valoii and raiding their settlements. Maybe it wasn't an ideal transformation, but it was more than they could have hoped for.

Rovan batted the air. "Yeah, I'm so scared."

She watched him trot away, kicking at random debris in the hall. For a moment she wished to be back in the refinery, where she could keep an eye on him. He may be a decent worker with enough ambition to get by, but he was no fighter.

If he died here, she would be responsible. Both in her family's opinion, and her own. Maybe pulling him out of Mizkov had been a mistake...

Vasi hurried back to her lab. The hallway was too cold, too dark. But if she could face this killer in place of Rovan, she would without a sliver of hesitation. The postwar zeitgeist might deem her *vihs* outdated, but it was more defence than Rovan possessed.

She checked the locks, just to be sure. Now, faced with a dozen benches loaded with various works in progress, shelves teetering under the burden of too many un-catalogued artifacts, and the high stained glass windows depicting flowing, bright feminine goddesses framed by leaves, Vasi began to think—was there a way to find this person before they had the chance to take Rovan?

Or should she just send him home? But he would never agree to return, not with the illusion of wealth... and there was still a part of Vasi that was relieved that he would never go back if it meant he would never know the horror of the resistance movement. The same horror she fought daily to forget.

Leave it to the security forces. You have enough to worry about here.

"Debt collection? Are you serious?"

Capra smirked and shrugged and slumped against the brick wall. She glanced around the wall, into the street—a habit she had been unable to shake since going on the run—and when she was satisfied that Alim and the army was nowhere to be found, she relaxed a little.

"Yes," she said. "A job is a job, right?"

Dannac pinched the bridge of his nose. His right eye closed, but the left remained open and twitched slightly. "I have acted as the bodyguard for the Bhagovan parliamentarians. I have assassinated Tamish agitators. I have broken into the banks of Yahrein to steal back what they took from us during the war. I will not descend to the level of... debt collector."

He had a point. They were a different class of undesirable. But this was the wrong time for caprice. "Easy for you to say. You're not the one stuck with bare feet and half of a stupid dress."

She had paced around the dingy lunch counter for an hour, and this had been the only job she could find. They needed to eat, at the very least. When she had spotted a grey-haired gentleman in the process of roughing up one of the men in blue, it had seemed like the opportunity they needed. And it was—the man was eager for some help.

It didn't take long for it to sink in exactly why the man was willing to part with twenty pistres each in exchange for completion of a "small errand."

Dannac went back into the street, and she followed him. "Listen, it's not so bad. It's just a simple eviction, you see. I mean, unless the man has the money, but I don't think anyone is expecting that."

He spun round and she collided with him. The thump reminded her of the sound of a body collapsing on a marble floor. "An eviction? Well, you would know about those, wouldn't you?"

"That was cheap."

"It was the truth."

She stared at him for a moment, and there would have been uncomfortable silence were it not for the otherworldly clanking hammering the air from all directions.

"Listen," she said, having already learned not to take these kinds of remarks too personally. "The man just wants us to kindly escort from the premises a single occupant who hasn't paid in months. We barely have to do anything, and he said he'll pay us half up front. Even if he stiffs us for the rest, it's still a steal."

He let out a low growl.

"Otherwise we might as well just set up camp here in this alley with these fine people here." She glanced to where three people huddled under a makeshift lean-to. There was a pall of smoke above them, yet the chemical burn in her nose could not be burning scraps of food or smouldering cheroots.

"Ten up front?"

"That's right. Ten up front, and that's for each of us. All we have to do is meet him at his property."

She braced for another of his diatribes about how he would only work for the rich, and only work against the rich, and how he would not profit from stomping on people who had nothing. She stared at the hazy orange sky, tracked the flying boat's course to the northern province that had been their original destination. She was somewhat disappointed, since she had never seen fjords before, or the large sea mammals she had heard about.

He simply nodded and said, "All right."

"What?"

"I heard some of the elites on the ship talking about this place. I think it would be best if we didn't have to sleep under a bridge tonight."

"What did you hear?"

"Mostly indignation about the crime rates and praise for the district's oligarch."

"Till Sevari?"

He nodded, and they continued their stroll through the city. She squinted at the smudged scrawl on the back of her hand and tried to remember their client's directions. He had mentioned something about an underground transport system, but he might as well have been directing her to the edge of the world for all she understood.

A few blocks deeper into the city, they found buildings in which the setting sun blazed through giant gashes in the masonry, and Capra was never sure which buildings were part of the city's fever of construction or which were derelict. But once they went west, towards what the nameless man at the lunch counter had called Corwood Park, Capra's sweaty clenched hands relaxed at the sight of the neat rows of townhomes. High rent areas, reasonable people. The guy from whom they needed to collect probably had just run into some bad luck and would offer no resistance.

She smiled lightly, and Dannac glared at her, as if the minute gesture were the equivalent to laughing at a funeral. "Why does everyone your age smile at their own abject failure?"

"I wasn't smiling at our failure. It's just that these rows of homes are almost like the little towns in Uvrow. It was cold there, but I really liked the pubs. There was always a good pub down the road from wherever you were staying."

"Do you ever stop thinking about the continent? Those bloody Little Nations?"

"No. It's all that keeps me going, Dannac. I thought you would have known that by now."

"I thought you wanted to own a restaurant. You can do that anywhere. If you were smart, you'd do it here in Blightcross. The business growth here seems unprecedented."

"I never said I wanted to own anything." But before she could drift into fluffy visions of her plans, she found the street in question and began to search for the address written on her hand. "It should be right here..."

She scanned the block for any sign of the grey-haired man they were to meet. She found him pacing in front of one of the townhouses, cracking his knuckles and wringing his hands.

"Sir! My colleague and I have decided to accept your offer."

"Ah. Are you sure?" He looked at Dannac for a moment, and the questioning lines in his forehead smoothed, as if the Ehzeri's presence had answered a silent question about how this woman was going to perform an eviction.

Capra extended her hand to the man. He ignored the gesture. He ignored her altogether, and she couldn't understand why, since he had given her his attention at the lunch counter.

"Now," the man said to Dannac, "I should tell you that this man has dispatched two bailiffs previously."

"What do you—"

Dannac raised his hand and cut her off. "Just the one man?"

"Of course."

"I have dealt with worse."

The man's eyes flicked to Capra. "She one of your healers? Is that your edge?"

Dannac nodded.

She tried again. "But—"

"Just one condition. I want all of the money up front. You can stay here and watch. I can assure you the fight will not last long, if he chooses to start one."

The man chewed his lip and fiddled with the buttons on his coat. All the while, Capra's gaze flitted between both men, and she wondered if she had stepped into a vivid dream where she had become a phantom. The men seemed to have an understanding, or at least Dannac was pretending that they did. Had the man thought that Capra were just a runner, just a secretary, for Dannac?

It was unthinkable.

But, she reminded herself, the rest of the world was not used to new ways of the Valoii.

"Fine." The man dropped four coins into Dannac's palm. She was about to snatch her share from him, but by now realized that the act was important.

Dannac kicked open the iron gate, and there was the sound of snapping metal. Capra skittered behind.

"Try not to damage the new wainscoting!"

She assumed that Dannac would know what that meant, because he casually raised his hand and said nothing to the man. They stopped at the door, where he pounded four times on the deep red wood.

"Can you see inside?" she asked.

"I can. There is only one person inside, upstairs." He knocked again. "And he is not moving."

"Maybe he's dead?"

He raised an eyebrow. "The dead appear differently to me, unless freshly deceased. This man is as orange as you or I."

Only now did she realize the implications of having left everything behind on the ship. She had no weapons, except the switchblade she always carried hidden in the ornamental band on her left arm.

Anyway, it was just one man who couldn't afford to pay his own rent. She wouldn't need an arsenal for that.

"Why did you ignore me just now?"

"The man expected it. Most do, Capra."

"It seems worse here. Back in the—"

"This is not the Little Nations." He gazed around the side of the house. "I think we should go around back."

So they left the porch, while the man from the lunch counter stood with his arms crossed and puffed on a metal pipe. They ducked under clothes flapping in the breeze, and nearly tripped over a couch that was inexplicably lying askew on the grass at the rear of the house. Dannac gave a quick nod, then smashed open the back door with his boot.

It would be quick, especially since Dannac could pinpoint the man's location through the walls. His strange sight almost made up for his attitude.

He couldn't see the colour of a person's skin, or pick up on their finer features. Still, he knew she was a Valoii. Why had he chosen to stay with her?

He took point, and went straight for the front of the house, as if he already knew the layout. She followed and fell into her usual role of sharp observer, which usually meant watching for panels in the floor that didn't look quite right, or authority-types closing in on their rear. But this time, she saw only dirt-smudged floorboards, empty shelves, and rubbish strewn about. There were no authority-types to watch for. This time, they were the authority. An uncomfortable thought.

They went upstairs, and Dannac's footsteps boomed throughout the house. Capra stepped lightly out of habit, and reached to her armband to retrieve the switchblade.

"Time to give it up," Dannac said. His voice echoed in hall.

He approached a doorway, to which he gestured with a jerk of his head. He stepped into the room.

"Don't make me—"

There was a sudden charge in the air, and a chill crawled beneath Capra's skin. There was an undefined grunt from Dannac, and thunder—

Dannac flew from the room and slammed into the wall across from Capra. She gripped her little knife and, after she saw Dannac shaking his head, showing he was still alive, crept around the doorway.

She poked her head around first. But a confused breath caught between her lips once she saw inside. She didn't expect that the force that had slammed Dannac out of the fight would be an obese, sweaty man, nearly passed out in the corner of a bare room. All around him there were smoked glass bottles, and a host of metal utensils—spoons and other devices she was too anxious to place.

"Whatever you do, do it now!" Dannac's voice was gravelly and weak.

She gulped. The man was just lying there, eyes bloodshot and mired by a sickly cloudiness, and she did not want to accept that he was also drooling. He raised a hand, muttered something, and she felt it again—

A buzz, a thrill, something to which she had been taught by her countrymen to react with deadly force...

It triggered her senses and training so that she dodged the man's etheric attack, and leaped across the room faster than the man's pathetic eyes could track. The room took on a surreal quality—it was the first time in nearly a year that she had needed to use the *vihs* sensitization instilled in her by the army. This man was an Ehzeri. A powerful one.

The skin on her forearms prickled, and she watched him for the subliminal cues she instinctively scrutinized every *vihs*-capable Ehzeri for by sheer habit of her training. She brought the knife into a ready position and widened her stance.

There was a dust storm that day, and her platoon had donned their dark green head scarves. The suspected Ehzeri compound was not much of a compound at all, just a collection of tents baking in the sun...

Her mouth turned dry, and she hesitated to strike. "Look... you've got a problem... I can see that..."

Dannac called out from the hall: "Don't talk to him, kill him!"

She ignored him. "There must be a place you can go."

The man shifted and knocked over several bottles. "Need more of it. Got to. You?"

What was he asking for? Medicine? No, there was something else wrong with him. She tried to think of her training, of what this kind of erratic *vihs* discharge could result from. Emotional turmoil, illness, inebriation, old age—

Whatever the cause, she had to act before the charge racing through the air and tingling her skin reached its critical point and the man attacked her once again.

She flipped the knife around, and was about to dart in close enough to put the man into a hold, when it came.

All she saw was a crackling light spread across her eyes. When a breath later she opened them, she lay crumpled in the corner opposite the Ehzeri. Her head ached, and any amount of light only acted as a hammer to pound the pain deeper into her skull.

Fat man, magic gone awry, paid in full...

There still pressed in her palm the reassuring bulk of her knife. There was still time to—

A metallic glint sailed through the room, followed by a meaty thud. She gathered herself, recoiled once she found the Ehzeri spewing blood from his head. A small hatchet stuck from his forehead.

Dannac stumbled in and helped her stand. "I told you to kill him." Her legs cramped, and she was instantly reminded of the familiarization training, of being intentionally attacked by a magic wielder. "You should be dead."

She leaned on her thighs and tried to catch her breath. "I didn't think we'd be sent to remove a *vihs*-capable squatter. I didn't think there was any of that going on here."

"Me neither." There was a hard note in his voice, more than usual.

"Do you gain satisfaction from taking down someone from a family who still has power? With a dull hatchet, no less."

He pulled the weapon from the dead man's wound and dropped it. "Come on, the man outside paid us to remove this person. He may be dead, but he is still here."

Vasi's nose twitched at the smell of the ancient book pressed against her face. Her eyes felt stiff and her heart jolted at the sudden awakening. When she opened her eyes, she found herself sprawled across one of her lab's many benches.

A pounding arose from the door. Frantic pounding. "Vasi, open this door right now. Are you in trouble in there? Hm?"

She stood, dazed for a moment. The dream was still there, like a translucent blanket draped over her perception. Blackness, like in that horrible painting she had been analyzing... complete blackness, as if she were in the painting's presence and being drawn into its abyss.

"Vasi!" More pounding.

Sevari. What did he want? She braced herself and concentrated on the heavy door's locks. It took more effort to move them than usual, thanks to the black dream dampening her thoughts.

Sevari stormed in, all polished boots and crisp brown uniform. He made a quick tour of the lab, heels thudding and hands laced at his back.

"What took you so long?" He picked up a book, began to page through it.

"Sorry, Leader. I was... indisposed."

"There is something off about you. Are you ill? Should I send for a surgeon? I had thought that your kind could heal yourselves, but perhaps there are some things best left to the medical profession."

"No. I am fine. I just..." Lying to Till Sevari was a bad idea. "I think the painting is affecting me more than I had thought. Even though it's locked in your museum, I felt drawn into it." She turned away.

"Damned Helverliss." He put his hand on her shoulder, which made her cringe. "All the more reason I need you to unravel the mad artist's secrets." He resumed his stomping. "Although, perhaps your visions may be a clue. Perhaps the painting's power is communicating with you. Or even some buried aspect of the artist himself. Maybe we could even manipulate him through this link..."

She thought for a moment. Sevari knew more about his obsessions than anyone, but even to an Ehzeri with far-fetched abilities, this seemed a bit silly.

He held his fist to his lips and paced. "What did you see?"

She shrugged. "It was just a crazy dream, Leader. I—"

"What did you see, Vasi? Hm? Tell me. It may be important. It may be the secret we both need to understand Helverliss and his horrible artwork."

That biting tone, that impatience, gave her a cold shiver. This change in pitch often preceded executions. "Okay, let me think. It was black, just like the painting. The abyss." Closed eyes, forced serenity. Sevari's agitated breath beat against her neck. Damn his nonexistent personal boundaries...

She relived the blackness, a sucking void that lived inside the enchanted painting. Nothing new.

"It's just the same thing over and over again, Leader. I doubt my impressions of the void is of any use to us."

Sevari snorted and shuffled his feet. "This project is taking far too long. How can one insane artist evade my entire research wing? Hm? I have studied for decades, and still this damned fool's work eludes me." With a sigh, he resumed his stomping course through the laboratory.

"We'll get it. It's not—" Like a bolt of lightning, an image shattered the void. An image of deep blue, of sensuous curves. She gasped.

"What is it?"

She barely heard Sevari, and was more concerned with focusing on the figure. Not a figure—a person. With... wings?

"It's an archon." Her voice trailed off. Of all things to see, why did it have to be this?

"A what?"

The archon turned, lashing its forked tail like an annoyed lion. A beam of moonlight splashed its face, illuminated sharp fangs. Vasi's chest rattled. She muttered, hardly audible, "I vowed never again..."

"What is this?"

She stumbled over her words. "An archon. She's beautiful. But..." An uneasiness came over her, and the image disappeared. Still a presence lingered inside her, as if the archon were watching. "Perhaps you call them angels. Whatever you call them, one must take notice if they see one."

"An omen, you say?"

She rubbed her temples. "I am not sure what it means. It could just be my overworked mind."

"Nonsense. Everything has meaning, Vasi." He hummed to himself, and his strange thought processes reared once again in his nervous tapping and jiggling. "Angels, really. Perhaps they are trapped in the painting, and waiting for us to release them. If he has trapped shadows inside, why not angels?"

"I don't know that—"

Sevari clapped loud enough that she flinched. "I had, in my studies, begun to doubt that these angels, or any divine force, really existed. Of course, there are the worldspirits, but those are merely ideas that move us, not actual beings with tails and fangs. Perhaps these archons, as you call them, are agents of the worldspirits."

"I really think that—"

"When things deteriorate to such a poor state as they have, perhaps the worldspirits, these intrinsic ideas, have no choice but to incarnate as the angels and direct us more deliberately. Yes." He stormed towards the door. "Thank you, Vasi. You have given me a lot to think about. Now, let's get back to work on that painting. Blightcross needs its power."

She lowered her head. "Yes, Leader."

Watching Sevari disappear into the hall comforted her some, but when she returned to her bench, something gnawed inside. It was as though the archon's gaze cut into her, all the way from beyond the gap. Was it judging her?

It had been years. Five, at least, since she had left what was now called Mizkov for Blightcross. Why now?

Stories. Nothing more. What mattered was here, now. And that just happened to be unravelling arcane secrets for a madman.

CHAPTER THREE

Capra tended to avoid jobs in which the task involved dumping bodies, so this one was a first for her. But it wasn't as if evictions usually ended this way.

Or perhaps here in Blightcross, they did. Whatever the case, anxiety about the encounter clung to her like the haze that permeated the air in this city. The money meant nothing; if she had been patient, they could have found something easier and more profitable.

She still couldn't make sense of this city. On one street, she suspended her guilty conscience as they passed a remarkable, asymmetrical building of grey concrete. Around it, traditional half-timbre designs dominated the block's architectural canvas, their squat windows betraying a deep jealousy of the new style. This was nothing new to her. What bothered her was the government notice pasted to the front of the beautiful structure: Condemned and Appropriated By The Decency Commission.

It seemed wherever she found comforting progressive elements from the Little Nations here, they were stifled by the shit growing around them.

"Look, a leather shop."

Dannac spread his hands. "So?"

"So, I left everything I own on that damned flying boat. I can't work as a thief or saboteur in loose trousers and a frilly blouse."

"Ah, yes. Your... work outfit."

How could the old bastard argue with practicality? She paused to remember her measurements, then darted into the shop.

The young man at the counter could only blink at her request. "It's not like any work clothes I ever saw. Are you sure this isn't for some unwholesome activity?"

She sighed. "I do a lot of climbing, you see. Climbing, falling, skidding, and everything else you could think of. This is what works. Now, will you make this or are you going to make me find someone else?"

The young man cleared his throat. Probably the kid was imagining what she'd look like in such an outfit. "Yeah, give me a few days."

"Sooner."

"A few days, lady. Look around you, everyone's wearing workwear from this shop. I got plenty of pieces to finish."

She stomped and rolled her eyes. "Fine. I'll come back in a few days, then."

Back into the street, she found Dannac with his arms crossed, gazing at the passing carriages. He turned to her. "What was his price?"

"A little higher than usual."

"Let me go in and renegotiate."

She placed a hand on his chest. "Relax. It wasn't that bad."

"Maybe not to a decadent Valoii, but we aren't really in a position to—"

She shoved him along. "Yes, we are. Now, what we need more than bargains is a damned job."

Two hours later, Capra conceded that they could only afford the most basic housing for the night. The prices at even mediocre inns were ridiculous. How could there be a housing problem when there was so much unused, barren space in this godforsaken place?

They settled on a four-storey brick inn, the name of which Capra couldn't read. At this price range, the name probably didn't matter anyway. On stepping into the lobby, she reeled with second thoughts and regret—she convulsed in a fit of sneezing, a strange tingle biting in her sinuses. Even more encouraging was the iron cage built around the front desk.

"I'll let you deal with this," she said, and further surveyed the lobby.

Dannac spoke briefly with the attendant, and before long, though not nearly long enough for her liking, they headed up crumbling stairs towards their room. A tackiness clung to her boots and made sticky sounds along the floor, and many rooms lacked doors. Some rooms held ten or more occupants, and there was a constant thumping and yelling that seemed built into the architecture. A few tenants appeared to be regular working people who could find no better place to live, but leathery faces marked with knife scars and talk of ransom and contraband fluttered through the halls, and the former must have been the exception in this building.

It wasn't all gloom and depression, though. They had escaped Alim, and the human stains existing in and around this building would insulate them if he aimed to continue searching for her. She might prefer a luxury resort, like the Baron had booked for them, but this was safer.

A table was the room's only piece of furniture. On the floor they sat cross-legged and drank short bottles of small beer. Capra had visited the water pump on the ground floor, and decided to pass on it. Of course, Dannac would drink anything, but she was determined not to let him put grey sludge into his body.

After a while, he said, "You need to stop stressing yourself over it. It is done. The man was near death anyway."

She looked up from the community newspaper, which she could barely read on account of her lax knowledge of the Tamish written language. "How do you know? He needed help, not to be killed."

"He attacked us."

"Maybe he didn't know what he was doing."

There was something wrong about Dannac trying to convince Capra, a Valoii, that killing an Ehzeri was necessary. No doubt everyone back home, on all sides, would at least have a laugh over it.

Wind, so hot... sun beaming on a dozen cavalry sabres...

"From what I have seen, this was not isolated." Dannac pointed to the paper. "There are many Ehzeri here. Many from empowered families."

"But why?"

"Someone told them that exchanging their birthright for temporary financial gain was better than fighting your people."

"Isn't it, though?"

He shook his head. "Individual use of *vihs* will deplete the Ehzeri familial power forever. That is what happened to my family." He was silent for a moment. "Since not all Ehzeri in each family are working here in concert with each other, it will only deplete what few family lines are left with the ability."

"They never told us that. All they did was allude to inbreeding or some other strange deviancy as the reason for waning Ehzeri power. Then there were the mystical explanations, and I think those were the most accepted theories."

He snorted. "God sees the *vihs-draaf* as wicked and unnecessary, just because of these machines?"

Capra shrugged. "It didn't make any sense to me either, but you don't argue with the academy instructors."

Her knees were getting stiff, so she stood and went to the rickety iron balcony. Across the way stood another eight-storey building of the same rectilinear construction of red brick their own building displayed. This part of town could not have been very old, since Naartland itself had been established for barely a century, yet these buildings already gave her an impression of being worn and tired, like an adolescent who had never eaten well. She longed for the grand cathedrals and palaces of the Little Nations. She loved them all—that year she had spent hiding, with barely enough to eat once a day, still made her smile when she reminisced about it.

There were arches, and ruins of aqueducts, and a vibrant new type of architecture to replace what had been destroyed during the war. The men in most of the towns she visited were affectionate, to say the least. The tea had more flavour, and she could just lie on the beach for much of the day and forget about the army, Ehzeri guerrillas, and the things she had willingly done that made her sick to remember.

She rested her hand on the rail. She felt something greasy and pulled away. Her hand was covered in a black smear of grit.

In the distance, there it was—the monolith. A clock tower, surrounded by bulbous buildings that reminded her of fungal growths on trees. Smokestacks rose from many of these bulbs, and in the waning light jets of flame spewing from them became visible.

Was it a foundry? Just what was it that was attracting people from all over the main continent?

It couldn't be a foundry. Yahrein possessed the best foundries in the world, and a project this massive would have caused upset back on the continent. All she had heard during her forced holiday was that Naartland was a nation of upstarts who took great credit and pride for the resources that had been lying under their feet for billions of years.

She had just assumed that they were talking about ore, but perhaps this was some new product...

When the chemical odour returned on a hot breeze, she wrinkled her nose and went back inside.

The two of them passed the rest of the night in silence. She assumed Dannac was performing a kind of Ehzeri meditation, and she busied herself with the newspaper. Since they could be stuck in Blightcross for months, even a year or more, she thought she had better improve her language skills.

Although both Capra and Dannac were disciplined enough to go days without food and maintain their concentration, neither were in the mood for a fasting contest, and the next morning they ventured into the streets. There was an eatery just down the road from their building, but Capra insisted they find something else after stepping into the place's sawdust floor.

"As you wish, your majesty," Dannac had told her when she refused to eat at the place.

By now, Capra noticed that the city seemed to cycle through three or four strange odours, and that her throat felt as though she had swallowed a washboard. Beyond the low buildings, there was another industrial-looking monolith, but these she knew were foundries and smelters. There were parcels of unused land surrounding them, and there was a peculiar red tinge to the sand.

"I have a method, you know," she said, as they cleared the barren area and came upon a collection of tents and shacks and tables, all barely visible amid the crowd buzzing around them. Most of them were women in dun-coloured cloth that covered their faces. The few uncovered faces showed nasty red sores.

There was some produce for sale, but most of the things for sale were things unfamiliar to Capra. She began to feel backward and stupid. She may have received a sophisticated, state-sponsored education, but did that matter out here? Was Blightcross also a centre for innovation?

Or was it all just distraction?

She saw trinkets stamped with the rose emblem that must have been the crest of Blightcross. Slogans—"strong and free"—on random items, like chamber pots and grain sifters. Symbols of the Tamarck deity called The Teacher, which was rapidly displacing its companions in the old pantheon and was responsible for much of the current disdain for *vihs*.

"The Teacher helps those who help themselves," Dannac said, and loud enough for anyone to hear. "Choice is the ultimate divinity."

Capra gave him a perplexed look. "You don't agree?"

"Choice for its own sake is vain. This is why my cousins and brothers kill your people."

"We are not a theocracy. We do what we do because of the war, not because of any spiritual high-ground."

"Well, I really don't care about it either way. It is kind of strange how these people seem to be constantly reminding themselves of what they already think, though."

They moved faster through the market. Now she noticed the market's neat rows of palms. For a single breath, the heat and palm trees whisked her back to the southern state of Heuvot. She had washed dishes there for three weeks, and again it was one of the best experiences she'd ever had, so for the moment she shut away the memory.

They settled for a bistro tucked into a side street that was not clogged with carriages. Buildings here were made of granite, and there were worn hints of intricacies on many of them. Instead of hammers, machines, and hurrying workers, the air shimmered with music.

Music and aromatics, like Parnas' clove cheroots and brewing shalep. Some of the walls in the alley were marked with painted slogans and strange symbols, yet no derelicts clogged the way.

It took a few seconds for Capra's eyes to adjust to the dimness. Wood planks creaked with each step. Still, it reminded her of better times. A string quartet played at the back of the place, and the well-dressed patrons seemed to take this strange music as commonplace.

"I feel uneasy here," Dannac said.

"You need to learn how to relax. This is the best place we've been since we left the continent. Now sit."

They took a table tucked into a corner. Dannac still didn't look half as impressed as Capra felt. The menu alone... overpriced, yes, but real cuisine, like the kind she wanted to create. It even took three quarters of an hour to get their food—a pace she could get used to.

At last, after having no complaints about the "extravagant" food, Dannac said, "There are men sitting here who have done nothing but read books for the last hour."

"Yes. I almost want to talk to the chef, because I have never made this particular—"

A woman placed a thin palm on the table and leaned in. "I will be blunt. Are you two free for the day? I would like to interest you in some work."

At this, Dannac appeared less uncomfortable. "A day?"

"Well, it will take the better part of this day to go over the assignment. It is quite complex, you see."

Capra eyed the woman warily. "What makes you think we are the sort who needs work?"

The woman gestured at Capra's tattered clothes. "Unless this is the latest style off the boat from Arjoan, you either need emergency treatment from one of these local dandies, or you've found yourself in circumstances that make available your... services."

Capra blinked for a moment. "Maybe we are not the types of people to offer you these... services, as you call them."

"Word gets around. Your little eviction of a certain korganum addicted magic wielder did impress your client."

That? It had been nothing to gloat about. And they had nearly been killed.

"Go on," Dannac said.

This time, she didn't want this woman's first impression to be that of a subservient female. "Yes, please do."

"At the north end of Orvis Dunes, there is a book shop. I think we ought to go there if we are to discuss business."

Capra exchanged a glance with Dannac and said, "Can you at least tell us the nature of your problem?"

The woman invited herself to sit beside Dannac in their booth. "My name is Irea. I am a patroness around here."

Dannac grunted and raised an eyebrow.

"I support many of the artists here in Orvis Dunes. I am a collector, you see."

The woman must have been around Capra's age, yet sported dense curls and a diagonally-cut dress of rich colours Capra had only seen old royalty wear on the continent.

"Artists? Is that what this street is?" Dannac asked. "The corner of the room where all of the workers have shoved the artists to keep them out of the way?" He chuckled.

Irea made a condescending nod and looked to Capra. "You are one of those war resisters I heard about."

Capra suddenly felt naked, and snapped her hands to her neck. It was too late, but she still didn't want anyone to see her tattoo. "I..."

"I am not going to call you a coward and turn you in. This is Orvis Dunes, after all."

"I think I have misunderstood you..."

Irea gestured to the quiet young men sitting in the other booths. "On this street, you would be hard put to find someone who didn't support your choice."

"Oh. Is that so?"

"Yes. And that is why I speak to you and not your boorish friend. We love what your country has done for women. I am sure it will spread in a few generations, even to a place like this."

"Wait, you love that they're forcing us to fight?"

"No, we like that your country has destroyed the gender barrier."

Capra shrugged. To her it was just an historical afterthought. It had always been that way.

She heard Dannac sigh and guzzle his stein of small beer. "What do you need? I won't take any more evictions. Not in this place, anyway."

"No, of course not. I actually am doing this on behalf of a friend of mine. A brilliant man..." Irea gazed into the dimness beyond their booth.

Capra waited a few seconds, and when Irea failed to continue, she cleared her throat.

"Yes. Well, his name is Noro Helverliss. Perhaps you have heard of him."

Both shook their heads.

"One of the greatest minds produced in this century. He is on the leading edge of all things—the sciences, the arts—to the point of becoming the enemy of the oligarchy in both the government and academic circles."

Dannac yawned and pushed around the remaining food on his plate, but Capra became absorbed in the woman's passionate tone. She leaned forward on her elbows, instantly reminded of tales from the Little Nations, of persecuted genius and doomed romance, escapes by sailing ship to unknown islands...

"He is depressed, you see."

Like a bottle of fine wine dumped into a drain, Capra's excitement became a confusion.

"So," Dannac said. "You want us to help him not be sad?" He laughed, shook his head, and stood.

Capra clapped her hand on his shoulder, and he sat once more.

"If you would let me finish," Irea said, and from this point on acted as though there were a wall separating herself from Dannac. "Till Sevari has finally snapped the last of what few strings of sanity kept his mind together. He has stolen one of Noro's paintings. The finest work of art ever created... all because it threatens this order he has created."

"What order? This is chaos."

"Come with me to meet the artist, at least. He is the most intelligent man you will ever meet."

The man sounded fascinating, but Capra still had to think of Alim and the army she had deserted, and the officials she needed to bribe for her freedom. "We won't continue until you give us an idea of what you can afford."

It was as if Capra had lapsed into an obscure Valoii dialect nobody had heard in three centuries. Irea cocked her head and watched them with blank eyes. Finally, she said, "Money? Of course. Helverliss can afford any price you name."

Dannac looked sceptical. "Yet he somehow finds himself in need of this kind of help? Are all the rich here not involved in the oligarchy?"

"Not all, sir. Helverliss has much support in certain continental circles. Most of his work sells well over there."

"But," Capra said, "why does he stay here? If the continent is more accepting of his ideas, I hardly see why he should live in Naartland."

"That is another problem entirely. I am sure he will tell you these things if he believes them to be necessary. Would you at least come meet him? Why don't I give you each some kind of... token to show my honesty."

"Such as?"

Irea glanced at Capra's chest. "Well, I was going to give you this amulet of mine—it is a one of a kind piece, but I see you already wear a much more unique piece and that my gift would only insult it."

"A hand-cannon."

Both women fell silent. Dannac was eased back on the bench, arms folded.

"Get me one of these new devices, and we will talk."

Here he goes again. Another of his impossible conditions reserved for clients he wanted to exclude.

Capra shot him a stern look. "No, I think that's too much to ask. Some better lodging, or a new set of clothes would be more than—"

Irea stood. "A hand-cannon? I had thought you would be more imaginative, my friend. I shall return in three-quarters of an hour with one hand-cannon, and appropriate attire for the lady." With that, she flashed them a self-satisfied smirk and cantered out of the bistro.

"I want to see what this is about," Capra said, once Irea was gone. "Don't discount it just yet."

"If you want to waste time, fine. But this woman is not going to find a hand-cannon. At least not in less than an hour."

He was right—even her former regiment had barely started to phase in the new weapons. The woman was rich, sure, but could Irea really find such a valuable and rare weapon on an hour's notice?

It didn't matter. Whatever happened, Capra intended to pursue it. Dannac could do what he wanted—it wouldn't be the first time they had split for a job or two. When later they met up and he brought more bruises than money with him, she'd have a good laugh at him.

A half-hour passed. For the next fifteen minutes, Capra nursed another small beer. She slammed it on the table, empty, just as the clock on the wall struck the hour. There was still no sign of Irea.

Dannac rose. "There are better jobs in a city like this. I'll go find one."

"Suit yourself. I'm going to wait a bit longer."

He strode to the exit, but collided with a patron who was on the way in. It was Irea, and in her hand she held a large rosewood box, and clothes hung from her shoulder.

"Sorry. I believe this is yours," Irea said, and thrust the box into Dannac's chest.

Dannac gazed at the box incredulously. Capra just sat back and smiled.

He returned to the table with the box.

"Go ahead, open it," Capra said.

He slowly pried open the lid. Inside, lying on a bed of red velvet and smelling of new oil, was a peculiar contraption consisting of a wooden handle and precision-machined barrel, complete with etchings of elaborate vines.

A hand-cannon.

At last, Alim stood at the call of the receptionist. He flattened his hair and tugged out the wrinkles in his clothes. It had been a long two days.

A guard, dressed in a blue double-breasted tunic with a wide leather strap across his shoulder, tapped a stud on the wall. The heavy, riveted metal doors creaked open. "Sevari will see you now."

Alim saluted the guard and strode in. Facing the window, Sevari stood behind a grey steel desk. There was a single green gas lamp on the desk. Strange symbols decorated the office, and Alim had the strange feeling of having walked into an Ehzeri's tent.

"Mr. Sevari," Alim said.

"How goes it in Mizkov?" Sevari continued to stare out the window.

What was the protocol concerning this man? Alim didn't even know Sevari's official title. "It is going well. Your... eminence."

Sevari chuckled. "The people just call me their leader. I am not born into this, or appointed, after all. I do not deserve that kind of pedestal."

Somewhat disarmed by Sevari's candour, Alim edged closer. "I need your help in apprehending a wanted enemy of the state."

"And an enemy of Mizkov is an enemy of mine. You will have my full cooperation."

"If you could just alert your police force—"

Sevari spun around to face him. His face was hollow and bony, and a trail of dark spots dotted his receding hairline. "Police force? My good man, this is Blightcross. We have no police force."

"No police force? But I saw uniformed men guarding your public transit stations."

"Those are real soldiers, Alim. I've cut out the middlemen. Blightcross is going to be impenetrable, you just wait. No more will we need to rely on Tamarck for protection..."

That, Alim remembered, had been one of Sevari's strengths in gaining popular support. It reminded him of his own country, although something seemed different about this place. "Good. Then you will alert your army to my situation?"

"Of course. In fact, I am going to give you a squad of your own to command in your search. I cannot just sit back while some agitator threatens production. These things must be dealt with swiftly."

Alim nodded.

"The world will become envious of Blightcross very soon, friend. If word somehow gets out that my district harbours dissenters like this Capra Jorassian and her terrorist companion, it would ruin us." Sevari dropped into his chair, and motioned for Alim to do the same. "The Combined Fuel Corporation of Blightcross sent me a dire warning against that kind of thing. The Industry Corporation is uneasy as well."

"I am not sure I understand, Leader."

"Oh, yes. You Valoii have not yet made the change to my system. Well, they are the cartels, you see. I have men from my government in each, and it makes for a harmonious economy and society. But it is these artists, you see. They keep spreading dangerous ideas. I have had to silence a few of them. Some... some are much too popular for me to deal with swiftly. And, with all of the immigration going on, the corporations are increasingly nervous that we might be importing dangerous ideas. Accidentally, of course. But one does need workers."

Alim's eyes began to glaze. None of this mattered, and all he wanted was to rush back into the streets to find Jorassian.

"But this is a good thing, my friend. I will put in a request to run a series of articles in the weekly about this brave Valoii soldier who has come to aid us in tracking down dangerous dissidents. The people will be very interested in the story. You Valoii soldiers have a certain reputation."

He nodded and did not disagree with the portrayal. It was, after all, extremely important. Justice knew no boundaries, and he took pride in being sent to the underworld and back if need be to ensure that Jorassian would receive what she deserved. "I would like to resume my search as soon as possible."

"Yes, yes." He pressed a stud on his desk. Thirty seconds later, a uniformed man stepped in, saluted. "Colonel, please arrange a squad to go on loan to this Valoii representative. Give him your best."

The Colonel's stance shifted. He did not even glance at Alim. "Leader?"

"This is important, Colonel. We have a rogue war resister loose in the city. This joint operation will engage the public. They will feel strong when they see us working together with the Valoii to protect this refinery."

Is that where he was? He had assumed it was the palace, but, remembering another domed, more ornate structure a few blocks away, it now made more sense. *That* was the palace—the golden minarets, the intricate tiles. This was the refinery. When he had told the transport worker that he needed to see Till Sevari, the worker had just handed him a ticket and told him which train to take. The stop had practically led straight into the refinery's courtyard.

So Sevari's office was in the refinery clock tower, and not the palace.

Strange. But Sevari was proving to be far from the average leader.

Sevari turned his back to them. "War is terrible, Colonel. I think you can agree to this."

The Colonel made a noncommittal gesture with his head.

Sevari faced them again. "And so, a war resister is the worst kind of criminal, see? We have only learned in the last three decades that refusing to fight only condemns the rest of society to more suffering. They lack a certain spirit you see? It is no wonder that our criminal is a woman. Only the male energies have the power for war and virtue."

"Yes, Leader."

"This will be the... the tone of this operation. Do you understand, Colonel?"

"Completely. I will send twelve of my highest trained soldiers to the clock tower within the hour. And I will make sure to dictate this story to a journalist. In the proper tone, of course."

Sevari waved the man out. "It is all coming together. The spirits are with us, I can feel it."

Alim's ears perked at the statement. "Sir?"

"The worldspirits, Alim."

There was an uneasy silence.

"Come now, there is no need to be offended. I am not religious. But the worldspirits are moving us into our destiny. That is not religion, it is... science. It is philosophy. A buried knowledge of which only full disclosure will allow us to advance."

"As you say, Leader."

Not a second after the door clicked shut from the Colonel's exit, the door flew open once again. A blond woman in a neat skirt sauntered in and dropped a folder on Sevari's desk. She left as silently as she had come.

Sevari picked it up casually. His bored, slack expression transformed into a serious frown, like molten iron poured into a mold. He brought the papers closer to his face, read for two minutes, slammed the folder onto the desk.

"Well, this is not going very well. Not very well at all."

"Sir?"

Sevari stood, and Alim did the same. "Come with me, Valoii."

So he followed Till Sevari, The Leader of Blightcross, out of the office and into a long hallway decorated with a purple carpet, numerous portraits, and chandeliers. At the end of the hall, they came to a round door, riveted all round, and fitted with a wheel at the centre to operate a seal mechanism. The Leader pointed to it, and Alim rushed to open the door. During the final turns of the wheel, a hiss issued from the wall. He recoiled at a burning sensation in his nostrils.

Opening the door filled the hall with a loud grating, staccato banging, hissing, all mixed with metallic footsteps and the shouts of workmen. This sealed door was the demarcation between Sevari's wing of the place and the actual refinery. Alim stared, speechless at the immensity of what he saw beyond the door. A labyrinth of pipes and catwalks, and he could not begin to understand how any of it worked.

"This facility stretches far into the desert," Sevari said. "There are seventeen different pipelines that all feed this refinery."

"I have seen the largest factories in Tamarck, and still this amazes me." He made tentative steps along the grated floor. A steady vibration shook his knees.

Sevari led him through the facility. "I would prefer it if you would wear your uniform from now on, except when you are working in the city and need to be inconspicuous."

Alim scarcely heard the directive. There were too many things going on around him to argue about it. "As you wish."

"Now, I did bring you in here for a reason. I have a potential problem with a large percentage of my workforce here."

"I don't follow you, Sir."

"They are Ehzeri, and they are becoming scared. A few of them have died. Murder, they say."

"Is it true?"

Sevari stopped and gazed at a group of workers across the way. They were huddled around a pipe juncture, and a shower of sparks bathed their work area, like a fountain of fire. What machine could do such a thing? Unless Sevari were employing Ehzeri for their *vihs*... but surely a man like him would not degrade himself. It must be some new machine. Each day there came to be new machines to replace the various *vihs* powers that were falling behind a curtain of obsolescence.

"The issue I have is how to deal with Ehzeri."

"Respectfully, Leader, if my people had figured that out, the border skirmishes would have ended and we would all be shitting rainbows."

Sevari ushered him along with a fatherly hand. "I am speaking on a purely psychological basis. I know of your extensive training. Even Tamarck is jealous of it."

"You mean to ask me how you should keep your workers in line?"

"I merely wish to find out how to calm them. They need to realize that they are safe in my refinery. I need them. You need them. Tamarck needs them. We all need these workers to be working in my refinery, and the more talk of Ehzeri murders floats around, the greater risk there is of them causing trouble."

Alim narrowed his eyes. "You mean, the greater risk there is of them leaving?"

"Whichever. I'm sure this could cause any number of production problems."

The conversation gradually died, swallowed by the quicksand of distractions around them. Sevari took the time to speak with many of the workers, and Alim had the impression that these were the collaborators—the ones Sevari could trust not to report back to the others. Very few of these were Ehzeri. Despite the complex social situation, his main question was what exactly did they refine here?

He was not up on his sciences or mechanics, but now he understood that many innovative mechanisms required fuel. Like a steam engine—which had been a miserable failure—only clearly more powerful. Coal was not enough. This substance, this fuel, was a kind of concentrated spirit that required much processing. He could only imagine the sheer scale of the operation. He had always known of the deposits of volatile liquids locked in the earth—the blood of the giants. To pump it across vast distances and dig wells...

It did not make sense. Yes, they had various engines to aid in the work, but back home, there was not even talk of developing similar deposits. It simply was not feasible or necessary, yet Sevari had created this monstrosity and his district had become a constantly mutating organism as a result.

Was the machine really supplanting the old ways—the *work?* Or was Sevari using the *vihs* in a roundabout way?

For now it didn't matter. These Ehzeri were out of Mizkov's badlands and the less of them there the better. Now he had something far worse than dirt-poor Ehzeri to apprehend.

CHAPTER FOUR

It tickled Capra to see Dannac descend into a subdued mood. If she didn't know any better, she'd say he was embarrassed that the woman had called his bluff. For ten minutes, he had traced his fingers along the glassy metal and wood of his new hand-cannon. As for Capra's own gift, she caught a quick glance in the mirror and shrugged. Her trousers were neither stylish nor practical, but by now she had realized that despite this group's forward-thinking nature, it still in some ways suffered from the backwardness of Tamarck-influenced style.

Style was the furthest thing from her mind as they headed down the Orvis Dunes to the bookshop owned by Noro Helverliss. The sun splashed across the horizon, stabbed by the black spears of Blightcross's towers, and it looked as though it would swallow the entire city if not kept at bay by these jagged silhouettes. When, ten minutes after putting it on, her blouse was damp, she began to wonder if maybe the sun were devouring them. The air flowed in her lungs with a stifling weight. At their feet, a thin black mud softened their steps. And even though there played snippets of good music in this part of the town, her ears still rang with the constant screeching and hammering that came from nowhere and everywhere.

The bookshop smelled of mould and stale shalep. There were towers of unsorted books, and the shelves themselves leaned enough that Capra stepped lightly around them for fear of causing a catastrophe. Cookbooks sat with philosophy texts, mathematics tomes with novels, and if there was any kind of order to it, Capra couldn't see it. Perhaps this Noro

Helverliss was such a genius that he could make sense of this chaos.

In one corner, a glass vase glowed from within. A flowing figure of a woman, tendrils of hair draped in sinuous curves. Capra ran her fingers along the serene, knowing face, traced the intricate details of the figure's leafy crown. It took her a moment to realize that this was a lamp, not just some sculpture.

Irea strolled through the stacks. "Noro? Noro, you bastard, where are you?"

There was no answer. Capra soon became absorbed in the room's paintings. They were like nothing she had seen before.

Figures, twisted and warped by what looked like evil magic. Landscapes that were deranged. Obscene colours and sometimes primitive, blocky figures and grotesque creations, inappropriate combinations like a desert cactus growing out of the body of an angel, or an eye set into an otherwise realistic portrayal of a stone hearth. Capra wandered around the shop to visit each painting, and was especially intrigued by ones that resembled nothing in particular—in fact, they looked rather like someone had spilled paint accidentally and called it art. Yet there was something sublingual, something that grabbed her and made her stand in a thrall, staring into the patterns so that her entire world framed this strange graphic—

"Capra!"

She tried to pry herself from the painting, but could do little more than shuffle her feet a few steps. It was Dannac's huge hand on her shoulder, pulling her away, that finally broke the trance. "Have you gone dumb, woman?"

She jerked free, and her breaths came in short rasps. "I..." A moment later, she began to feel normal. "What?"

He led her to the open loft, where they found Irea and a thin, stoop-shouldered man sitting in low chairs and gazing at the store below.

Irea rose and said, "Capra, Dannac, this is Noro Helverliss."

Helverliss inclined his head slightly and raised his mug. His frock coat and trousers hung as if he were a skeleton.

The mad, obsessed intellectual, baking under gaslight and forgetting to eat, surviving on stimulants. Capra had fallen for more than one in the past—

"Mr. Helverliss," she said. "I am intrigued by your paintings."

"Those are my early works," he said in a raspy voice. "I really dislike most of them."

—although admittedly, those men had been younger and just a bit more charming.

A chill raced through her. There was a strange depth to Helverliss' blue eyes. She could only think of lightning storms when she looked into them.

"A woman like you is hard to find," Helverliss said, while his eyes traced Capra's figure.

"Most of us wear trousers back home... practicality dictates, Sir."

"Ah, yes. Mizkov." He lit a cheroot and sighed with a stark heaviness.

"Now," Irea said. "About your painting, Noro."

"Oh." Helverliss blew a thick cloud of smoke from his nostrils. "My best work. Sevari sent his thugs to take it from me." He inhaled for a long while, eased back his head. "I should have never showed it. I should have never showed it."

Just listening to the man made Capra tired. While Dannac took a seat next to Irea, Capra forced herself to stand.

Helverliss went on: "I called it *Akhli and the Shadows*. Superficially the painting is mostly a canvas of flat black, with a simple red emblem in the corner."

Dannac made a disgusted grunt. "How is that art? And why would an important man like Sevari care about a black canvas that portrayed nothing?"

"You stupid cretin," Helverliss said. "Nothing of its kind exists. If Sevari were smart enough to just sell the damned thing he would be able to build another refinery and double the output of that monster in which he has burrowed himself."

Dannac shifted in his seat. The muscles of his jaw rippled, and Capra knew the only reason he had not struck Helverliss was because of the gift Irea had given to him.

"Was it like the one downstairs?" Capra thought for a moment, remembered how it had transported her to some unknown landscape. "I felt it... I mean it was amazing, it's just a few splatters of colour but..."

Helverliss waved his hand, as if she had oohed and ahed over a vulgar caricature. "It was nothing like that shit." He sighed and took a few quick puffs on his cheroot. "But yes, my work from that point on does involve aspects that go beyond mere appearance."

"There is more to his work than superficial images," Irea said. Her tone reminded Capra of a translator. "While Tamarck and Naartland bask in their infantile return to folklore and bastardized aesthetics, Helverliss has used Ehzeri tradition in an innovative way."

Dannac shook his head. "Tradition? My people do not create paintings like this. Ours look like the things they are supposed to be."

"Yes. But your people also possess certain techniques. Surely you know of them? For most of our history, we have used *vihs* in some capacity or another. The war should not have changed this. Just because certain political forces have deemed *vihs* as corrupt and out of date doesn't mean it is true. I find it a remarkable tool for modern art."

Capra grimaced and motioned for Irea to abandon the issue. But it was too late.

"I know nothing of what other families are capable of, or what most of us used to possess a century ago. I was not fortunate enough to belong to a family capable of managing what little power remains."

Helverliss let out a frustrated sigh. "In any case, much of my work is infused with... well, let us just call it magic. The viewer is affected in ways traditional art can never achieve. *Akhli and the Shadows* was a portrayal of the legend most of us know. But instead of glorifying Akhli for some sacrifice he clearly never meant to make, I showed the darkness. The darkness of the blood pits in the desert, the darkness of the shadow beings he locked underground forever. Akhli was not an innocent boy. I believe Akhli was complicit in the chaos. I believe he was playing with our reality, as if it were a game. He was a sadistic creature, and I wanted to show the similarity between Akhli's darkness and that of the shadows."

"That is ridiculous," Dannac said.

"The painting is the first and only glimpse mankind can gain of pure darkness. Without harming themselves or others, that is." His voice became shaky, and he paused to smoke. When he resumed, his voice regained its steady ennui. "And so Sevari thought this was a threat to his order, his stupid vertical trade union, his distaste of modernism. He stole that painting and other works of mine. Some of it theoretical, and my only copy. But all I ask is that you return that one painting. Sevari must not be allowed to keep it." Helverliss flashed a sardonic grin. "The fool could hurt himself if he's not careful."

Aside from the fantastic details—an artist who somehow found a way to utilize *vihs* for his work—it was a familiar request. Now Capra began to slide back into her routine. The mining scam had thrown her off; she was not at heart a confidence trickster, although they had resorted to that in desperate times.

Within the month she would be back in the Little Nations—perhaps Prasdim, near the Sparkling Sea—working as a chef, and all without having to worry about Alim. Not only that, but if the painting she had seen downstairs was his idea of a shit painting, she could only dream of what this piece would be like. At once she began to picture Akhli skipping around the plains and stumbling upon the shadow men while they set their final trap to rid the world of the fire giants. Did Helverliss really know what they had looked like?

No, she realized, Helverliss did not possess some knowledge of the giant pits, or if Akhli had survived when the traps had collapsed on top of him along with the shadow men and the fire giants. Nobody could. But he did know a lot about *vihs*, and that alone was remarkable.

"There is one other thing I would request."

Both gave the man expectant looks.

"I want out of here. Sevari has barred me from leaving, and not even the human traffickers here will have anything to do with me, no matter how much I offer them."

Dannac sounded intrigued, for once. "Where would you like to go?"

"Anywhere. Even the shores of Tamarck. At least I could pass through there before anyone realized who I was. The Bhagovan Republic might appreciate what I have to offer."

At this, Irea appeared uneasy, but she said nothing.

"That is one place we won't be going," Dannac said. Capra just shrugged—she did not care either way.

"Whatever. Anywhere but here. I had thought the climate here could change, that at least the academics in Naartland would be willing to discuss things with me, but their business is only to buttress Sevari's policies with their own rationalizations. I need to leave, and I assume that you two will be leaving once this is all over as well."

"That would be correct," Capra said. "So, maybe a better idea would be to skip the painting and pay us for getting you out of here."

"No." Helverliss scrunched his face and gritted his teeth, then returned to his laconic state. "I have to have that one painting. Everything else the man can keep—though if there were an opportunity to recover it I would gladly take it—but you must retrieve that piece. I am willing to pay you ten-thousand pistres. In gold, if you prefer."

Dannac's head dropped slightly, and the two stared at each other, both slack-jawed. Ten-thousand was more than they had made in an entire year of work.

So many works, and not enough hours in each day to work them. Vasi gulped the last of her tea and nearly squashed a frail scroll she had yet to copy with the mug. Once her heart calmed again, she looked back to the notebook in front of her. The more she studied, the more it felt as though she knew this Helverliss personally, and he was not the kind of man she would befriend. One of these volumes must hold the secret to his technique. Perhaps he had written the formulae in code.

... and it is my contention that the great Yahrein philosopher had his head on backwards. The so-called "worldspirit" of his did not come out of nothing and start shoving us mere humans around to fulfil its bizarre desires.

The totality he spoke of arises out of the material world we find ourselves in, and that is what moves society. From the ground up, not the other way around, and in an opposition-based process of tension and release...

She squinted and rubbed her temples. Thousands of pages, hundreds of hours, all without uncovering a single passage relating to *Akhli and the Shadows*. If she had to read another thousand pages of this, she wondered if her head might explode.

Sitting around too long, that was the trouble. She needed stimulation, so she left her lab, locked it dutifully, and began to wander through the clock tower. Her head swam with a sick ache around her eyes—one that reminded her of a fever but came from staring at books for hours on end. That was the one good part about her first job as a labourer in the refinery. At least she moved, and used her skills regularly for practical, important tasks.

Around the corner was a small balcony. She stepped onto it, and hopped onto the stone wall to lie on the narrow strip. She knew she wouldn't fall, and it made her feel as though she were hovering above the city. The whole district sprawled below, and it was the kind of stimulation that kicked her thoughts back into their usual rhythm.

A strange thrill raced through her. What if she jumped? Imagine flying over the city, whether by *vihs* or some other means. Like the flying boats, only without tons of iron between herself and the air. Like an archon...

Damn, there it was again. The archon returning to her, taking liberties as though things had never changed. *Go away. I made my decision long ago. Never again.*

But she should have known that it took more than words to banish the archon from her mind. Now it flew in the moonlight, as they were always portrayed. Wings fully spread. Staring into her, judging, even mocking. Divine but flawed tricksters, playing with the material plane as though it were a toy... what did it want from her? But the image became buried in her drowsiness, leaving her with half-formed thoughts and questions.

An hour later, Vasi awoke drenched with sweat and sun-seared eyes. Beneath those sensations a strange inspiration nagged her, probably brought on by the dream.

Archon, archon... *damn you, go away. I have work to do.*

And somehow she dragged from her sleep the important thoughts she sensed, like plucking a drowning child from the water. What if she wove a visual working of *vihs* into the canvas? If her power could merge with the painting, it might expose some clue she had missed. A written invocation, or a burn mark, or anything that might point to how this strange object worked.

She dashed through the halls, feet cooled by the smooth granite, to find the special vault where Sevari stored his most prized pieces. She worked the locks with little more than a thought and found the mysterious painting encased in glass. The rest of the displays were artifacts Sevari wouldn't entrust even her with—an enchanted gauntlet, one of her people's spears said to have been carried by the only man to have battled one of the fire giants before they had disappeared, and a host of other legendary items.

Again it drew her in, demanded that she approach it and acknowledge its existence. She drifted towards it, falling into a trance. Then came the whispering chatter, the voices urging her forward, but uttering no word she recognized. It chilled her and excited her, the tingle in her limbs both from anticipation and fright.

There it hung, complete with its strange gaze. Black.

Each time she looked at it, she tried to imagine that the shadow men, or the giants, or even Akhli, somehow appeared in that evenly-painted canvas. But no matter how hard she squinted, cocked her head, or crossed her eyes, nothing became visible. All she gleaned from the piece was utter blackness.

Maybe that was enough. The way it spoke, the way it grabbed one by the throat and—

Before she could begin to analyze the painting further, the entrance rattled and two men walked in. She spun round and found Sevari striding in, flanked by a handsome young man with—

Never mind. He was not handsome, but a monster. A tattooed monster, one of the Valoii murderers.

"Vasi," Sevari said. "Having any luck?"

She lowered her head. "I was just going to analyze the painting's *vihs* vibrations again. I had an idea..."

"Very good. Now, this is Alim, and he's come to help us."

She looked up at them. "Help us?"

Sevari spoke to Alim for a few seconds, low enough that Vasi could not hear. "There is a rogue Valoii in this town. A... well, a murderer."

Vasi pondered this for a moment. At least he admitted there was a threat to his workers, for once.

"And, this fine Valoii here will be helping me track her down so that we may bring her to justice. Do you see?"

"I understand, Leader."

Sevari pulled her closer, put his arm around her. "The others look up to you. You are successful in their eyes. Some are becoming nervous about the deaths."

Only now did the magnitude of her carelessness hit her: how idiotic was walking around the dark halls alone, without a single care other than her banal work? Then again, with the inexplicable return of the archon, perhaps she'd have protection. More protection than she wanted.

"And so, you can see that there is nothing to worry about. Many of the deaths have been ruled as accidental, and if there is a murderer, you can bet that it is this rogue Valoii that our friend here will be apprehending within the next few days. He is hot on her trail, you see. If this murderer aims to harm any of you here, rest assured that I will protect you."

She thought of the boy she had known who had just been found with a neat hole in his forehead. "But Leader—"

"Now, does that really sound like something to worry about?"

"I—"

"Does it not make more sense that perhaps this hysteria might be causing workers to be lax in their safety practices? Do you recall how dangerous the refinery is?"

She bowed and reminded herself not to tell him exactly why the refinery was dangerous, because he'd only see her pointing out his lax standards as an insult. But it was Alim who commanded most of her attention. Blood raced in her ears, and she found her fists clenched at her sides.

Murderer.

"Answer me, Vasi!"

She met Sevari's eyes. "Sir?"

"I asked you to spread this calming message among your peers. I cannot have them scared of prowlers and knife attacks and so on. Alim here is more than capable of taking care of this rogue Valoii, though I still would urge you to doubt that she is really prowling around this refinery and killing its workers. It is a bit absurd, isn't it?"

Before she could answer, they began to amble around the room. Sevari gave a running narrative of each exhibit—the tourist versions, anyway. She knew these objects better than she knew her own family these days, and there was more to them than romantic tales.

With the Valoii murderer and Sevari gone, she went back to the painting. Only now, she saw nothing but a field of black set in a minimalist frame. Her thought had washed away under Sevari's nattering like lines on the beach erased by lapping waves.

Murderer. That's what had distracted her. She didn't believe Sevari's smooth evasions. It was always the same, and only the issues changed. First it had been working hours—of course he had convinced them to agree with him by trying to paint them all as lazy and unwilling to do their part. Since most of the immigrants here had dealt with those accusations their entire lives, they had quickly stopped their criticism. Then there was the issue of ventilation in certain areas, and Sevari's excuse had been that in such tough post-war times, all had to make little sacrifices to rebuild society, and in turn, they had all felt bad for speaking up about the growths in their lungs.

This was more of the same. The only thing that made her wonder was Alim. Was there really a Valoii soldier hiding in this city? One of those war criminals who had done something so deplorable that even the Valoii generals could not let it go unpunished? It would not be the first time. The only thing worse than a Valoii soldier was a rogue one. Even the generals had limits to their genocidal practices.

She left the room and slipped into the clock tower's halls again. Every few steps she glanced past her shoulder.

And here, she realized that Rovan staying here, waiting to be murdered or killed in an accident was hardly worth it.

Some things were more valuable than money. She alone could make enough to support the family. Rovan's wage was nothing compared to hers, so what was the point in him risking his life in the refinery? Hadn't it been selfish to bring him along? Even if the kid had gotten himself mixed up with a resistance cell, he'd never know the terrors Vasi had lived through.

Sometimes, being born without any *vihs* capacity was a blessing.

She stopped at one of the immense windows of stained glass. In front of her loomed a colourful depiction of a winged boy holding a sword. Below him were the black pits in which the fire giants and the shadow men had perished. Tamish versions of ancient texts. She would never understand how they could deify this Akhli character.

Idiots.

And it was these same idiots who couldn't even read sacred texts properly who were charged with keeping Rovan safe.

Not worth it.

She hurried to the ground floor. Through the security checkpoint, three sealed bulkheads, and into the refinery. She had forgotten the thick air, the constant noise, the confusing array of machines and pipe. A few minutes into her trek, her nostrils filled with a greasy film.

When she could not find Rovan at his usual station, she pulled aside his supervisor. "Where is he?"

The man spat a black wad over the edge of the catwalk and further smeared the grease on his face with his hand. "What's it to you?"

"I am his sister. I have to speak with him. It is urgent." What if this man were the killer? She let go of him and put a few steps of distance between them.

He sneered, hardly enough for her to notice, but his tone filled in the rest. "Oh, yes, it's you. They reassigned him." The man grumbled to himself and spat again. "Only just started getting things right, and now Sevari is so impressed, he's got Rovan on one of his little projects. Bloody sheepfucker ought to make a new project out of fixing his pit-rotted pipelines. Golden Ram be damned, there's a break every day in the line west of here."

She froze. "Little projects."

"Aw yeh, you know, his spooky studies. Bastard. He's a bloody bastard." The man lowered his goggles and said, "But, ah, don't tell him I said that, love." He then turned back to the valve he was fixing.

She leaned against a guardrail, put her hands to her ears and tried to work out why Rovan would be reassigned. But in this place, complex thoughts often melted under the aural assault of the refinery.

Damn it—good luck convincing Rovan to return home now. He wanted gold rings and a mechanical carriage loaded with women to buy and sell, and with this promotion the kid would catch a glimpse of enough money to obtain it. Then he would never leave, no matter how crazy or unsafe the place became. He might even join Sevari's political party.

Still, what could Rovan offer to them? Was he hiding latent skills? Perhaps her family possessed more power than they had thought. Technically possible, though she doubted it. Damn, if her family caught wind of Rovan coming into power, they'd do the same thing to him as they had to her. Perhaps this was why her mind kept showing her the archon. It could be a warning, but for Rovan's sake.

She hurried into one of the elevators, and emerged back in the cool darkness of the clock tower. Once she returned to her pile of Helverliss' works, her shoulders dropped and the piles of books and sculptures and paintings loomed like an unclimbable peak.

Bloody distractions. The greatest challenge of her life, this strange painting, and it had to be mired by contingencies and distraction. She could unlock its secrets, she knew she could. Given enough time, anyway...

Rovan was the reason for doing this mindless research. She did it so that they would all have something for the future. Her mind flickered with images of Rovan lying in a pool of blood, barely visible to the rest of the staff. A bleeding ghost.

Perhaps someone in the city would have heard something about this killer. Most of the people involved with the city's underbelly would never cooperate with Sevari. Only an Ehzeri could stand a chance at coaxing information from the underclass. And besides, she had stayed locked in this tower for how long, three months? All without a single trip into town. There were old friends to speak with, pubs crawling with bits of questionable facts, and of course, most of the newspapers never made it into the refinery. Were there others dying in the streets, or did the killer only strike at the refinery?

What if she could find the answer? If she couldn't unlock Noro Helverliss' painting at the moment, she could at least find this killer, since all Sevari would do was cover it up and allow it to continue.

"We should not be staying at that shop, Capra. If the law here has already raided his place, they will come again."

Capra led him around the market, gazed at the gimcracks and utensils for sale. "I see what you mean, but I almost think a good night's sleep is worth it." She grinned at him.

"Spoiled brat."

She rolled her eyes at him. "Well, I'm no good to you tired. Somehow I doubt you were having a good time in that ghetto we slept in."

As she predicted, he didn't argue. With the coins Helverliss had provided weighing her down, she turned her eyes back to the merchant stalls. She picked up several trinkets, only to set them down after realizing how useless they were.

"Bastardized Ehzeri items," Dannac finally said. "They look nothing like the real thing."

But there were hundreds of Ehzeri clogging the dirt streets and shoving the same objects into their black-stained bags, so maybe they were good enough.

Capra looked at her white blouse and saw the same vague smudges. There also was a grittiness between her teeth. By now she had conceded to living with it and stopped spitting to rid her mouth of it.

Towering above the market was a triangular metal structure—a crane, she decided—that began to creak and whine. There was a tiny cabin at one end, and a plume of black smoke issued from a pipe.

"Is there a man inside that?"

Dannac nodded. "I sat next to a man who was an owner under the industry corporation here, whose concern built these machines. There is a man inside who controls it."

She shivered, visions of being cramped inside a tiny metal barrel on top of a giant tower. Then again, the fact of its height hardly mattered. The worst part was the small space. It might as well have been a closet or one of the raid shelters in which she had spent countless hours of her youth hiding with her parents.

Explosions. Dad with his hand over her mouth. Days inside, darkness, three people sharing a few slabs of unleavened bread. The dirt walls closed in, men shouted outside—

"We need one of these."

Dannac's voice snapped her back into the crowded street. In his hand he held a length of rope.

She paused for a few seconds while her heart slowed to normal. "I don't even know where we'll end up with this job." She glanced at the crane. "But as long as it doesn't involve one of those, I think I'll be fine."

Dannac gave her a puzzled look and dropped the coil into her arms. She glanced away, into the desert beyond the market, where a lone ox stood on the cracked earth. In a moment of utter serendipity, the animal's horns formed a perfect circular frame around the sun. If only she could look at it directly—it would be a rare sight of beauty in this otherwise ugly land.

Dannac could look straight into the sun without harming himself. What would it be like? Would it be the same as if a person with normal vision were able to glimpse it? Or would his strange sight miss something? Or would it see something natural sight could not?

"Powder for the hand-cannon," he said, and took the lead. "Though I wonder if it is widely available here."

They passed a group of Ehzeri, huddled and making the low intonations of a collective working. She began to guess what they were doing—healing, cursing, fixing, sharpening. It was nice to see them not conjuring war spirits or turning themselves into bombs.

She handed him the bag of coins. "You do the shopping. We need to find out where this bloody painting is. I want to get out of this place."

With that, she pushed through the dirty robes and boil-pitted faces that eyed her with suspicion. She checked her cravat to keep her tattoo covered. For her entire adult life, that ink had defined her. It didn't matter what lived beneath the ink; people would see the tattoo and that would be all they saw. Just another olive-skinned warrior-fanatic from Mizkov, just another piece of meat to hold a crossbow because those stupid Valoii could not properly crush or negotiate with their enemies. And a woman, no less.

She left the market area and went through the quieter streets around Orvis Dunes—the old, crumbling buildings that still showed a hint of classical design. If only this were Tamarck, where the corruption ran so deep that she could simply pull aside a government official at random and pry from him where the paintings might be held. The guards in the streets here maintained an impossible posture, a cold expression, and sneered when anyone even appeared to approach them.

Stoicism, duty, virtue—she could very well be back in Mizkov. Given that, pulling aside one of these guards to bribe would only work if she wanted to end up dead or in prison.

A whistle cut through the air, and she stopped mid-stride. There was a man across the street, and he was gazing at her. She tucked her amulet down her undershirt, and touched her arm for the reassuring bulge of her switchblade, and jogged to meet him.

He had bloodshot eyes, and his hands were jammed into his dirty coat. His lower lip was swollen and showed a scabby gash that extended down his face. "You want some?"

Capra stepped back, brought herself out of his reach. "Do I want some what?"

"Korganum. You want it?"

"Depends. What is it?" Judging by the man they had killed earlier, it didn't seem like the kind of thing she'd like.

"I got cheap plugs of cavo root. You want that? No tax on it, no tax. Cheaper than in the store. Or buy the korganum. You look like you would like it. Oh, try it. So good."

Cavo, sure. But this korganum stuff sounded like it might be that acrid smelling garbage everyone was cooking in the alleys, and that was far from the harmless, aromatic stimulant she enjoyed. "Tax free cavo?"

"Oh yes. Yes."

Cavo... at once her mouth watered, and she began to fidget. Because of the Baron's old fashioned curmudgeon views, she had not chewed any for days because it was unladylike.

But could a person trust this broken man? Maybe he was selling something else entirely. Then again, tax free... and they did not exactly have their fortune yet...

"You there!" Both startled and glanced down the street. It was one of the men in blue leather. He reached to his side, and Capra wasn't fazed—

A hand-cannon. Not a club or short sword, but a hand-cannon.

"Halt! Stop!"

Another tall, rectangular building, and almost as high as the clock tower. It must have been new. Vasi could hardly believe it. Had she been locked inside for that long? The skyline no longer stretched into the desert, broken only by the refinery's trail of pipes extending far into the outlands. Now, blocky structures chopped the horizon into a strangely ordered field of orange sky and ominous black rectangles.

Had Sevari tacitly discouraged her from leaving? Nobody had explicitly said it was forbidden, but there was always an excuse. This project needs to be completed, that report must be completed and delivered to the administrator, oh, you could go but you might miss the special meeting we had arranged and you are a good team member, so...

But she was out now, in the streets she used to prowl during her days as a mere refinery labourer. She skirted the worker camps at the edge of the Orvis Dunes, and smiled at a restaurant that smelled of the roasting skewered meat she remembered. One would think that by now, they would serve the Ehzeri food at the refinery.

The owner always gave her extra, because he said she reminded him of his niece back in Mizkov. Yes—and he did possess the *vihs-draaf*, because she saw flashes of it when he assumed nobody was watching. Whenever she asked him why he was selling spiced meat byproducts instead of practising his skills, he had shifted the conversation back to which condiments she wanted with her order, or how her little brother was doing.

She rounded the corner to find an upper-class lady speaking with one of the korganum pushers. The rich succumb to the same hell as the workers...

Too much money around, no direction for it. Where does it end up? In that man's pockets.

Then the martial shout of the guardsman came like thunder, and the withered man bolted into the alley. She leaned into a lamppost and watched.

The guardsman raised his weapon, and a boom shook the block and hammered her ears. The rich lady took off as well, but in the other direction—towards her.

A red cravat. Such vanity. And here she was, dashing across the street, her silly red fabric flapping in the wind. Did she really think that the guardsman had any interest in her? Newcomers. Must be just getting started on her addiction.

Vasi scowled at the woman as she ran past. The cravat now hung loose at her shoulders, like a priest. A comical sight—

What's that on her neck?

—if it weren't for the Valoii army tattoo.

Vasi's heart thudded, both from her memories of what those symbols represented and her theories about the refinery killings. Sevari was actually right for once—here was a narcotic-addicted runaway from the Valoii army.

Vasi broke into a run. She narrowed her eyes and took after the woman. When her legs slowed and began to cramp, she clenched her jaw, grasped the amulet around her neck, and called upon the ancestral powers to propel her legs faster and erase her fatigue. Waves of heat flowed through her, each current gathering in the amulet at her chest and catapulting into her muscles.

The woman ran all the way down Orvis Dunes to the Palms. Probably an attempt to lose her non-existent pursuers in the buzz of the market.

Once the woman slowed to a walk, Vasi eased around, through her fellow expatriates, and bumped into the woman she had followed.

"Excuse me!" Vasi said.

The woman was panting and clutching her chest. "Yes?" she asked, in between heavy breaths.

"I could not help but see what happened back there." What was she doing? If the woman were guilty, she ought to just smite her there and go back to her job. But could she be sure?

"Yes? Well, good for you. I did not know that there was a policy here against... speaking with men on the street."

Vasi extended her hand and guided the woman away from the busy stall. "You look lost."

The woman flashed a quick smile and adjusted her cravat. "I just was looking for some information. And some cavo would be nice."

Vasi shuddered. Valoii were different, yes, but were their women really crass enough to chew cavo? "What sort of information?"

"I am new here, you see. I was told that Leader Sevari possessed an extensive art collection, and was interested in viewing it." She coughed. "I am a professor. Of... art. An art professor from Prasdim."

Vasi widened her eyes. "An art professor. Impressive."

The woman's demeanour suddenly shifted. "Why thank you. Now, we all know how Sevari obtained his works. I am uninterested in his politics, and am here strictly in the interest of high culture."

Now the Valoii flipped her tight braid from her shoulder, crossed her arms, and sank into the wall behind her. Could she be telling the truth? But the tattoo... then again, she could have escaped, or served her term uneventfully and become an academic elsewhere. Could she forgive the woman, were that the case?

"So, I wonder, is there any chance of viewing them? Do you know of anyone I can talk to to arrange a special viewing? Does he have a publicity coordinator or someone else I can speak to?" The woman tapped her chin for a moment and glared at Vasi. "Or, maybe if you just pointed me in the collection's general direction, I could figure the rest out myself."

"I do know about the collection..." Maybe this wasn't the killer she had wanted to find.

"Good. You can call me Capra." She uncrossed her arms, and there was a golden glare at her chest. Once Capra shifted so that the glare ceased, Vasi saw the amulet at her chest. As Capra talked more about herself, Vasi heard none of it and became transfixed by the amulet dangling from the other's neck.

Bronze and gold, sapphires, all in a complex knot meant to signify a certain family bond.

An Ehzeri clan.

An emblem specific and exclusive to a single clan.

An emblem specific and exclusive to Vasi's clan.

Who did you kill to obtain that, Valoii whore?

Vasi cursed herself for empathizing with the woman. Capra did not deserve the kind of death Vasi had planned on dealing to her. Only Sevari was capable of plunging her into a hell that could approximate what animals like her had done to Vasi's people.

The archon within her stirred. As imperfectly as it had been conjured and grafted to her soul, her family had at least imbued a healthy appetite for vengeance. No matter how she hated it, it was still there, and clearly she could never truly run away from her past.

Perhaps the archon would gain satisfaction soon.

Capra supposed that her new friend was staring at the old, gaudy heirloom because it was the kind of thing that looked more expensive than it was. If the amulet weren't the only thing she had left of her life back home, she would have just given it to the poor Ehzeri.

"I just need to know where these paintings are, Vasi. If, that is, they actually exist."

"Then you are in luck." Vasi appeared to strain for something, probably a word. Neither of them spoke Tamarck very well. "I... I will lead you right to them."

"Good. Where will we be going?"

Vasi pointed west, to a gold and ivory dome that was overshadowed and buried by the industrial fever surrounding it. "The palace."

"The palace..." Nobody had mentioned this palace. But, she reminded herself, intellectuals like Irea and Helverliss often were too self-absorbed to notice these kinds of things. If they had just done a bit of basic research, they could have saved her a day's worth of fruitless conversations with shady characters. "Well, I would gladly pay you for your trouble. My university has given me an expense account for just this kind of thing."

"You are too kind, Professor." Vasi took a deep breath. "Meet me at the western end of the Palms tomorrow at noon. I will accompany you to view these exhibits."

Capra thought for a moment. Vasi looked familiar, but then most of her people reminded Capra of that one family—

It's a compound, it's a compound. It's one of their training camps. If we destroy this one, their ability to attack will suffer.

It's so damned hot. Just want to get it over with and get back to the base for some water...

When Vasi turned to leave, Capra reached out and said, "Wait. I don't want you to come with us. Just tell me where the damned things are."

"Why?"

"Because. There are things you would do best to avoid. This... art business is one of them."

Vasi's posture stiffened. "I must personally escort you."

Great. Now they had to deal with an outsider. There was no way they could show up with their gear and not look suspicious. "All right. Here's the thing, my friend. My colleague and I need to break into the place. That would be why I want you to stay behind."

"I suspected as much. You hardly look like a professor. You are hardly older than I am."

Capra sighed. "Good. Now that we have that over with…"

"Yes. I want to help. Like I said, meet me here tomorrow and I will lead you straight to the collection. It is hidden. And without detailed instructions, you will never find your way through the palace."

Capra grinned. "Perfect."

CHAPTER FIVE

"A woman bumped into you in the market after you ran from a guardsman, and you hired her to help us?"

Another one of Dannac's scathing glances raked Capra from across the loft. Had they not worked together long enough for him to trust her judgement?

She eased back in the soft leather chair. "That's right. We'll raid the palace tomorrow, map out our escape from this awful island, and be out of here in two days."

She held out her hand and snapped her fingers. A second later, there was a plug of cavo careening for her head, and she caught it without raising her gaze from the paper in her lap. "Thank you."

The familiar cavo-tingle filled her mouth, and she parked it in her cheek. The article she was reading concerned her people's struggle against the Ehzeri attacks. Part of it was an alleged firsthand account of one of the guerrilla raids. In particular, one of the occasions where the attackers had employed *vihs* with devastating results.

Devastating results she remembered with a depressing clarity. She heard the sounds, the booms and cracks, the roaring jets of fire, all pounding her parents' settlement while they huddled in the shelter underground. She heard the chilling crooning of Ehzeri fighters ready to overload their own bodies with *vihs* in order to cause maximum damage.

But then this account veered into tales of cannibalism and sexual deviancy. Things nobody could possibly believe. And it concluded with a note praising Blightcross' own Ehzeri population for their denial of such horrible ways. That answered Capra's question of why anyone would publish such a scathing report in a town full of the very people it decried.

Oh, it was not you we think are monsters; only the ones who are stuck back in your homeland. Keep doing what you are doing! We love you!

"Why are you wasting your time with that trash?"

She set it on the table, next to her lukewarm shalep. The front page showed a headline lauding the tireless bureaucrats of the Blightcross Fuel Corporation for improving working conditions, as well as a short note of congratulations to the Publications Commission for becoming the most widely read stable of periodicals. "Because there's nothing to do until tomorrow."

"You really trust this person?"

"She was one of your own."

"That means nothing, especially here. I would not trust most of them to brew my shalep. They have been bought, and the few here who still have their power are only going to permanently deplete their families back home."

She began to wander around Helverliss' loft. There were uncleaned paintbrushes, lying stiff in strange places, and she accidentally stepped on an incomplete sketch lying on the floor. "I still don't get that, Dan. It just makes no sense. I can understand that certain groups have more capability, and of course that the war wiped most of them out. But this family link thing your people have sounds rather silly."

"The strict code and familial binding was supposed to keep us strong. And it did, until people started to come here and use their power individually. I do not claim to understand how it works. Nobody knows a damned thing about *vihs*, and anyone who claims to is a liar. Our system also ensured that catastrophes like what happened during the war are impossible. We would all have to agree to wipe out an entire race."

"Have your people not agreed unanimously to wipe out the Valoii? I have heard of strange tactics. Ingenious ones. Raising your young, gifted countrymen from birth to become fighters, to transform them into weapons. It really shows what can happen in times of desperation."

Dannac said nothing.

Best let the man brood as he always did. She went downstairs and decided to peruse the mess of books. There had to be something interesting amid all the junk.

She traced her finger along each shelf and examined the titles. Most of them left her baffled—*The Pyramid Of Iathecan Analysis, On Folklore And Nationalist Revivals, Vihs: The Joke Of Reality And Why We Cannot Laugh*, and one that made her chuckle, *Magic As Phallic Desire*.

After pacing through a few shelves, she stopped and accepted that she would find no romances or retellings of old legends. There were stacks of outdated journals, going back fifteen years at least, and all of them concerning art, science, and literature. There were university publications, and a small section of brightly-coloured books with the same mark she had seen on the weekly she had just read.

Definitely nothing she would want while relaxing on the rocky shores of Prasdim. Then again, if she were actually able to get back to Prasdim to lie on a towel, she would read the most boring academic text and feel damned great about it.

On one of the walls, her eyes fixated on another painting. This one showed at least something resembling a person, though it was too vague to call it a man or a woman. But the ghostly form stood amid a backdrop of grey-blue tendrils. It was like a fire made of deep blue storm clouds, and her lips parted as she shuffled towards the painting.

This painting's impressions leaped into her mind with a kind of sophistication that the one before lacked. Now she understood why Helverliss decried the other one as crude. She began to feel as though the stylized figure were dancing in her own mind, and she began to cycle through happiness to sadness and curiosity and horror...

The image overtook her vision so that she lived inside it, or it inside her. The blue fire began to take on shapes— people she vaguely recognized, and voices whispered to her.

Dad? Who are those men?

Her parents' old place near the demilitarized zone in the foothills, where derelict Yahreinian equipment rusted in their buckwheat fields. A broken wall, and a group of men in sagging caps like her dad's, sleeves rolled up to their elbows and who was that man they had pinned against the crumbling wall...?

Traitor traitor traitor traitor traitor traitor

The voices of her grandfathers and their grandfathers, whirling blue figures, spirits, flying in formation over the mountains that had been their ancestral home, and all at once she felt her throat spasm and her eyes flood but she did not understand why...

He wanted to hurt us, honey. He can't hurt you now. It's okay. Stop crying.

But she shouldn't have seen it—how had it happened? Nobody that young could have understood it. There were men, there was a broken wall, and there was a thump, and there was blood.

You think this excuses you? Shall we all just walk away because we saw something horrific? Everyone has seen something horrific. It is simply the times in which we live.

And she called aloud, "Who the hell are you to judge?"

She hardly expected the answer, and even less expected to be yanked out of the painting's strange world, to stand once again in a musty shop surrounded by academic drivel. "I did not mean to judge, Capra."

She wiped her eyes and once they focused, she saw Helverliss standing under the painting. For a second, she saw the two flow into each other, as if both were ink being swallowed in a whirlpool. "Sorry... I..."

"No apologies, young lady. It is what I had intended my art to do."

"What?"

"This painting. I neither wanted a fully subjective piece, nor a static objective work. This was one of my first pieces that could place abstract concepts directly into the viewer's personal experience. My work exists both inside and outside—it is neither solely dependent upon the viewer, nor is it meant to be viewed with cold distance in isolation. It is a fine line, I know, and many have said I have failed to do what I have claimed, but I of course disagree."

She stared at him for a moment, tried to think of what any of that might have meant. "I... felt..."

"Why do you run?"

"What?"

"Why do you run? And why would you trust your friend with your life?" He began to pace and glanced at the painting.

"Mr. Helverliss, I—"

"Not my place, I know. But that particular painting explores concepts relating to compassion, although what actually occurs when the viewer experiences this work is hardly reflected by such an inadequate word. Most people do have similar reactions, but rarely as strong as you."

"But I was inside the picture. There were these things... and I saw my dad and these other men..."

He grinned. "Yes. I cannot tell you what it meant, but I have wondered since meeting you what event could be so moving that you would take off across the world with your sworn blood enemy. I know why he trusts you—because he is truly insecure and lonely, and is extremely flattered that you have not stabbed him in the heart like any good Valoii would do. But you are more complicated."

She tried to meet his eyes, but afterimages of the painting's illusions crept into her mind. Was it a buried memory? No—it seemed familiar now. It could be her mind playing with her, or the painting manipulating her, but she had the strange idea that memory was an integral cog in the machinery of her mind. It had always been there...

What are you doing, Dad?

Around the man's neck was a golden, knot-like emblem. Knot—that was all she could remember, and that she thought it was pretty because there were stones in it and she liked shiny stones...

"Oh, shit." She brought her hand to her mouth, and with her other hand, grasped the amulet around her neck. *Heirloom my foot.*

"I do not mean to pry, Capra. I am sorry."

She composed herself. "No, I appreciate it. I think your works are brilliant, though I don't understand most of them. I mean, my favourite works are just the old masters... this is so new to me. Your work is not all handsome nudes and pictures of fire giants leering at maidens." She flashed him a nervous smile.

"Well, it is not meant as a tool for psychoanalysis, but sometimes it does end up contributing to some insight. I hope you at least have enjoyed the experience."

"Psychowhat?"

Helverliss sighed and guided her away from the painting. "A new science of the mind."

More new sciences, and all for what? To replace the *vihs*? To feign understanding and build machines?

She had to give Helverliss credit for his observations. The only odd thing was that the painting's vision had not been a remembrance of the day she had decided to desert the army, as she would have thought would happen based on Helverliss' explanation of the painting. In the vision she had been a child, and with each trudging step up to the loft, she wondered more if she had been destined to become a traitor from the very beginning.

She flopped onto a couch, and Dannac gazed at her. What was he thinking? The stupid jewel in his head just sat there and glistened the same whether he was angry or sad or randy or whatever.

"So what was your answer?"

"What?"

"Helverliss asked you why you decided to stay with me. I disagree with his assumptions about myself, but I am curious about your answer."

With a swift jerk, she shot upright. "You were listening?"

"Small shop."

"It's a stupid question. You're my friend, and that's it."

"If you say so. I thought it might be atonement for the Valoii phosphorus grenades that stole my sight, but maybe that was too obvious and simplistic for someone like you."

Ridiculous—if that were the case, she could have chosen another of his people to befriend who wasn't such a bitter old twat. She shook her head and lay down again. She was loyal, people could depend on her, and why did it have to be more than that?

She was loyal and dependable.

Traitor!

Vasi hesitated at Sevari's door and gazed at the carvings. The figures came alive in the deep red grains, symbols became literal in shining varnish. They were the old legends, processed by Sevari's delusions and twisted to convince Blightcross natives that they were something special, a violent establishment of difference. Akhli's descendants, all alive on the man's door, holding spears, slaying fire giants, leading armies, ascending to heaven...

She thought of backing out, but she had already told Sevari the important details. For a moment she imagined the sizzle of Capra's flesh disintegrating under her own devastating working—a *vihs* conjuration of the white fire that had maimed so many of her people. But she was disciplined. Unlike most of her age, she was able to detach, to become an instrument, to withdraw from passion so that all she did was move according to what the divine asked.

One of those requests, Vasi knew, was justice. There was a right way and a wrong way to achieve justice, and part of doing things the right way was denying the archon's seductive promise. The cost was too high.

She held her breath and knocked. A moment later, the doors buzzed and opened. Standing at ease, in the green double-breasted jacket and trousers, black beret, and knee-length boots, was Alim.

"So, you have her, do you?" Sevari poured some liquor into a glass and offered it to her.

She sniffed it and shook her head.

"Very well. I thought that perhaps you might relax a little. You've been one of my best assets, Vasi."

"You know we do not drink that kind of spirit, Sevari."

He chuckled. "Yes, yes. I just thought this might be an occasion for exceptions. Now, are you absolutely sure this person you met was the one my friend is after?"

She nodded.

Sevari gestured to Alim, who passed him a dog-eared piece of parchment. "Here is a portrait of the woman."

Those fierce, dark eyes, military-style tight braid, insolent smirk, slightly bumped nose... "That is the woman I saw."

"And you planned to take her to the palace?"

"Yes."

"Why the palace?"

She stammered, then recovered. "It was the first thing that came to my mind. They were looking for confiscated treasures, and I wanted to keep them far away from the clock tower to keep us safe from them. The palace seemed a decent place to corner them. The underground vaults of the armoury connect with the catacombs, if I am not mistaken."

Sevari clapped, and she flinched. "Yes! Then she will be out of the streets, and the take-down will be seen by nobody. There will be no panic or fear. Wonderful."

Alim cleared his throat. "Sir, I thought you wanted this to be public knowledge. A publicity maneuverings."

"Yes, but only in a way we can control. Anything could happen when we take her down, Alim. We get her first without telling anyone, and then we will send the appropriate story to the Publications Commission once we figure out how best to profit from the event."

Alim bowed his head. "As you wish, Leader." He then broke his rigid stance and rubbed his jaw thoughtfully. "I had thought we would find out where she was staying and raid the building. Sometimes the simplest approach is best."

"I respect your opinion, good soldier. But as of yet, she has committed no crime in Blightcross. Do I want my people, who have been living in the shadow of Tamarck since this island's modernization, to believe that I am simply the poor idiot who holds the tail while Mizkov copulates with their livestock? No. It should appear as though I am protecting these people from a deranged, highly dangerous fugitive. And an incursion into the palace to assassinate a freely elected leader is just the kind of think I need."

"But Leader, you don't—"

"Let us never speak of my living arrangements, now." Sevari's face dropped its serious tightness when he turned back to Vasi. "So it is settled then. Good. You all know where to be tomorrow?"

Vasi and Alim muttered their agreements.

"Perfect. Now, Vasi, I trust you will go back to your research until then. I need to know what that painting means, how we can use it. What secrets it might hold for me... I can almost see the message meant for me, but I think I am too close to see. That is why I need you, Vasi."

"Of course, sir."

"The worldspirits have chosen you. I can just tell that you are the one to unlock this monumental power. Helverliss was a fool to treat it as mere philosophy, as some kind of finger-wagging at what he dislikes about us."

She endured ten minutes of this rhetoric before Sevari sent her back to the lab. A while later, one of the peons brought her a meal from the Leader's personal kitchens, as had been the routine since her promotion to the research staff. It was her favourite—well, her new favourite. A Tamarck dish consisting of beans and some kind of meat. At first, the thought of going against The Blacksmith's Edicts made bile rise in her throat, but after she had made the leap to actually eating the unholy combination, she had never looked back.

But, as she worked her triangular implement around the food, she thought of her grandparents back home. Were they still practising? Was she diverting all of the family's power? They would not say in their letters. They just wrote as though *vihs* did not exist.

Maybe because for them, it no longer did.

Because of her. But given the choice between living as a slaughterer of thousands and depleting her family's power, the only reasonable choice was the latter.

I can make it up to you. I will save the image of Capra Jorassian suffering in my memory, and you will witness the justice first hand once I come home.

Alim seated himself across from Sevari. More than once he came close to voicing his scepticism, but by now he knew it was futile. This oligarch didn't much care for clashing opinions.

"How loyal are your employees, Sevari?" He was already weary with the show of decorum. "Really."

"You worry that this is too easy? That the big bad Ehzeri is going to hurt you? This is Blightcross. They are not Ehzeri anymore. They are my employees, and some of them still have the old powers. I am all they have here. You can trust them."

Odd how the man who was responsible for the death-knell of magic and thaumaturgy with his campaign of mechanization still concerned himself with the *vihs*. Never mind concern—the man blatantly employed *vihs* in his refinery.

"I admit that I do not understand your mysticism. The whole world is changing as a result of your industrial efforts. Your public stance is very different from what I have seen here."

Sevari touched a stud on his desk, and panels in the wall rotated to reveal several abstract paintings. "I would advise against staring directly at them until you have some time to deal with potentially disturbing concepts. But these paintings are infused with magic, and have amazing properties. Properties no machine will ever approximate. Yes, I move to replace what little magic practice is left with machines, because I control how much fuel these machines receive. Magic still exists, though. It does not go away because we become afraid or suspicious of its use. There will be new applications for it, and I believe the worldspirits move through me in sorting out how humans should best use this tool."

Alim squirmed and fidgeted. What could anyone make of such a theory? As if powered by some spring of eternal vigour, the Leader continued, and after a few more minutes of this, the words took on a watery quality. Alim feigned interest with a mechanical nod every few sentences.

Let Sevari believe in his spirits. Let the whole damned world be run by these grotesque engines, or let it be ruled by disciplined practitioners of the classical arts. The facts were startlingly simple: Capra Jorassian was a deserter. She deserved to die.

He glanced at one of the paintings—at first just a glance, but then his eyes were pulled to it once again, and soon he was mesmerized by the red and black pattern of the one directly behind Sevari.

He thought he saw forms—people—writhing in agony among horrible paint splatters. A woman with shorter hair, and a military tunic. Pleading and pain chiseled her face into a pale masque, and Alim wanted desperately to give this woman whatever it was she needed to end her suffering.

Jasaf...

Then an explosion of red paint, and she was gone.

"Alim? I say, friend, I told you not to look at them for very long."

The vision disappeared, and Alim's heart rattled as though he'd sprinted across the desert. "What?"

"Your face is covered in nervous sweat, good soldier. Here." Sevari tossed a handkerchief to him. "Who did you see?"

Alim hesitated.

"Come now, it is best to talk about it. This is why I had to confiscate these paintings, you see. They are awfully powerful and upsetting to many."

Jasaf...

Alim's shred of solace had come from knowing that Jasaf had died quickly, and that she was not suffering in the great beyond. But that painting had shown the complete opposite—his wife twisting and squirming and her face strangely set in a kind of stone—

"My wife died during a particularly brutal raid on an Ehzeri base."

"Ah. Yes, that is the kind of thing most people are reminded of with that particular work. I myself become haunted by the assassination of my friend when I look into that picture. And there are always the war memories..."

There was a long silence—Alim wanted to leave and be alone but found himself without the will to move.

"There, there, friend. Let us get you a drink—"

"Jasaf was a surgeon. All she wanted was to keep her comrades alive when we were sent into the madness for no good reason. She never harmed anyone, not even one of those Ehzeri maggots..."

"Well, it is a shame, what goes on there. It is a good thing more and more of them are coming here to work—"

Alim slammed his fist on the desk. "Jas was the surgeon assigned to Capra Jorassian's squad. If Capra had not deserted at the time she did, Jas would still be alive. She was supposed to protect Jas... she didn't do that... she used the confusion as an opportunity to run away..."

Another eerie silence passed.

"And this is why you are after her now? Do your superiors know about this?"

"Of course they do. They set up a special unit to track down these deserters. As soon as I saw Jorassian's name on the list of targets, I volunteered. I did not sleep for months just so I could get through the list fast enough to be assigned to her file."

He stood, straightened his damp wrinkled uniform. "And now it's time."

CHAPTER SIX

"So the terrorist and the collaborator are ready to go. Wonderful." Helverliss looked both from head to toe and showed no expression.

Dannac ignored the slur, and Capra assumed this was because she had caught him reading some of Helverliss' letters and essays, most of which sympathized with his people.

Capra tightened her boot lace, took a quick inventory of her standard kit. Small hand tools rested in a pouch on her belt, and in her satchel she carried rope and a few charges of small explosives. "Remind me to find a dealer after all this," she said. "This is the last of the stuff I lifted from the army."

No weapons hung at her side, which satisfied the latent pacifist within her soldier's mind. Since Dannac now carried a hand-cannon, and she'd learned a certain amount of finesse over the last few years, it seemed pointless to add the unnecessary weight.

She paused at the rumbling in her gut—either it was from the way Helverliss brewed his shalep, or she was nervous.

No, not nervous. Excited.

"I imagine this contact of yours aims to lead you into the underground vaults," Helverliss said.

At once Capra stiffened and shuddered. "Vaults?"

"Blightcross District sits over several ancient ruins. Part of this includes a network of solid metal vaults, and the palace joins with them."

"Underground? Like how deep?"

"Deep enough."

"How large are they?"

Helverliss smirked as if he could look directly into Capra's heart and stare at the growing knot of worry. "The passages are large enough for the average man to stand. Barely."

"Ah. Great."

"I would have guessed Sevari would keep his booty locked in the armoury, but I am clearly wrong."

With a small thumbnail of what the painting looked like—basically a black square, so the framing was more notable than the dark smudge it contained—the two left Orvis Dunes. For the first time since arriving here, Capra revelled in the breaths of cool air. A shard of sun burned on the horizon, and she saw carriages slow to the side of the road at residential buildings, where men with soot-blackened faces hopped out and switched spots with fresh workers just now emerging from the buildings. On the side of the horseless carriage was the rose emblem. It seemed that she could go not a block without glimpsing the crest.

And gradually, as they walked and the sun rose, the noise marched back into the air. Of course it had never really disappeared—Capra's poor sleep the night before proved the tired joke about Blightcross being the first city to ban the use of beds and soporifics—but now the drone of machines reached towards its peak.

"About Vasi," Dannac said. "Watch yourself when we are with her."

"You don't trust one of your own?"

He was silent for half a city block. "Let's just say I know her type. I would rather just leave it at that."

Dannac, always so cautious. It seemed a miracle that he had grown to trust her. Maybe he didn't?

Neither had forgotten about Alim, and with wordless understanding they kept to side streets wherever possible. It meant the trip would take an extra half-hour, but by now Alim must have recruited Sevari to his task, and every soldier they met was essentially Alim's agent.

"I wonder what they have hiding in there." Dannac gazed over the roof of a pyramid church. This block of the city brooded in the shadow of an immense white wall. Above it stood what Capra had assumed was another of the city's towers, but now, closer to it, she saw otherwise.

It was a tower, but made of metal tubing, and canvas stretched between the trusses, billowing and drumming with the wind. A guard stood on the wall—she had assumed he was a statue at first.

"It must be the armoury," she said.

"Maybe your friend is wrong and the painting really is in there. Helverliss is an extremely intelligent man. I would bet on his advice before some Ehzeri stranger's."

"Could be, but the palace looks pretty beaten up. I think their security might be shit, so we might as well give it a try. If not, I'm sure there will be something else in there to make it worth our while. Palaces are full of good stuff."

"Sure. But something about this place bothers me."

She tried to laugh, but it came out more like a cough. "It's this whole city."

"No, there is something about this... armoury. When I look towards it, I am nearly blinded."

She glanced at the strange structure. It looked normal, in that all she saw was a strange structure of canvas and metal tubes. Like a tent... "Maybe it's temporary."

"But why?"

"I have no idea. Maybe it's just a giant statue of Sevari and they're still working on it. It's probably nothing."

They made it to the arranged street without garnering any attention, and Capra began to search the crowd for Vasi. Numerous times they were accosted by salesmen in frock coats that looked as though they had at one time been expensive, but now were blackened and bristling with frayed threads. One asked if she wanted to buy a barely-used starting ember, and she wanted to ask the man what in the hell a starting ember would do for her. Before she could find out, Dannac swatted him away. Another approached them with an offer to read her fortune, solve her marital or sexual dysfunction, cure her of her monthlies, or any combination of the above for fifty pistres per half-hour. The little man received the same treatment as his predecessor.

"Can we walk a damned block without being told to buy something?" Dannac said, as he stared down another potential salesman. "Maybe if they bathed and learned how to overcome their nervousness, they might sell something."

"They're thieves. They're like us, Dannac."

"Bah. There is a difference."

"They are also addicts. They're sick."

He gave her a dismissive sneer. "Your friend is not coming. We should beat one of these thieves into telling us where to find the painting."

"Give her time, Dannac. I bet—" She caught a face in the crowd near the centre of the square, instantly recognized the woman's slender face. "Vasi!" She raised her arm and began to wave.

She fixed her eyes on Vasi, and was relieved when her new friend joined them. They quickly left the busy square, with Vasi leading them through narrow alleys they had overlooked. There was barely room enough to accommodate Dannac's shoulders. Their denim clothes scraped against the walls, emitted a strange chirping-rubbing.

"Vasi, please walk faster. I get uneasy in places like this..."

Vasi picked up her pace, but soon slowed again.

"There is where the leaders live," Vasi told them, after they emerged from the main streets into a less dense area. There was another wall here, but this time it was precise masonry and wrought iron, with sculpted lamps at each post. Farther down the road stood their destination, its dome dingy and pitted. "And there is the palace."

She would have expected the two Ehzeri to spark a conversation, but neither so much as looked at the other. Later, after this was over with, she would pry him for the story. Was she an old friend? Jilted lover? Had she done something offensive to his slightly old fashioned sensibilities?

"The palace is not really a palace any longer. Since the Leader took power after the war, it has become the district's administrative hall."

"The great Leader drove out the tyrant monarch, eh?" This was the first thing Dannac had said directly to Vasi.

Capra wrapped her cravat and tied it tighter than usual to keep it out of the way. She caught Vasi eyeing her with the steely gaze of the mountain lions that used to stalk Valoii herds—

At once she stopped herself. That was her people's conditioning; turn the enemy into an animal. The girl was probably just nervous or hungry.

Or she had caught a flash of Capra's tattoo.

Never mind—it was too late to worry about first impressions.

They walked right in the palace door, much to Capra's surprise. They passed through unchallenged, the standard guard postings deserted. On the floor were spots of discoloured marble, as though furniture that had decorated the palace for centuries had only recently been moved. Their footsteps reverberated as if they walked in an empty colosseum.

Signs dangled at each juncture, pointing them either to the District Court, Corporate Headquarters (all branches, including Mercantile Union), Complaints Commission, Office of the Governor General, and—

"Sevari Family Memorial?" Capra asked out loud, though she had not meant to.

Vasi knitted her brows at her and nothing further was said about the subject.

They passed offices littered with parchment stacks. Deeper into the halls, they wove around stray carts loaded with envelopes and boxes. They did pass the occasional office person, but nobody said anything to them.

"So, Vasi... have you done much of this kind of thing before?"

"No. But I am desperate."

"Sorry..." A thunderclap crashed outside. Another strange desert storm. "I thought Blightcross was a desert."

"Often there is dry lightning, and sometimes storms. It is not a lack of rain that is totally responsible for the desert here." Ahead lay a junction that either led to a rear exit, or a storage wing. "To the storage area. Here is where you must pick the locks. These doors are automatic, so they will lock behind us."

Capra gulped and opened the case on her belt. "Look, I know you must have seen my tattoo. I want you to know that I ran away because I couldn't live with what we were doing.

You have to know that I have nothing against your kind. I like your music and—"

"There are regular patrols by the lone guard here. We must move."

Just like that? Not even an acknowledgement of the awkward fact?

She looked at Vasi for a moment, thought of ways to press the issue, to make this Ehzeri acknowledge that Capra had done the right thing. But what else could she say? Besides, there would be a better time to explain herself than now.

Capra began to work the lock. She slipped one of her tools inside, felt a familiar layout specific to a certain foundry in Tamarck. The reason for its familiarity being that the last time she had probed this particular arrangement of tumblers, she hadn't been able to do it.

She took a deep breath, forced herself to concentrate on the tactile sensations coming through her implement. A few seconds into it, the room tilted and spun, and her stomach wrenched.

"What now?" Dannac asked.

"Damn." She stopped and her hand shook enough to cause a faint rattling inside the lock. "It's just a weird feeling." She inhaled deeply and went back to work, despite her unsteadiness. The thunder rumbled in the outer walls again, and this only seemed to make the feeling worse.

She tried to picture the inside of the lock based on what she felt. Concentration could usually override minor discomfort.

Except this time.

"Can't you work any faster?" Vasi asked, an edge to her intonation.

If it weren't for the damned dizziness, she might be better able to visualize the lock's mechanism. But each time she built a semblance of understanding, a tide of vertigo buried the fragile picture. A bead of sweat crept down her forehead to the tip of her nose, and she breathed heavily.

"Capra?" Dannac sounded concerned, for once. "Maybe we should just blow it up."

She didn't answer. A sharp pain cut from her jaw into her forehead, but she kept her teeth clenched because it helped to ground her. The other two began to mutter and complain, their voices lost in the faraway world from which Capra's strange sensations had removed her.

One click. Good.

Sweat stung her eyes. But who needs eyes for lock picking? She pressed on, and it clicked again.

After she figured out the next piece and moved it with her picks, there was a clicking sound in the wall and the door swung open on its own, under some unseen power. "Looks like I still have it, even though I could visit the privy..."

Vasi returned at the head of the group, and they traversed through a hall lined with numbered rooms.

"You look pale," Dannac said.

"Probably nothing. I felt like this on the airship too, and look how that ended up."

"Perhaps it is the storm. My sister often became ill during storms. We have a word for it. Cloud sickness."

"That's silly, Dannac. I bet it's the air here. All this black smoke..."

"Smoke does not cause sickness."

Now he brandished his hand cannon, and Capra wondered if he wouldn't be disappointed if they made it out of the palace without him needing to blow apart a man's head.

"The vaults are down here," Vasi said, pointing to a trap door. On the wall behind it was a panel of studs. "A mechanical lock that uses numbers."

Capra let out a silent belch of sour air and approached the mechanism. "Bloody sheepfuckers, what do I do with this?"

She ran her hands along the panel and studs. Ten metal studs, numbered zero to nine.

Think, think...

"The famed Valoii army training fails you? Unthinkable." Dannac snorted and raised his weapon.

"Shut up, Dannac. This is different. Some kind of complex mechanical... what power does all of this use anyway? Some tamed form of *vihs*?"

Nobody answered. She turned back to the panel and pressed a few buttons. Each stayed depressed, until she pressed a fifth one, which seemed to slam each one back out again with a sharp clang.

She kneeled and put her ear to the panel. When she touched her head to it, she heard whirring, the metallic grinding. "It's all gears. Clockwork, driven by engines." She brought out her tools and began to pry off the panel.

It was ridiculous—the entire complex veined with little shafts and cams, and all just to operate elevators and doors. Yet with the panel off, that is what showed in the wall cavity. The brass buttons remained, fastened to levers and cams whose connections became lost in the web of gears and sprockets.

With her small tools, she began to probe inside the cavity. "You have family here, Vasi?"

"Pardon?"

Dannac sighed. "She does this when she works sometimes. Inane chatter. At least, until things go wrong and she goes dead silent and one has to scream at her to get an answer."

"I... brought my brother here last year."

"Sounds like you regret it." Capra bit her tongue—perhaps it was too soon in their professional relationship to make such assumptions. "I mean, well... Hey, I think this thing is actually pretty simple in the end..."

"I wish there were other options, but this seemed to be the best idea at the time. I am sure you know what trouble a young man can get into back home."

"Hey, I know what it's like to leave home and wonder if you'll ever go back. But I guess both of us probably would do best to stay away from home for good." She glanced to Vasi, who was staring at her again. Or, rather, at her chest, where the amulet had fallen out of her shirt and dangled. "My dad gave it to me." *And where did he get it from?*

"Really?"

She smashed one of the thin brass shafts with her pliers, and it snapped. "Is it familiar to you?"

Vasi broke eye contact, and Capra shrugged away the odd conversation to return to the panel.

"We move farther back into the vaults. Ambushes near the entrance are something she will be watching for." Alim forced himself to concentrate on his men, rather than marvel at the sheer immensity of the underground fortress. It had taken them nearly an hour to reach this point, even at their martial jaunt. But they had come too far—just ahead lay the palace entrance, and he knew that by now Capra should be just beyond the ceiling, tinkering with the security mechanisms.

They took position near an intersection—two groups behind each wall. "Turn off your glow torches," he said, and twisted the band on his own to separate the two reactive elements inside.

"She will not hesitate to engage you hand-to-hand. We are taught to kill with any means, even if our shins have been blown off. She is agile. She has above average lower-body strength." This last point he knew from experience, from them all taking part in school sporting events. Staring at those thighs, wobbly with a teenaged drunkenness over girls' legs...

What was he thinking? He no longer knew her. Mizkov no longer loved her; she had thrown away her citizenship. She was something else—not the girl he had sat in detention with, not the girl who had introduced him to Jasaf.

"Do what you will to the Ehzeri, but I want Capra for myself."

A grave thought overcame Capra, after having failed to decipher the mechanism: what if one of the incidental (*she thought*) cams she had snapped (*because it seemed like it would make things easier*) was an essential part of the wretched thing?

"Is there no other way in?" she asked.

Dannac grimaced. "You can't do it?"

"You can't always win, Dannac. So many pieces, I hate to think of what would happen if someone had to repair this. And it looks like someone is going to have to—"

There was a creak in the floor, and Capra jumped back. Her tools fell and jingled at their feet.

The opening in the ground raised with the grinding of stressed metal, as if the entire jumble of gears were being forced to act against their design. Once the trapdoor was open, Dannac fished in his gear for a glow torch and began to step into the abyss without question.

"Vasi?"

Vasi echoed Dannac's silence and descended behind him. Why had nobody said anything about the woman's power before?

Then again, it hardly surprised her. The Ehzeri avoided certain discussions, and calling attention to their abilities was one of them. Perhaps it was a way to keep the mystique alive after the practice had become a skilled trade rather than a mystical endowment.

Inside the vaults, Capra saw just enough room above her head to stave off her panic. The halls were long enough that the light of their glow torches became lost in the void ahead. At least there was somewhere to run if the walls started crushing her...

The sick feeling was still there, and she stopped for a moment to collect her wits after a particularly bad wave of nausea and head pain.

Vasi approached her, torch brandished like a weapon.

The green light seared into her already throbbing head. "Hey, not in the eyes!"

"We must hurry." Vasi hesitated, forehead drawn tight.

"Let's just keep going. It will pass."

Vasi looked about as calm as Capra's stomach. Could it be intuition trying to grab her attention with these sick feelings? Like her grandmother who talked about omens and thought that every minor ache was a portent sent from the gods? If it were, they ought to be turning back as fast as they can.

"Stop." Dannac held up his hand and shut off his torch. Capra and Vasi took the cue and extinguished theirs. "I thought I saw something. A strange variation."

She whispered to Vasi, "His eyes are dead. The jewel in his head allows him to see, though it seems through a different plane from what we are used to."

"Where did he get it?"

Capra thought for a moment. "I had just assumed your people healed him. I never asked him about it."

"I have never heard of such a working."

Odd, but it was not as though the Ehzeri were the absolute last group to possess magic. Someone else could have done it.

Dannac gestured down the hall. "Come forward, but keep watch. It is probably just a vent for warm air—sometimes that can show in my vision."

"He sees air?"

Capra shrugged. She was starting to notice a strange pallor in Vasi's face. "Maybe there really is something in the air down here."

Vasi met her eyes again. There was something different this time. A weight plaguing the girl, and more than most Ehzeri usually displayed. No, not a weight. A kind of fire.

The last time she had seen a pair of brown eyes cut a slash of hatred was the night the army ordered her to murder. The night she had decided that it would be the last time.

Something wasn't right.

"Dannac..."

"It is clear. Shut up."

"No, Dannac, stop." Vasi was now at their rear. Capra suddenly felt as though her back were naked, that at any moment Vasi could unleash an attack.

And it would only take one such attack.

The back of her neck prickled. What could she do? If she were quick enough, she might slit Vasi's throat...

There had to be an explanation for it. Vasi just wished there were more time to find one. She was too accustomed to working things out at her leisure, thanks to Sevari's lenity towards his research staff.

Alim should be waiting a few steps ahead, and ready to take Capra down with his squad of loaned killers. His gnashing teeth and angry eyes when he had spoken about this operation were far from the Valoii soldiers' legendary stoicism. What was really the reason behind this? One thing was for sure, Capra was not like the other soldiers back home—even her own people wanted her dead.

The eyes... Capra's eyes said it all, or did they?

The archon twisted in her mind. *Forget it. Kill her. Kill them all.*

She bit into her lip until she tasted blood, as if swallowing her own would satiate the archon. Capra wasn't what she appeared to be. Killing her might not be the right thing to do. Not yet, anyway. And she would never do it if it meant she had to bring that corrupted archon back into existence.

Nothing else Vasi knew of could turn the dark eyes of a Valoii into a pure blue. And the storm...

Dannac was right, without even knowing half of what he had said. Couple Capra's eyes, the fact of the thunderstorm, and that she carried an Ehzeri family's emblem around her neck...

But how? How could an Ehzeri grow up to join the Valoii and kill her own people?

She had to find out, and there was no way Vasi would trust Alim to keep Capra alive long enough to discover why she was showing symptoms of the cloud sickness, why she was in fact suffering from the work-lust, the *vihslag*, the thundery eyes, unnatural blue...

Pent-up *vihs* with nowhere to go, aggravated by thunderstorms. A banal rite of passage among Ehzeri teenagers.

They were fast approaching the trap. She had to decide in the next ten seconds.

The dread only deepened—now at her back she felt a kind of tingle, a sense of... doom?

But this was more than that. She unsheathed her knife, popped the blade. There was a strange light dancing on the walls now, and it came from behind them.

She went to Dannac's side, her mouth dry like the cracked earth. "She's preparing an attack. I have no shielding. I never expected to face another Ehzeri again, damn it."

Dannac calmly drew his hand-cannon, this being his only reaction.

"By the look of it, she has already finished her meditations and is just waiting to strike."

Dannac whispered, "Perhaps this will be the instance that finally depletes her family forever and the working will fail." There was an odd sincerity in his voice, as if he knew this from personal experience. "If you get the chance, rip from her neck the amulet she wears. It will look similar to yours."

"What amulet? I saw none."

"Anyone who still has power uses the family amulets to channel the common reserves. She no doubt has one under her clothes."

The implications of this had barely come apparent to her when behind them Vasi called out, "Duck!"

Both instinctively dove to the floor, and Capra skidded across smooth concrete. There was a crack and a blue flash, and the sound of men crying out in pain and surprise. She lay there, hands covering the back of her head, breaths rapid and rattling.

When she stood, knife at the ready, Vasi was ahead of them and gesturing frantically.

"What's going on?" Capra twitched with a strange anticipation.

Dannac joined her. "She released an attack. Obviously her family is well powered."

"But what is this about?"

Vasi waved down the hall. "There is no time. Follow me— the men will only be out for twenty minutes."

Men? What men? The men who had screamed, but who were they?

Unless...

"You knew... Vasi, you bitch!"

Lying on either side of the next intersection were soldiers in blue leather. Except Alim, of course, whose uniform brought unpleasant memories and a cold chill racing through her flesh. She stopped for a moment, kneeled at his side, and peered into his open, unresponsive eyes.

"What did I do to you, Ali?" She bathed his face in torchlight, and now that he was unconscious, saw the man she had known, rather than the bitter, mindless tool of Great Mizkov. "What did *they* do to you?"

Dannac's voice boomed and echoed in the corridor. "Either slit his throat or run."

The thought to kill Alim had never occurred to her.

It was ridiculous. Murder was one thing she could and would run away from.

She bent down and kissed him on the forehead, then sprinted to catch up with the others.

They emerged from a hidden entrance in the alley next to the palace, which had been covered with wood scraps and old sheets of canvas. They had run the entire way through the catacombs, fast and hard enough that none could squeeze any words in between panting breaths. Capra had tried to make sense of it all—a traitor who led them away from the trap, and her own unwillingness to kill Alim.

They leaned on their thighs and caught their breath. Capra's own breathing reminded her of the mechanical cacophony around them—rattling, laboured.

"Did you do it?" Dannac finally asked.

"Of course not. He's my friend."

Dannac chuckled.

"He is. I think the army did something to him. Alim would never turn into such an obsessive, hateful person."

"There is no hope for your generation." He stretched and gazed at Vasi. "You have some explaining to do."

Vasi shook her head. "Alim has reinforcements stationed all around the palace. I suggest we split up."

"Why should I trust you?" Capra asked.

"Because I just saved your life. That man wants nothing more than to see you suffer. He is ready to die for it."

The words stabbed Capra like a Valoii phalanx. "What are you saying?"

"I am saying that you need to hide for the moment. Give up your search for this painting. You will never find it."

Dannac stepped between them, shoving his hand-cannon back into his coat. "We can sort that out later. I would not doubt that she speaks the truth about Alim's reinforcements. We should just agree to meet at Orvis Dunes in... say four days. At noon." He smiled, and Capra caught the subtle jab at her leisurely pace during most mornings.

"We aren't giving up. Not after that..."

When she peered around Dannac to address Vasi, she was gone.

"Great."

Dannac grabbed her shoulder. "Pick a direction and run."

So she did.

CHAPTER SEVEN

Alim brought himself upright in the infirmary bed, and realized that the humiliation hurt more than the surprise attack's waning hurt. "Sir."

Sevari entered with a disappointed look, but turned the expression into a hollow smile. "The surgeons say you will be fine. Now, what happened?"

It was a question he had asked himself a hundred times. There had been the sound of footsteps in the corridor, then...

"We almost had them. And suddenly the attack came, through the walls. It was *vihs*, without a doubt."

"Vasi told me the same thing. I guess Capra's friend is more than just a sour face connected to a jumble of overdeveloped muscle, eh?"

"You think it was him? I suppose it's possible."

"Well, who else? Capra? She has no such power."

Alim rubbed is forehead. "No, she does not. But there could have been another culprit."

"I hope you do not mean to incriminate my loyal Vasi. She would never turn on me."

Alim swung his legs off the bed, wiggled his toes. "I was going to say that perhaps they hired another."

"Witnesses said nothing of a fourth intruder."

"Then it must have been Capra's friend." He stood and put on his beret. "Any sign of where they went?"

"None."

"Are my men in good health?"

Sevari nodded.

"Then I have to get back into the streets. But this time, I'm doing it my way. No uniforms."

"As you wish. I will send a note to the Publications Commission. This is a great opportunity for us to legitimize ourselves further."

Alim paused. What an odd thing to say. "You need to legitimize yourself?"

"Well, you don't admit it in public, but the reality is that in this situation, I do."

The more Alim worked with Sevari, the less he liked him. What kind of place was this? Blightcross was a part of Naartland, yet Sevari acted as though he owned the whole damned place. It made no sense—all he was doing was divvying up this slice of desert and feeding it to his friends.

But the people were free.

He made to leave, and as he came to the door, Sevari stopped him. "I may require some more of your expertise in dealing with my workers."

"I am hardly an expert, Leader."

"You are too modest. Now, how do they behave when threatened?"

Alim briefly recalled the military's mandatory course in Ehzeri relations. "Depends on who exactly is threatened. In general they keep silent. They hate to acknowledge their own tragedies, yet they are obsessed with them at the same time. Families with power will try to avoid confrontation if possible because they are afraid of squandering it. Depleted people will lash out. They have nothing to lose—in the eyes of their god, they have been forsaken and all they can do to redeem themselves is destroy as many heathens as they can before they die. In modern terms, you could call it simple class tension; one group fearing to lose what they have, another group with nothing and capable of desperate violence."

Sevari stepped aside. "Interesting. Are they paranoid?"

"Not exactly. They are pragmatic people, and incredibly anxious as well. But ever since the war, I am told, they have become distrustful. I guess you can't blame them, considering how every army on the continent exploited them."

"Indeed. Well, I hope to avoid a potential disaster, but if they begin to feel threatened, I believe I will be able to anticipate a bad situation." Sevari stepped aside. "Thank you, Alim. Good luck out there."

She tried to act as though nothing had happened, but in the silence of the museum, Vasi was so distracted that staring at *Akhli and the Shadows* failed to bring about its strange visions.

Was Capra the murderer?

Every fibre of her being wanted to say yes, to be able to transpose her people's collective angst onto this one rogue Valoii and cleanse them by slaughtering her.

Or was this the archon's influence? Where did her justified anger end and her family's horrible working of hatred begin?

Damn them, did they really think their troubles could be solved so easily? In times like this, she tried to picture the ceremony. The gathering of family members, the ritual, the sky—it must have lit up like the Day of Creation with all the power it would take to create their own archon. Their own weapon.

No, she was lucky to suffer this kind of amnesia. It was enough that she felt the archon within, that she had not truly cast off its bloodlust. It was enough that she wanted to rip from Capra's chest her still-beating heart and expose its charred corruption and blackness.

But, unlike the Blacksmith's eternal labour to sustain the earthly plane, it would not be a divine sacrifice. It would be petty murder.

Focus, damn you. There were more important things. Like this painting. She owed Sevari a solution to the painting's bound energies, and this would always take precedence over capturing the Valoii. Once she completed it, removed the power, mastered it, the notoriety would eclipse the promise of a cash bonus.

But the damned thing was so complicated. Every time she shut her eyes to envision the tapestry of *vihs* living inside the frame, it was even more dark and alien. The few times she mustered enough concentration to follow a single thread, it split into another, and that branched again. The red and black twine continued into infinity. She could not manipulate them—they had no beginning and no end.

It was a void.

There was the feeling of utter otherness, of something foreign. She wanted both to turn away from it and ask it for its desire.

What do you want?

What do you want from me?

Why do you not answer?

There was nothing there, but there had to be...

She opened her eyes, tried to banish her connection to the working. Breaths came shorter and shorter, panting... a shaky hand pressed to her throat.

If this void existed, where was her God?

Darkness, dark like the Golroot river, dark like the thick poison pumped into the refinery.

Maybe some kind of holy illumination could unravel this conundrum, but it would take time. Any longer in this chamber and she worried that her body would disintegrate and her soul would fall to the ground in a cloud of poisoned sand.

She hurried back to her own lab, where she began to pick up the hose and tunics and petticoats strewn across the floor. Weeks had passed with her tripping over junk and nearly destroying valuable pieces, and cleaning would help ground her after the encounter with the painting.

Each item she tossed into a gunnysack. When she took one last look inside, there was a Koratian artifact sitting atop her unmentionables, along with two other random objects. She hardly remembered picking up her clothes—the banal act had failed to distract her from her troubles.

After returning the misplaced things to their shelves, she headed down to the clock tower's laundry.

Past the stained glass angels and into the elevator, its brass gleaming like the day it had first been installed. It was probably polished every night by people she had known back home.

The machine started its descent, and she clutched the brass handholds. As with every foray into the complex bowels, she closed her eyes during the descent.

When the rumbling ceased, and the telltale bump signalled that the elevator had arrived, Vasi opened her eyes. She swung the laundry bag over her shoulder and grasped the door handle.

And, as though she had taken a ride into an underworld of unseen horrors, like in the painting, Vasi's arm became paralysed and her throat tightened and a sense of dread urged her to run.

Her hand twitched. It felt as though the void had followed her, as if it were watching her and waiting for her to do something... but what?

Paranoia. Paranoia and that is all. Paranoia started the war, paranoia decimated our people. Calm yourself.

A relaxed breath, and she opened the door. It slid soundlessly on its bearings, and all she saw ahead was the harsh blue corridors of the basement, lit by bare gas. She sighed and smiled to herself. How stupid—

As she moved to take her first step, an arm dropped down from the shaft above. She dropped the bag. Jumped back, once more grasping the railing. "Hello?" It could be a maintenance worker, after all.

"Hello?"

She took one step forward. Above, there came the sound of a loaded sack scraping against metal.

At first, it was a blur of darkness—a disruption, like a large bird flitting across a window. Then came the thud, the sound of a side of beef cut from its hanging. A body, twisted in a cruel pose, jammed against the elevator exit. The eyes showed no pupils or iris. There was a perfect hole between them, and from this a line of dried blood ran down his face. The mouth gaped, cheeks hollow like a victim of the consumption.

Only, it was not the consumption. It could not have been; only days ago, this same middle-aged Ehzeri had knocked on her laboratory door, arms loaded with the reams of paper and jars of ink she had requested from the office. They had chatted about a refinery committee tasked with organizing this year's Festival of the Divine Furnace. She had politely declined, citing her workload. He had nodded understandingly, and they exchanged pleasantries for a few minutes until she had dismissed him and forgotten his name in the time it took him to reach the elevator.

Another male, dead the same way as the others. Why? This man had crossed no one.

She dropped the bag and carefully stepped over the body. The sight of a corpse itself did not faze her. Her hard swallowing, sandy mouth, and wobbly knees came from the fact that someone else would die, and then another, and another, and she could not see any reason for it to stop. It was all too familiar. The archon had started the same way— taking a person here and there, not making too much trouble. Would this killer find the same bloodlust?

What if it were her? The archon...

Impossible.

A hundred different theories offered a simpler, more sensible solution. Worker solidarity was gone. This was not an event, but just part of a process. It happened with the militias back home, it happened everywhere: the degeneration into violence. While when she had arrived at the refinery, all the labourers bonded by way of their universal suffering, hope, conditions, and aspirations. She should have known that could never last forever.

Was it worth it to stay?

She hurried through the basement, asking if anyone had seen Rovan. Each time a worker claimed to have not seen him, her heart sank. He could be rotting in a waste pipe...

When she found him, he could argue all he wanted. They were going home.

Provided, of course, that her brother still lived.

Capra, having inherited her father's tendency to categorize things, had long ago assigned different stages to her current career. These categories, or levels of proficiency and experience, elevated what in vulgar terms was called "thief" to a respectable vocation.

Though she had only been in the business for about two years, her current self-appointed title was "security consultant."

She had started as an apprentice.

An apprentice in this business—of being an outcast, a malcontent, a scoundrel—partly paid his dues by the time honoured practice of sleeping in ditches when necessary. "When necessary" was usually most of the time, barring any contingent success in actually stealing anything valuable enough to pay for a room.

And this glorious morning, when Capra awoke with a stiff neck and dirt in her nostrils, she reminded herself that she was still a security consultant, even though she had spent the night in a ditch.

It was not really a ditch, but a space under a small foot bridge. She had wandered the streets past the Damwall area, with its perfect walls and houses that could never be robbed by the seething mass of cretins who lived on the outside, and ended up down here when she had run into a squad of soldiers.

She stood, made sure she had collected her things. At once she scrunched her face at the metallic, bitter taste in her mouth. She spat several times, and when it persisted, vowed to find a pub and burn it out with a few shots of plum liquor.

She climbed up the embankment and crossed the bridge. Why had she pointed herself in this direction in the first place? They had split up, running... Vasi had left them before they could glean a fraction of what had happened...

It was no use trying to make sense of it. But it wasn't as if there were anywhere better, so she continued to walk south. No giant towers loomed here—those were now at the skyline to her back. This area was eerily deserted, yet the air still vibrated with noise. Rails ran parallel to the disused road, and she felt the rumbling of a locomotive in her feet.

Only once before did she remember riding in a train, and it was one of the failed steam-driven ones. Luckily, it had not exploded during their journey—

The journey. Out of the mountains and into Mizkov. Like cattle.

Later she would learn that her family had held out in the years after the war and tried to keep their place in the mountains, but Yahrein was serious about keeping the mountains clear of Valoii, since the treaty had awarded the ancestral lands to them.

She shivered as the iron beast gained on her. Two lamps shone at the engine's front, and out of twin smokestacks jets of pure black trailed. She braced for the strange hiss of the steam-drive, but when it came, it was even louder and more aggressive—a banging, a growling, and the whole thing was like a mountain ram mad from winter starvation, breath steaming from its nostrils.

But instead of snow-capped mountains and trees, she walked among scorched earth. Here, in the empty lots, heaps of red sand sat in rows. There was no winter here, and surely no sheep, and the smoke was not the innocent breath of an animal, but an expression of extreme heat and dirt.

Now farther into the area, her denim coat became a soggy oven. She shrugged out of it, and the sun broadsided her shoulders with a pleasant warmth. Only minutes later, it seared her shoulders and neck. Except, of course, the scarred patch on her left shoulder, which felt nothing.

Would the danger really dissipate in two days? What if waiting only allowed Alim and his allies to gather their strength? And what about Vasi?

An hour later, her once tight plait now a frizzy, damp sketch of her military neatness, she found the factories. Tall barbed fencing cut the desert into giant squares, with industrial castles rising out of the sand. Plumes of vapour joined the city's haze.

Ahead, there stood several strips of low buildings. One of them had to be a pub or a café. There were men in rough brown overalls coming in and out of them. Something was different, though. They were taller, and she found not a single Ehzeri cloak among them.

She stopped to gaze at the different businesses. Any concerns about Alim and escaping Blightcross drowned in Capra's thirst. Damn, one of these places had to sell a good drink—

There was a bell tone behind her, but she ignored it. A rumbling. A skidding sound, screeching. When at last she turned to find the commotion, she sprang to dodge the carriage speeding towards her. Too late.

Capra rolled onto her back. Whatever she lay on, it was reasonably soft.

Noise, impact... the last thing she remembered.

She sat up, rubbed her head. A cutting pain seared the left side of her head with each touch. When her vision cleared, she found herself in a small room, planted on a medical bench. There was a pong of ether and the odour of alcoholic plant tinctures.

The door squeaked open. Was it a prison surgery? Bloody hell...

She rubbed her eyes, gritted her teeth, prepared for the worst. The man who walked in wore brown coveralls and a flat cap. He looked out into the hall before shutting the door.

Capra stood. Wobbled a bit, steadied herself on the bench.

"The surgeon says you're fine. Said your knockout was more from shock than the impact of the transport."

The man's biceps rippled through a dingy undershirt. Capra didn't want to find out whether or not she could take him in a fistfight, and slipped her hand behind her to the tray of implements lying beside the bench. There—a scalpel. Plenty sharp. It would be over in two seconds.

She shifted aside to cover the action. "Is that so?"

He stepped forward and reached out to her. Capra failed to react when he snaked his hand round her back and grasped her wrist. He took the knife from her hand. "Relax. Everything is fine. It was just an accident." He dropped the knife onto the tray. "You shouldn't walk in the middle of the road."

The road... now she remembered. How stupid she had been, now that she recalled the heavy iron machines that rolled through the streets in Blightcross. She eyed the man for any clue about who he was. He didn't look like a prison guard, but one could never be too sure.

"I'll get to the point," he said. "I'll forget about the knife. I think I can understand where you're coming from."

At the same time, she both felt somewhat eased and more tense at this frankness. "Where am I?"

"A machine parts factory in Redsands. When the driver hit you, he assumed you were one of the workers here, so he loaded you into the corporate wagon and took you back. When I came to investigate the problem, I realized that you had no identification."

She backed away.

"Relax."

She'd relax when she left the place and found Dannac. There wasn't much point in staying at this factory. She moved to leave.

The man barred her with his arm. "Whoa, wait a second, honey." Now he leered at her. "Where do you think you're going?"

She bit her lip and held back the urge to flatten him. "As you said, I'm not one of your employees. I shouldn't keep you any longer. Sir."

"My name is Laik and I sure as hell am not 'Sir'." He smiled and let go of her. "I'm a foreman here."

"How nice. I really must get going."

But he blocked her again. "You aren't from here. That much is clear."

She said nothing.

"I'll be honest. There aren't enough people on my shift working. I need cleaners."

She blinked. "Excuse me?"

"I need cleaners. If I can't find any good workers, the management is talking about allowing Ehzeri into this factory." He grimaced as if he'd swallowed a mouthful of glass.

"And you think I want to work as a cleaner in a factory?" She almost laughed.

Laik pointed into the hall. "Let me show you the place."

"I'll save you the trouble by saying no thanks."

He clenched his fists and breathed heavily. "Look, Valoii. I know things are different in Mizkov, but here, you treat a man with respect. Do I make myself clear?"

"Get out of my way. I can't think of any way to have an intelligent conversation with someone like you." She shoved him aside and strode into the hall. The floor was shiny and reeked of cleaner, and she passed many a bewildered man along the way.

Who did that guy think he was? She could hear his heavy steps thump behind her. He didn't know how damned lucky he was. These Naartlanders clearly didn't know much about their allies if they would toss around a Valoii soldier based on her gender. Hell, a single platoon of *Kommzad* could probably find a way to lay waste to the Blightcross armoury without much trouble.

She passed through a glass corridor, and below was the factory floor. Giant vats of glowing orange, like the Blightcross sky melted into a pot. Chains everywhere, men with blackened faces. Sparks showered the concrete floor. And unlike the rest of the city, she saw no Ehzeri workers.

Now she had to find the way out of this damned place. But she slowed when she tried to think of what to do after leaving. She had a few days to lie low, to keep out of the public and wait for Sevari's attention to drift to some other injustice.

Before she could work it out, a hand grabbed onto her collar and jerked her to a stop. She whirled and let fly an open-handed strike. The attacker caught her hand.

Of course, it was Laik. "Calm down."

"You just don't get it, do you? I don't belong here." But, on the other hand...

"That's right, Valoii. Which makes my offer all the more generous. Only Naartlanders are given work in the factories. If I weren't so nice, you'd be sent back to the city to work in the refinery with all the other immigrants. And nobody wants that."

He let go of her, and she began to catch his subtext, which was the only reason she didn't snap his neck. "So you're desperate enough to keep Ehzeri out of your cleaning crews that you'd let a Valoii in, is that right?"

There was an odd flash in his eyes; a smugness. "It's a premium job. You could do much worse." He grinned. "And I think you have."

The comment snatched her breath. She glanced around and stepped closer to him. "Cut the nonsense. What do you know?"

"Me? I know that I'm short on cleaning staff and you're right here, probably jobless, and in need of a place to stay. Got me?"

A minute of silence, an appraising stare. Laik's expression held fast. Did he know who she was? Or was he just desperate for workers and bluffing?

No matter how much she hated the backwards men of Naartland and Tamarck, Capra reminded herself that these cultural problems didn't necessarily make the individuals who perpetuated them untrustworthy. At the worst, most were probably just ignorant clods. The facts were that the authorities were after her, and Redsands was a nice distance from the heart of the city, and the exclusive status given to these factory workers meant that the authorities probably wouldn't think to look for her here.

It was only for a few days.

She winced once more, then said, "I think I get you, Laik."

Dannac told himself to stop worrying about Capra—she was capable of keeping her mouth shut in dire enough circumstances. She did possess basic reasoning skills, and knew when her opinions needed to be silenced. Sometimes, anyway.

After they had split, he had taken the opposite direction and eventually came back to Corwood Park. He remembered the address from the eviction days earlier, and was pleased to find it still vacant.

He stood in the townhome's living room now, partly hidden by the wall and gazing out the front window for signs of Alim and his men. He fought hard not to be lulled by the halcyon air of Corwood Park, the peaceful order of these apartment blocks. The order had come at a cost—it had to. It always did, like the rows of Valoii houses in the foothills, where the cost had been a thousand Ehzeri lives.

He could see into the homes across the way—the glow of their ovens and furnaces, blobs of colour spread into vaguely human forms, as if his vision saw into a world made by Helverliss' perverted paintings. Ever since the Valoii attack that had left him blind, it was as though it had bounced him into a different reality.

Maybe the world really was completely different. Did the human senses lie?

He stopped himself from descending into a philosophical mania. There were soldiers after them, and he could not enjoy the comfort of squatting in the townhome forever. In fact, just down the road he noticed three forms heading purposefully towards the place.

He slipped away from the window and gathered his pack on the way to the rear of the house. Best not to take chances—places to live were in short supply here, and one night's vacancy was probably pushing it.

He went into the small back yard and hopped over the fence, into the gravelly square of the neighbour's yard. He did the same three more times until he emerged on a main road continuing east.

Ahead were the cranes he had glimpsed from the flying boat. They were shorter cranes than the ones at construction sites. Cranes for cargo. He sped to a jog, headed towards the harbour. It would be as good a place as any to hide. Lots of cargo, transient workers, slackened enforcement.

When he looked to the river, it barely stood out against the sand on the other side; the water was warm. Far warmer than a river ought to be. It must have been the way the refinery straddled the river, likely using the water in its processes.

He went to the water's edge and walked along the quays. Minutes later, he found his tentative goal: a group of depleted Ehzeri huddled near the ground, tossing around a pair of dice.

They stopped as soon as they caught sight of him. Gambling bastards. Gambling and charging interest—two things expressly forbidden by the Blacksmith. Perhaps his people were better off with these weaklings rotting away across the ocean.

"Good day," Dannac said.

A short man whose cap was askew and smothered his small head approached. "I'll be damned, the cursed one with three eyes. I had thought you to be a myth."

"Who did you have to betray to get back your sight, anyway?" asked another man.

Dannac reached for his hand-cannon, but stopped short of the concealed holster—it might be best not to advertise the weapon at this point. "I need a place to stay. Perhaps a very small loan to cover provisions for a few days as well."

"Loan?" The short one snickered. "Yes, let me just confer with the other board members of this fine financial establishment."

The man's companions guffawed.

He began to circle the short man, cutting him off from the rest. "I remember you."

"Oh, really?"

"Yes. The raid about three years ago. Ilagam, near the foothills."

"I see, I see. You must have read about it in the news, because I doubt the son of a coward who squandered his family's power in Tamarck to entertain our oppressors would have the courage to fight with us."

Dannac stepped closer, pushing the man further away from his friends. The others looked on, expressions unchanged. "I was there when a certain group of fighters were directed to join the *vihssat* at the head of the attack and defend him so that we could at least take out their command. I was there when that group saw the numbers of Valoii, and realized how utterly useless they were despite their big talk and love of violence and collection of blades and pathetic bombs that never work. I saw you all surrender. I know you, and I know what pathetic, unworthy trash you all are, and I need your help."

The little man blinked and Dannac saw a shift in the man's complexion. "It was a stupid attack. It never would have worked."

"It did, in the end. We did win, no thanks to you."

"And two days later, the Valoii came with more men and maybe a new war engine and squashed hundreds and took the land as if nothing had ever happened."

Dannac said nothing.

"In a way, maybe your father was smart. He did what he wanted with *vihs*, he followed his heart. He did not risk his life fighting for nothing."

"Like you."

"Yes, if you like. What do you want?"

Dannac smirked. "I told you."

"I can give you no loan. I know some businessmen who are always needing help, though."

"What kind of work?"

"Smuggling."

He shook his head. "I don't need any more attention from Sevari's people. I need something legitimate and safe."

"Legitimate? Smuggling is the most legitimate thing going on in this town. Everyone knows it happens, everyone agrees with it. If you contract yourself out as private security, you will deal with more papers and officials than if you just do what everyone expects and deliver a few packages of contraband to the armoury."

The armoury—they had to be joking. He said nothing to the man, instead letting the silence speak for him.

"Yes, the armoury. That is all you need to do. It is not nearly as hard as it sounds."

"If this is so accepted, why is it illegal?"

"Why must you ask so many questions?"

Dannac thought about it and gazed at the freighters bobbing in the river. Perhaps the man was right. His stomach growled, and he was thirsty. He had grown used to comfortable conditions, thanks to Capra, and besides did not trust that he could fall asleep in an alley here without being robbed or murdered.

"Fine."

For now, at least, it was fine. But what would he do if Capra failed to show at their planned meeting? What if they never reconnected?

Could he find the painting without her? Or would he be stuck with these other Ehzeri? He could smuggle himself off the island, but then he would be back where he started: on the continent, a wanted terrorist, and utterly alone. His own people had become careless and apathetic concerning matters outside fighting the Valoii, and the rest of the world was convinced that he wanted to destroy everything of value to everyone.

The little man led him around the quays to a yacht. Its sail showed a Tamarck folk-art depiction of a fire giant, all orange and red, with a long tail ending in spikes.

For the first time in a year or more, he felt the isolation. The sense of being cut from the rest of humanity because he could not see them. Had he really grown that dependent on Capra? She had made him feel normal, and even made him laugh at his own misfortune once or twice. Now he began to sink into a hard coldness that he hadn't realized he had overcome.

He focused back on the yacht and forced himself to forget about the issue. This was reality—everyone was alone, including himself.

CHAPTER EIGHT

In one day, Capra had graduated from apprentice to journeyman by pure virtue of sleeping on a rusted cot rather than a ditch. Laik had put her to work right away. It was a first for her, this sweeping of metal shavings and scrubbing lavatories.

Most of the women on her crew lived at the company hostel. Even with the broken spring that had jabbed her skin and the rank smell of the place, it was an improvement over the previous night.

She stood at the communal sink, scrubbing the grit from her fingernails, when Tey, one of the cleaning ladies, came in.

After a while of just watching Capra, Tey said, "There is something different about you."

She dismissed it with a limp wave. "Like what?"

"It's not your accent, or the strange words you choose. We get the occasional foreigner marries one of the men. A lot lately, now that this oil business has taken off. The men can't find a woman who will put up with their drinking, so they bring them over from the continent or the islands." Tey squinted. "But you have the walk of a single woman. So what are you doing here?"

"The walk of a single woman?" She shook her head and chuckled. "Are you kidding?"

"I kid you not." Tey's tone grated against Capra's good humour. So maybe making fun of these people's superstitions wasn't the best idea.

She looked over her shoulder. "It's complicated. The work isn't terrible, and... it suits my needs for now."

Tey nodded. "We do have it better than everyone who comes in from outside. But do you know how many times I have considered going down to the quays for quick, easy money? And this work is so boring. The rules..."

"I really have no problem with it. The work, anyway. It's dirty but better than other jobs..." What she had a problem with was the way the men behaved, their boorishness, the way they walked around in their coveralls like they owned the place just because they knew how to arrange the equipment in a way that produced more machines. "I mean, compared to what I am used to, it's nothing." Capra shut off the water and dried her hands.

Tey's eyes widened. "I knew it. You are not just a lucky Valoii who was able to grab a job at a place that hires no immigrants. You are a pirate or a princess or something, aren't you?"

Capra rolled her eyes. "That's ridiculous. I was just tired of the continent and wanted to live here for a while."

"To live in filth and grime and sweep metal shavings for the men? When your own society would have the men doing just as humiliating work?"

"Actually, none of the work is humiliating to us."

"See? Why did you leave, then? Oh, tell me everything. I'd die to hear of something beyond this stupid factory."

They left the lavatory. A massive wall of window panes stretched across the hostel's main hall; a dingy field of squares. From here the factory dominated the view, black and sweating against the red sunset. For a moment, Capra was reminded of tales of the underworld. There was even a river here, just like the one that led into the land of the dead.

But maybe it couldn't hurt to put some of Tey's curiosity to rest. Superstitious people could often turn on a person for the silliest reasons, and forcing them to guess was usually one such reason. "I am working towards becoming a chef, you see. I just need to save some money first." It wasn't exactly a lie. It's what she wanted to do. And she did need to save money before being able to settle into such a life. The part about using money to call off Valoii assassins was just a minor detail.

Tey appeared to stifle a salvo of chuckles. "A chef, you say?"

So Tey wasn't born yesterday. Better give her something, then. "Exactly. No more, no less. But instead, I have to run."

"But you were able to see so many things, and the danger..."

"What of it? And I can see as much as I want as a chef. Really, there is nothing so special happening beyond the rule of civilization. Crime, base urges, avarice..."

Capra was downplaying her own life and it felt strange, but she partly believed it. Not so with Tey, who pouted at Capra's remark, as if confronted with a tear in her little world—a world preoccupied with the romantic and grotesque. The other women showed the same signs—all their talk centred around salacious situations, murders, and preposterous stories from the continent, and they were all extremely conservative underneath these fascinations.

Capra, of course, was not immune: she did enjoy the gossip about rogues and romances and stories about rough men taming the Blightcross desert and fighting with Tamarck's king over sovereignty, and of Sevari's lieutenant, Iermo Juvihern, who was one of the most romantic figures in recent history. Iermo had been a privileged surgeon from the continent—Prasdim, she thought—who had given everything to join Sevari's coup out of some mysterious loyalty to the man, or his ideals.

The women here spoke of brutality as virtue. Tey had been happy to tell Capra about Fasco, whose fame lent his namesake to one of the city's roads. This executioner would round up all suspicious characters he could find, and each week he would take the worst of them personally across the Golroot River's bridge and into the area of the desert known as the Hex. Anyone who entered the Hex contracted a condition that rendered the skin pocked and burned, made their hair fall out, and inflicted a kind of sickness. Fasco was horribly disfigured from his weekly forays into the Hex, but continued to bring anyone he saw fit across town and deposit them there to either find a way out or perish from the invisible death that permeated the desert.

Even now, Capra could still see the gleam in Tey's eye when she spoke of Fasco the Executioner; Fasco the Just. A wistful sadness, or regret.

"You seem disappointed, Tey."

"Aw, it's nothing." Tey no longer smiled, and her voice dropped into a monotone drawl. "You're just so feisty. I thought you'd be itching to take on the men, take down this factory... something, anyway. Something big, you know?"

She was nonplussed. These were conservative women— everyone in this part of the world was. They should be comforted by Capra's denial of romantic savagery, yet Tey seemed to feel threatened by an outsider's insistence that civilized behaviour was revolutionary, and that crime was conservative and stagnating.

"Listen, Tey." She bit her tongue and reminded herself that these people were, at heart, honest. "Can you keep a secret?"

"Oh, yes. Yes, I can." Tey's disappointment vanished like a wisp of steam in the wind.

"Have you ever heard of a Baron Parnas?"

"Well, yes. Everyone has. He owns several oil field service outfits and serves on the labour relations council."

Capra put on a devilish grin and began to recall the scam that had stranded her in Blightcross.

"It started with a conversation I overheard at a chemist's back in the Little Nations. The Baron had come to pick up a tincture of Hypericum and struck a conversation with the apothecary there. He was lonely and depressed, which I gathered from the prescription alone. I listened more, and he talked about his wife who had left him for a young aristocrat who was both more handsome and wealthy, and of course the Baron was left in a shambles ever since. I arranged a dinner with him by posing as a wealthy heiress, and from there I began to exchange letters with him."

At the mention of love letters, Tey's face brightened, and they strolled through the hostel's halls. The setting sun sprawled across endless glass panes.

She left out the part about being hunted by Alim and trying to steal priceless artwork. The Baron's scam was enough to satiate Tey's hunger for romance.

"I had a husband once."

Capra indulged in a breath of relief. Deflect away, friend. "You don't say."

"Oh yes. Lousy bastard. Wouldn't drink a drop of beer, made him sick. A bit of a pansy, he was. In more ways than one. But that wasn't the worst part..."

An epic narrative ensued. One packed with grisly details and tittering, and Capra couldn't help joining in with Tey's stupid but contagious laugh. Only when they reached their room did she remember the situation's gravity.

A moment after they arrived, the lights winked out. The room plunged into a gloom lit by scraps of red light seeping through rectangular slits of windows. Women were already lying face-down in their beds, others rubbed strong-smelling salve into their knees and backs. Tey began to undress.

Capra looked around at the bedtime rituals. "Listen, I'll be back in a bit. I just have to go for a walk or something. I usually go to sleep much later."

"Oh, no. You cannot."

She cocked her head. The night before she had been so exhausted that she had gone to sleep the instant she came within falling distance of a bed. "What do you mean?"

"Well, you cannot just wander the hostel aimlessly. It is not allowed. And you can't leave the compound. Did you not learn the rules?"

"Rules?"

"Leave must be applied for in advance. And they never give it unless you have a decent excuse. Of course, each month you can have two days in the city proper."

"And if I become ill?"

"There is a surgery here. Quite large, actually. It even serves some of the rural populations."

Capra sat on her cot and took a deep breath. She felt trapped—they might as well have shoved her into a closet.

Deep breaths.

Closed eyes.

And then came a wave of rage against the bloody sheepfuckers and their damned rules. But she swallowed it. "Why... why don't I just take my monthly leave now?"

"They never do that. Never. You want those two days, you have to wait a month. Now, let's get you into bed. No sense agitating over it, after all."

"Are you joking?"

"Why no, missy. Get to bed—if you keep this up, someone will complain, and then what? Do you want them to send one of the men in here? Because you can bet they will."

"From the sound of it, you guys could use a servicing from them."

She stood and stormed towards the exit.

Tey called out, "You only get one chance, Capra!"

Who did these people think they were? Capra thought of the posters she had seen pasted everywhere on the continent boasting of the great opportunities in Blightcross, of the wealth to be had and the freedom to enjoy. What the posters left out was that in order to obtain this unending wealth, one would have to go to bed when they were told.

She slammed the door behind her and calmed slightly at the illusion of openness coming through the grid of glass. Now that she was out of the barrack, what would she do? Perhaps leaving the factory wasn't the best idea—there were security checks and besides, it would take a while just to reach the barbed wire fence circling the complex.

"I think you should head back into the barrack."

The voice belonged to Laik, and carried from the extreme end of the corridor.

"Laik, this is ridiculous. I am not a child."

"You are a woman. We do not hire you to reorganize the way we do things."

"Is this entire place just a big joke?"

"You owe me, Capra. I own you."

She clenched her hands into fists and stomped towards him. "The posters you people plaster all over the continent mentioned nothing about your stupid rules. Even Tamarck is not as backward as you."

"You are free to leave, Capra. This is not a dictatorship, like your land."

"Then let me leave."

"Go ahead. You can go to the refinery and enjoy your twilight years while you're still young, because the average lifespan of a refinery worker is forty. And, of course, they never report all accidents and deaths. I would guess the average is more like thirty-six."

She bit her tongue. Why bother arguing? It would only have been for a day or two. But the bastard was wrong, and he would never realize it if nobody told him.

"Besides," Laik said, a smart smirk beaming across the room. "You are much safer here."

"What?"

"You heard me."

She grabbed Laik by his coveralls and shoved him into the windows. He struggled, but she applied leverage enough to keep him pinned. She quickly turned him around, wrapped his arms round his back, and mashed his face against the glass. "What do you know about me?"

"I know you are running from someone. I could probably find out by talking with the Corps captain here and asking about any unusual security bulletins." Capra applied more pressure, and he coughed. Once she eased back, he said, "I heard a manager talking about a special joint operation between our forces and a Valoii soldier. They aim to flush out a war criminal. Then I remembered how you Valoii let your women fight for you. It doesn't take a genius to figure out who you are."

"Say a word and I will throw you into one of those vats of molten metal."

"Oh?" He kicked his leg and twisted so that Capra tumbled to the ground. He grasped a handful of her hair and jerked her head up. "I did you a favour, and this is how you repay me?" He punched her across the jaw. "No wonder Yahrein wanted to kill all of you freaks." He raised his hand to strike her again, but this time she caught his hand and flipped him over.

"Then why did you bring me here?"

He smiled, in spite of Capra's advantage. "Because now I own you. I have my own personal slave living right here in this factory, or I get a reward from Sevari if I turn you in. Either way, I profit."

"And if I kill you?"

"You won't, though."

She spotted a weakness in his hold, and braced herself to snap his neck.

No—the whole point of running from the army was to stop killing. She could have made a fortune as an assassin, yet she chose to avoid adding to her list of personal atrocities. Laik was not worth that compromise. She could still kill, she knew, but not over something so petty. Laik wasn't worth *that* much to her.

It was this momentary lapse into contemplation that slackened Capra's grip enough for Laik to throw her from him, and he followed this with a kick to her gut. She gasped and rolled around in the dust.

"Give up now, and we can forget this happened. All I want is half of your wages."

Did he really think she was going to stay long enough to make that worthwhile to him? "Sure."

"And I will be notifying the security personnel to keep watch for unauthorized leave takers. If you leave, I will tell them who you are, and they will find you before you clear Redsands."

"Sure."

And with that, she stood up, ignored the aching ribs, and limped back to her barrack.

The ass was going to get it.

Dannac tried not to let the yacht's subtle bobbing in the water lull him into sleep. For some reason, he found it soothing. The sitting room was quiet and the plush couches offered a heavenly embrace to his sore back. The little man sitting across from him—the Ehzeri whose name he did not want to know—offered no conversation, either.

But sitting around accomplished nothing. He sat up and cracked his knuckles. "I am beginning to wonder if this is an elaborate ploy to waste my time."

"He'll be here in a moment. He's very busy."

"Who is this person, anyway?"

"A senior partner in the industry. This boat belongs to Kervin Rawles."

"I have heard the name, but I cannot place it."

"The transport mogul. Probably you in some way used his services in coming here."

"And he owns this ship? He deals contraband?"

The man set his feet on the coffee table. "Everyone knows what he is into, and that is partly why he is so famous."

"And, no doubt, why he is so successful in the world of legitimate business."

A moment later, there was the sound of footsteps on the deck above, which carried across the room and descended. A man emerged from the door.

It was someone Dannac had never counted on seeing again, much less in Naartland. He stood and offered his hand to the old acquaintance. "Yaz?" he shook the man's hand, heart thrumming from this surprise.

"We were wondering about you, Dannac." Yaz clapped his hands together and examined Dannac from head to boot. "You are looking well. I trust the operation has stood the test of time?"

"It has." Dannac removed the scarf from his head to fully reveal the jewel.

The little man said, "This man is looking for some quick work. I told him about the shipment... you know, the job to take the stuff to the armoury."

"Yes, yes," Yaz said. "You can go."

The little man left, and Yaz gestured to the narrow flight of stairs. "The top deck is much better suited for entertaining."

Yaz showed him to a deck that overlooked the harbour. There was a table already set with appetizers and a bottle of amber spirits. "I am sorry I cannot offer you plum liquor." He paused for a moment. "You are still on your righteous kick, right? Still not mixing legumes with meats and all that lovely stuff?"

"I am not here to drink. What I am interested in is why, Yaztherew, you are captaining a yacht owned by a man who is the very antithesis of the Bhagovan Republic's ways. Have you defected? It seems to be in fashion these days."

Yaz stretched and eased back in the chair. "Defected? Heavens, no. I am on a deep cover assignment."

"Tired of the front lines?"

"My superiors pulled me out of Mizkov. Supporting your people's struggle is becoming something of a liability, given the ever increasing unity of the other governments against us."

Dannac reached for a honey-covered pastry. "I am curious as to what you are doing here, but my predicament matters more. Perhaps you can help me. Of course, I am willing to perform your delivery, as the little twit said."

"Forget about that. I could not care less about the pies Kervin Rawles is stuffing down his gullet. No, I am afraid I am only here to spy on Sevari's little paradise. Assess their industrial capacity, that sort of thing. Very boring. What about yourself, Dannac? You seem to have given up the fight as well."

The honeyed pastry melted in his mouth, and the spirits Yaz was drinking suddenly looked appealing rather than blasphemous. But momentary pleasure was fleeting. "I became tired of running from Valoii death squads. I tired of fanaticism backed by incompetent action. I just left and went out on my own."

"Just like your father, eh?"

Dannac scowled. "Without getting into three years of theft and bodyguard work, let's say that I have become stranded here. My... partner and I."

"Stranded? I could offer you passage out of here, I suppose."

Yes—he should have realized as soon as he saw Yaz that this could mean an end to their problem. "I would be grateful."

Yaz stood and gazed at the field of dark water dotted by lights from the boats, like the night sky mirrored. "The Bhagovan Republic of Arnhas sympathizes with your people, Dannac. We wish to help in any way possible." He faced Dannac. "Did you know that our researchers are tracing the Ehzeri back thousands of years? We believe that we are in fact quite related. Both our peoples date back to the Ildra culture."

"Fascinating."

"But to be completely honest, old friend... sometimes there is such a thing as doing too many favours. For example, your sight. We still have yet to see any returns on that investment."

"You said it was a gift."

"Of course. But, naturally, we had thought it would be beneficial to our cause as well."

Dannac rose—just a small reminder of the discrepancy between his bulk and the other's. "I fought our mutual enemy."

"Yes, yes. Now, what were you really doing in Blightcross?"

He told Yaz everything about his misfortune with Capra and their mission for Helverliss, right up to the pathetic trap Vasi had led them into, only to suffer from a sudden change of heart.

"Breaking into Sevari's prized collection?" Yaz rubbed his neat beard and hummed for a moment.

"So, you see how it would be much appreciated if my colleague and I could avoid such a problem. At this point, we do not even know where this collection is. I have a feeling it is in those vaults."

Yaz came within biting distance of Dannac's face and touched the jewel embedded in his skull. Dannac did not flinch. "Here's the thing, Dannac."

"I do not like that tone."

"Listen, loyalty is a funny thing. It is not always convenient."

"What are you saying?"

Yaz paced around the deck. "Dannac, I think this is a good opportunity for us to gain some valuable information about Blightcross. Your jewel, that thing that allows you to see, can also remember what you see. This is why we gave it to you, after all. You are an invisible eye for the Republic."

He opened his mouth to speak, yet said nothing. Had he been that naive? Had he really thought that the Republic field operative who had saved him and brought him to the Republic's advanced surgery was motivated by compassion?

But sight was sight, and because of this, he could see where he otherwise should be blind.

Still, he felt used. Now his sight would never feel like his own. He would forever be in the presence of this undefinable other, this abstract thing overlaid upon his own consciousness. The Republic.

Yaz continued, his slightly apologetic tone now replaced with a matter-of-fact coolness. "Sevari is much too paranoid to keep his precious things—especially things of a mystical bent—in some generic vault with the district's gold reserves and emergency grain supply."

"You know where it is, then? Do you want it for yourself?"

"No, you misread me. I mean that if you can get to his collection of mystical nonsense and confiscated art, you will have penetrated his security. There will be any number of answers to questions my department has about this strange place."

He crossed his arms, raised an eyebrow.

"You have a new mission: continue on your original plan to liberate the artwork."

"If you want me to do this, what else can you offer me? I had thought you would help us avoid this very situation."

"I do not enjoy doing things like this, Dannac. But I am afraid I can offer you nothing except your own continued existence for this favour. If not, I will just have to sign a termination order."

Dannac grabbed the table and tossed it over. A cascade of pastries and liquor pelted Yaz's feet, yet the man remained still and composed. "The jewel in your head, stupid. Did you think it was a gift free of any controls or safeguards on our part? Yes, I can kill you with the flick of a switch. You are still my responsibility, after all. I have kept your control mechanism for these last few years because I knew you would return to us someday."

"You son of a bitch—"

"If I die, the man who takes my position will see your file, and I have made several notes to terminate you if I am killed, as I doubt anyone else would have the patience to deal with such a rigid, old-fashioned man like yourself. So please do not kill me—if only for your own sake.

"Now, tonight I will set your eye to record all that you see from hereon in. You will find this collection, and get a good look at each piece. You will also capture in your vision any targets of opportunity, such as pieces of technology, documents, schematics. Do you understand?"

Dannac grunted and flexed his fingers and wished to tear off Yaz's arms and throw him overboard.

"Do you understand, Dannac?"

He grabbed Yaz by the collar of his coat, pulled him close. He saw a sudden change in colour in the man's head. With this type of vision, he could see fear flush a man's face even when the skin was too dark to show it under normal circumstances.

Yaz struggled and wheezed. "You... will not drink the finest whiskey, but you will threaten a man who gave back your sight? That is some moral imperative you have."

He shoved Yaz into the upturned table and made to leave the yacht. As he approached the stairwell, he stopped at the sound of coins hitting the ground behind him. At his feet sat a pouch of Tamarck pistres, the drawstring slightly open so that the silvery glimmer of coins stared like misplaced eyes.

"Go buy yourself a good night's sleep and a decent woman."

The void—a thing for which no words existed except words like "void" and "darkness"—all negatives, none really denoting any property other than the lack of something. The more Vasi tried to work out the various inversions of her thoughts, the less she understood *Akhli and the Shadows* and the disturbing way Helverliss had worked *vihs* into it. *Vihs* was power, it was *something*, yet he had used it to create absence and void.

She walked around the lab, hands pressed to the sides of her head. Who could think under this kind of pressure? It was impossible to work when she could not even convince herself that Rovan still lived. Where was he?

The moment she found him, they were going to leave.

He would kick, he would holler and call her names, but when he grew up to be a real man, he would thank her. It just was not worth it to stay.

And this, she realized, was probably why she could no longer even give the appearance of continuing Sevari's research without losing track.

There was a knock at the door. She shut her eyes and envisioned the small hole in the door. A tunnel of light bored through the blackness behind her eyes, and she saw Rovan standing at the entrance. She immediately willed the locks to unlatch, and the door to open.

"Rovan, you shit. Where have you been?"

"Working, just like you."

She touched his face and examined him for signs of damage, as one would a piece of fruit, until he shrugged away from her.

"I'm not a kid, Vasi. I make a lot of money now."

"That does not mean you are any stronger, smarter, or wiser."

He gave her a cocky grin and invited himself to tour her lab. He picked up an artifact, examined it, and put it down disinterestedly.

"Rovan, I have some news. We are going home."

He went still, and Vasi sprinted to him and snatched the charged idol from him, set it back on its shelf. "What do you mean we're going home?"

"Have you not been paying attention? Young men are being killed here, for no good reason. These are not accidents, Rovan. They are just randomly killing Ehzeri males."

"I work for Sevari now. On the fifth floor of the clock tower. Nobody will kill me. They all want to *be* me, not kill me."

What was with this kid? Did he really think that nobody could be murdered in the tower? It was off limits to most people, sure, but that would not stop a killer from sneaking in to murder its inhabitants.

"What exactly do you do here, anyway? You have no power, Rovan."

"You people are too arrogant to carry things, put things away, deliver things... I help out in ways you refuse to. Sevari doesn't judge. He has more in common with me than he does with you." There was a strength in his voice and sparkle in his eyes, as if he'd found the ideal father. He reached into the satchel he carried and produced a sleek obsidian cylinder. "This is why I came. Sevari wanted you to have this."

She took the cylinder and nearly dropped it. There was a familiar resonance within it, but she could not quite place it. "What is it?"

"He told me to tell you that Section Three had a breakthrough and that this would help you figure out how that painting really worked. He said you needed to use it for an experiment."

She weighed it in her palm. Yes—just the other week, she had written in her progress report that without some kind of detached energy, she could not observe directly how the painting's energies affected a conscious being. At the moment, she was only relying on how it directly affected herself, and unless she submitted to the painting's weak, yet seductive pull into a very real darkness, her empirical observations would continue to be flawed.

"You mean they found... detached energy?" she asked.

Rovan shrugged. "You're the magician, not me. I just do the real work."

She held it up to the gaslight. There was a slight glimmer inside, and again she could not shake the feeling of either having done this before, or having seen something like this before, or...

"So Section Three was able to synthesize it? From what? Raw *vihs*? A kind of artificial..."

"I have no idea, sister. Still want to leave?"

"Yes, I do." But this changed it all.

"Well, I'm staying here. Only a fool would give this up."

She stared at the cylinder, gazed at the glow inside. Finally, something to feed to the void, something to watch it devour. Again she closed her eyes and opened herself to the world of *vihs* reflections and flow.

She saw scenes—dry land, sagebrush. Any Ehzeri would feel homesick when faced with such landscape set in front of a mountain backdrop. Land not even their Valoii oppressors were allowed to inhabit. Ehzeri faces—emblems of a different family, since the knot was much different to hers and it was decorated with emeralds rather than sapphires. Someone talking to her—

No, not talking to her.

"Stop being so sensitive—my father does like you. You would not have married me if he did not approve."

A woman, talking to someone—

The scene faded and in came another, this time a view from the flying boat. Now thoughts came into her mind: *It must have cost a fortune to purchase such a craft, and to give us free passage... how fortunate are we?* Below she saw where the ocean met the land, and the smokestacks of Blightcross smouldering in the distance, and the river delta.

The thoughts were not hers. She had come via sailing ship.

Another scene played in her, eclipsing the others.

She saw her laboratory door, that slab of security. She saw it open, and watched herself greet whoever this was, and take an envelope from these strange hands that were not her own.

Her eyes fluttered open, because she recognized the scene. Not only that, but the flavour of energy within the crystal.

"Rovan? Where did you go?"

The mail clerk. But how?

Section Three had not synthesized an energy that could mimic a human. They had just killed the mail clerk and stuffed his consciousness into a piece of obsidian so Vasi could feed it to the painting and watch what happened.

So Vasi could feed the shadows.

"Rovan?" She went into the hall. The empty hall.

She locked the door, double-checked it and jammed an unused chair against it.

There was no crazed Ehzeri-killer loose in the plant. It was Sevari and his attempts to gain some impossible mystical clarity, some divine justification for his actions.

Rovan was his new pet.

Sevari the killer. Who knew what the maniac could do, even to a favourite employee. Everyone knew about the memorial he had created for his family. This was the kind of logic that could drive a man to kill his friends in order to preserve them.

She snatched a bag from the coat hook and stuffed it with food, extra coins, and a few artifacts that would give her power a short boost if needed.

Maybe Rovan would not agree to leave until it was too late, but could he fight his big sister, the huge man with the jewel in his head, and an ex-Valoii stormtrooper?

CHAPTER NINE

There were two different lunch breaks at the factory. The one at noon, where the skilled workers, like Laik and his crew, took thirty minutes that somehow lasted forty-five, and brought their company-supplied lunches onto the factory floor to eat wherever they wanted. The other lunch break was for the ladies and young men who did not produce directly, whose drudgery made sure the factory ran smoothly. This one started two hours later, lasted for fifteen minutes, and was confined under the low ceiling of the auxiliary cafeteria.

It was during one of the noon breaks that Capra swept out a corridor and saw the men on their break. She saw Laik among them, overall straps hanging at his sides and showing his barrel chest. He ate a giant sandwich in two bites, and, ten minutes into the break, began to gesture wildly at the others. Another man stood and raised his fists.

Tey came wheezing by, under the weight of an overburdened dustbin.

"What are they doing?" Capra asked, as the men organized into a circle.

"Beating each other for fun."

"Why on earth...?"

"'Tis what men do. Really, are your men all eunuchs in Mizkov?"

Capra forgot what she was doing and watched intensely. Of course it was stupid, at least to a Valoii, but something else about it intrigued her.

"We don't fight each other in Mizkov. Not even for fun. Well, there is sparring for instruction, but..."

She watched Laik pound another man senseless, and afterwards they shook hands. Why would they either act like friends when they hated each other, or fight each other if they were friends?

They went quiet when Laik spoke. They moved out of his way, they cheered him on.

These men fought to reinforce notions of status?

"Is that why they do it?" she said out loud.

Tey let out an inquisitive grunt.

"They gain respect—it is a way of distributing surplus status among them."

"You have some strange terms, Capra. Get back to work, otherwise you'll run afoul of the boss again."

"What do you mean, again?"

"We all heard about the tiff in the hallway with Laik."

Capra peered over Tey's shoulder, and once she was sure no-one else was listening, whispered, "What did you hear, exactly?"

"Well, Marta said she saw him beat you, and of course she had her own problem with the man. She's married, you see, but of course that never stopped Laik. Then there was that gutsy woman who actually learned a trade and joined his crew, and of course he pinned her down and speared her with his dangler..."

Tey's words soon sounded like a string of disjointed sounds, and all Capra could think of was how to use this situation to her advantage.

"... and he is on the Board, too, so what can you do?"

Aha. "A board? Which?" Before Tey could answer, she said, mostly to herself, "Never mind. A board is a board, and here it seems everyone who has any power is on some board. Which means he may be able to get me to Sevari..."

"Sevari? Till Sevari? Our Leader?"

Capra nodded and caught the gaze of a supervisor searing the air between them from across the shop floor. She shoved a handcart loaded with machine parts out of her way and pretended to sweep under it. That had been the man's scathing criticism—Don't just sweep around things, you lazy cow. Move them and get all the rubbish underneath.

She did this now with a smile, and the supervisor left.

"Ah, I was just joking around."

Tey giggled. "Oh, I see. He is a handsome man, isn't he, that Sevari?"

"Maybe, but I think he's a little old for me."

"Don't let that stop you, dearie. If you can do it... I hear he has not taken a wife... ever. Could you imagine living in that palace with him?"

Had Tey even seen the palace lately? And it hardly seemed like the residence of their great leader. It was a collection of offices. Perhaps he lived behind the gated walls of Damwall? That would make more sense—the politicos of Tamarck also chose to live in exclusive residential developments, rather than in the palaces and mansions owned by their king. Or, for that matter, the houses in which everyone else in the nation lived.

"I have been to the palace, Tey."

"Ooh?"

"All I saw were offices and signs either pointing me towards or warning me about the Sevari Family Memorial."

"Ah, the memorial. Poor man."

Capra stopped sweeping, face screwed into a puzzled grimace.

"Well, just the way he lost his whole family during the war. No wonder he searched the wreckage for their bodies and did what he did. Still visits them once a week, like clockwork."

Part of her did not want to know what exactly a man like Sevari was capable of doing to a corpse. Actually, most of her did not want to know.

The conversation dissipated under the pressing matters of dustbins and dirty floors. Capra found drudgery oddly meditative—after a while, the action seemed to perform itself, and her mind could drift as it wanted. Her dreamlike trance flitted between inane thoughts of what Laik might look like in a dress, how much money she might have left after finding Helverliss' precious artwork and paying the army to leave her alone, the travesty of using corn starch to thicken a sauce instead of a roux, desserts, pastries, shalep with spices, like they drank in the south...

Then it came: a screeching whistle to which every skilled worker answered by dropping his current work, removing his helmet, and forming a line at the exit. The noise snapped Capra from her meditation, and for an instant, she strained to remember where she was and what she was doing, and she gazed at the factory floor, head slightly askew and eyes wary.

"I know it would be nice to go with them, but we have two more hours left." Tey emptied a bucket into a trough of black sludge. "Besides, they're just going to drink their dinner and become loud. The smell will not improve either, I'll wager."

Capra handed her broom to Tey. "Just a second or two, all right?"

"What?"

She spotted Laik among the workers and bounded after them. In her path was one of the vats of glowing orange inferno, and a blast of heat baked her face. Damn, these short breaths. Something was different, because she would never become winded so easily. Would she even pass the army's physical standards test now? She had the disturbing feeling, as she huffed along after Laik, that were she to try the ten-minute run, she would fall on her face, or at the very least, double her time.

"Laik," she said, trotting alongside the man. His face was black and shiny.

"Get back to work."

She wanted to grab him by his overall straps, but held back. "You are on the board, is that right?"

He sighed and rolled his eyes and prattled on in monotone, "If you really must raise some issue, go to the clerk at your barrack and request form 23-C." He met her eyes. "But I would advise against it. Someone like you should think twice about crying to the authorities."

She pulled him out of the lineup, and was surprised when he offered no punches or public humiliation. "I can make it worth your while. We both know I am not going to stay here for long."

"I know. But I have debts, and I want your wages. I also want to fuck you silly, and will probably call in that debt before you leave."

She growled.

"There, there. That's what I like."

"You pig."

Laik put his hand on her waist. "I have personal connections to Sevari. I can have you in his torture dungeon in the time it takes you to scrub the privy after I shit in it."

"Personal connections, eh?"

"You think I am going to let one of his mindless Freedom Corps jackasses take you in, and conveniently forget that I was the one to capture you? Never."

Another worker chuckled on the way past them and knocked Laik with his shoulder.

"Now get out of here. You leave before I'm done with you, and you're as good as dead."

He shoved her into a pillar, and she gasped from the impact. "See you tomorrow at lunch, Laik."

But he was too far away to hear. Just as well—it would have more impact if she took him by surprise.

"But why Blightcross, is what I wonder." Tey crossed in front of Capra, hands on her wide hips.

Capra simply shrugged and dipped her mop into the pail of brown water.

"Well, really, why are you hiding here?"

By now, Capra imagined that Tey had constructed a composite of her, based on morsels of conversation, rumours, and observations. The woman's questions had become more specific, and like this one, referred more to the things Capra had not said that both implicitly acknowledged.

Capra pushed her bucket across the tiles, leaving dark streaks, and paused to stifle her gagging before going to work on the next lavatory stall.

"You could be a dancer in the Orvis Dunes, or a courtesan. How did you end up here, a pretty thing like you?"

She cringed, and not from the mess in front of her, but at the things she had told Tey. Maybe it had been a mistake to talk about random things like her most embarrassing moment at the academy as a teenager—a complete bastardization of one of the most famous ballets from the continent, and the ensuing five years of humiliation it caused.

After hearing that, Tey's suspicion faded, and she began to act strangely... as if they were friends.

Friend. Now a foreign concept, since Dannac wasn't exactly the kind of man with whom one could gossip and joke around, and the only friend who had meant anything to her was back in Mizkov. It felt strange to garner such interest from Tey.

"I could never be a dancer. I screwed the performance up, remember? I fell three times, and gave the boy who was supposed to catch me a broken nose. Not good."

She had left out the part about practising for six hours each day for the next three years and performing it again flawlessly. It was probably best not to appear arrogant among simpler people.

Tey snapped her fingers. "Aha—it's treasure, isn't it?"

"Pardon?"

"The people who used to live on this island... there is gold buried somewhere in the factory. It has to be true, because if anyone catches you digging for no reason, they haul you in and you never want to touch a spade again."

There was something sickening about the way the limp wet mop sloshed and sucked at the floor, and there also was the dilemma about whether the smell was worse than the possibility of tasting it, should she try to avoid the odour by breathing through her mouth. She wrinkled her nose and took shallow morsels of air.

"I want you to know, I won't say anything. I probably said that before, but heaven knows turning you in won't make my life any better."

She stopped. "Well, thanks. You are... a good friend."

The only trouble was, did she deserve one? Not even a note to Jasaf, not even a goodbye, just wait for the damned explosions to distract everyone and run westward.

And Capra had not looked back.

She wondered what Jasaf was up to, if she were still in their unit. Her mandatory service would be almost finished. Damn—she should have asked Alim about her when she had the chance. Maybe rekindling the old days would have been powerful enough for him to abandon his chase and let her be.

Out on the factory floor, the sounds of hundreds of men's feet tromping around in unison boomed through the walls.

This was it. Lunch time.

"Tey, I'll be back in a bit. Can you cover for me? Say I cut myself and was at the nurse's station."

"You don't get to use the nurse's station. None of us do…"

"Tell them it was really bad. They have to understand."

"They will not—"

Capra dropped the mop and darted to the shop floor, where the men had gathered in a circle, the same as yesterday. She skirted around their sweaty, broad backs, waiting for the fights to begin. One of the ladies had said something about matches during the evenings, but since it was difficult to leave the women's barracks without attracting attention, she thought the afternoon fights were the best opportunity.

Perfect—Laik was full of sandwich and wild urges again, and entered the circle. A smaller man came from the opposite side of the clump. The smaller man started the fight with a blow to Laik's kidney. Laik reeled, and returned with a lunge. He brought the other into a headlock, and seconds later, the man dropped to the ground like Capra's soggy mop.

The men grumbled amongst themselves:

"Boring."

"Gut him, Laik!"

"I seen better fights between cats."

She waded through the crowd, ignoring their crude comments. She emerged inside the circle—the inadequate woman at the very heart of the men's exclusive enclosure. She steeled her gaze and didn't wait for an invitation to shove Laik into one of his underlings.

"You stupid whore. Get out of here, this is for men only."

"I am in the circle, Laik." She punched him. The men laughed.

"You hit like a girl."

"Thank you."

He lunged again, his form eclipsing the glowing strands of pouring metal beyond the ring. She dropped to the ground on her elbows and hoisted herself up to kick him, and he flew into the spectators. But this time, instead of waiting for him to come again, she flew at Laik and rammed her knee into his rib cage.

The crack of his bones sent a chill through her, but also a childish satisfaction.

Now his face gleamed red, and he clasped his hands together and smashed her in the jaw. "I don't know what you think you're getting here, slut, but you will regret it."

Her vision filled with a sparkling blizzard. The next instant, his bulk flashed into view and pinned her shoulders.

Now the men hooted, as if they had never seen a real fight between members of the opposite sex. He chortled and punched her.

Crack.

Crack.

A delicate note of blood on the back of her tongue.

He paused. "You must be mad, woman."

Crack.

She caught his hand. "Where is it?"

"Where is what?"

"Sevari's collection. That's all I want to know."

Her arm began to shake. "What do you want with Sevari's bizarre obsessions?" As if offended even by her choice of transgressions, he bared his teeth and grabbed her throat. "You make no sense to me. You come here to hide from someone, try to best me, and all because you want some worthless scribbles and sculptures?"

She choked and sputtered. Blackness encroached on her vision. Her hands flailed, and she instinctively went for the hidden switchblade. She manoeuvred the blade against his belly, jabbed him just enough to make him stop.

Laik looked down. His maniac grin softened. "You're a cheat, too."

"I know what you do here. I heard it all. I have no idea how corrupt your bureaucracy is, but I know that the women are far too timid to tell anyone, on the off chance that rape and assault against a worker is actually legal in this godforsaken pit."

"You can't prove anything."

"Do you want to take that chance? There are ways. Suppose they interrogate you with truth serum. There are many ways to catch scum like you." She pushed the blade harder. "And the only reason you are still here is because they are too afraid to talk."

"You still cannot prove anything. And you are guilty of more crimes than I am."

It was true... it sickened her to hear it, but she knew every bit of it was the truth.

"Jorassian? What are you waiting for?"

They had nothing. They lived in huts, they lived in the harshest, most undesirable areas of the new Valoii homeland. Their eyes showed fright—never mind that they also blazed with vihs. It was the Ehzeri equivalent to flinching, and you do not answer a flinch with a volley of phosphorus grenades...

She gritted her teeth and felt the knife dig into Laik's flesh. "Forget it. This ends now, and you give me what I want, or I kill you."

There was a silence, as if the crowd had heard the remark. Laik's thick arms relaxed for an instant, and Capra struck him with her elbow. She then pressed the knife against his throat.

"So you..." He licked his lips and stuttered. "So you cared nothing for those women, then? I will keep doing as I please if you leave this place to find your treasures. You would be willing to let me continue to do that, if I just gave you what you wanted? Is that right?"

"You sheepfucking bastard..."

"You've done it dozens of times before, Jorassian. Move out!"

It wasn't right.

But that kind of recognition is meaningless when you do it anyway.

"Yes. Come on, slit my throat, you cunt. Answer to the Corps, answer to Sevari's expert torture surgeons—you won't make it two steps from my body. I am sure they can show you the stupid mystical garbage you risk your life for from the comfort of a spiked mattress."

So killing him was out of the question.

"How many have you killed? Hm? Just for a few pistres? Did you pose as the nanny and fuck the overworked father and take him for all he was worth, then kill him? Things like that?"

She wanted to tell him the truth—that she had killed no one since leaving the army, but decided not to downplay herself. "Where is it?"

"Really? You are that shallow? These poor abused women mean nothing to you?"

She swallowed hard. "I am no good to them as your slave or hunted by Sevari."

"If that makes you feel better about yourself..."

She pressed the blade into his skin, watched a sliver of blood creep from his skin. She then released him and skittered back. "It's over."

The group's voices rumbled again. From what she gathered during her jostling through them, half were impressed with her and made fun of Laik, the other half thought she was a diseased, disturbed woman and that Laik ought to have finished her.

The factory seemed to spin, and her sight was still blurred. As soon as she hit the wall of sewage reek in the lavatory, she made a mad sprint for the pot she had just cleaned.

"Capra?"

It was Tey.

"Concussion. I'll be okay." Another nauseous wave came, and she was reminded of her experience aboard the flying boat.

The stall darkened, and Capra assumed it was just Tey coming to her aid anyway. "Really, Tey, just one more and I think it'll be done." Another flood of bile in her mouth—

"I know a man who works at the Pavilion of Machines just outside of Redsands." Deep and gravelly, gravelly like her own voice at the moment.

She wiped her mouth and turned around. Once she realized that it was Laik, she reached for her knife again.

"Relax. I am an honourable man, Capra." There were a few seconds of a strange silence. "This man designed and maintains the mechanical fire giant at the pavilion. He talks a lot, if you catch my drift. His name is Tilas Feyerbik." Laik's eyes darted around the room.

"Laik, I..."

"Get out of here. Say nothing about me, the information I gave you, or your overblown accusations. Take the back way out. I have arranged for the guards there to be indisposed for the next while."

"You're scum, and suddenly you become this noble gentleman?"

He shook his head. "Unwritten codes. Perhaps your society is too honest with itself."

"Men like you are respected, while the real men are ridiculed and singled out?"

"Get out. You have your information. Your eyes are clearing up—I didn't hit you hard enough to send you to the surgery. That is not our intent when we fight."

"I don't believe that. Not for a second."

"I never asked you to."

Never one to question when things turned in her favour, she shoved past him and found Tey wrestling with a handcart whose wheels squealed under a load of cracked parts. Tey stopped and looked mortified after she saw Capra's face.

"Oh no, you look like you've been through the ringer. What happened?"

Capra touched one of the cuts on her jaw. "Nothing, really. Look, Tey... I have to go." She thought of the day she had left the army. At least she barely knew Tey, and they had little in common.

"So soon? Why?"

"Just... for a while. I promise to come back." Though her voice said otherwise, and Tey didn't appear to buy it either.

"But where are you going?" Tey's eyes brightened. "Found whatever you were looking for?"

Capra slid her hand through her damp hair. "Get out of here, Tey."

"What?"

"This city. Get out. Go north, to the resorts."

"But they pay much less there."

"This place takes more than it gives, Tey. You have to realize that."

Tey scoffed at the comment and waved. "Sure, for a petty middle-class woman like yourself. But I know what the real world is like."

The woman's insight surprised Capra. Perhaps she should have kept quiet. She hurried past the lake of molten metal and through the metal-grated halls to the side exit, just as Laik had told her. For once, she took his words at face value. His voice had dripped with resignation, and she knew it wasn't a trick.

Victory? The voice of a beaten man?

Dannac would say: "It had nothing to do with you challenging the little order they have in the factory. It had everything to do with your incessant nattering and stubbornness. Some people can only handle so much insistence that Capra knows all."

The monotonous road out of the Redsands area only made her relive the past two days. Tey would be okay. It was incredibly self-absorbed to think that everyone she left behind would suffer from her absence.

Wasn't it?

Raid after raid, Alim became more weary of the ridiculous rumours that wasted his time.

I saw her at a bistro, serving shalep.

She's my next-door neighbour. Very noisy at night, you see. I would love for you to remove her.

Part of the problem was that there were so many Ehzeri here, and to the Blightcross natives, Capra's olive skin and dark eyes belonged to the entire immigrant population. They would describe her vaguely, and of course sneer at the mention of what they thought was a "big nose". Alim began to wonder if these people saw others as caricatures, as if under some bizarre hex.

He paced in Sevari's office alone, waiting for the Leader to return. The old-style, arched window let in the city's dusty light, and from here Alim traced the pipeline; massive cords of sinew stretching far into the desert. Parts of it disappeared under the sand and emerged miles away, like stitching.

"Alim," Sevari said, heading for his big leather chair. "How goes it?"

"You're late."

"More paranoia among the workers. Bodies, bodies... You know how it is. Everyone thinks they're going to be next, as if the entire universe is out to get them."

Alim thought to ask about these strange murders, but Sevari's casualness meant it was probably best not to ask. Accusing the man of murder, or at least being complicit by inaction, would do little to help the situation. "Your intelligence section has given me a few reports. I have followed up on many of them."

"And?"

"Capra is nowhere to be found. I believe she split up with her partner, and I want to get to her while she is vulnerable. Without that man protecting her, I can take her easily. But your troops seem to have more paranoia and imagination than investigative skill."

Sevari frowned and scribbled madly on a slip of paper. "I think your nation's training might be more to blame. This is the monster your people have created. An army of strictly volunteer soldiers is the only way. There is something to be said for creating an army strong enough to destroy one's enemies, but not so well trained that they can become a liability."

"They do not train us to be liars. I think Capra came into that on her own." He held back his defence of Mizkov's policies. People outside did not understand, and they never would. "There's one report I do have at least some faith in." He dropped the pages onto the desk.

Sevari glanced over them. "You think she is in Redsands?"

"Not any longer. This is just third-hand, and I'd rather not waste my time pursuing that aspect. But read more."

There was a silence while Sevari skimmed the pages. "Working for Helverliss? What on earth for?"

"What I have learned is that Capra is attracted to romantic figures. In the Little Nations, she engaged in a short and furious tryst with one of the continent's most famous composers. She is selfish and craves excitement, but is not reckless enough to take pleasure in her military duties. I imagine she felt pity for Helverliss, and sees him as some kind of martyr."

"And your point in all of this?"

"I came here, Leader, to request your permission to arrest Noro Helverliss."

Sevari laid the papers on the desk and folded his hands. "I have wanted to arrest that man ever since the Shield Party took power after the war. But one must learn from the mistakes of Tamarck."

"Sir?"

"Of appearing to be a ruthless tyrant. People tend to get uneasy when you start arresting popular men like Helverliss. And, I will give Helverliss one bit of credit: in his philosophical ramblings, he mentions that engaging opposing ideas in such a way will only bring me closer to my own negation."

Alim stared blankly.

"Let Helverliss be, that has always been my strategy. Keep an eye on him, yes, and do not allow him to possess power, but otherwise, I will hurt myself by giving his supporters more reason to hate my government."

A buzzing sounded behind the desk. Sevari grumbled and pressed a stud on the panel, and in walked one of his assistants. "Just a minute, Alim."

He took this as his cue to stand and give them space, so he went to the window and watched one of the flying boats circle above the city.

A moment later, Sevari joined him at the window box. "It seems that dissent is in the air these days. I wonder if your rogue soldier hasn't brought some mysterious disease with her that causes this madness."

"Sir?"

"My best researcher has disappeared. I can only assume because she was scared."

"Vasi? The one who set up the failed trap?"

Sevari nodded slowly. The stupid man showed no indication of seeing the connection. It could be misplaced optimism, but it seemed obvious. Vasi might have been helping Capra all along. The two events had to be related. And it made more sense—all reports about Dannac stated that he had showed no *vihs* capacity—his father had squandered it all. Vasi must have saved them from his trap. But why?

What could make an Ehzeri even think twice about sending a Valoii to a prison?

"How powerful was this girl?" Alim asked.

"Quite. She is highly sensitive to *vihs*. She's my main researcher for *Akhli and the Shadows*. Nobody else has even been able to look at the damned thing, let alone analyze it and isolate its power."

"So your research is effectively stalled?"

"On this project, yes." Sevari slammed his hand on a shelf. "I was ahead of myself in thinking that I would soon understand the worldspirits and what they desire. At least Section Three has finally found a technique to complete our defence modernization plan. But I would prefer the secret to the painting over my army's equipment any day."

Alim stuffed his hands into his pockets and began to walk about the room casually. "Sounds like you could use help from Helverliss."

"I think I understand you. We should probably take his little coven as well. That rogue contessa who finances him ought to be brought in as well."

"I'll get right on it, Leader."

At the smooth paved entrance to the Pavilion of Machines stood a bronze and brass arbour. On its front, Capra read, quite slowly: *Pavilion of Machines - Established 8756 U.E. - Pritalvihs Wehk Glostrikkz.*

That last sentence was in Old Karabac—a language those of the west used when they wanted to appear serious and scholarly. She had learned some phrases in her travels, and it seemed to declare something to the effect of *Realpower - Progress - Pureness.*

Beyond the signs and maps of each attraction was a spectacle Capra's experience could only compare to a menagerie of machines. A giant wheel of metal, rotating silently but for the chugging of the engines. Other spinning sculptures were set on pedestals, and dozens of young couples, parasols in hand and children trailing, strolled the glimmering metal walkways.

Closer to the big wheel, Capra now saw baskets at the end of each spoke, and in these, people. Smiling, laughing people. She shivered. It was bad enough to travel by flying boat for three days. But to sit in one of those rickety metal skeletons? For fun?

Now she searched among the spinning blades and engine-driven faces and grotesque, living metal for the mechanical fire giant.

Everyone had their own vision of what a real fire giant ought to look like. Nobody had seen one for two thousand years, and the old drawings were simply a starting point for everyone else's imagination. Capra imagined a sentient reptile, with spiny tail and a tough round armour covering its back. It would stand as tall as some of the monstrous buildings in downtown Blightcross.

At last she found it—a brass and iron figure standing three-times the height of a tall man. Its eyes sparkled with each movement of its head, and she saw that they were large diamonds. The tail swished and flicked without so much as a squeak from its metal segments. Capra's heart thundered at the sight—deep down she knew it was fake, but realizing this did nothing to dispel her awe.

The thing looked at her, and she swore there existed some kind of intelligence, the kind of divine, primal awareness that made the fire giants such a powerful myth.

Myth—it hardly seemed like one now. She chilled at the thought of someone bringing these ancient figures to life. This thing seemed more than just a collection of metal bits, although that's exactly what the artist had intended.

She read the plaque on the thing's pedestal. *Fire Giant, by Tilas Feyerbik.*

That was her man. But.

Why did that name sound so familiar?

The fire giant now opened its mouth, and from it came a clicking sound, followed by a hiss. There was a flash, and Capra jumped back to dodge the fire spewing from the sculpture's mouth. She soon shook her head and felt like an idiot, since the flame didn't reach beyond the surrounding chain barrier.

Tilas Feyerbik... A memory came to her, a bulletin of some sort—surely from before her escape.

Before she could recover the memory, a panel in the ground opened, and out popped a semi-bald man, with thick spectacles and wool trousers held by braces. The bit of hair around the side of his head stuck out, and his pockets bulged with screwdrivers and hammers and spanners.

Feyerbik... it was a name from Yahrein.

"How's she working now?" The man stepped over the chain and examined one of the leg joints.

"Excuse me, are you Feyerbik?"

He lowered his glasses. "Well, yes." There was something hesitant in his voice. "Will you liking it, eh?"

The sentence construction—Yahrein. Then it hit her—this was one of the men that MDF special forces were still trying to hunt down for trial.

This man was a war criminal. No wonder he looked uncomfortable—he knew a Valoii when he saw one, and he was backing away slowly.

"I am old, do you not see? I can not take any of it back... I can take none of it back..."

She reached out to him. "I... I'm not one of them. I just wanted to know about Noro Helverliss."

"Eh?"

She gestured to the fire giant. "It's beautiful. And it doesn't make a single noise, not like some of these others." She stepped over the chain and ran her hand along the beast's leg.

"The engines, they are below. I tell them, 'give me one just for him, he cannot share with the other sculptures' and they give it to me. Special exhaust, I run it around underneath. Noisier over there, but you enjoy looking without the engine noise, right?"

"Yes."

He gazed into her eyes. Should she feel sick or feel pity for him or kill him? Now that she had abandoned Mizkov, nothing seemed clear, except that she needed to sever her ties with them fully so she could live how she wanted. This man had been an accomplice to mass murder—one of the Yahrein scientists who devised experiments to merge men with his engines. He created strange magnetic weapons that destroyed entire Valoii camps. So many people would give their lives for a meeting like this, and she could not help but feel conflicted and sad.

"It was a different time, Valoii," Feyerbik said. "A different time... There was *vihs* everywhere. We thought... with all the decline in morals, that our proud nation was being corrupted by a mass concentration of bad *vihs*. It was insane. But it might have been true."

She looked away. Because of her age, her only point of reference was the turmoil left by the war's end, and her parents' stories. "There is very little of that among the Valoii, you know. We are a pragmatic people. We do what is necessary to survive, and we can do it without any special powers. Perhaps it was your own people corrupting your culture, not us."

"Oh yes, I have heard all of the theories, right up to Helverliss' idea that the *vihs* doesn't exist and never did in the first place."

Clearly this man was an intellectual like Helverliss, and could babble on just as well, so she decided to cut to the main issue. "I am working for Helverliss. I need to find his paintings and steal them from Sevari. I was told that you know where Sevari is keeping them."

"Ah. Sevari." His face darkened. "Blightcross is no different from my old society. It is painful to watch. The same mystical revival, the same fetish with production..."

"You know about the paintings?"

"Hmm, yes. That is what scares me. Not that Sevari has the same temperament as my former leaders, but that Helverliss is actually capable of delivering the kind of power my people sought but were too ignorant to find."

She glared at him.

"The collection is in the clock tower. That is Sevari's cocoon. I designed all of its mechanisms, and was a contributing architect." He sighed, and she compared his weariness with that of Helverliss. "I had thought Sevari was a good man, after all he gave me a second chance here. I never guessed he would be just more of the same."

She turned to leave—this was all she needed, and she feared further discussion with Feyerbik would only force her into the dutiful hatred she knew had been planted somewhere inside her.

"Hold on, Valoii." He replaced his glasses. "If you are stupid enough to enter Sevari's haven, at least stay out of the building proper."

"What do you mean?"

He pointed to the hole in the ground and ducked back inside it. She followed him into his workshop, where he rifled through a stack of yellowed papers, many with brown rings of shalep stains.

He passed her a leather tube, but she did not take it.

"Go ahead. You will need it."

"What is it?"

"The schematic. For the clock mechanism."

She took the tube, but scrunched her face in confusion. "Why should I care about the stupid clock?"

He grinned slightly, almost sadistically. "Because, Valoii, you are going to climb up her. Climb through her, I might say. It is the only way, trust me. The refinery is the most secure part of this entire nation. You will not just walk in or cut through a window after climbing up the tower's face. You have to go up through the mechanism. It is the only weak spot."

Her jaw slackened. The man had to be insane. "No way."

"It is the largest, most decadent design ever built. The tower itself is built around a tower of gears and cams, all ending at the clock. The tolerances should allow a girl of your size to squeeze through, though it will depend on your sense of timing."

"Whoa, wait. You want me to climb through a bunch of gears?"

"Yes."

And she thought a couple of hours in the raid shelter was bad.

CHAPTER TEN

The historical buildings of this neighbourhood, no matter how rundown, gave her a warmth and ease, as if there were an invisible shield around the district. Even so, Capra knew Orvis Dunes was about as safe as anywhere else in the city, and the comfort was a superficial one.

There was something different about the place. The cloud of shalep fumes and cheroot smoke was less than usual. She stopped to listen for the string trio. All she heard was the endemic groan of the city, and the soughing of hot wind.

Even better—she found a poster on a lamp standard, warning the public of the dangers posed by some criminal named Khapruh Jerazuhn. If these people's refusal to adopt proper Valoii spelling weren't offensive enough, below the warning was an artist's conception of her.

The artist had exaggerated her nose, and stretched her face in a comical fashion. It looked like a copy of the drawing Alim probably was using for this purpose, only warped.

She tore it from the standard and ripped it beyond recognition. Not that anyone could recognize her from that drawing anyway.

It was noon. Would Dannac show up?

Of course he would. He was incapable of forgetting. Then again, he could be locked up in a prison somewhere, or lying in a ditch...

She rounded the corner near Helverliss' bookshop. But she quickly rolled back around the corner, because a squad of soldiers blocked the sidewalk around Helverliss' shop. It could only mean one thing.

Shit. He's the one with all the cash.

And here she had been wanting to renegotiate her fees, on account of the extra-dangerous, panic-inducing necessity of climbing through the heart of the clock tower. Now there might be nothing in it for them, not even enough to cover their expenses.

She crouched and covered her profile with a shaking hand. Her mind raced to concoct an alternate plan. There was always the resorts to the north, as she had advised Tey to pursue, but good luck wrangling a flying boat ticket now, and forget trekking through the desert. A sailing ship might take them, but still, that would require money and a foolproof disguise.

When Dannac came into the alley with his own look of shock, she couldn't be bothered to stand. She just shook her head at him and frowned.

"What is this?" he said.

"They got him."

"But why? Why now?"

"It's anyone's guess. I don't suppose it matters why. We're done."

He appeared disturbed. "Done? But..."

"You of all people should see why. We're after Helverliss' money, remember?"

"Yes, but..." He hesitated. "Maybe we should go for the painting anyway. For... for ourselves. He did say that it would fetch a decent price."

She stood and peered into the street. Was he kidding? At least with Helverliss, they knew the painting had value and that he would pay to get it back. But what if it were worthless on the market? "If you want to get an appraiser to swear that the thing has any market value, go ahead." She watched him for a moment, noted his fidgeting and quick breathing. "Okay, something's not right. You're taking this worse than I am."

"You have never turned down such an opportunity. Maybe you're the one with the problem."

"Me? Look, something else will come up, it always does. And anyway, I don't really want to have to go into that tower's mechanics, because that's the only way to get inside the tower unnoticed." Just thinking of squeezing through it like a worm caught in an engine kicked her heart into a stutter.

They said nothing for a while, and Capra listened for the troopers' voices. They were equally as quiet, except when the occasional patron passed by and the men shouted at them to get back.

But minutes later, just when the silence was becoming a tense moment between the two, the voice of a woman called out behind them.

"It was my fault."

Both snapped from their daze.

"Vasi?" Capra squinted at the figure striding towards them.

Vasi joined them and spoke lowly. "I left Sevari. I can only assume he was frustrated with his research. I was ready to finish it, to unlock the painting, when I realized..."

"What's wrong, Vasi? What did he do?" Capra took Vasi's hand.

"Sevari has been killing us for research. He wanted me to feed the souls of my own people to the darkness inside that horrible painting so I could finish the work." Vasi's eyes began to glisten, and Capra fidgeted and touched her awkwardly in an attempt to comfort. "I saw the man's memories. Did Sevari not think I would sense that? Section Three was supposed to be researching constructing synthetic spirits, not ripping real ones from their owners."

"Synthetic spirits? What is all of this about?"

Dannac grunted and sighed. "Just like the tyrants of Yahrein. Perverted studies, all meant to give them new reasons to rationalize their insanity."

Vasi flailed her arms and turned around. "I hardly care about that. I came to you because of my brother. I tried to get him out, but I can't find him, and I'm just so afraid he's being used by Section Three, and I didn't know what else to do. I can't deal with that painting anymore, not knowing what horrors Sevari is able to produce."

Great timing. As far as she was concerned, this job was over. She tapped her jaw and began to think of excuses. "Vasi, it's just that... there's no more profit in it."

As soon as she finished the sentence, she jammed her eyes closed and winced. Dannac would have something to say about such a callous remark in maybe three... two—

"Once a Valoii, always a Valoii. You see, Vasi, even the good ones will let you down sooner or later."

It felt like one of Laik's crushing blows hammering her chest. They just didn't understand. How could they? They were the ones she had been hiding from in that stupid shelter, it was them who kept attacking and just would not stop, with their hoarded powers and terrible hatred—

Vasi sat on a broken crate. "Do you people think you are justified in what you do just because of what Yahrein did? Do you think they did not do the same thing to us?"

Capra jumped into her usual defensiveness. "What does that have to do with anything? That's history. I'm talking about right here, right now. I'm sorry, I just don't see why we should risk our lives in that tower anymore, now that Helverliss is gone."

"And where do you think they took him, Valoii? Do you think they took him to the armoury? To that stupid palace? No. Helverliss is in that tower with the painting."

Capra considered this. It did change things, provided that Sevari didn't execute Helverliss. She could still, in theory, succeed. The tough part was that she had already started to feel a kind of relief that she would no longer need to climb through that tower's machinery.

"Perhaps she actually enjoys this life," Dannac said. "Is that why you are stalling?"

"Dannac, what's happening to you? Where have you been these past few days? Something isn't right. You can usually see the sense in being cautious, and now you want to run headlong into the most secure facility this side of the ocean."

He began to walk towards the markets. "Perhaps we should leave this place before spilling our deepest secrets with soldiers in earshot."

Dannac cursed under his breath and kicked at the garbage littering the alley. The girl was too perceptive for her own good. Correction: too perceptive for him to hide anything. His mind drifted between thoughts of telling her about his involvement with the Bhagovan Republic's secret police, and simply distancing himself from her and cooling their relationship to one of strict professionalism.

Now she walked with her head low, with an uncharacteristic heaviness. Normally, he would be telling her to stop looking so haughty and try to blend in, and here she was looking like a sulking desert rat.

"I am confused," Vasi said to him, and she was also stealing glances at Capra. "Will you help me or not? Rovan could already be in their laboratory, being drained into a crystal. Or maybe Helverliss has some obscene ritual to use him for."

"Of course. One way or another, we will go to the refinery. If your brother is alive, I will try to free him."

"You alone, though? Your partner seems to have given up."

"We'll see about that."

They came out of the alley into the fringes of the markets. Dannac ignored a particular huckster who was trying to sell him a feather duster by declaring that everyone who used one of his dusters had an interesting story, and his ultimate pressure point was to ask the baffled passerby "what's your dusting story?". Also, he would ask, "How do you flick the duster?" as if the banal act were some stunning act of individual expression.

Dannac suppressed the urge to punch the man and led them deep into the crowd.

"Capra grew up in one of the heavily disputed zones. She has probably seen a lot. She is very able, but in the end she is fragile."

"You feel sympathy for her?"

"No, but are we not supposed to forgive? We have a common goal: to be free of her government's pursuit—me as an alleged terrorist, she as a deserter—and live unremarkable lives."

She gave him a puzzled look. "Dannac... do you not recognize something different about her? Did you not recognize the amulet she wears?"

"It looked Ehzeri, but I assumed she just pillaged it from one of the notches on her sabre. I never asked about it, because I did not want to know. It is history." He made sure Capra was not within earshot.

"No wonder she is confused and makes up for it by being impossible. She is Ehzeri, not Valoii."

He stopped. "What?"

She pointed to her own amulet, and for the first time, it was clear to him that they were exactly the same. "I had not paid any attention because my family is drained and no longer has their own knot... are you sure she didn't just take it from one of her victims?"

"No. If she did, it was coincidence. Look, in the palace, she was feeling ill. You were right, you know. She did have the cloud sickness."

"But she is much too old. That only happens to teenagers."

"She has been repressed, Dannac. That is why she still reacts to thunderstorms on occasion. A teenager, even a clumsy one who never really learns how to use *vihs*, eventually learns how to handle the buildups when they happen. Provided they are at least given some direction as to what's happening to them, which Capra has never had."

It was ridiculous, yet he could see that Vasi truly believed it. But she didn't know Capra. She was forgetting about the tattoo hiding under that red cravat, and that only moments ago she had defended Valoii atrocities, if only in that argumentative way she was prone to.

"Look at her. She looks Valoii."

"Open your eyes, Dannac. Is there really so much difference? We come from the same people. The people here can't tell the difference, unless the Ehzeri is wearing their garb. But nobody does these days. Strip all that away, and what are we left with? People of the southeast."

"She and her kind do not believe in the Blacksmith's eternal toiling for our benefit. That could be why *vihs* diminishes—her people and their Tamarck allies refuse to acknowledge the divinity of the Blacksmith. Unlike our people." Even the slight implication that Valoii and Ehzeri were the same made his veins boil. How could that be possible? They were opposed. The same could not exist as its opposite, could it?

Best kill the conversation altogether. There were more immediate concerns, like how he was going to get into the tower if Capra refused to go. "I am sure there is an explanation for why she suffered the cloud sickness and why she carries your family emblem."

Vasi shook her head and dropped the issue, much to Dannac's relief.

"Yet you care for her?" she finally said, just as Capra was catching up to them.

"When it is convenient." He tried not to think of Yaz's interest in them, since it was obvious that Yaz's superiors would love a chance to interrogate a Valoii like Capra.

He just hoped he could find a way to avoid handing her to the Republic.

When Capra joined them, Dannac and Vasi made as though they had been discussing Ehzeri things. She had a look of contrition about her.

Perhaps, underneath Capra's incredible drive to run, there was something more. Something besides the indulgent guilt that sustained her.

Vasi whispered, in their native tongue, "Would she be more likely to help if she knew she was related to me?"

He eyed Capra for a moment, read the rare glimmer of right in her eyes and tense mouth. "No. Just wait."

Capra folded her arms and flicked a wisp of hair that had escaped from her plait. "I'm sorry. I... well, if your brother won't leave that stupid clock tower, I guess we should go get him. And Helverliss. And the painting."

It was an almost perverse setup: by all accounts, this room could be a public museum, with a rich blue carpet and little cards affixed to each glass box to explain the exhibits to casual observers. Alim had always hated museums, and folded his arms while Sevari looked on with a childish grin.

The perverse part was Noro Helverliss, chained to the grey stone wall at the back. It was almost as if he were an exhibit himself, and Alim had the sickening suspicion that Sevari really treated him as such.

"Here he is, Alim," Sevari said. He paced around the gaunt man and tugged the chains. "The great Noro

Helverliss. The man who has sat in his little shop for nearly a decade, whining about every little thing that occurs in my district. As you can see, he is a pathetic creature; an 'intellectual', a nattering voice full of answers to questions nobody wants to ask."

Sevari's tone reminded Alim more of a curator dispassionately highlighting weaknesses in an historic piece of artwork than the voice of a jailer.

"I give up. Why is he here? Is it secure?" Alim took notice of the apparatus bolted to the wall. It hadn't been there last time.

"He wanted so much to have his works returned." Sevari took his prisoner's jaw in his hand. "Now he can be with them, as he so desired." He stared into Helverliss' bloodshot eyes. "Isn't that right, hm? Are you going to tell me what you did to that horrible painting of yours? That blasphemy against Akhli's legacy?"

There was a silence, and Alim watched the prisoner's face. Helverliss made no expression, and he seemed a mannequin hung as decoration for a travelling horror show.

"I should think that it might be better to hold him in the interrogation room, with the contessa."

But Sevari ignored the comment. "You see, he knows his life's work has been mostly impure philosophizing, and it is probably by dumb chance that he had stumbled upon these terrible ways of corrupting *vihs* for his strange urges—"

"You have no idea." It was Helverliss, and he spoke slowly. "Akhli has no legacy. That was the entire point of the legend. He did not turn the shadow men's trick upon themselves and destroy the primordial races. They had already buried themselves. What do you think fuels your machines? The stuff of their deaths. Akhli is merely the point at which the two species negate each other and unify: humanity."

"Preposterous. Akhli was a warrior. Humanity existed alongside the primordial races. What you say is ridiculous."

Helverliss let out a rattling laugh. "Akhli's appearance marked an admission by the divine in its own failure. It was a reconciliation with meaninglessness. And that painting you are so obsessed with was meant to reacquaint us with that void."

"The shadow beings," Alim said, without being fully aware of it. "Shape-shifters, manipulators. Why would we want to be familiar with them?"

"Haha. Because people like you use myths to coerce whole populations into idiocy. I wanted everyone to see the void, the lack of any virtue, that any divine force must necessarily embody. And somehow this despot has come to the conclusion that there is some kind of big power waiting for him to master in that painting."

Alim stepped closer to the prisoner, and for the moment forgot about Sevari. "And is there?" At the same time, he wondered why he was allowing himself to be captivated by this mystical nonsense. Mizkov did go through the motions of a state-sanctioned religion, but national unity was served more by their new militarism than half-hearted adherence to Akhli's Church of the Teacher.

"Never mind all that, good soldier. Leave that to me— don't expect the truth from him just yet. He is of a nervous, suspicious constitution, and my specialists still need to break him properly."

Two guards stormed in, and between them stood the woman they had arrested along with Helverliss.

Sevari rubbed his hands together. "Take a good look at him, Ms. Irea." He took her shackled hand and jerked her in front of him. When he spoke, he leaned into her, lips at her ear. "See how he is now? Reasonably intact? The more information I lack, the more skin and blood he will lose."

Irea kept her head at its haughty angle. "I hate to disappoint you, but even I cannot get Noro to divulge his secrets. I just give him money and hang his paintings where I like."

"Oh nonsense, nonsense. Why must you harbour this childish resentment? Even your parents realized why we needed their land. They were glad to be of service to me. Perhaps you should take their lead and cooperate."

One of the guards said, "She could use some treatment."

The guard's sadistic grin made Alim step between them. Torturing women—not while he had any say in the matter.

"Relax, Alim." Sevari released Irea into the guard's custody. "Her family is far too integral to the class peace I have created. I would never torture someone like her."

At least that. Strange how Sevari's moods seemed to shift like the sand dunes in a storm.

"I will, however, execute her humanely should she prove uncooperative. Her family would understand."

With that, the guards left with the woman, leaving an altogether nasty taste in Alim's mouth. One he had to swallow and choke back, because in the end Sevari's rule was none of his business. He took one last gaze at Helverliss, then turned to leave.

"Wait a moment, my good friend."

"Yes?"

"My security personnel have been having a problem with some of the workers. It is to do with these murders they keep talking about."

Again? Sevari was becoming an increasingly boring waste of time. Perhaps deep down he was a lonely man. Did he somehow feel that Alim was the replacement for his fallen lieutenant?

"What kind of problem?"

"Oh, you know, the usual. I was wanting your professional opinion on how best to tighten the reins on the Ehzeri without spooking them further. I need them to stop fighting amongst each other. There is a growing divide—the labourers versus the *vihs*-capable workers."

They left the museum, and much to Alim's annoyance, Sevari led him into the refinery. Only this time, he veered from the main area into a quieter, more secure section.

"Sir, I do have work to do. I have tightened the area around which Capra and her friend will be found."

"You want to get back out there, eh? Well, I won't keep you long. You know I use the *vihs* in my research laboratories in the clock tower. But I also employ *vihs* in the refining process."

They stopped at a large iron door fitted with a massive combination lock. Sevari took a key from his belt, turned it, then began to spin the rings. "The problem is that the people beyond this door believe the workers are jealous and are killing anyone who might have the power, or even once had it, or is related to someone who uses it openly."

Sevari opened the door, and beyond was a long chamber. Pipes ran through the entire section, and all along each wall stood person-sized alcoves. Around either side of each alcove was a knot of smaller pipe that joined with the larger ones.

Alim made a few tentative steps, like a pack animal unsure of the ground. His breath caught in his lungs when he saw the people standing in each alcove. Motionless, blank faces and a strange glow about them, like nighttime fog curling around a lantern.

"What have you done?"

"Maximized production. With the sad state of metallurgy and the sciences, could I have really brought this facility into the world-leading producer of fuel without a little magic?"

"A little magic? You must have two-hundred of them locked in there. Are they being harmed?"

Sevari rolled his eyes and waved to his machines. "They are on for just twelve hours each shift. They are well taken care of. Now, about this tension in my refinery..."

Alim stepped towards one of the alcoves. The person inside glowed with *vihs*, and his eyes were stark, glowing gems. They could have been statues.

He turned away, took a deep breath, and straightened his back. "You have to be careful. They do have a history of violence between different groups. I'm not surprised you don't have more of a gang problem. My best advice is to begin a campaign among them that systematically disavows any differences between them. Sponsor cultural events, that sort of thing. Smooth out the variations between different groups by reinforcing the few things they all have in common. You need to avoid aspects specific to a certain knot."

"Knot?"

"Yes. Families, sects, whatever you want to call them. For example, the Hakerz—the one with four interlocking circular knots and emeralds—will celebrate the supposed occasion of Akhli passing through their ancestral pastures, but you will never catch another group acknowledging this. In fact, they find it offensive. So do not choose this as a refinery-sanctioned event. It will divide them."

"Interesting. Go on."

"You also need to make it appear as though this killer is being brought to justice. Increase the visibility of your security personnel. Have them perform random checks. They'll be unnecessary, but the appearance of security will outweigh the few who are bothered by such intrusions. Despite what the Ehzeri say, they do respond to displays of authority, as long as they are comfortable enough."

He made uneasy steps around the chamber, while Sevari prattled on about metallurgy, his accountant's peculiar birthmark, and his own mother. It looked as though the room swam with a mist, a kind of almost-glow that one didn't exactly see but perceived nonetheless. His neck became hot beneath his collar, and his clothes felt as though they were choking him.

He steadied himself against an empty alcove, but was horrified that he even touched the monstrosity.

"Something the matter?"

Something the matter? The haze, the war-vihs collecting, the only warning they ever give before they destroy whole villages...

"Nothing, sir. I really must be going." He buried the images of Ehzeri attacks and told himself that here, they were harmless—they were being used, and the haze was just a byproduct of their collective work. Peaceful work.

"Oh, so soon?" Sevari looked a bit sheepish, and for some reason, this juxtaposition with his status as a dictator made Alim shiver.

He moved to leave. "We know that Jorassian has passed through my perimeter of surveillance. I must close in on her now. Perhaps another time." He bowed.

"Oh, it's too bad, really. I have these dancers, you see. Imported from Prasdim."

Alim stopped and clenched his jaw. He hadn't so much as looked at another woman since Jasaf had come home as a casket of unidentifiable body parts, and the infuriating part was that somewhere inside, past his discipline, was the urge to take Sevari's offer.

"And, of course, the finest cuisine you'll find anywhere."

Well, perhaps it could wait just a few hours...

What was he thinking? He began to feel sorry for the man, but forced himself to leave. He had not come to the other side of the world to befriend the famous Till Sevari. Leave that for high-society-obsessed whores from Prasdim.

Without any windows in the place, Helverliss could only guess at the time of day. It had been what, late morning when they had come? He had barely put on the first pot of shalep when the foreboding knock rattled through his shop, all the way to his loft.

It had not been not a friendly knock, or an inquisitive one: those lacked the hardness of the clubs the Corps carried. It surely had not been hands striking his door.

He twisted in the chains, shifted the weight on his feet. He coughed and spat as far as his weak breath would throw his mucus.

Yes, it was a cruel inversion. One Helverliss could actually appreciate for its philosophical value. It was just too bad that it required him to be chained to the wall. He felt like one of the exhibits there, and was sure that this was all Sevari saw in him.

Would Sevari bring in his academic allies to witness the fall of the heretic philosopher? They would love to see his complete ruin here. The Divine only knew how many times he had blown their theories to pieces in small journals. With him imprisoned, they were completely unopposed, except for the legions of scholars east of Tamarck with whom Helverliss had a theoretical kinship. But nobody bothered to listen to them. They just didn't exist to the people of Naartland.

Even in light of this disaster, though, he could not help but smile at the sight of his masterpiece. There it was, encased in glass no doubt made unbreakable by some charm. There, a beacon of nothing, plain black. From this distance, the voices still touched him, and the painting's tendrils of notions flicked from the canvas and tickled his mind. Except, being the thing's creator, he was not alarmed or surprised. He just leaned against his wall and grinned.

Let Sevari do what he wanted. He would never accomplish this—the successful capturing of something so sublime, so universal. The ethereal shadow beings.

Nature's negative image.

The shadow and opposite of primitive libidinal life embodied by the fire giants—pure intent, malicious, manipulative intelligence, and for all that, still caring when viewed from the right perspective. Civilization itself.

He pulled at the chains once again, despite knowing that they would never yield.

If only he could conjure the power once again, he might break them.

The great Leader returned, this time without the Valoii. He spent minutes just staring at Helverliss.

Oh what Helverliss wouldn't have given for a chance to sit down with Sevari, to apply the new analytic techniques to his strange mind. What kind of pathological processes were at work? What kind of coping mechanism was this descent into mystical mania?

Finally, Sevari spoke: "Here is what I need you to do, Noro. I need that power inside me. I know it is the darkness. I must take it within myself and conquer it."

"You are mad. It does not work that way."

"It does! When I transmute the raw death contained in that painting—the demise of everything divine in the pits after Akhli tricked the shadow men into falling into their own trap—I will be complete. I will be Akhli himself, the master of both divine forces."

Helverliss laughed, and a sawing-gnawing plagued his ribs.

"Imagine possessing the primal force of the fire giants along with the cruel intelligence of the shadow men. You must have thought this when you created this horrible painting."

No wonder there had been increasing instances of vague anti-religious mania in some circles. It was naive and silly, but Helverliss did see how fervour like Sevari's would necessarily create its antithesis in the assurance of atheism.

"Kill me," Helverliss finally said.

"Kill you?"

"Yes."

"My good man, why would I do that?" He reached into his coat and produced a writing pad and a pencil. "Will you just dictate to me the *vihs* procedures you used to access this darkness?"

"Never."

Sevari hummed to himself. His eyes flashed with a kind of random blinking that would have disturbed Helverliss had he been healthy.

Then Sevari hit him.

"Well? What have you to say for yourself now?"

"You don't deserve to know how I did it. I'd sooner give the secret to one of the tyrants in exile from Yahrein than you."

Sevari then reached to his belt and unfurled a flail.

CHAPTER ELEVEN

It would be fine. Capra had faced her fear before. This usually ended with her shivering in a cold sweat and sometimes even with the task complete, but she could still overcome the fear.

Not likely, but probability wasn't one of her strengths.

She squinted at Feyerbik's schematic, which wasn't much more than a decorative grid of random lines in the poor light of the pub.

"So they are hiding war criminals here too?"

"Shut up, Dannac. That's the last thing I need right now. He wants to make up for what he did. And he dislikes the Leader."

"Does that make it okay?"

She rolled up the schematic and shoved it back into its tube. "I really don't care right now, Dannac."

There must have been something in the air. Something besides the miasma that one moment smelled sour and metallic, only to shift with the wind into a sickly sweet odour. What else could account for Dannac's sudden personality change? He was always uptight, but this was different.

And why did he keep making eyes with Vasi? She watched their new companion nurse a glass of water. Every so often, Vasi met Dannac's eyes with a flash of conspiracy.

Finally, she could take it no more. "What? What is it?"

Both just shrugged, and she wanted to slap them.

She ordered another small beer. The selection of ales and lagers at this particular pub tempted her, but they weren't rich yet, and she also needed to keep her wits sharp.

"Okay. So I need to know what your brother looks like if I'm going to pull him out of there."

Vasi looked puzzled. "Why? I am coming with you."

"Oh no. Haven't you been paying attention? The only way in is through the clock's machines and drives and whatever else these things are made of."

"I was going to lead you right in. I am an employee, you know."

It was tempting, but she knew it was impossible. "You're an enemy of the state now, Vasi. You have to realize that. You can't show up at the front door." A waitress who would barely look at the three outsiders slammed Capra's small beer on the table. "Gee, thanks honey, thanks a lot." Even this didn't garner anything more than a slight sneer from the waitress. "Anyway, how might I find Rovan?"

"He is in the tower somewhere. He does errands for the rest of us... I mean, for the tower's staff. That means my section, Section Three, the medical research group, the archivists... the tower has so many floors." Vasi fidgeted and made marks in the condensation on her glass. "Rovan is just like any other Ehzeri boy. He has dark curly hair. He's a good boy, Capra."

"I know, but what would happen if I knocked out some other boy and brought him to you? Would we just call it even and hope the kid is willing to pretend to be your brother?"

"I see what you mean."

She slid a napkin towards Vasi and dropped a pencil onto the table. "Can you draw him? Ehzeri are great artists..."

"I cannot draw to save my life," Dannac said. Capra stuck out her tongue at him.

Vasi pushed away the paper. "It would be no use." She stared at Dannac once more, then took Capra's hand. "But there is another trick that might work."

Dannac grumbled. "I wouldn't..."

Before Capra could question the remark, Vasi squeezed her hand and said, "Try to block the noise from your mind. Try to think of what a waterfall sounds like."

"Huh?"

But as soon as she did, there came a strange fog, thick enough to blot out the pub around her. She could still feel the pressure of Vasi's hand, but otherwise the fog had completely consumed the external world.

"What do you see?" The voice came from nowhere; the same unseen dimension from which came the sensation of Vasi's hand.

Capra's heart jolted. She stared into infinity, into nothingness; just a greyness and fuzzy light light.

"What have you done? Where did everything go?"

"Good."

She wanted to stand and run, but the conflict between her presence in this void and her idea of reality paralysed her.

The greyness twisted and knit into an apparition. A boy. On his face was the makings of a mustache, and on his fingers were gaudy rings of copper and cheap stones. He crossed his arms and looked on with a capricious smirk.

In the next instant, her surroundings flipped back to the pub. A passing waitress shot her a look of disdain, and Vasi was hunched forward, mouth dropped open and eyes wide.

"Did you see? Did you see Rovan?"

Now Dannac leaned in, eyeing Capra with an appraising stare and rubbing his chin.

Capra blinked and waited for her eyes to adjust to the low, yellow light. "About my height, gangly, bad mustache, lopsided smile? And a really ugly ring on his finger. Like ridiculously ugly."

There was a silence while Dannac and Vasi gazed at each other for what seemed a long while. "What? What just happened?"

"Capra, you just—"

Dannac raised his voice. "It is an Ehzeri trick. Illusions. Most are susceptible to them."

Vasi cut in again. "But—"

"Really, that is all. Vasi."

Had it really happened? It seemed like more than an illusion. She guzzled the small beer and touched the table and bench to ground herself in reality. Solid stuff—the stuff that never disappointed her, always existing as it should. How could the Ehzeri continue to persist in their imaginary world? If she had to spend her life competing with the foggy universe of appearances she had just glimpsed, it would drive her to insanity.

"Okay. Well, at least I'll recognize him when I see him. So Dannac will come with me, and once we find Rovan, he'll take him down the clock mechanism, and I'll find Helverliss and his painting."

Dannac cleared his throat. "Good. Except that we are not sure that we can climb down the mechanism."

"What?"

"I saw your schematic. The way the gears are arranged seems like a person could only get away with climbing up through it."

"Then how are we supposed to get out?"

"I was thinking of jumping out the window."

Vasi smiled, probably assuming it to be a joke.

Sevari stopped at the mirror before leaving his office: he had to check the knot of his tie, make sure his trouser creases were neat and crisp. He straightened the Corps campaign ribbons on his jacket, and checked the positioning of the rose emblem band on his left arm. His boots had arrived earlier that morning shined to his exacting standards, and one of the servants had plastered his hair with pomade.

It was the fifth day of the week. It was, he reflected as he marched to his personal elevator, too bad that such a happy occasion be spoiled by such sadness.

But duty was duty.

Just as he reached the hall containing his elevator, he stopped to greet young Rovan, who carried a large yellow envelope in his hand.

"This is from Section Three, Leader. They say everything is in order."

Such a sweet boy, that Rovan. "I am in a hurry, young man. Just go into my office and put it on my desk."

The boy's eyes went wide. It probably sounded like the stuff of myth to the boy, that kind of directive. "Me? Go into your office?"

He ruffled Rovan's hair. "You've been doing such good work, my boy. I trust you more than my caucus. Section Three would be nothing without your contribution."

Rovan's face flashed with an uneasiness. Sevari stooped and decided that Rovan's loyalty was worth a few minutes from his schedule. "Is everything going well for you? Are the others giving you trouble?"

Rovan shook his head.

"Then why the long face, son?"

"It is nothing. Just... they've become scared of me."

"Because of your success?"

"I guess you could say that."

The boy could barely make eye contact with Sevari. He assumed this was just the way boys Rovan's age behaved—it was an awkward time. Having never produced children, this was unknown territory.

Rovan continued: "Leader, do you know what Section Three does?"

"Of course. Spiritual research. Experiments in intelligence. And their success is going to ensure that my district is the best defended district of Naartland. We may not have armies of thousands, but we do have something almost as good."

The boy appeared even more conflicted. But after a few seconds of contemplation, he appeared to brighten some. "Anyway, I'll go drop this off."

"Good show, little man!" Sevari patted Rovan's head.

Children could be strange at times, couldn't they? It was probably harmless. Clearly he was a hard worker, at the very least.

Once he descended into the dank pit of the tower's basement, he stepped into his private rail car, built just for the trip between the refinery and the palace. The engineer bowed his head with appropriate solemnity, as he had been taught, and said nothing during the trip.

At the palace he found found, as always, a contingent of minor bureaucrats hungry for him to sign a ream of forms and bills. They were everywhere, and when he quickened his pace, they followed even faster, a ragged drumbeat of office shoes.

He could take no more of this pestering, and halted. "Must I remind you all that this is my day of grieving?"

In half of a breath, the secretaries and caucus members and administrators and maintenance men shut their mouths. Their eyes all went wide, as if they all knew of this collective crime they had committed.

"Get back to work, all of you." Sevari removed his pocket watch, glanced at its face. "I am going to be late if this continues."

The staff inclined their heads in unison and shuffled back to the offices and meeting rooms. A minute more of their pleading and wasting his time, and he would have ordered the fat one with the soprano voice shot as an example.

He ducked out of the main halls into the polished marble and brass corridors that had linked the throne room with the rest of the palace. While the offices and public areas were crumbling, this section shone like a mirror hall and smelled of incense. The old throne room, which now housed his memorial, was like an island in the immense hall. First, he took the circular walkway that skirted the glass enclosure. This was as close as anyone else, even his old friends when they were alive, could come to the memorial.

He then inserted his special key into the giant iron door. A hiss of pressure sounded, and he inhaled the sickly odour of preservative that had long ago become the harbinger of fond memories.

There, on the wall, sketches and paintings he had commissioned and placed in the hall leading to the Sevari family's resting place. His mother's flowing hair, his sister's innocent smile, the old days when things made sense and people were honourable... Such beautiful paintings. Such wonderful times...

As he neared his family, he tugged at his lapels and once more patted down his hair.

A voice called to him in breathless moaning. "Till? Till? Is that you?"

Mamma always spoke first. He went to her pedestal, where his mother's torso stood set into a complex array of machines and *vihs* capacitors. An iron lung next to the pedestal wheezed and the tubes connected to Mamma's back fluttered with each hiss of the machine.

"It is me, mother."

"Pa's outside. Told me to. Told me to."

"What did he tell you?"

She paused while the respirator hissed a new breath. "Told me to get you to. Early start on the harvest."

"Yes, mother. Harvest time already. What will you do with all those apples?"

"You can make a pie. You can make a jelly."

"Mmm I like pie. Would you make me a pie?"

"You can make a pie."

He bent to inspect his mother's face closely after noticing an ugly speck on her skin. Yes, there it was—a blemish on one of her leather replacement panels. And her makeup needed redoing.

He went on to his sister. This one was in much better shape than the others, both physically and mentally. It still wasn't clear to him exactly why he had chosen not to have the rope burns removed from her neck. It just didn't seem right to erase that horrible event.

Luckily, her voice was fine. "Till, you're back. Listen to me, you have to get me out of here."

He nodded, the movement as mechanical as the limited jerks of his family. "Yes, it's terrible what they've done. But I'm here now." This one he was able to make eye contact with, since the engineers had been able to preserve much of her face so well that with the help of the specially calibrated lights on the wall, they gleamed with the same inner life they had before the war.

"Get me out, Till." She shifted on her post, and the respirator made a sucking sound. Her eyes flashed with a different kind of recognition. "Till?" She looked down at herself, at the functionless legs, the arms that could only move slightly at the elbow. "What have you done?" More jerks and jolts. "I... I cannot move. Till, help me."

He angled around to inspect the wires running into the back of her neck.

"What kind of hell is this, brother?"

Everything looked fine. They did say there could be lapses into the present with the bodies that had suffered little real damage. He patted his sister's head and moved on to his favourite one of them all: Iermo Juvihern—his only friend, and probably the only reason he had been successful in wresting power from the Tamish governor.

Sevari had told the engineers to make Iermo as whole as possible and spare no expense. The dead revolutionary sported the same old uniform style that Sevari wore on these occasions. Every three days, a maintenance man would come and dust off Iermo, make sure his medals and cap brass were in perfect shape.

"Iermo, how goes it today?"

"We finally did it, didn't we? They are conceding. Sailing back to Tamarck."

The routine never changed, but Sevari's smile and warmth was as genuine as the first day he had glimpsed these restored bodies. "Yes. The King of Tamarck's cabinet has allowed him to pull out."

"They think these engines are a passing fad, eh?"

"They don't know what they are leaving behind."

There was a faint whirring, gears grinding, while Iermo cocked his head. "I see things sometimes, Till. Sometimes I think it is the future, what we made. But other times, I think it is some ghost. A grimace of history itself, as if none of my life ever happened."

"Iermo, it is normal to become so confused with life." His tone became haughty and pedantic.

"It wasn't what we wanted. My hallucinations, I mean. I saw executions and you shaking hands with the king of Tamarck himself. You gave it to him, Till. Is that going to happen?"

"No, Iermo. Blightcross District is its own autonomous nation. It always will be."

"We will defend it. Even the Hex. It is all ours."

Sevari nodded and clapped his hand onto the living mannequin's shoulder. "That is the best part, my friend. Now we are fully secure." He made sure to leave out certain facts—things that Iermo's living corpse could not process. "The worldspirits have caught us in their movement, their silent weaving."

"Always with these damned spirits, Till." Iermo began to stutter, then recovered after his respirator chuffed. "It'll be the end of it all. It was about the people, Till. Forget about these worldspirits. Things just happen as they happen; there is nothing behind any of it."

Sevari had heard that same sentence several times before during his pilgrimages. "You could be right, Iermo. Luckily I was also speaking of our dream. Remember it?"

"Yes, of course."

"It is done."

"Really?" The thing's eyes brightened, and more than should have been possible given its state of living death. "Bring me to see it, comrade."

"Maybe in time. There are still some last minute additions. It needs a mind."

"You have discovered a way to give it one?"

"Of course. You told me that my pursuit of the worldspirit was nonsense. Here is where we reap the rewards."

And, once Helverliss capitulated, The Autonomous Naartland District of Blightcross would dominate the ethereal as well as the physical. A new centre of power—neither the dispersed concentration of *vihs* that the Ehzeri used to be, nor the industrial giant of Yahrein, but their ultimate synthesis...

Never again would anyone be able to repeat the horrible war that had driven him to this grotesque attempt to cope.

He knew it was insane, but that didn't mean it wasn't comforting.

Helverliss could see only the painting, its black glare from inside the case just a few steps out of his grasp. Everything else was shut behind a greyness. His bare feet felt tacky in the congealed blood puddle in which he stood. He would have laughed at the rubber sheet they had put under him if he were capable of laughter.

At some point during Sevari's torture—perhaps around four-hundred lashes—he had broken out in hysterical laughter. But it couldn't last forever, and now he was simply existing, bled of any emotive substance.

The bastards... the bastards...

Reversal, reunited with his prized work but not in the way he wanted...

He spat a blood clot to the floor and began to realize that it was all futile. Everything he'd ever done.

They wanted the painting? They wanted to know what horrible secrets lay beneath the canvas?

He grinned. The pain itself bled away. It bled away because Helverliss was losing any connection to the scarred thing he watched in the reflection of the glass cases. It bled away because Sevari had orchestrated his own doom, and ultimately, despite his crippling depression and self-imposed distance from reality, Helverliss could only take satisfaction in becoming the instrument of Sevari's downfall.

A nice reversal, Sevari. I am with my paintings.

He bent to pick up the note pad, dropped it twice between stiff bloody fingers, and began to scrawl.

The complex signifier he scrawled nearly matched the one he had placed inconspicuously in the corner of the painting. Had he been meant, by some strange process, to do this? The decision to tame the power using these signifiers that were beyond language itself, could represent it in its totality, had puzzled him. At the time he had not thought that he would need to access the shadow beings by any means other than *vihs* manipulation.

Now he saw why.

All he needed now was to finish the last few strokes that would open up a void between his symbol and the one marking the painting. The metalanguage, the thing that the cutting-edge theorists ridiculed, the rip in reality that he could effect with mere pen strokes...

He chuckled, rattled his chains, rattled his bloodsoaked lungs. Sevari had spent a fortune on these Ehzeri slaves because he thought *vihs* could unlock *vihs* based on a silly assumption.

Only the gap between these two monstrous symbols of meaning could draw the shadow men from the painting— they would gravitate towards the space opened up by the symbols themselves. The only way to unlock the painting had nothing to do with utilizing magic.

And so he filled with an almost childish smugness as he scribbled the last dot needed to complete the character.

Take me quickly, primordial tyrants.

In the air between the two symbols, a long jagged gash of black opened. A dark mist poured from the rift, this broken welt in reality, as though he had taken Sevari's flail and lashed a wound in the universe itself.

The first being slipped from the rend and floated towards him. It was a slim, black figure, and as it edged closer, the blackness coalesced in mid-air. First, it collected into a solid form, or at least the illusion of one. It then dropped to the floor, as though it could obey gravity on a whim.

Helverliss grinned and thought of the peace awaiting him, of an end to the ridiculous condition of existence. How best to enter oblivion than by being dissolved by the shadows?

But once the shadow being took on the form of a human, he pressed against the wall and could no longer grin at his own unique death. A human was too familiar, too banal, and too brutal.

This one wore a black frock coat and leggings, along with a black hat. It reminded him of Sevari's officials, only with a dour severity. Though he was shaking and stifling bile creeping up his throat, Helverliss could not avoid the thing's eyes. Eyes of a cold blue, and besides the unnatural shade, showed all the fine details and veins of any normal human.

"You," the shadow man said. Helverliss flinched, but the shadow merely gazed at him inquisitively.

"Send me back. Send me into that rift."

More black shapes slipped from the tear. The painting lost much of its richness, and patches of faded red and green showed through the dwindling matte finish—an abandoned failure, which he had covered with his masterpiece.

"Is that what you really want?" The shadow's tone was confident and steady. It could have been any one of the haughty artists from Orvis Dunes, or one of Sevari's office managers. "I do not think so." The shadow brushed a gloved hand over Helverliss' chest, and one of the bleeding gashes healed instantly. "Hmm. No, you are not the best choice."

"Best choice? Please, this is agonizing. I want you to destroy me. You are going to destroy everything else, are you not? Destroy it in your own way, to achieve your uniqueness?"

"Hah. Is that what you think?"

"But the history…"

"We do not destroy, Noro Helverliss. We take, we create, we possess and consume. The fire giants are destruction and base urges."

"But I thought…"

"You thought wrong. They are thoughtless. They are not noble. They exist as instinct made flesh, and of course they can only react superficially to any ordering presence, like us."

"Void does not order!"

"Oh no? Did you not yourself write that your concept of zero is twofold? That there is the true void, and the notion of the void, which is a form that encircles it? A form of the void that thereby gives order to it?"

If it were not for the chains suspending him, Helverliss would have reeled and fallen from the sudden attack of dizziness. He frantically searched his mind for his theories and formulae, for the theories of others, even for religious explanations for what the shadow was telling him.

"You honestly do not care for the outside world, I see. Even if I wanted you, I doubt it would work out."

The shadow slowly walked out of the room, while its unformed brethren continued to flow from the tear and dart through the walls.

"Come back, you ridiculous shade. I made you."

The shadow stopped, stole a glance past his shoulder, and resumed his slow walk towards the door. "They tell me that there are better candidates here. People who want to make something of themselves, people who have a desire to direct and own this wincing cringe of truth you believe to be reality."

"And who might that be?"

The shadow shook its head and disappeared into the hall.

Capra barely noticed her companions once dinner had arrived. They had been acting strange since Vasi had wowed her with the silly illusion, and her only thought was that it was an Ehzeri thing.

She stuffed a fragment of boiled potato into her mouth. Watery and starchy. This wasn't the 4200s. It wasn't like salt was a war-inducing rarity these days.

"I will never understand how you can eat as much as you do." Dannac poked at a bowl of soup, and to her knowledge hadn't actually put any of it into his mouth yet.

"The army told us that this was what you do the night before you do any really strenuous work. Athletes do it, apparently." And how could she argue with that? Although, the food here lacked seasoning and she knew she could cook a thousand times better than whomever had tossed this dish together. "I mean, it makes sense. Doesn't it?" She choked on a tendril of chewy spinach. "They can't even cook spinach here."

"So the Valoii faith does not warn against gluttony?"

She shrugged. "Back home we spend a lot of time in little shelters without much to eat. I don't know about everyone else, but after going through that, I'm not going to starve myself. Not that I'm blaming you two for it." Both peoples faced lack, she realized. But the Ehzeri dealt with it by rationalizing their starvation, rather than Capra's occasional gorging to make up for lost meals.

Another boiled potato and slab of ham later, Vasi jumped from her seat. She gasped and stared across the pub.

"What is it?" Capra scanned the pub, found only a tired waitress with a skin condition attempting to appease three parties of loud beer hounds at once.

"I am not sure... look, that man over there. In black."

Dannac reached inside his coat. By now he must have been burning to try his hand-cannon in a real situation.

"It's just a banker or factory owner. What's the problem?"

She watched the man lean into a table and whisper to a lone patron. They calmly left the pub together.

Vasi shook her head. "No, something is wrong. Those men did not know each other."

"So?"

Vasi made to follow the man in black, but Dannac caught her sleeve. "Perhaps you are tired."

"No, it is something awful... it feels like *vihs* only not—"

There was a scream just beyond the far wall, which faced the alley. A few patrons startled at the sound, but they soon settled.

Vasi tore free of Dannac and rushed outside. Capra dashed behind her, nearly catching the door with her face.

She had expected to find the man who had left with the other man in black lying against the wall with his throat slashed. They emerged into the alley only to find the same man strutting towards the main street, alive and well.

"I'm not sure what just happened," Capra said.

"Look," Vasi said, pointing to the sky, where ribbons of midnight rippled against the deep red of late afternoon.

The forms, which had been flying in unison, scattered and rained on the city. Capra shivered, though why she could not begin to guess. She had seen it all—massive explosions during Ehzeri attacks, whole cavalry divisions wiped out in a flash. A few black smudges on the sky could be anything, and probably nothing to worry too much about.

Although, there was a strange familiarity this time. "Do the Ehzeri fighters ever use *vihs* that looks like that?"

Dannac shook his head. "The number of capable people willing to give their lives is so low. We never resorted to fancy tricks like this, whatever it is. I can see no advantage to this. Valoii would not think twice about it, so it cannot even be called an attack against the enemy's mind."

"Then what is it?"

And just what was Vasi's problem? Capra watched her, and the girl made no indication of being aware of the outside world. Her neck was bent awkwardly, like a puppet, and she stared into the sky. Was this some miracle?

Vasi clutched her hands at her chest and began to gasp. The shapes flitted about the sky like a swarm of bats, hovering and flying circuits until finally stopping to plummet to the rooftops.

"It is..." Her face turned ashen.

"What?" Capra wrenched Vasi's trembling hand from her chest.

"They've done it. They've actually done it."

"What?"

Vasi faced Capra, lips faintly quivering. "They've unlocked the painting. Whatever forces Helverliss had bound to it are free." She rubbed her temples. "I have been working with these forces for months. To feel them free, and swimming through the air all around us..."

"What are they?"

"Shadow men. Anything that exists is their target—it is their nature. They must absorb everything into them. With them roaming free, their blind urge to dominate all matter means everyone, everything belongs to them."

"Can you control them?"

"Of course not. I was unable to grasp the concepts." She faced the looming clock tower. "Now Rovan is in grave danger." She stomped, sending a cloud of dust to weave at their ankles. "I knew we should have left. Left before any of this happened."

Capra exchanged glances with Dannac. She whispered to him, "Does this mean we can't get the painting back? Does it still exist?"

Dannac grunted. "Does Helverliss?"

It was a good question, and she had wanted to avoid addressing the possibility that their rich benefactor was dead.

"We have to hurry." Vasi bounded off, northbound towards the tower.

"Come on," Dannac said. "The clock tower awaits."

For the time being, she couldn't think of a better idea. But there had to be a reason beyond loyalty to his own people that drove Dannac towards the tower without his usual deliberation. She was the reckless one, not him.

CHAPTER TWELVE

Usually, Sevari fell into sublime joy when he gazed at the city from his window. It rose high enough to elevate him far above the layer of smog around the city, as if it existed in its own heaven. But no longer. Now the strange shadows swam through the smoke below like minnows. Sevari stepped around his office, searched for some answer to the phenomenon, and ultimately found himself back at the window.

There crawled a sickness in his gut—the cause of these shadows had to have been Helverliss. But with the elevators malfunctioning, nobody could reach the floor to question him.

Could it be the worldspirits? Could it be that maybe Sevari himself could see them? The people moved through the streets and worked and chatted as normal. There had been no alerts from the guardsmen, no catastrophe.

Perhaps this show was just for him. A display of power, a sign of what would soon be his once he came into the secrets he deserved. He rubbed his stomach to quell the uneasiness roiling below his heart. Surely the elevators should have been repaired after so long.

He headed into the hall, and as he hurried to his elevator, realized that perhaps he ought to try appealing to Helverliss' intellect instead of torturing him. The man was brilliant, after all. As much as he was a thorn in the Shield Party, maybe he deserved a token amount of respect and dignity.

The door lay just around the corner. There was a draft of cold at his back, and he felt his ears twitch, so he turned around.

Only an empty hall stared back at him.

For a few steps he moved faster, until the same eerie sensation harried him again.

Seconds passed, with his breath shattering a strange silence.

When he could take no more, he called out, "Who is there? Show yourself."

Thump thump thump thump

"I said show yourself. I haven't time for this nonsense."

Thump thump

"State your business, damn you!"

"Hello, Mr. Sevari." The voice was young, petulant. Out of the shadows near a window sill stepped his young assistant.

"Rovan? What are you doing up here?"

There was something about the boy... was he more mature? The way he carried himself, the way he swaggered, the look in his eyes. "I wanted to tell you something."

"What is it now, boy?"

"I am in charge."

Sevari wanted to laugh, but the boy's words weighed on his ears with a certain gravity. A ludicrous gravity, given the boy's age. What did the kid know of power?

He didn't have time for games. Perhaps becoming attached to the boy had been a mistake. It was just that Rovan showed so much ambition, so much fire and passion. He reminded Sevari of himself.

"Funny boy, Rovan. Now, I have some work to do. There are things going on that you cannot comprehend just yet, my boy." But when he turned to leave, his knee slammed into an invisible force. He cried out and tried to pass through the barrier, but his limbs would not move beyond the invisible line. "What is this?"

"I told you, Leader. I am in charge now. Shall we go back to your office?"

"This is the kind of thing that will get you killed, Rovan. If you have come into some latent ability like your sister's, we can arrange a far better way to channel it."

"Ha. You would bargain with me? The hero who made Blightcross free? You aren't so tough, I see."

Now Sevari screwed his face into the same hard scowl depicted in the many romantic portraits and paintings of himself atop white horses with the King of Tamarck cowering at his mercy. "Listen here, you will release me at once. All I need do is press one stud to call a whole platoon of troops to my location."

Rovan circled him, his steps rhythmic and resounding in the hall against the constant drone of the tower's gearwork. "Poor man. Did you think you were the only one who saw horrible things during the war?"

"What do you know of the war? Hm? You weren't even an impure urge in your father's groin yet."

Rovan went still and for an instant, his image changed to that of a tall man in black coat and hat.

Sevari shut his eyes, shook his head. When he opened them, Rovan was back to his old self.

It was just that now, two men in black, tailored outfits flanked him.

"Who are these men? Hm? What have you brought into my home?"

The three strange people now began to circle him. Could it be the worldspirits? Were they testing him? No, something far worse.

"Shadows. You are the shadows, aren't you? From the painting?" His gut began to lurch. "Did that fool release them?"

How could he be so naive? He might as well have given Helverliss a regiment to command against him.

One of the men in black said, "We thought you were more like us, but really, Rovan is more suited."

He could only respond with a confused mumble.

Against what he would expect, the shadow men said nothing and paced while Rovan spoke. "They need a leader. A figurehead to remind them of why they are here, to anchor them. They chose me."

The boy was no longer Rovan. It was a trick—the shadows were the agents of lies and they had taken the boy's body. "Rovan was like one of my own, you ghouls. I will ensure that you... things will suffer for taking him."

"Come, back to our office. I'm willing to share it with you, Sevari." For once, Rovan looked sincere.

"Really?"

"Yes. We would cease to exist without this world of men. Therefore, it will remain intact in some respects. Besides, the people here seem to trust you. It will be a joint operation. Blightcross will become the envy of the world once the shadows overrun this already admirable society."

"What is your aim?"

"Whatever we want. That is the only rule. There will be competition among us, and brothers will be pitted against each other."

"I do not understand..."

"You will."

Alim looked up from his spyglass. Below, the streets bustled as usual, and he only hoped that nobody would be injured once they fired upon their targets from the rooftops. "What is it, Corporal?"

The soldier knelt and removed his cap. "Strange things, Sir. Things I ain't never seen, and we've seen plenty here."

The black streaks? It could have been anything. Some strange industrial byproduct, or a scientific phenomenon.

"It is nothing to worry about, Corporal. We have more immediate concerns."

There was no answer, unless a heavy breathing and glazed eyes was the soldier's reply.

"Is that clear, Corporal—"

The soldier's knees buckled, blood gushed from his mouth. Behind him stood another soldier, whose mouth was half-curled into a bizarre expression somewhere between a smile and a grimace.

Alim drew his short sword just in time to parry the soldier's unwieldy blow. "What the hell is wrong with you, soldier?"

"I want."

"Want what?"

The soldier took another swipe, which Alim dodged. His heel jammed against the small ledge, and he flailed to keep his balance. A mere step from dropping to his death and a murdered comrade at his feet—he had to shove away these thoughts and focus.

"What have you done, man?"

There was an odd glaze over the soldier's eyes. And now, inexplicably, since they had secured the rooftop, a thin man in black business attire watched from behind the soldier.

"Who are you? Someone arrest this man." Alim raised his sword, and despite that the man immediately in front of him was a trained killer, the one in black was what chilled him.

"I am in command now," the soldier said. "You are too weak. The strong are better suited to lead, don't you think?"

One false move and he would tumble over the edge to his death. "I'm warning you one last time, soldier. Stand down."

The soldier crept forward, and Alim slashed. The blade bit into the soldier's abdomen, and he did not so much as wince before he fell to the ground. Alim averted his gaze from the body and faced the stranger in black.

"You there—what have you done to him?" He peered behind the man. The rest of his men were propped against the little wall, heads slack and eyes closed. There were two other squads stationed atop other buildings on this block, but they were already in position and watching the ground.

The man turned his blue eyes to the freshly slain soldiers. "You always knew better than your commanders, Alim."

"I have no time for this. What have you done to my men?"

"The officers who command you are part of their own little club, aren't they? If only you could just expose them for the leeches they are." The man shook his head slowly. "Sitting back and taking monetary benefits from the very men who own many of these weapons factories. Buying more and more weapons to hand over to men like you. Brave men. You deserve so much better."

Alim's fingers relaxed slightly, the sword slipping in his grip. The man's voice seemed to pacify his racing heart and soften his hard readiness—who was he, and how could he know Alim's deepest held thoughts? Was he a foreign agent who had read a dossier filled with minute details and analysis by one of these new mind-bending practitioners?

"Look at all of the waste here. These factories, this corrupt regime. The world needs heroes, Alim. You are that hero."

What an odd thing to say. Except in Tamarck, of course, where heroic rhetoric flowed from the King and the elected officials like the industrialized wine they jettisoned on all sides of their borders to war-torn nations begging for affordable products.

"See? You are humble. We can just let that part be unspoken. Follow my direction, and we will accomplish great things." The man touched Alim's shoulder, and Alim wondered why this had not triggered him to hack off the man's arm at the elbow. "I want you to go to those men lying back there and kill them."

"No. I won't." As if it were a reasonable request he just couldn't perform, as if they were talking about cutting a deal for a bushel of grain. Why was he suddenly so blasé about this bizarre conversation? The fact of his questioning this should have kicked him out of the trance, but...

"Greatness is hampered by leeches such as them. Go ahead—they won't feel a thing. They are already unconscious."

He was right. They would not feel the blade across their throats, and with them gone he could do so much more—

What was he thinking?

He needed them.

They were real people, not pawns, not objects like this man was portraying. This person was an agent of self-satisfaction, a ghoul of narcissism.

Alim shoved the man away and readied his sword. "I do not know who you are, but flattery is rather amateurish."

"Fine. Do it for Jasaf. You want to gut her—the woman who could have saved her had she not fled like the coward she is. Cowards are the real criminals. Those who will not stand up to the call of duty, those who are afraid. I will help you make her pay. You cannot just bring her back to face a trial and sterile execution."

"You seriously think I have so little self-control that I can't resist your appealing to visceral fantasies? Do you not realize that..." His mind went alight with bright images of Capra hoisted onto a cross and left to rot in the sun.

Punishment.

"You were saying, brave soldier?"

Alim turned away from the man. "I was saying that you have no power over me." He then twirled, sword at throat-level to end this man's stupid chatter.

His blade passed through the stranger, and Alim stumbled wildly. "What are you?"

Three more, identical to the first, appeared from high above—black streaks, like tar poured from high above, filling an invisible casting of their human forms.

This was a kind of magic on which Alim had never been briefed, and with his special status, he possessed access to all the bulletins.

"This one lacks the ability to have any fun," one of them said.

Another said, "Enjoy yourself, Alim."

Alim began to step back, and mentally mapped out his escape to the stairwell. "I can do that just fine on my own, thank you."

"Admiration, that's why you do it. You want to be able to do as you please once you're an old, decrepit fool just because you served, isn't that right? Well, take that respect now. You deserve it, Alim."

The more he spoke with these ghosts, the more they made sense. He had to get out before they started to make too much sense.

He clenched his jaw, waved the sword, and bolted for the stairwell.

He was prepared to engage them, but sailed past, too afraid to look back. The strangers' laughter seeped into his skull even as he blew down the stairs and ran through the leather shop on the ground floor.

Outside, he craned his neck every which way, eyes darting around but finding no sign of the ghosts. Had he imagined it? What if he had come under some spell and actually murdered his own men?

This city boiled with a thousand poisons, like an alchemist's lab. Perhaps a tainted meal, or maybe there were chemicals here that entered the body by touch, and he had descended into a madness. But there wasn't time to explain it. This was the street through which Capra was heading, and his men were poised at the rooftops surrounding the block with orders to take down her Ehzeri companions with as many cannon shots as necessary.

Twenty men, all firing hand-cannons from every angle—it would be a hailstorm given the ambiguous accuracy of these new weapons.

Rather than run to one of the other buildings, Alim chose to hide and observe the capture. A man on the ground was a good idea anyway.

Everything would be fine, as long as the hand-cannons did their job.

Alim took comfort in these grounding thoughts. Until, that is, he saw the three identical men in black wending through the afternoon crowds, all eyes trained on him.

"What do you want from me?"

They did not answer.

It was as though the moment in the pub had bounced Capra into some strange shadow of the world she had known. First the strange man in the alley, then a sky writhing with shadows. Walking through the city only deepened the disconnectedness. Queues spilled out of the underground terminals and into the street, and the place seemed more chaotic than usual. She peered over a railing at an open section of track. There were people in the middle of the tracks raving at an invisible audience. Twice she observed horseless carriages tipping and crashing and erupting into a pile of burning metal and black smoke. There were brawls on every corner, and every so often she noticed flashes of the same smartly dressed man, only to lose sight of him in the next instant.

"I hardly see the point of buying clothes at a time like this," Dannac said.

Capra stopped in front of the leather shop. "If I went into a giant machine wearing these, I'd either be pulled into the mechanisms and pulverized, or nude. I'd prefer to avoid both."

"And what am I supposed to do?"

"And me too?" This was the first time Vasi had spoken since they left the pub.

"You'll have to strip to your underclothes, at least," she said to Dannac. "And you're not coming, Vasi. Remember?"

Vasi looked contrite, sullen. "Right. I forgot. Sorry."

They came to the shop, and Capra quickly darted in. She found the man at the counter in a daze, glaring out the window.

When she was finally able to catch them man's attention with a wave, he said, "Yes? Oh, you're the lady... hm." He reached under the counter and brought out a folded bundle tied with string. "Now, I don't know what someone like you is going to do with this, but it seems like something unsavoury."

"Sir, it's strictly a vocational garment. Please, I have to hurry."

"Vocation? Bah. I been making work attire for fifteen years here, and I never seen something like this."

"Well, now you have." She dumped the coins on the counter and snatched the bundle from him.

"Strange things happening today." The man shook his head and examined each coin.

"So these crashing carriages and random fights in the streets are not usual for this city?"

The clerk lowered his glasses and gave her a sceptical look. "I just had a bunch of men scrambling to the roof. Then one scrambling down. They're from the Corps, I imagine. I think they've finally gone crazy too. Everyone has."

She gulped. "Corps?"

"Nice young man, immigrant like yourself. Intense fellow, though."

"Shit." She stuffed the bundle into her rucksack and bolted out of the shop, but it was too late.

The block roared with stuttering thunder, followed by the patter of hailstones pounding the dirt road and brickwork. Cannon fire? She flattened against the wall and searched the scattering crowd for her companions.

So much for the safety of big city anonymity. Was Alim so single-minded that he would let innocent bystanders take the brunt of their fire, just in the hope that he might capture her?

She readied her switchblade, though the attackers were hidden, and, she assumed, occupying high ground. Her knuckles blanched under her anxious grip on the blade.

She sensed something wrong, and it wasn't just the booming guns aimed at her comrades. It was worth the risk to step into the fire to find Dannac and Vasi, and luckily Alim's men appeared to need more practice with their weapons. Years ago she had taken part in a similar ambush in an attempt to assassinate an Ehzeri resistance leader, and their crossbow assault had destroyed the enemy in five seconds. This was highly unprofessional, and Alim could have had them all killed in an instant if he'd followed procedure and had the right people.

The packed crowd shattered into splinters, the people scrambling in every direction. Soon the block was empty. A ghost town, only one trembling with cannon fire. A naked dread, as if she had been stripped of all defences, spurred her into action. She dashed behind a dustbin, only to find the hiding place already occupied, and she collided with a crouching man. The two rolled into the street, where cannon shot continued to pepper the ground.

When the dust cleared and they stopped rolling, she startled and jumped away from the man. She readied her switchblade and tensed.

Shit. Alim.

She prepared for a fight to the death. "Alim, this is madness. Your people have injured innocents over your stupid orders. Am I really so important?"

Alim brushed dust from his sleeves, but did not make any threatening moves. "Capra, they've gone insane."

"What?" Was this a trick? A way to bring down her guard?

Without warning, he lunged and tackled her. They rolled into an alley, and she fought hard enough to end up on top. She pressed her knife against his throat. "Don't make me do it, Alim. There are strange things going on. The only way to stop it is to find Helverliss."

"I don't give a damn about Sevari or Helverliss or anything to do with this horrible place. I am not returning to that tower. Sevari is of no use to me at this point. He was getting on my nerves." He coughed. "What are you waiting for, then? Hm?"

"What's happened to you, Alim? The service changes us, but not like this. You're not even on the front lines anymore."

"I—"

A cannon shot pelted the ground, a mere fingernail's width from his head. "My soldiers have been corrupted. They are firing at random. They fired at me, they fired at everyone else..."

"Why? Does it have something to do with those shadows?"

"Shadows?"

"Sevari has unlocked the painting. He released whatever it was that Helverliss had bound to it. It seems as though these shadows might be affecting the people here."

"The men in black."

She cocked her head.

"They wanted me to do things. Horrible things. They thought it was a game, but at the same time they were... extremely serious about it. They seduce you. They offer a kind of greatness." He paused, ground together his teeth. "What have we done?"

Above, there still swam the ribbons of shadow, all weaving and darting, hunting, and diving towards their targets on the ground.

Now, on the rooftops, she saw Sevari's men in blue, standing on the ledges. In unison, they stepped off as one would the last step of a set of stairs, and plummeted to the ground. They fell into a heap, and for a moment Capra sighed and began to collect herself again, if not slightly confused and horrified at the mass suicide.

But that lasted only the few seconds necessary for the soldiers to stand, however wobbly. They began to load their hand-cannons and form firing lines. A dozen men in black stood behind the soldiers.

"What the hell is going on, Alim?" Vasi would know, but where was she? And Dannac?

Of all the people to be stuck with, it had to be Alim. The worst part was that she still felt a hint of comfort at a familiar face, even if the man wanted to kill her.

The phalanx of hand-cannons advanced. Unless this was some convoluted trick, Alim would have to cooperate with her.

She jumped from his chest and extended her hand to him. "Come on, there's no use fighting these people."

Alim's mouth gaped for a second. The two met eyes, Alim's blazing with a fervour she knew he was consciously tempering. Just when the moment began to slide into an uncomfortable exchange, he gripped Capra's forearm, and she pulled him to his feet.

The soldiers began to bellow crude remarks. *Sheepfuckers! Suck on this! You stupid cunt, get back in the kitchen where you belong!*

Alim nodded and the two broke into a mad sprint away from the shadows and their puppets. Fatigue crept into her lungs and muscles, but when they passed a crowd of men playing a round of darts with an elderly man tied to a lamppost as their target, she quickly found the wherewithal to overcome a few stitches in her sides.

"The rules are strict," someone said. "We will, after this game, divide the group by virtue of their scores. Landing your dart between the eyes will earn you an automatic spot in the new Council of Ten-Thousand!"

Rules? It was chaos.

Another voice: "We will once again establish the rule of law, just as we did with the Fire Giants."

They rounded a corner near a park decorated with white columns, and they decided to hide among the false ruins. She dropped to her knees and panted, mouth parched and throat burning. "I wish I had paid more attention in our religious classes, Alim. I have no idea what these people are talking about."

"The shadows," he said between gasps. "Wanted to organize nature the way they saw fit. It could have been perverse, like this, or it could have been heaven... but the fire giants resisted their taint, and fought back."

"What a choirboy you are."

"Understanding the religious differences between us and the Ehzeri is a tactical advantage, Capra. You should have paid attention."

In this one moment of discussion, this exceptional suspension of their relationship as defector and hunter, Capra felt like she had before she had left the army. Before they had shipped her to the Red Sector to help quash the never-ending rebellion, before she had witnessed what really happened in Red.

"What are you smiling about?"

She erased her out-of-place grin. "Nothing."

"Well, you obviously found something funny about depravity in the streets and the shadow men ruling the natural world."

"It was nothing. Just memories. Ghosts."

He grumbled and peered around the column, into the madness. "What do you know about this? Were you going to stop it?"

"I'm not exactly sure. I was on my way to... well, maybe I shouldn't tell you these things. You are, after all, in bed with Sevari."

"These things don't acknowledge our allegiances." He drew a deep breath and gazed at her with blatant malice flashing in his eyes. "We can sort that out afterwards. Neither of us will gain anything with Sevari's madness spreading into the streets through these shadow men."

"I just have a hard time trusting people with the same tattoo I have."

"Don't bring up issues of trust, Capra. You are the one who has spent the last three years running from the law of your own people and surviving by leeching off the rich and their petty whims."

How could he know all of this? She could only blink and wonder which of her secrets he had uncovered.

"Oh yes, Capra. I know a lot about you. They gave me everything I needed to track down the war resisters. I know what you have stolen, what you have sabotaged, and three of the five men you were involved with."

She felt her cheeks become hot. "Five? You need to go back and do some more investigating, Alim."

"What was that?"

"Nothing."

They were copulating in the middle of the road, faces caked with oil and soot, bodies writhing in ripped clothes and smearing puddles of engine grease. Dannac seriously considered putting them out of the misery that seemed to have overtaken them.

"I had no idea this was what they wanted," Vasi said. "If I had known, I would never have agreed to work on the project."

The makeshift bandage on her back was bright red and beginning to leak. "Stop and let me change the bandage. It is still bleeding."

She shrugged away from him. "I will be fine. We need to find Capra."

"The shot could be laced with poison."

She shut her eyes and shivered for a moment. "I am not poisoned, and if I were, most poisons are easy to remove."

They moved on, while everyone they passed either fought or groped or ate dirt and a dozen other inedible things.

Dannac shuddered as he realized that were it not for this depravity, the ambush would have been successful and they would be dead. "I should not have left her behind."

"We had no choice. You know she can take care of herself."

A flying boat roared overhead, and in its wake, several black specks fell to the ground.

Passengers.

"You seem to be able to take care of yourself as well."

She jolted. "What?"

"Any of our fighters could recognize what you are. Sevari must be either truly insane or too stupid to check out the people he hires. I imagine the line of discipline that prevents you from levelling his clock tower is thin."

She butted against him, apparently not satisfied that none of the deranged people around them cared about her secrets. "It is not the way to fight. If they had given me a bow and shoved me onto the front lines, I would have stayed to defend our people. But the archon they turned me into..."

"Relax. I left them too, remember? I just wonder if you ever stopped to think that a weapon like yourself placed in a place like Blightcross could be more disastrous than anything you ever saw in Mizkov."

"Don't you think I've thought about that? It haunts me every day. Sevari's work helps to keep me focused and stable."

Thank the Blacksmith for that.

They dodged a clump of revellers and turned onto a side street. The oddness seemed to be collecting, organizing itself along the main arteries of the city, and Dannac thought it best to avoid any more confrontations with these corrupted people.

If, that is, they still were people. Perhaps he would do them a favour by killing them. The thought persisted in his conscience—was it right to let them fall victim to these shadow men?

He sidestepped a headless corpse. Around the next corner, they drew back at the sight of a dozen black-suited men patrolling the street. Dannac pulled out his hand-cannon, heart racing. Their eyes swept the block, at once both vacant and searing. A depraved laughter rattled above on a metal staircase. He coiled into a ready stance, like a flinching reptile. Hanging over the railing, the gibbering idiot above stared with crossed eyes and brandished a cocked crossbow in one hand, and a corn broom in the other. Dannac aimed the cannon between the man's eyes and held his breath.

"Dannac, what are you doing?"

He kept stone-still. "Get behind me. There are shadow men in the street, and a fool with a crossbow in the balcony."

"Let's just keep going. He's not well. I doubt he can even aim his weapon."

But the man blew a lock of his hair from his eyes and raised the crossbow. Dannac ground his molars and squeezed the trigger. The shot slammed his arms, and the alley was a thunder-filled canyon. The round shattered the man's face, and sprayed the wall behind with the pulp of his head.

Dannac nodded with satisfaction, reloaded the cannon, and gestured to the street. Vasi could stand there and stare if she wanted. While he might with Capra, he wouldn't try to reason with Vasi.

Finally, she rejoined him, her head kept low. That is, until they passed a group of shadow men, and she let out a quiet, startled noise. Dannac tried to stare them down as they passed, but they did not break their gaze.

When they passed, Dannac could barely admit to himself that he had held his breath and recited prayers in his mind. But the apparitions made no move against them.

A few blocks later, Vasi broke the eerie silence.

"You would have to worry about your friend less if you would just let me tell her the truth."

"She is not one of us."

Vasi flinched at a guttural sound coming from one of the alleys. "How do you explain her ability? Her sensitivity to the storms? The family knot around her neck that is identical to mine? We are related, she and I. It is..."

"Crazy. She stole it from the body of one of the hundreds she has killed."

"I thought that at first, but I cannot believe it now. She is not the type to carry trophies. It could really be a family heirloom, like she said. Only she doesn't appear to know the significance of it."

He wanted to cover his ears, or her mouth. What Ehzeri could even imply that one of those Valoii monsters was actually one of their own? True, he had accepted Capra out of necessity and in the end had grown to appreciate her friendship and expertise, but he could never forget who she really was. A few symptoms of cloud sickness and the ability to receive *vihs* images in her mind did not replace Valoii blood.

"It is wishful thinking. Sevari has worked you to the bone, and the stress of your worrying about Rovan has taken your ability to reason. Capra cannot be one of us."

She stopped. "You think I am this delicate little *chuzka*, don't you? Do you have any idea what I can do? The things I have done? I am not imagining things. Capra is Ehzeri."

"If Capra is Ehzeri, then use your witch-sense to find her so we can stop wandering aimlessly. I do not like delays. I must get to that tower."

"You seem very interested in this tower. Are you an engineer?"

"No."

She made a little noise, then kept quiet.

Was having sight worth doing dirty work for Yaz and the Republic?

"There she is." Vasi skipped towards a plot of short grass decorated with benches and granite columns.

"Are you joking?"

Obviously not—there she was, cowering behind a column. With another man.

Another Valoii.

He grabbed Vasi and guided her behind one of the columns. "Are you insane? That is the Valoii."

"The soldier Alim? I know. It seems they have reconciled for the time being. It would be foolish not to, given the state of things."

"You are much too trusting."

"That is what you think." She gave him a look of utter defiance and tore free.

"Wait, just do not complicate matters by speaking of your bizarre theories. We have enough to deal with as it is. All right?"

She nodded, and they approached their comrade.

Alim shot to his feet, hand on his sword hilt. Capra stayed behind the column, since she was hardly equipped for a fight.

In hindsight, they should have picked up one of the hand-cannons dropped by their attackers. They could not be that hard to figure out, could they?

"What is it?" she whispered.

"Four of them."

"Four of what?"

"Men in black."

"But not humans with axes and cannons?"

"No."

She stood. "Perhaps they would negotiate. We could gain the upper hand. I'm a good talker, Alim."

"I know that."

"So let's see if we can outsmart them."

He ducked back behind the column. "There is no outsmarting them. There is nothing to negotiate with. They are shadows, Capra."

"Then how are they walking towards us? How are they driving the city to madness? Alim, they have to be intelligent, they have to be capable of listening and comprehending."

"I don't pretend to understand them. That's just what they are. Sevari could tell you what their power is—something about the space where something isn't being more powerful than the thing that fills that place. It's all mad, and we'd best get moving."

The only question was of where they could run. To the south, the main street began to pack with these men in black, all standing beside or behind a depraved worker or mother or child, as if guiding them in some obscene ritual.

To the east, Capra glimpsed the likely source of the sulphur reek she had noticed. Rising above the low buildings were the cargo cranes, and beyond these the Golroot River pushed its sludge towards the ocean. Across the bridge stretched a dead expanse of desert, broken only by a single grey monolith—the prison.

"I say we go towards the docks, at least," she said.

"Why?"

"Because most of the shadows were concentrated on the refinery and the centre of the city. At least, in the air they were. We get out of the fray, regroup and come up with a better idea."

They scrambled from column to column, and Capra could not ignore a strange sensation at her back, as if her awareness were pulled partly out of her body and could sense the phantoms pursuing them.

Once they cleared the park, it was as though they had walked into an arena of death-sport. The streets were empty of business and wagons, blades and hammers lay in pools of blood, men swung barbed chains, and legions of the shadows watched dispassionately like bored patricians barely staving off their ennui.

Capra skidded to a stop. "We're surrounded."

"We might pass through them. They appear occupied. Almost as if there's some plan to play out, and they're filling roles and establishing some new structure. If we don't fit with it, they'll ignore us."

"You mean kill us?"

Alim shrugged. "It seems even the victims of this death have taken on a role. Look."

He might have been right, but why would anyone choose to be subservient? A lean, strong man who must have worked in the foundry and lived through his share of fistfights, somehow struck down by a teenager with a hook on a rope and a nasty grin. Even a greying, wrinkled lady found a way to bury the point of her parasol into the throat of a young man in business attire. Why would these people accept their deaths?

Alim drew his sword, and Capra still held her little switchblade.

He whispered, "Walk slowly, don't look at the shadows."

"Alim, are you crazy?"

"If we run, they will notice us, like cats. They can't see worth a damn, but when something makes sudden moves, they will take notice and pounce."

It almost made sense. Enough that Capra obeyed and tried to block out the mad raving and gang beatings and copulation. It was as if the city itself were writhing in a fever-dream, legs and arms squirming in the streets, a complete breakdown of language and all of the basic assumptions one took for granted if they were to function in society.

They decided to head for the darkened alleys wherever possible. Capra hated the feeling of walls flanking her. She stepped around human waste and puddles of spilled beer.

The alley residents were slumped against the wall. An inhuman reek hung over them like localized extensions of the smog above the city. Would they attack her? If they did, perhaps it would be a cry for help, a way of ending whatever had come over them.

Wouldn't they be better off dead?

She caught herself in the middle of that thought and cringed. It was not her place to decide.

"What happened to my friends?" she asked, since conversation would help to keep her nerves in check.

"My men were taken by the shadows minutes before you came into the ambush. By then, they didn't care who they killed, it seemed."

"Is that a yes?"

"They disappeared in the crowd. Maybe they were hit, maybe not."

That didn't sound very encouraging, but she then remembered that Dannac was armed for the occasion, and that Vasi could hold her own. She might even have healing abilities.

Wouldn't that be handy about now? And why weren't the city's Ehzeri fighting back?

Had Capra possessed those skills, she would jump at the chance to fend off these shadows. Although, it was probably more complicated than simply firing random bolts of thunder at an enemy and destroying them. Who was she kidding—she had no idea what it was like. No Valoii of her generation did, not even the instructors who drilled them on how to recognize this or that type of attack, how to spot a *vihs*-enabled person, how to counter them with certain elements.

How to kill them.

Just a few steps from the alley's end, and the beginning of the docks, Alim jolted to a stop.

"What now?"

He said nothing, readied his sword.

"Shit, are you kidding me?"

She brought her hands up, muscles tense and vibrating. She stepped to Alim's side, and saw the impasse: four soldiers, each with large axes and hand-cannons stuffed in their belts.

"We've received orders to round up any suspicious characters," one of them said.

Alim said, "I am working under Sevari, you dullards. Let us pass."

"All men who look like you do are to be interrogated."

"Men who look like me?"

"There are agents here, Sir." The soldier advanced, licking his lips and raising his axe. "They told me about the agents. They say that you are one of them. I must interrogate you, Sir."

"This is ridiculous—"

Capra tapped him with her elbow. "He's been corrupted, Alim."

"Thought it was worth a try, anyway. You never know."

"Never know? Look at him. He's a lunatic."

Four against two—it wasn't so bad. Scientific studies had confirmed that Valoii training could enable the average person to take on three trained Tamarck infantrymen at the low end. It would be over in a matter of seconds, with these bastards at their feet and—

A small axe sliced through the air and grazed her arm, and she reeled. Alim jumped into them, and Capra rushed in, striking with her fists. She landed a blow against one of the soldiers' jaw. He stumbled once, and slashed again with his axe. She whirled and drove her knife into his thigh, twisted, and tossed him to the ground.

She was about to finish him when she caught a flash at the other side of the alley. She planted her boot onto the man's throat and glared at the shadow men approaching from the other side.

"Alim..."

He was busy with two soldiers.

"Alim, they're here..."

He killed one, and knocked the other to the ground before finally acknowledging her.

One of the shadows stood an arm's length before her. She raised her knife. Met the thing's eyes—blue, almost glowing. And mesmerizing...

No, don't fight. Just listen to what he has to say.

Her grip slackened, and she looked upon the shadow man with a calm that chilled her, but there was nothing she could do to fight it.

"I wanted to tell you something, Capra."

"Yes?"

"I wanted to ask you not to tell anyone about what you saw here."

"Oh?"

The thing nodded. "It is a secret, you see. If you tell anyone about this event, everyone will know. We will be very disappointed in you. Can you hold that secret?"

"You're killing them." She heard her own voice as childlike, singsong.

"No, Capra. We are helping them. Don't you want to help people? You would never kill an innocent again. If you tell anyone, more will die. This is a secret, and I need you to keep it."

"Why?"

"Because I know you will."

"That doesn't even make sense."

The shadow man took her hand, and from his palm came a cold shock that slithered into her lungs, froze her breath. She tried to snap her hand away, and only gave a pathetic tug.

"Now that you know our secret, you have to help us. You belong now. Isn't that great?"

"I belong?"

"That's right, you can stop running now. You can take part in parades, and we will give you a medal. Come to the tower. We need one like you to fulfil a new role."

Beneath his words swam some other meaning—a feeling of regret, like her own, a wistful desire for home, for the ability to belong once again, and not in the superficial way she thought she had in the Little Nations.

I did not want to leave. I had to. Why won't they forgive me?

"Yes, you understand now, don't you? We can take you to the tower now, if you like."

From behind the shadow man came two real men. Over one's arm dangled a set of shackles.

"For your safety, of course," the shadow man said.

This made sense to her clouded mind, and after a second of hesitation, she pressed the lever on her knife to retract the blade and clipped it to her armband. "For my safety, yes." She presented her hands, wrists limp.

A warm feeling came over her, as though she were going home, going back to her parents' townhome in Lagaz. They—

or someone—would tell her that it was okay, that she did the right thing by leaving and that they were all so sorry they had made her—

Just get it over with. Reach into that satchel, pull the fuse, and toss it into the hut. You don't even have to look inside. Nobody ever does. Just throw it in. They are murderers, remember.

—fight their enemies, made her contribute...

And in an instant, this strange mirror world she had dropped into, where the shadows spoke truth, where she was going to belong again, shattered with the sound of a hand-cannon roaring across the alley. The man with the shackles spurted a fountain of blood from his head and fell, and seconds later, another shot rang through the alley, and there was a meaty thud as the other man's chest shot a plume of blood and bone fragments.

There was the sound of a familiar voice hollering at her, but her ears rang and she reeled, in a daze from her encounter with the shadow man. Sound swirled around her, none of it discernible.

One more crack sounded, and the shadow man vanished.

At the alley's end stood Vasi and Dannac, and in his hand was his new toy, its barrel tonguing the air with a thick wisp of smoke.

"Capra, answer me. Are you okay?"

She stumbled forward, and suddenly the dreamy wash that had overtaken her senses left her entirely, and she once again lived in the stark reality of pitted concrete, shit-stained alleys, and black smoke.

"I think so." She touched the gash on her arm, smeared blood between her fingers. "What just happened?"

Alim came beside her. "You were almost taken by the shadows."

"As if things could not get worse," Dannac said, with a glare towards Alim.

She winced. "Relax, Dannac. I think it's safe to say there are bigger things to worry about than allegiances in a border conflict across the ocean." She rubbed her eyes. "How did you scare off the shadow, anyway?"

Vasi smirked. "I charged his cannon shot. It seems to disintegrate their manifestations for a while."

"What is the situation like back there?" Alim asked.

Dannac was still glowering at him. "We were pushed eastward. I would advise against turning back, since they are concentrating around the core of the city."

"Look, the cranes have stopped moving. The harbour and ships are deserted."

Capra moved to the crest of the hill leading down into the port area. What specks she saw below moving around the docks were leaving the area, either walking up into the city or hopping into carriages. No noise or smoke came from the cranes, and under many, shipping containers dangled in mid-air.

And, strangest of all was that there were no shadows hovering above the harbour, as there were deeper into the city.

"Why, I wonder?"

"I wouldn't question it right now." Alim took one last appraising glare at Dannac, and slid his sword back into its sheath. "I say we go down to the harbour."

"And after that?" Vasi raised her head as she walked past Alim as if he were the mongrel servant of a feudal palace. "We have to find a way back to the refinery."

"We could take one of the boats," Dannac said.

Capra thought for a moment. "I don't like putting ourselves in such a vulnerable position."

"I agree." Alim gestured to the bridge. "That area is completely deserted." He traced his finger along the riverbank, back to where the refinery's egg-shaped structures and pipes met the river. "If we go along the other edge, perhaps we could arrive there without meeting any opposition."

"That is the Hex," Vasi said.

"I heard about that." Capra recalled Tey's stories. "We would have to take Fasco's Road, through the slums, and then cross through the desert on the other side. It killed Fasco, so it would probably kill us. And I doubt the prison is going to offer any help to us."

Alim looked confused. "Fasco?"

Capra relayed what she could remember of the story, and Vasi filled in the missing parts.

"Well," Alim said, with a stupid grin. "Did it ever occur to you that the reason the shadows are staying away from the dockside slums and the Hex is because of this taint that killed the executioner?"

Both women glanced at each other, and Capra caught the same sheepish grimace on Vasi that she knew she was displaying.

"And if this Fasco character made the trip once a week for three years before dying, maybe one trip through the Hex would not be enough to kill us."

CHAPTER THIRTEEN

The walls of Sevari's office loomed from all sides, now giving him the impression of a miserable cave. No longer did he gush over his traditional decor, the comforting artifacts on his shelves, or the expensive stonework of his monument.

Even his perfect chair was tainted. His workingman's throne, the perfect firmness of the seat, the perfect angle of the back... how he used to sit in it for hours and research the old texts or work into the early morning designing his new policies...

And now he stood beside his window, while the boy spun around on the chair as though it were a carnival ride. The chair squeaked and creaked.

"Careful, Rovan. That chair is expensive and meant for work, not spinning."

"I am working, Till."

He dug his fingernails into his palms and ground his teeth. Best ignore the little things. He had to remember that the shadows had chosen Rovan as their leader. He still could not determine if the boy had one of the shadows inside him, or if he were simply a rotten little shit.

"So what do you intend to do, hm? Will you just sit here while your friends ravage my city?"

"They are multiplying, Till. It's just a little upset for now, that's all. You'll see." Rovan kicked the desk, propelling him across the room on squealing casters. "You're lucky I'm giving you this opportunity. The shadows will fix everything. We'll be rich."

"Rich? Is that what you think this is about? You think they are genii who have come to grant your juvenile wishes?"

"You're spoiling it. Stop being such a downer."

If he kept trying to reason with Rovan, he'd drive himself mad. Rovan was too young to understand the primordial force of the shadow men, of their mission to re-form heaven and earth according to their every whim.

He knew what to expect. First would come the depravity in the streets. If there existed any plant matter in Blightcross, it would also have been corrupted. Then a darkness would descend, and life would seem to disappear after everyone had destroyed themselves in their mad attempt to achieve order. Then the shadows would be made real again.

That was what the first people had written.

Without the fire giants, there would be no opposition to them.

Sevari went to his former desk and reached for the row of call studs.

"What are you doing, Till? That's my desk now."

"I am just calling for some assistance."

Rovan jumped out of his seat and jogged to the desk. "I can call. What do you need? Another pie? I can get us pie."

"I do not want pie." But, on second thought... "Actually, yes. Send for pie."

"Ha. They told me that you like pie."

"Did they?"

Rovan shut his eyes for a moment, then bounced back to the chair, where he began to spin again. "It'll be here in a minute. You know, I think I want some statues made. They should go up all along the main road leading to the refinery."

"Is that so?"

Rovan began to describe the statue, which would depict himself in golden armour, holding the biggest hand-cannon they could make, his right foot resting on the severed head of a fire giant. Sevari simply nodded and scribbled behind the desk. With luck, the hasty note would be legible.

It choked him to accept that he had made such a grave error in dealing with Helverliss. But the situation could still be brought under control. Locking up Helverliss with his own work had been the stupidest mistake he could think of, but after he wrested control from Rovan and his shadow friends, he would return to leadership more powerful than ever. The silent weaving of the worldspirits perhaps worked in mysterious ways, and in the end, this turmoil may even have been necessary for further progress.

He crumpled the note in his hands and clasped them behind his back. When the servant arrived at the door with the pie, he darted across the room to meet him.

He took the pie, and slapped the note into the servant's hand. "Take this to the guard lieutenant." The servant unfolded the note, and Sevari clapped the man's hand shut. "Go now, and ensure that he gets it." He glanced back to Rovan. "Do you see?"

The servant's eyes widened, and he spun on his heel to leave.

As long as the servant could perform basic functions, Blightcross might still have hope at containing the shadow beings.

"Well? What are you waiting for, Till? Hand over the fucking pie."

Ooh, you will regret choosing such a naive, ignorant clod as your anchor here, shadows.

He calmly set the pie on the desk—*his* desk—and took a slice.

Too much cinnamon, nothing like Mother's. If he were alone, he would toss it in the trash, but Rovan was a suspicious creature much like himself, and he thought he'd better choke it down for the sake of appearances.

"They say that you have this thing about pie, you know. I wonder if it's true."

"Who says this?"

"My friends."

"They are hardly friends, Rovan." As soon as he finished the sentence, he winced. It had been reversed—Rovan was the Leader now, and he had to abandon his pedantic tone, or risk the wrath of the shadows.

"Hah! You'll learn, Till." He ate half of the slice, tossed it across the room, and picked up another. "Hey, stop stressing. I won't turn on you. I'm like that guy you love so much. Iermo, that's his name, right? We're like a team of heroes, aren't we?"

The son of a bitch. Was Rovan serious, or just trying to goad him into a confrontation?

"Yes, Rovan." He made a difficult swallow. "It's quite like that."

Now he went back to his window to gaze at the armoury. A cloying spicy taste hovered in the back of his throat, and he wanted to throw the boy to the ground below, but his one bit of solace was the steel and canvas towering above the armoury. More accurately, what lay beneath the temporary covering.

The guard officer unfolded the paper, leaned into the light of the hallway lamp, and squinted at the hen scratch in watery faded ink.

Attn Guard Personnel please hurrb expadoto massc— gramma to defer cite and kill shallot mom...

"I haven't any clue what this means," the officer said to the servant.

"Sevari was under duress, I think. Whatever these phantoms are, they have corrupted one of the Ehzeri workers. It seems I now take dessert orders for the boy, instead of Sevari."

The officer snorted. "That's ridiculous. The Leader must be bluffing or biding his time."

"He looked desperate. Are you sure you can't read the note?"

He adjusted the paper's angle and tried again. This was not the firm hand of Till Sevari, and not the stern, impeccable penmanship of the many execution orders the officer had taken. It was a hasty cry for help, as if he had been unable to even look at his work. It was frantic and, like the servant suggested, desperate.

Attn Guard Personnel please hurry expedite deployment of mechanical golem to defend city and kill the shadow men and their pawns. Use any means to deploy. You have full authority to confiscate fuel necessary Section Three must be informed you may threaten execution if refuse to press into service please hurry.

The officer shoved the servant out of his way and ran for the nearest signalling station.

The damned thing wasn't ready. Were things really that bad? It was supposed to defend against a surprise attack from the Bhagovan Republic, or even Tamarck, should they decide that they wanted the district's fuel for themselves.

But would it really work against these phantoms?

Though she didn't want to admit it, Alim was right: by the time they reached the waterfront, they found only doors swinging on hinges and crates sitting in the middle of the road, waiting for the cranes above to lift them. A few times, she swore she caught glimpses of the shadow men, only to focus her eyes and find nothing out of the ordinary.

It wasn't completely deserted, though. Capra caught the flicker of a lamp in one of the windows as they made their way to Fasco's Road. After a short debate, she broke from the group and went inside.

The shelves were stocked with chains and rope and hooks. At the counter stood a woman close to her age with sunken cheeks and dry, frizzy hair.

"What happened here?"

"They all left. Them things came, started talking to everyone. Told them things I ain't ever heard before. They sounded like preachers or aldermen."

"Did they talk to you?"

The woman coughed in a way Capra had only heard from lung-rot patients and phosphorous grenade victims. She backed away accordingly. "They won't come near me. One of them said something about the ethers or some such garbage. If you ask me, it's just a ploy by the government. Aw yeah, they just want us all to move out of here so they can build more pipes or whatever they want to do. That's the word out at the estates, anyway."

Capra recalled overhearing conversations in the city about "the estates", this spoken with a note of disdain. "The slums, you mean?"

The woman spread her hands in a defensive gesture. "Not my words, missy."

The slums—the area off the south end of Fasco's Road. A whole population of people untouched by the shadows, but tainted by what, exactly?

"The owner here went along with the others. I don't know why, but I doubt he'll be back today. Maybe that Sevari's going to lock 'em all up and cook them in his great ovens, who knows?"

"I think you should just close up and go home for the day."

The woman made a noise that could have either been laughter or a retch. "You ain't from this area, are ye, missy? You got a job down here, you make the most of it and get yourself as much time in a clean space as you can. I ain't a going back unless I got to."

On one shelf Capra spotted a bottle of oil. Never one to argue with a nagging in her gut, she bought it. She was, after all, going to climb through a running machine, and the last thing she needed was to be caught in a seized gear.

Back outside, she expected to find either Alim or Dannac cast into a gutter with a broken neck, but she found them strolling down the deserted cobblestones together. Perhaps it was the mediating presence of Vasi between them that stopped them from destroying each other. Dannac would never join a Valoii. Capra was the exception, and the first few months together had involved more than a few fistfights.

Something was bothering him.

"You decided to join us," Alim said when she took position on Dannac's side of Vasi.

"She was alive. Barely alive, from the sound of her, and the shadows didn't want her. Apparently the slums have been untouched. Anything along this end of Fasco's Road."

"So there is something in the air."

Deathly cough, pale, peeling skin... "Something not entirely good for us either, I'm thinking." She stared at one of the boats bobbing at the quay. "You know, we could sail out of here."

"No," Dannac said. "Rovan could still be alive. Besides, look out to sea. They are patrolling the delta."

She shielded her eyes with her hand and glimpsed the shadows circling far in the distance, as though the world were inverted and they were leaves swirling in ocean currents. Whatever force kept them away from the Hex did not extend to the ocean.

"Helverliss was in a bad state, wasn't he? Don't you think he did this out of desperation? I can't imagine what Sevari must have done to him."

"He has to be alive," Vasi said. "I cannot fix this, and neither can any of the other researchers."

Alim began to walk faster. "And we cannot leave if these things are not dealt with."

Capra sighed.

"It's your own fault. None of this would have happened if you had just stayed with the army."

"Shut up, Alim."

In the space of a block, they passed from the cluttered colonial stone of the waterfront into the desert. It was as though they had travelled from Tamarck to the heart of Mizkov, all in a few strides. Here the old thoroughfare joined with Fasco's Road, which stretched into the distance, accompanied only by a splatter of huts and canvas tents along its south side. Capra could barely make out the bridge from where they stood at an abandoned guard post.

"It starts just a few minutes down the road, I think," she said.

"The unnamed invisible thing that's supposed to protect us?" Alim asked.

Dannac cracked open his canteen and sat on the side of the road. "Better drink and rest, if we are to walk through a desert that will make us sick."

She wasn't tired, and she stood under the shade of a palm. Damn it, they were getting closer to the tower. Never mind this stupid Hex, or even these shadows. All she could think about was the clock. Having never been inside a giant clock, she envisioned a grotesque contraption of swinging axes, misshapen cogs, and random plates of metal that pressed into any available space for no apparent reason. She dug in the sand with her toe, reminded herself that there were worse things to overcome before the clock would be a concern. But still...

The others didn't care about the tight spaces. What was so different about them that they could do the same thing without any of the anxiety she felt?

Maybe Helverliss knew the answer, with his mind-sciences.

"Here." Alim handed her a canteen. "The heat doesn't seem to drop overnight very much, unlike back home. I don't quite understand why yet."

She paused for a moment, then gingerly took the canteen. "So."

"Hm?"

"I mean..." She could still do no more than stare at his boots. He was from home, both an oppressive force in her conscience and a source of comfort. "How are things back home, anyway?"

"What do you care?"

She turned away from him and wiped the sweat from her face. "Jasaf. Is she still in the service? She should be out by now, I would think. Unless she volunteered for more, but she never seemed like the type to make it a career."

A silence came over them, as if the hot wind in their faces had burned away any possibility of conversation. Sure, Jasaf probably felt a little betrayed by Capra's desertion, but it was not uncommon and they had talked about the issue a few times.

When the silence dragged for longer than any decent person could allow, she held her breath and met his eyes.

Red, watery eyes, and his brows were knitted and straining.

"Alim? What is it?"

She backed away, and suddenly felt sick.

He stepped towards her, blinking and with his hands knotted into fists. "You want to know about Jasaf? She's dead."

Dead. The word echoed inside her, in the canyon that had torn through what she had assumed to be true. It only widened, it seemed.

"When the Ehzeri fighters arrived with three adepts and the explosions tore through your platoon, you took the opportunity to run."

She nodded, although what did that have to do with anything?

"You didn't really think of what was going on at the time, did you? Just that there was a confusion, and that you could run without anyone noticing."

"Alim, what are you getting at?"

He lurched forward and gabbed at her cravat with both hands to pull her close. "You were supposed to watch her. She was a surgeon, for God's sake."

Her throat welled with an aching sadness, and Alim's grip wasn't helping. She pried his hands off.

"You killed her, Capra." There was a broken note in his voice, but also a rage in his eyes.

"That's crazy. I wasn't the only one in the whole damned regiment. It was a brutal attack. Command miscalculated, and we should never have gone in without more information."

"Rationalize it all you want. She was right beside you until you ran away."

In an instant she saw burned-out flashes of the day she had fled. The explosions, the weight of the crossbow in her hand, the clouds of sand kicked up by the men at the front of the clash, filling her nose and mouth and god damn it she could see nothing, not Jasaf, not anyone else, just a cloud of dust and the reek of burning flesh, the same as when she had inhaled the odour of her own skin burning from a misplaced phosphorous grenade—

"No, it was confusion all round, Alim. You know that. I had lost Jasaf before I even decided to run." And yet she had never, not once, thought that anything might have happened to her friend.

Was there something missing? Had her memory become corrupted to ease guilt?

She let go of his hands and fell against his chest. "I can't remember. I can't remember what happened. It was fast, and only the day before they had sent us into Red—or what they thought was Red—and made us kill them. All of them." She looked up at him. "They were old women and boys with broken legs who were useless as fighters to them. And you know what? When I came into the doorway of the stinking hut I was supposed to engage, they were happy to see me." She let out an ironic laugh. "They said, '*Selvaz! Selvaz!*' when

I knocked down their door and pulled the fuse from my phos grenade. They wanted me to help them."

Alim put his hand on her back, almost as if he were reciprocating her gesture. Part of her wanted to believe he wouldn't kill or arrest her once they dealt with the shadows. "It could have been a trap. They have done such things before. You couldn't have known."

"I did know, Alim. I obeyed the order anyway because I didn't want a stupid reprimand for insubordination. What is it, fifteen lashes per offence?"

He shoved her away, sent her skidding across the sand. "So you abandoned Jasaf just because you couldn't deal with the horrible reality every one of us has to deal with? Do you think you're the only one?"

"I just..."

"The Valoii are on the verge of extinction and you think you have the luxury of moral superiority?"

"It wasn't like that, I—"

He cursed under his breath and clutched her shoulders. A torrent of guilt and grief had dulled her reflexes, and she offered no resistance when he slammed her against a tree. "I should just kill you. Forget the trial, forget the army."

And what could she say? She couldn't bear his hawk-like face, his pained eyes. Tears began to seep through the dam of her eyelids. She imagined Jasaf alone and confused in the blowing sand, wondering where the damned stupid bitch who was supposed to protect her had gone. Damn it all, not once did she consider...

She swallowed a knot of pain. "There's nothing I can say, Alim. There's nothing anyone can say. I did the wrong thing." His grip lightened some, but his expression still screamed murder. "I did the wrong thing and I'm sorry, and I don't know how I'm going to live with what happened, now that you've told me."

Dannac's voice boomed from under a palm tree. "Watch it, soldier boy. Do that once more, and I will saw off your head with my utility blade."

"Forget it." He gave her one last shove and stormed away.

But as she slumped down the smooth bark of the tree, bottom sinking into the sand, it was hard to keep any anger towards Alim. It was probably the worst thing that could have happened to a person who had deserted the army to *save* lives, not take them.

She hung her head between her knees for a while, until the flow out of her eyes dried and she could regain a semblance of her composure.

A half hour later, after much contemplation, she joined the rest under the tree, though she made sure to sit as far away from Alim as possible.

"Are you okay?" It was Vasi, and her voice did sound somewhat sincere.

"I'm fine. I just didn't know that my leaving had affected anything. In the army, everyone's just a soldier, we're all the same, we're all citizens... there should have been plenty of others to fill in the blank spot I left."

"The Blacksmith is tasked by the Divine to work on our behalf, so that we may use his pure power to engage fully with the life planned out for us. There is a structure we cannot see, Capra. You do not leave a blank space to be filled by another. Your actions resonate through the entire frame."

"It's a nice thought, and I wish I could believe the way you do, Vasi."

"Who says you cannot?"

Capra said nothing because she hardly understood Valoii faith, let alone the Ehzeri's version.

She caught Dannac with a look of concentration, and his ear turned to the city. She watched his eyes dart, and stood when he shot upright to survey the city looming above the riverbank.

There was a faint noise—engines—that cut in and out with the soughing wind.

"What is it?" she asked.

"Do you not hear it?"

"Engines. The city is always buzzing with engines, Dannac."

She plucked from her belt pouch a pair of field glasses. Now that Dannac had pointed out the noise as something exceptional, she paused to listen.

It was a roar like that of a flying boat, of many engines in concert. But there were no flying boats around, besides the deserted one at the quays. Through the glasses she scanned the city, where the only strange sight was the shadows overhead.

The rumbling was unchanged, until a roar of clattering rose over the wind. The cacophony vibrated in Capra's chest, and the sheer volume seemed to spark a primal fear in her—despite that the source was far away and probably no threat, the very idea of something so huge made her nervous and sent her heart into a tapdance.

It was like a cannon, only instead of vanishing like explosions did, it wound down. Seconds later, the noise rose back to its peak, and this happened several times.

"Do you see anything?" Alim asked.

Capra went back to the glasses and tried to block out the terrible noise. Was it some industrial accident in Redsands? No—nothing there, from what she could see. A problem at the refinery? No change in the black smoke there, and no flames.

As she passed the glasses along the city once more, she caught a strange glint, high above the armoury. A glow of red sun against metal and rivets. There were eight pipes at the top of this structure, and each pumped smoke into the air, and the louder its engines, the more black it belched.

"It's that contraption at the armoury." But most of it was hidden under the canvas, and at the moment, it just seemed like another tall building.

"But what is it?" Alim asked. "Sevari said nothing of it."

"Perhaps it is not his doing."

Capra lowered the glasses. "Or maybe it is."

There it was, the pride of Blightcross. The engineering marvel, the most advanced weapon in existence. Sevari barely hid a vengeful smile; it was still too early to show the boy any sign of the shadow men's impending downfall.

As per Rovan's orders, there now stood at either side of the door nude Ehzeri women, handpicked by the boy himself after two hours of parading them in and out of the office. Every so often, one of the human manifestations of the shadows would enter and speak with Rovan, but Sevari could not make out what they were discussing. It was impossible to tell who was directing whom—was the boy really in charge, or was his very placement in power part of some greater plan?

Never mind. He could drive himself insane trying to understand what the shadow beings aimed to do. They were transforming his city, he knew that much, but no more than that. The texts had spoken of the shadow beings and the fire giants as dependent upon each other, as unitary. He could find no reference that pointed to what the shadows would actually do had they achieved dominance over the giants.

No, the important thing now was the golem. Iermo's dream, now made reality. From its many cannons it would dispense the ultimate punishment on these depraved beings.

If he could beat them, they would have to submit to him. Submit their power.

With its cannon shot made from metals mined in the Hex, nothing could withstand this superior weapon. The only hitch would be if the thing's mind were still too far into the experimental stage to drive the machine.

"I hope you enjoyed your work with Section Three," he said to Rovan. "Did you?"

"Not as much as I enjoy these girls. Section Three was boring, and I didn't like the mess it made."

"Mess?"

Rovan gestured to one of the girls, who hurried to sit in his lap and stroke his face. "Don't you know what your own researchers are doing, Till?" He laughed and began to grope the girl. "You're ruining my mood. Why don't you have some more pie?"

Sevari withheld any remarks and watched his machine. Sooner or later, the shadows would tell the boy about the weapon, and he hoped that by then it would be of no consequence.

"I think I want a wall around the city. One that goes right to the oilfields. That way the other districts of Naartland can't try to steal our wealth."

"Is that so?"

"The shadow men love the idea. They're going to get started as soon as they're finished. What did they call it? The Initial Trauma."

Initial Trauma?

"How come you never thought about putting a wall around the oil? You're not so smart, are you?"

"Evidently not, Rovan. Evidently not." Sevari gazed at the golem, and his gut swam with anticipation. They must be just getting down to the final dozen engines in the lower quadrant. Soon the canvas would roll away and the golem would take its first steps and fire its first salvos.

CHAPTER FOURTEEN

"Well, I don't feel any different." Capra made a few more steps down Fasco's Road, waving her hands through the air. If there were some invisible force there, it wasn't one she could feel.

"Neither do I," Vasi said.

If Vasi couldn't sense it, what could it be? Didn't Ehzeri sense all beyond the physical world?

Dannac pulled from his belt the hand-cannon. "I would worry more about these slums ahead than the air."

She slapped his arm. "Put that away. They're probably just normal people who haven't benefited from Sevari's refinery."

Despite what she had just said, she came into a nervous readiness, and wished for a crossbow or sabre. She had seen slums before, along with the desperation, violence, and inhuman struggles inherent in them. Ehzeri camps, Valoii ghettos, it was all the same.

Here, there were crumbling wells and rusted machines fitted with warning placards. As they walked Fasco's Road, a dozen Ehzeri stopped and watched them with suspicious eyes. Many held broken hoes, jagged pipes, and rakes.

It was hard to understand the pride Tey felt about Fasco and his road. This was his legacy. A community of people unified by the mere fact of their peeling skin, of the boils on their faces, of their thinning hair.

Alim shoved her along. "Let's move it. You don't want to end up like that, do you?"

"What do you care?"

"As long as Helverliss and his phantoms are taking this district, I care enough to shove you when you stand around and wait to catch this sickness everyone has."

"Why don't we get it over with now. Are you going to try to bring me in after this?"

He kept quiet. Just as well—deep down, she preferred to avoid bad news until it was unavoidable.

The bridge lay just ahead, and beyond, the horizon wavered in layers of orange and red, with an occasional strand of industrial smoke intruding into it.

In the distance, the prison brooded amid heat waves, barely visible.

"Maybe we should go to the prison for help after all. It's right in the middle of the Hex, and there isn't a shadow within leagues of it. Could be worth a try."

Vasi said, "No. This is not a normal prison. There is one warden, and a handful of mechanics to fix it."

"What kind of prison is not staffed with armed guards?"

"A mechanical prison."

The three of them gasped. It sounded ludicrous.

"It is... new. I know people who have escaped and survived the trek through the Hex." She gulped. "But after they reached the city, they did not survive long. There is nothing like this prison, I can guarantee you. Their meals are given by machine, they are disciplined by machine. I barely understand it myself."

"Look at the distance," Dannac said. "It almost appears farther to the prison than to cross the desert to the refinery."

"By foot, the trip from the prison is usually one way." Vasi shielded her eyes and gazed towards the refinery. "This is the best way for us. Besides, what help would prison guards offer?"

Vasi was right. Capra had to remember that any official was more likely to lock her up than to help her break into the refinery.

They pushed cautiously along a road thick with hostile glares. She tried to keep her eyes forward, and focus on the sound of beating grit-laden wind, but she could never deny her curiosity.

She glanced to one of the wells and observed a boy hoisting a water bucket. Her heart leaped when she realized that hanging from the boy's torso was a third arm. There was coughing and retching and moaning, and several men lying in the sand with broken manacles on their wrists.

One tent rattled and rippled, and a muffled scream issued from within the flapping canvas. Capra shook her head and stepped off the road without thinking. She drew her knife and stormed towards the squalor.

Dannac jerked her back, sighed.

"Let me go. Listen to what's going on here." The screams became louder. "It sounds like a child."

He gestured to the ground in front of them. There were faces of shredded skin, red, blistered, some displaying tumescent lumps and barely recognizable as human. Stained sand, shit everywhere and corpses bleaching in the sun. "You can't help them, Capra. The problems here aren't so easily fixed. If they were..."

Dannac's arm was stronger than Capra's nervous will to attack the person in the tent, and she joined them back on Fasco's Road.

The images of the place haunted her as they approached the encampment's edge. "In some ways, this is more than either of us has seen, Alim. Worse than the Ehzeri ghettos, or those eerie drawings of the Yahrein death camps our parents endured."

He gave a sympathetic expression, but it was short-lived. He narrowed his eyes, straightened himself. "Try to avoid a crisis of conscience until after we reach the bloody tower, okay?"

Damn him, damn the army's programming. Why couldn't they have just brainwashed them into being killing machines? Why did they have to remain thinking, feeling soldiers who had the unfortunate compulsion to defer their morality for the sake of the mission, only to have to deal with it later?

And damn it all, Capra wasn't even good at it.

Crossing the bridge outside the slums helped her focus and forget about the misery behind them, but she would never forget that haunting variety of despair. None of the plaques and memorial crests carved into the covered bridge's pillars could wash Fasco's Road in a lustre of law and order and decent folk. These were the stragglers and escapees of a mad, obsessive justice and everyone must have known it.

She could easily be one of them. She was, after all, a criminal.

Before she could descend into another bout of guilt and internalizing, her foot jammed against something hard in the sand. She jolted back into more immediate concerns, such as landing without getting a mouthful of grit.

When she brought herself to her knees, she scanned the ground for the culprit.

It was a hand.

She scrambled back and kicked sand into her companions' faces.

"What is it?" Dannac asked.

She pointed to the hand. "You're not going to touch it, are you?"

But it was too late. He grasped the hand, and began to dig through the sand. "This man is alive."

They all joined in and pulled the man out. Sand caked his skin, and even in this heat, Capra's hand warmed on touching him. He was bald, and he reeked of machine oil.

The man slowly opened his eyes, though just barely. "How far to the city?"

"Farther than you'll be going," Alim said. "What are you doing here?"

As if he didn't know. Naive little Alim...

Capra knew how it would end, so she walked away. They were too far into the Hex to take the man out of it. Was this the kind of death they all faced? Her stomach already wrenched with an intermittent churn, and it could be the Hex getting to her already. Or a sickness over news of Jas' death. Or a combination of both...

One thing she knew—this man had been dead the moment he stepped out of the prison and into the desert.

Just as she predicted, the others left the man where they had found him. Alim came to her with an almost optimistic look, and she was puzzled. It wasn't as if the dead man had been a rich, dead traveller loaded with things they could use. The man had possessed nothing. Just a pointless death.

"What are you so happy about? Was he an Ehzeri?"

"Yes, in fact he was. But that's not why he's proved useful to us."

"And why was a dead prisoner useful to us?"

As they trudged along the river, they debated. They debated the reliability of the prisoner's reports—mainly that the prison itself had gone mad and that the mechanics either didn't care, or were behind the craziness. The warden's voice had disturbingly come through the horns throughout the prison speaking of new rules and perverted desires, while the restraint machines in the cells locked into disciplinary action. The man had escaped to find help to repair the prison, not to save himself.

They argued about this because Alim pointed out an inconsistency in the story: "If we are to believe that the prison has become corrupted, there need to be shadows in the area." He pointed to the sky, and of course no shadows fluttered above the desert. "This man heard stories and tried to play us for fools."

"You're not listening," Vasi said. "I told you about the underground areas of the city. They are far enough underground that the shadows were able to avoid the Hex and connect to the prison through them. So the prison was not immune to the shadows. And, I say that these tunnels are our best way to the refinery."

Capra's head spun, and she stumbled. The desert turned to a smudge before her eyes for a few seconds. "Is anyone else starting to feel a bit off?"

The others grumbled but didn't answer. Could she blame them? They all had seen what this Hex did to a person. Thinking about it was the last thing they needed to do.

"And what are we going to do, then, once we reach the refinery? Will we swim across? Our skin will fall off tomorrow if we do that."

Alim stormed up the steep dune they were climbing, took the lead. "I've been inside the tower and looked down at the river. There are pipes and other structures that span the water. I'm sure we can cross and enter through these."

"But—" Vasi began to say, before Alim interrupted again.

"You honestly think that these shadows have crawled underground and turned a mechanical prison into an abattoir?"

Vasi dropped out of the argument, and for an hour they trudged through the desert, silent as the stagnating hot breeze. But when they came to a sharp dip in the land, Capra could only stop and gasp.

"I had no idea this was here," Alim said.

It was a gully, and it bristled with tall, brown columns of rock. A forest of stone pillars, much too large to be made by mankind.

"There is a similar place back home," Vasi said. "It's not nearly as large, though. They say it was created when the Blacksmith struck a mountain range with his hammer."

Capra went to the nearest rock, ran her fingers along it. Rough, crumbly, dusty. "Limestone?"

"I doubt it matters what it's made of," Dannac said. "We should keep moving."

She gazed into the stone labyrinth. "Through this? We don't know the layout of the place."

"Going around will take more time than we have. We should take our chances going through."

For a moment, she wanted to ask Alim what he thought, but she stopped short of saying anything. The one good thing about this limestone maze was the shade it offered. They might even get through faster, now that the heat had lessened some.

The place sparked Capra's imagination. The structures made her think of ancient ruins, and it disappointed her when she reminded herself that these were just natural formations. But Vasi seemed even more disappointed.

"What's the matter?" she finally asked.

Vasi trailed her hand along one of the columns. "I was just thinking that if I had been able to understand Helverliss' stupid painting, none of this would have happened. I would have understood the chaos inside and convinced Sevari that there was nothing else in it and that it ought to be destroyed."

"Would he have listened?"

"Maybe not. But I would never have allowed this to happen. I just wasn't smart enough to do it." She sighed and brushed the dust from her hands. "There must be something missing. An element to the painting I haven't sensed, or looked over. Something to bind it all."

"Well, I'm sure Helverliss would know. I'll be sure to ask him, once I free your brother."

Deeper into the strange place, the formations stretched above like towers, and now they walked in dark shadows, slashed by an occasional whip of harsh sunlight. Were they even heading in the correct direction? It was impossible to tell, now that their world was a city of limestone monoliths.

A dead city.

There was a sound. A hissing-grating, and it jutted out from the eerie silence. Capra stopped. "Did you hear that?" And when the others began to answer, she held up her hand and shushed them.

There, again. She drew her knife and turned a slow circle, scanning the columns and boulders for the source.

"There is nothing here, Capra." Dannac clutched her arm. "You do have an imagination."

"No, there's something. I heard it."

Vasi knelt and drank from a canteen. "Capra, I can't sense anything."

Great, now she looked like a fool. It wouldn't be the first time, but at least this instance was harmless—

Across the path—a flicker of movement. She motioned for the others to halt again, and she crept forward. Her eyes locked to the rock tower nearest to her, a nervous sweat seeped onto the knife handle. Listen.

Nothing.

Alim finally spoke. "Capra, this is stupid. We have to move faster than this."

Before she could answer, something moved behind the stone. This time, she saw it clearly. A form, about three times the height of a man, and its colour was identical to the rock behind which it hid.

She darted back. "Now tell me there's nothing there, Alim."

The thing stepped into full view. A hideous thing, standing on two legs as a man, but with a grotesque, snouted head. Its bulk bristled with spines at random intervals, and birdlike legs propelled it faster than something of this size ought to move.

Dannac drew his hand-cannon.

Capra darted onto an adjoining path. "I wouldn't bother." She whirled round, called out, "Run, you idiots!"

And so they did, propelled faster yet by inhuman growls at their backs. Damn the air here—she wheezed and fought stiff lungs to dash through the maze.

The thud of the beast's steps beat against serene quiet, punctuated by the scuffling of Capra and her comrades. When her legs began to cramp, and the others' footsteps began to sound much too far behind for her comfort, she darted behind a column and peered down the path.

Seconds later, the other three joined her, faces red and panting. The creature's grumbling and shuffling sounded around them.

"Where is it?" she asked.

It didn't surprise her that Alim was the first to catch his breath. "I think we lost it. Must be confused by the geography."

She listened. "It sounds like it's... I can't even pinpoint the direction."

Dannac said, "The rock formations must be affecting the sounds." He scanned their perimeter, hand-cannon at the ready.

"What on earth is that thing?"

"Perhaps this Hex does more than kill," Alim said.

Before anyone could ponder this, a giant fist slammed into the rock, barely a finger's width shy of Capra's head. She dove and rolled across the dirt. It was when she rolled to her feet that she caught a glimpse of the thing, and her heart nearly stopped at the sight. The creature's skin bulged with half-formed heads and misshapen limbs, and its eyes were spaced much wider than any normal living thing she could imagine.

The worst part about it was the eyes. They were too intelligent, with a human glimmer and a deep green sheen.

She snapped out of her shock when Dannac shoved her along the path, and she began to run again. She wanted to yell out, to tell them that continuing along this long, straight path was sheer idiocy. Running was more important.

She passed Dannac and Vasi, pulled beside Alim, but soon fell back again. Then her foot found a jagged rock, and she tumbled to the ground. *Shit.*

A mouthful of dirt, and a bolt of pain in her leg. She cried out, her voice echoing eerily in the dead city. She watched as they turned a corner, apparently unaware of her fall.

The creature slowed its advance. Its slavering maw dropped, showing rows of dull teeth. It was as though the thing wasn't built for this kind of hunting. Its teeth reminded her of a person's—definitely not flesh-tearing teeth.

And that would make it hurt even more.

Though it seemed pointless, Capra stood, weight transferred to her left foot, knife clutched under icy knuckles. "Listen, you son of a bitch..."

A disturbing recognition flashed in the creature's eyes. Capra's heart hammered on as though she were still sprinting. But the creature's lucid moment was short lived, and it lashed out with a three-fingered fist. Capra tried to dodge it, but the fist clipped her shoulder, and she spun into a rock. The knife skittered into the dust.

"Alim? Anyone?" She wiped a drop of blood from her brow and knelt to scoop a handful of sand.

Once the creature approached her, she tossed the sand into its face and bolted away from the rock wall.

This brought her two steps away from the wall, until the creature slammed her again, apparently unfazed by her sand-attack.

She still had her little satchel. Her thoughts scrambled to think of what she carried that could help. All the while, the thing sniffed at her and brought its head in close.

Damn, nothing useful. A few bricks of explosives, but they wouldn't help now.

"Dannac?" Now her voice wavered. What she wouldn't give for a crossbow, or a suicide tablet. That horrible dog-giant-man-thing's blunt teeth and meaty hands could only offer a carnival of hurt.

The maw edged closer. She squinted, tried not to look. Nervous hands searched the ground for a rock. She flung a stone into its face. It bounced off the thing's skull, eliciting a short grunt and nothing else.

It couldn't end like this. Not in this hole, this awful island full of bad air and bad food and bad attitudes... she cringed and felt humiliated.

And the uncomfortable silence shattered with the crack of a cannon. Her heart clenched for a second, then she opened her eyes. The creature sniffed the air and seemed more interested in the noise than in her.

She crawled on hands and knees until she felt enough confidence to run. Standing in the middle of the path was Dannac, and he held the cannon awkwardly while trying to reload it quickly.

Damned ankle. Her usual sprint had been slowed to a jog by the jarred ankle.

"It's just going to catch us, Dannac."

He closed the breech and rested the barrel on his elbow to aim. "Not if I can help it." He breathed calmly. The creature approached at a trot, and when it came within spitting distance, Dannac fired.

The shot blew a chunk of skin from the thing's head, but it roared and pumped its legs still faster. Dannac took Capra's arm and they fled.

"You won't get enough shots in to matter," she told him. "Damn, if only I had rigged these damned explosives into something useful."

"You have explosives?"

"Yes, but no way to detonate them."

"I could arrange something, but there's no time."

She winced at the ache in her ankle, tried to speed her gait. The creature was almost at their heels.

Dannac reloaded as they ran, whipped around and shot once more. The creature slowed for a few steps.

Capra searched the rock for offshoots of this passage. It was solid—no way out. They rounded a corner, and ahead she found Vasi and Alim.

Standing still.

"What's the matter with you two?" she screamed.

Then she saw why. A dead end. The rock wall spanning the path did have a shallow cave, but even at a distance, she could see that it offered no escape from the creature.

Damn...

Alim drew his sword as they reached the end of the path. She gave him a grim nod and glanced at the little cave.

"I have explosives. Any ideas?"

Dannac fired again, and the round bit into the thing's neck. It slowed its bounding and roared.

She brought out the charges and showed them to Vasi and Alim. "Any takers?"

Vasi bit her lip. "Give me those."

She handed them over, though if it were any other situation, she would have thought twice about giving explosives to an Ehzeri.

"How powerful are these?"

"I... I can't think right now. Powerful enough."

"Will they blow this wall?"

"Well, yes, that should be enough. The rock isn't that hard."

"Good. Now go."

With that, Vasi stepped forward and made a strange crooning sound. The monster reared and squinted its knowing eyes. What was Vasi going to do?

If she knew anything about this bizarre scenario, it was that watching would just get them killed. She collected Alim and Dannac, then darted around the path, behind the creature.

A few seconds later, there came a roar. Then a crack, and a rumble. Earth moving; landslide muttering.

Back towards the wall, all she found was a cloud of dust and a pulverized pile of rock. No Vasi.

"What did she do?" She gasped and pushed a strand of hair from her eyes.

Alim tugged off his gloves and shook his head. "Ehzeri are known to enjoy martyrdom."

"Typical Valoii ignorance," Dannac said, voice gravelly.

Capra ignored them and stepped towards the rock pile. She waved away the dust, saw one of the creature's legs poking from the rocks. It twitched and gushed red onto the surrounding rock like a fountainhead.

Not only did the blast kill the beast, but now the way was clear. And when Capra stepped to the top of the rubble, she saw open desert. They had reached the end of the rock valley.

Damn you, Vasi. There had to have been a better way.

Now she vowed more than ever to find Rovan, if only to tell him the news.

Alim and Dannac scrambled to the top of the pile.

"We've already wasted too much time in here," Alim said. "We'd best move on, or risk contracting the Hex."

It was true, but Capra wished she could at least find Vasi's body, bring back her amulet for Rovan. It pained her to think about the boy. "I can't believe she did that..."

She knelt and poked at the rocks. What kind of person could decide to destroy themselves with a split-second decision?

But wait—something odd in the rocks. A fragment of uniform ridges. Curved, tooled. She picked up a rock fragment, stood. "These formations weren't all natural. Look at this." She turned over the rock and revealed a deep, chiseled symbol. Three circles, each touching the other.

A voice said, from behind, "I noticed just before the explosion."

She whipped around. Vasi stood among the rocks, arms crossed. Capra's jaw dropped.

"What?"

"You're not dead."

"No, I am not." Vasi flashed a hint of a grin. "Sleight of hand. The creature was easily distracted by illusions. I caught some fragments in my back when I ran from the explosion, but nothing I can't deal with."

Capra wanted to embrace Vasi, but didn't. "Well, that was some trick."

"There was very little magic involved. Just enough to set off your charges. There is more to me than *vihs*, you know. Now, I have seen that symbol on dozens of Koratian artifacts, but I don't know what they mean. Three is a strange number to me."

"What do you mean?"

"Duality is nature. The third is out of place. And these ruins predate the colonists, yet they show the same symbol. There was religious imagery here. Archons... the true archons... and the sacred demiurge. "

Capra gazed at the symbols. "True archons?"

Dannac shook his head, and she took this as one of his cues to drop the subject.

Alim cleared his throat and gestured to the open desert. "I hate to break up the lecture, but the shadows are still destroying the city and blocking our escape."

With that, they resumed their trek through the Hex.

A few hours later, Capra slowed and clutched her abdomen. Something was wrong, and she had the feeling that they were reaching a point which if they passed, the sickness would kill them. She looked to Vasi and winced. With Dannac's strange mood ever since they had split up days earlier, Vasi seemed more of a friend than he did.

"Something wrong?" Vasi asked.

"I'm starting to feel it. The Hex, I mean. Aren't you?"

"A little."

"Why would I feel it so much more than everyone else?"

Vasi looked deep in thought. "The men are larger and stronger, despite that you could fight them both at the same time if you needed to. And me... well..." She appeared to struggle with something. "Let me show you something. Just a little trick to strengthen your resistance to illness."

"Oh, come on. Are you kidding me?"

"No, why?"

"Ehzeri don't just reveal their secrets to ex-soldiers. And I'm the last person who should be attempting these tricks. I don't really believe in it." This despite that her adult life had been spent snuffing out this power and dodging its attempts to kill her, but the rest of the world was abandoning *vihs*, and she thought humanity couldn't do this fast enough.

"Do you want to survive or not?"

"I'm starting to think none of us are going to survive if we don't find those tunnels you mentioned. Alim is an idiot."

Vasi ignored the comment and began to direct Capra into a series of guided thoughts. The odd part was that she asked that Capra focus on the amulet she wore.

"It is just an aid to focus. I have one too, under my shirt. It helps to... it just helps to ground the practitioner."

More nonsense. About the only good thing about it was the way it broke the monotony of the desert and distracted her from thinking of the Hex. When she finally cast aside her cynicism and made a concerted effort to focus on her amulet and visualize it as a quilting point for the *vihs* that flowed behind the invisible structure of reality, an odd sensation buzzed beneath her skin.

"There's so much of it," Capra said, after glimpsing mentally this vast network of energy, like rivers of lightning.

"It is deceptive. Not all of it will flow through your point, you see. There is a network, and if you..."

"Family connection?"

"Yes."

"But I am not Ehzeri."

"Well, everyone's place in the structure comes with a small amount of individual power... anyone can learn to use it."

She would not pretend to understand it. The grids and webs of *vihs* formed a structure too awesome for Capra's sharp disbelief to shatter. Not only could she see them in the immediate area if she really focused, she could also follow them beyond the physical space and trace them back to even more convoluted knots.

Her own web joined with another. This one glowed less brightly than the others she had seen, and compared to the cords extending from herself, they were dull, barely glowing.

"Vasi, am I draining someone else? I don't think this belongs to me." She didn't know why she asked the question, but it was the first thing that came to her.

"You need to do this, Capra. Draw it into you, envision it flowing through your blood and protecting your flesh from harm. Repeat these thoughts as much as you can."

"That doesn't answer my question."

Vasi skipped away, down the crest of a dune. "I must concentrate to find the nearest entrance to the vaults. I think if Alim actually sees them, he'll change his mind about going underground instead."

What was going on here? So far, Alim had been the most straightforward with her. It was almost easier to deal with him knowing that he would be after her as soon as it was convenient than trying to understand Dannac and Vasi's strange behaviour.

Dannac knew what the stupid girl was doing. He watched them walk with their closed eyes and foreheads lined with concentration.

That could have been him, accessing the power. How different would life have been if he had been born into a more responsible family? Imagine wielding the *vihs*, and what an Ehzeri who refused to be subjugated could do with it.

He screwed his face into a bitter frown while he watched Vasi guide Capra through the procedures he had never been taught. Anyone could learn how to connect to the power—this didn't mean Capra was one of them. She would see it as a toy and use up whatever was available to her in a short time, just like most non-Ehzeri who took the time to learn. What made an Ehzeri was the way in which they could act collectively and multiply their power to near infinity, not the mere ability to call upon it. An individualist like Capra would never be able to join with another in such a way.

Let the girl convince Capra of the lie. She would see soon enough that it was just nonsense, and that a simple protection working was not proof of anything but that Capra had the aptitude to access the power for a short time.

There was a reason the Ehzeri called it "work-skills". To everyone else, it was just wish fulfilment.

He guzzled some water from his canteen and gazed towards the refinery. His vision wavered and he could barely see through the haze of fuzzy specks that had plagued his sight since stepping into the Hex. There was something in the air, but was he seeing it?

"Look," Alim said. The Valoii had scarcely said anything to him since they met, and Dannac was thankful for this. "Whatever is making the engine noise is moving."

Dannac looked back to the armoury. Now, the temporary structure was gone, and he saw what lay beneath: a giant.

He watched it take its first steps, engines blaring with each movement of its gigantic legs and arms. "Impossible."

"I wouldn't believe it if you told me, but there it is. I had heard of plans for such things, but never anything this large. How did they solve the problem of brittle metal, I wonder?"

"Yes, well, whether or not this is a good thing depends on who it aims to attack."

It didn't take any special communique from Yaz to know that the Republic would be extremely interested in captured images of the machine. It was the kind of thing they would view as a threat, and they would immediately scramble to build their own version.

And they would want to know how such a backward colony like Blightcross could devise such a thing, and they would assume that it was a Tamish plot, and they would assume that every Valoii in existence knew about the plan.

In some ways, he hoped that Capra would die an honourable death before he had to make the decision to hand her to Yaz.

"Here, I found it." It was Vasi, and she was kneeling in the sand, scooping it with her hands. "The vaults are shielded from the Hex. This is our way to the refinery."

"They are also connected to the armoury, as you said." Dannac bent to help her. Capra seemed in a daze, standing there with her hands wrapped round her war-trophy amulet. "Do we want to risk an encounter with Sevari's men?"

"Sevari's men will be too busy with the chaos in the streets."

"Do you really think this is not what he intended?"

Vasi's digging became frantic. "I know Sevari better than most." She looked away. "I know him well enough to know that he does not enjoy... this chaos. Even if the shadows promised that it was related to some higher order that would become apparent, he is too stubborn to change his mystical views. He will think that these shadows are the antithesis of the worldspirits he believes in, and are trying to stop the world from turning or some such ludicrous thought."

He glanced at Capra again. Perhaps Vasi's help had aided her in staving off further damage, but nobody ought to be that shade of pale when labouring in the heat. No healthy person, anyway.

"You truly believe these vaults are protected from the Hex?"

"I know they are. And when we run into shadow men down there, you will believe me."

Helverliss had sensed the presence there for some time, but only now could he gather enough strength to raise his head and open his eyes. At his feet was a pen and the piece of paper, and he vaguely recognized his complex drawing as his sore eyes focused.

In front of him stood another man in black. "Good evening, Noro."

"Have you come to end my suffering?"

"I am here to gain information, Noro. Things you are hiding from us."

"I cannot hide anything from you."

"Come now. You have uncovered secrets to the human mind. Secrets to your own peculiar way of relating to the world around you. I know you have learned how to bury your knowledge."

He thought for a moment. "Ah. Things have changed over the millennia, haven't they? You're no longer satisfied with the primitive order you began to create."

"Very astute. The boy is fascinating, but we do not understand him. His desires are strange. For example, he does not copulate with the girls he has seized, but orders them around. He does not kill his subordinates, but asks favours of them. He is more interested in gazing into the mirror than any real act of fulfilment or dominance. This is all new to us."

There was something odd about the situation. The shadows should not be asking these questions, and he should be dead or turned into one of their pawns by now.

Could they really be confused by the current state of humanity? In the end, all of his philosophical advances and those of his colleagues amounted to little. How much had really changed since the last time the shadow beings roamed the earth? Perhaps it was not understanding they lacked, but context...

He drew just enough breath to speak. "You cannot properly exist without your enemy."

"The town is teeming with humans, and they are performing admirably. The lack of plant life makes things much easier for us, as well. Less to transmute, you see."

"No—not humanity." He did some quick mental figuring, using logical formulae he had devised in defining the relation of objects, substances, and subject. "You are un-life."

"That is right. And humanity is life."

"Humanity is not life."

The shadow man gave an inquisitive motion with his head.

"Not in this equation." Helverliss laughed. The impotent fools—let them run themselves into oblivion. He might even come out of it alive, whether or not that was a good thing. "You are missing something."

"And this is?"

"You'll love this, shadow man. You're missing the fire giants."

The shadow man drew back, face wrenched with disgust. "We killed them all. Their remains have become your people's fuel."

"You are the same, shadow man. The fire giants are the wild, untamed force of nature, and you wretches are their negative, not humanity's. You wanted to change their natural order, of the jungles and oceans, into cold precision." He chuckled more, relishing his revelation. It would make a great lecture, and the thought of actually living to complete it for once made him happy, rather than depressed. "And so, my friend, that is why things are not quite right with you. You have denied yourselves the very thing upon which you depend for your continued existence. Your other half."

"This cannot be true. We wish to destroy each other. The same does not destroy itself."

"But your mistake is in thinking it destruction. There are mediating circumstances, after all."

"Such as?"

"Man."

The shadow man looked even more disgusted. "Man is but a thing to be directed by his betters. You need direction and plans. You need confidence in yourselves, you need the seduction of individuality to coax you out of bed."

"Do you not remember the legend of Akhli? What do you think that was about?"

"He tricked us." The shadow gazed at the painting, or what was left of it. "And we learned from it. That is why rather than talking to you humans and letting you push us into our own traps, we force you to enjoy yourselves."

"Is that what is going on out there? You have it wrong. You see, Akhli was the mediating circumstance between the two opposing forces. In the end, they were... subsumed, and mankind began to flourish. It was a way to deal with the ultimate impotence of the two monolithic forces, of this primordial yet divine lie..."

Now his weak heart began to thud. There were so many avenues of thought opening to him after this realization, and he could barely scribble on the paper scraps at his feet.

Were these shadows, along with the giants, actually man himself? A kind of dream image? A universal delusion or hallucination?

Perhaps reality itself possessed a psychology, and this could give rise to such hysteria...

How would he reconcile the relationship between the three? It could take years to work out.

"What you speak of is impossible. If that were true, our return would also bring about the return of the giants."

Helverliss grinned. "I do believe you're getting it, friend."

Of all the oversights regarding the mechanical golem project, Lieutenant Baq Gorvanian never would have guessed that talking to his crew while the damned thing was running would be one of them. Engine noise drowned out everything, even the sound of his own heartbeat. His legs felt like chutney after standing atop the bloody machine for twenty minutes.

He waved at the technician standing on the other shoulder of the mechanical beast, and after minutes of futile flailing at a man too deep in his work to notice, stepped within smacking distance.

He shouted to the technician as loudly as he could. "Those first steps were far too shaky. I believe one of the gyroscopes is faulty. Do you have another?"

The technician grimaced as he wrenched tight another bolt, then wiped his brow. "Gyroscope is fine, Sir. I just had the thing's head opened up, ain't nothing wrong in there. The first few steps are bound to be a bit wobbly anyway."

They had only a few more minutes before the golem would finish its warm-up and they would have to either scramble down from it, or find some crevice to hide in once it engaged the shadows.

"I want to be damned sure that this machine is in order before it grows up and wanders into the world." He ran through the golem's schematic in his mind, searching for any system his team might have missed. "Maybe the bloody fuckers put a drunkard's brains into it."

He stepped back to the golem's head and removed a panel. Inside was a human brain, and next to it, an obsidian tube. Golden wires connected them.

It all looked as it was supposed to, and he snapped that one shut. The final task was to test fire the cannons and flame-guns, so he opened an auxiliary panel next to the main one. Inside were several studs and a few gauges and counting mechanisms.

He fiddled with them, and the sixteen engines responsible for the arms growled to raise them. He pointed them away from the city, hesitated for a moment, and pressed a stud.

The thing shook with a thunder that rose above the engine noise, and the special cannon shot trailed smoke as it arced towards the desert. Next, he tried the flame-guns. There was a hiss, and a spark. Flames leaped into the air, a distance that seemed half the length of the main road through the city. Flaming dust ran down the golem's arm—more of the ore from the Hex mixed into the fuel for extra damage, like the cannon shot.

Where the flame bit into the sky, the shadows parted. Gorvanian didn't know if the fire was damaging them, but at least he could be sure that it made them uneasy.

After shutting the panel and returning the golem to its own devices, he reached into his satchel for the signalling horn he had brought. He blew it, and began to climb down the golem's side.

There was one technician below him, climbing down the ladder. This was the worst part—no matter how precise their casting, the exhaust pipes were not perfectly sealed, and climbing down the side of the golem was an exercise in holding his breath for as long as he could. Also, his head was a hand's length away from the multitude of engines.

His foot met with the technician's hand. But the man below did not look up or say anything. He seemed transfixed by something in the distance.

Great—they must have forgotten about something. Someone always remembers when it's time to finish up and everyone thinks the work is done. It was probably the gyroscope, just as he had mentioned—

And he caught in the distance a jet of flame, not unlike the one he had just seen leap from the golem's arm. There was a creature nearly the size of the golem itself, stomping through the oilfields and heading towards the city.

He hollered several expletives, knowing fully that nobody would hear him.

At the sound of the bell tone under his former desk, Sevari sailed towards the panel of studs by sheer habit. Rovan rolled to block him.

"What if I don't want to answer the door right now?"

"Forgive me, Rovan."

He stepped aside, and Rovan rolled the chair back in front of the desk. "So how do I let them in?"

"I would not dream of directing you, Leader."

"Just tell me how to do it, Till."

He pointed to the correct stud, and Rovan slammed his thumb on it.

In walked Lieutenant Gorvanian, whose haggard eyes hardly so much as flickered over Rovan behind the desk. His hair was plastered to his head and greasy. His uniform was black and his skin did not escape this trend, either.

He was panting and trying to speak.

"What is it, man?" Sevari asked.

"Fire giants."

Sevari darted to the window and gazed to the city's outer reaches.

It had to be an illusion. No human since the time of Akhli had seen one of these creatures.

The spiked tail, the hardened back. Fire spewing from their mouths, a look of utter savagery in their eyes, which he would expect should not be visible from this distance but eerily, they were.

Gorvanian shook his head. "How is this possible? They were all destroyed. We have their remains in our museums and in our engines."

Sevari clapped and sneered at Rovan. "You see that, my boy? Hm? Will your friends be able to drive them away this time?"

Rovan spun round in the chair, and a bearing squealed. "There's no Akhli this time. That's what is different. A few overgrown turtles don't worry me."

"They look more like lizards to me," Gorvanian said.

"Whatever they are," Sevari said, "they are forcing the shadows to retreat." He pointed out the window, where a dozen giants swatted and belched fire into the shadows circling the city. Some of the shadows veered away from the giants, only to careen squarely into the path of the mechanical golem's attacks.

He held his breath while the golem moved to fire. What a perfect test of the weapon—now the city would see the golem in action and when this was all over, no army would dare invade.

The golem raised its arms and Sevari could make out the minute adjustments as Section Three's artificial mind thought and aimed just like any ordinary soldier. The engines blared with each movement, and when the automatic cannons boomed, Sevari felt a thrill spread through his body.

"Look, the golem's fire is just as potent as the giants'."

Rovan jumped from his seat, shoved Sevari from the window with his shoulder. "No. How can fire hurt a shadow?

It makes no sense." He growled. "Well, this is shit. I want someone to tell me how this can happen."

Rovan grabbed Sevari's lapel, and this time Sevari had no desire to appease the boy.

"Tell me, Till. What's going on here? Where did these giants come from?"

"Perhaps if you would let me out of this damned office, I could find that out!" He snatched Rovan's hand from his jacket. "Helverliss must have called upon them after realizing what a fool he had been to try to keep these secrets from me by unleashing them."

For the first time, Rovan looked as though he could cry. At least the little bastard knew when he was beaten.

It would only be a matter of time before the giants and the golem forced the shadows to surrender.

No amount of slow breathing and exercises in calmness could bring Capra's heartbeat to a reasonable level. She walked with her hands against either side of the tunnel, keeping herself steady and simultaneously reminding her of the tunnel's cramped size.

Also, the last time she had come into these smooth, metal tunnels, Vasi had turned on them.

The one good thing about the tunnels was that after Dannac had dispatched two black-suited men with his hand-cannon, they were reasonably sure that the Hex no longer posed any danger.

"You still look ill," Vasi said. "I wonder if the Hex got to you more than you realize."

"Ah, no. I don't do well in tight spaces. Once we get out of here, I'll be fine."

"Until you have to climb through the clock."

"Well yes, that goes without saying." She cringed. But that was different.

Wasn't it?

It took them another hour to cross under the river. Vasi used her skills to place them as close to the refinery as possible, and according to her, that was in the workers' camps surrounding it.

"I thought there was housing in the refinery complex," Alim said. "I've seen them."

Vasi rolled her eyes. "Most of the workers do not last long here. If you stay for two years, you can live in the proper housing. Transients and new workers must stay at these camps." She gestured to the ceiling, glancing at Capra. "We should hurry into the open air, eh?"

"Please," Capra said.

"I will go first." Dannac muscled through them and reached for the trap door release. "Provided they have not built a boiler or a pipeline on top of this exit."

The door groaned and greasy dust rained on them. There was a rush of air, and the soft red sunlight splashed into the chamber.

Along with this fresh air and light came the sounds of men hollering, women screaming, and other inhuman, sibilant whispers.

And the most tremendous booms and cracks Capra had ever heard.

"It's like an artillery division," Alim said. "Only louder."

Dannac pushed his arm through first, then tentatively peered over the edge. A second later, he ducked inside again. "The camps are in a panic. Shadows are everywhere. And there is something fighting them, now."

"What?" Capra asked.

"Giants."

"Impossible."

Vasi pushed to the ladder. "How can they have returned?"

Now she felt on the outside of a joke that the whole class understood. "Is that a bad thing?"

"I would say it means we are saved," Dannac said. He then hoisted himself above ground. Vasi followed.

For a flash—the time it took for her mind to grasp the words—Capra was elated at the thought. But the feeling did not last. "I'll believe that when I see it."

So she came into the open air, both relieved and horrified. She dodged bits of fire, and stepped around writhing, charred men. She readied her knife, but wondered if it would be of any use against the wild men thrashing about and attacking both random people and inanimate objects.

Then she heard a roar and a rumble carried through the dirt under her. She peered through the smoke at a dozen or so hulking forms approaching the refinery's sprawl. A chorus of inhuman screeching pierced through the drone of the machines, and she could also make out the sound of crumbling brick.

Giants.

She caught up to Vasi and kept close. Vasi could keep them all safe, couldn't she? The giants must be an apparition—something conjured by magic. They could not be real.

"Cowering behind an Ehzeri," Alim said.

She waved her little knife. "Look—look what I have. It's all I have, and see those bloody hulks breathing fire and smoke and swatting down the buildings? They don't seem to care who they kill. So yes, I'm going to hide right behind this sorceress because she's the only one here who can fight these things."

Vasi scowled. "'She' is also just a human, like these others who are burning to death."

With each thundering step, the giants strode the length of a city block. Capra brought her arms to cover her head and sidestepped the rain of embers floating to the ground. Bits of glowing fire fluttered around like burning ash in a wildfire.

But somehow, fighting a wildfire with the army seemed like a better idea than what they were doing.

More than the flyaway embers, Capra also sidestepped a man whose gnarled club bristled with rusty nails. She tensed and prepared to kill him, but he sailed past and began to attack another worker.

"What the..."

"They've chosen sides," Vasi said.

"What?"

Vasi guided them behind a wooden shack. Before she could speak, Dannac drew his hand-cannon and said, "They must fight. And those who were not corrupted by the shadows have decided to side with the giants."

"Why isn't anyone running?" Capra glanced past the wall and shook her head at the men, women, and children clashing among derelict shelters and rusty barrels.

"Do you not feel the draw? I can hear the giants. They want all of this gone, they want a return to the jungles, and they will destroy anyone who does not share this vision."

She watched his face. "And do you share this vision, Dannac?"

"Right now, we are better off fighting on the side of the giants. At least they cannot take human form and lie to us."

"He has a point," Alim said.

Capra flailed in frustration. "Who said we were fighting anything?"

"Look around you, Jorassian. Even if we get Helverliss and Rovan out of the tower, all we would be doing is moving them into more immediate danger. At least they are safe for the moment."

"No, we have to get into the refinery."

Everyone went quiet and stared at Dannac.

"But you just said we should fight," Capra said.

He turned away and massaged his temples. What was his problem, and why now? The giants would only advance, and the shadows would only become more desperate and deceptive.

She grabbed a handful of his jacket and pulled him close. "What's going on, Dannac? Look around you. Now is not the time."

"I have to go into the refinery. Otherwise they will kill me." He lowered his voice. "Arnhas. The Bhagovan Republic, that is."

"What has this to do with them?"

He tapped his jewel. "This. They gave me this, they gave back my sight. Now I am their spy."

"What?"

"It is complicated and the details don't matter. I had the misfortune of meeting with one of my handlers the other day. He has set my eye to capture images."

"They want you to spy for them? At a time like this?" Such a tool would be invaluable to a lot of people... especially her own.

"They want to take advantage of the situation."

A swarm of flaming pellets peppered the shack, and she slid down to her knees. "Then refuse to do it. They can't make you."

"Like I said, they can. Yaz can order the eye to kill me." He scowled at a passing group where each human walked alongside one of the shadows. Now the things just floated along, apparently no longer needing to keep up the appearance of walking. "These shadows need to be kept in check, though."

"Vasi isn't coming into the tower with us... maybe she could use a hand down here."

"I know what you're thinking. But I need to capture the inside of the refinery for Yaz." He went silent for a moment.

It would be a standard maneuver for them were it not for Dannac's predicament. She would have just slipped inside the building in question while he took care of the heavy lifting, fistfights, and in a few cases, religious debates. He was good for all that. But if he were to stay behind and fight the shadows with Vasi, she would be left alone with Alim...

Maybe his predicament wasn't so bad after all.

Dannac snapped his fingers. She was about to question him when he reached to his forehead and pulled free the jewel. Left behind was a brass socket, and at the bottom of this glistened a host of tiny jewels embedded into the metal. He handed the jewel to her, but she could only cringe and back away.

"Take it with you," he said. His natural eyes twitched.

"Are you mad?"

He lowered his weapon at a passing shadow, fired. The round did pass through his target, but that wasn't the point.

"How?"

"About all I can see with my right eye are shadows. Vasi can help me with everything else." He pressed the jewel into her hand. "Make sure you give this thing a proper view." He looked to the tower. "And if you get the chance, give me an overhead look at the battle. It will help us organize these fighters."

She held it gingerly, as though it were an eye made of flesh. "You can still see through it when it's detached from your head?"

"Flashes of images every few seconds. Enough to gain a decent picture of the battle." He turned to Alim. "And enough to know if your partner here is trustworthy. If you betray us now, Valoii, I will know. And I will kill you."

"She is still Valoii, Dannac. She's as trustworthy as I am. Take that however you wish."

Capra ignored the banter. Now it was real, not just a plan that was forever going to happen "sometime later", and thus was nothing to worry about.

The clock awaited.

CHAPTER FIFTEEN

Capra struggled to keep up with Alim. It wasn't the burning lungs holding her back, but the clashing blades and crazed cries. She watched the men slashing at each other, gouging out one another's eyes, and her muscles tensed in anticipation.

Finally, Alim looked back and said, "Don't worry about them." He passed one of the corrupted workers as if the depraved battle were a figment. "We haven't chosen a side. I don't think they'll be interested in us until we try to stop them." And here, he stepped straight into the path of a shadow man, and Capra's breath caught in her throat until the shadow simply glided on towards the fray.

It sort of made sense, but she still couldn't keep herself from glancing over her shoulder and maintaining a hyper-vigilant state.

The screams and clashes and booms from the huge machine's cannons all blended into a soup of sound. Her throat was irritated and seemed about the diameter of a wheat stalk, as her sprint forced hot smoky air into her. It was as though they were in the Blacksmith's furnace, consumed by divine fires with all of the other sinners. Burned as fuel for the righteous, for there was work to finish.

She caught the eye of a teenaged girl in singed rags. The girl held a length of rusted pipe and made challenging gestures to the shadow man standing near her. In her eyes Capra saw a glow of leaping flame. Was it from within, or just a reflection of the fires?

The girl began a chant—guttural, almost animal. Behind, hundreds repeated her words at a steady cadence.

Capra shoved Alim forward, and the two bolted from the scene. Neither of them had experienced anything so strange in their service.

"What in the holy forges was all of that?" she asked, once they reached the refinery gates.

"Now you're using Ehzeri expletives. Nice, Capra."

She went through the open gate and prodded a body clad in blue leather armour. She picked from the dead man's belt a hand-cannon and passed it to Alim. "I don't know how to use this, and I don't want to know."

The chanting persisted in her mind. She wanted to go back and listen more, to understand it. She stood there, dazed, staring at the clock tower's base.

Why had she come here?

Shadows were trying to create an unnatural world. She ought to be back in the fray, killing the shadows and establishing the rule of nature once again—

"Capra!"

"Huh?"

"I said, where is this mechanic's entrance you mentioned?"

She tried to penetrate the chanting reverberating in her head to retrieve the schematic she had memorized. "Don't you hear it, Alim?"

"Hear what?"

"The chanting."

"In the distance, yes. It sounds awful."

For an instant it seemed so clear. He didn't hear it because he had already been corrupted by the shadows. And the only logical thing to do then would be to kill him, to kill him with fire...

She pinched herself and tried to block the strange thoughts. "The entrance is around this side. I'll take point, since you're the one with the cannon." She glanced over her shoulder. "If I can really trust you."

"We don't have time for this."

They really didn't, and so Capra cut through the fog in her memory and remembered exactly the distance from the front gate to the small door set into the side of the tower. Next to the tower stood the monstrosity of the refinery itself. Pipes, bulbous structures, smokestacks, all of it glowing under the fading sun like a palace of iron, and Capra found herself examining these strange buildings more than the spectacle of the clock tower.

She tugged on it to no avail. She threw her pack to the ground and rummaged through it for the right tool.

"Might as well try it out," Alim said.

She barely had time to slip out of the way before Alim trained the cannon on the door. There was a loud crack, and a hail of wood splinters, and a squeal as the door flung open.

They ducked under the low frame and entered the heart of the clock. The air was thick and smelled of oil. They didn't escape the noise, either, as the clattering gears more than made up for their distance from the chaos outside.

At the centre of the room, a ring of shafts rose from below the floor. These terminated in cogs, which then drove crown gears. It seemed simple enough. But when she looked up, the shafts and gears bloomed into a rising, vine-like assembly of man-sized gears.

She threw down her pack and unfolded the suit she had bought. Alim glared at her, one eye squinting.

"Well, you have to think ahead, Alim." She gestured to the gears above and began to unbutton her blouse. "It's a deathtrap. You're going to have to dispense with some of your finery, soldier."

"I will not."

Now nude from the waist up, she stuffed the shirt into the pack, even though they likely would not come back to retrieve any of it.

She peeled off the rest of her clothes and began to step into the leather suit. "Come on, then. Self-consciousness is a luxury, remember? You know better than to put your own embarrassment ahead of the survival of your people."

"These are not my people," he said, and began to unbutton his shirt. Every few seconds, his eyes drifted towards Capra struggling into her leather.

"Might as well be." She at last thrust her arms in, and tightened the laces. "What's the matter now?"

"Nothing."

"It's the suit, isn't it? Look, I've been surviving by breaking into things and being where people least want me. I've learned a few things. This was one of them." She then clasped her armband back to her arm, and plaited her hair as tightly as possible.

The jar of oil came next. "Be quick and rub this all over me. It'll be a tight fit up there."

Even in the dim gaslight, his face showed a slight shift in colour. "Capra, this is ridiculous."

"Alim, grow up. I'll do you too. It's messy but you don't want to get snagged between metal teeth in here." A burst of cannon fire thundered outside. "This is for real. Grease me up."

He sighed and took the jar. He coated his hands in the thin oil. Now behind her and rubbing her shoulders, his touch made her flinch. He was in a perfect position to snap her neck. Here she had unknowingly caused the death of his wife, and was forcing him to rub her with oil...

She felt his hands stop around the middle of her back. "Alim, I'm serious. My behind will be one of the areas most in contact with the machinery. Every part of this suit must be lubricated." Under other circumstances, she would laugh. Even now, she let out a tiny chuckle. His hands shook as they stroked her, at times showing an interested pressure, other times backing off as though she were a poison-skinned amphibian.

Accomplishing full coverage of her front was even more amusing: his wide eyes and clumsy touch reminded her of the younger men she had teased on the continent. A deep frisson tickled her when he applied the oil between her legs, and she did catch him spending more time than necessary around her chest.

"Interested, Alim?"

He withdrew and grimaced. "No. I am... I am disappointed."

"What?"

"With myself."

She shook her head and grabbed the bottle and began to coat his bare skin. She worked quickly, as though she were a surgeon who knew too much of the anatomy to sexualize every encounter with another's body. Still, the excitement from his touch hounded her in the background, and she did try hard to remember the chaos outside as she worked her hand around his buttocks and thighs.

She fanned herself and closed the jar. "We might still need the rest, in case any part of the machine seizes and blocks us."

He cleared his throat. "Yes. Sounds like a great idea."

"These gears are not just the mechanism for the clock at the top. These shafts drive every other machine in the tower," she said, recalling the schematic. She caught his face in the wavering gaslight and smoothed a forgotten glob of grease across his cheekbone. "Now, I intend to follow it into one of the elevator shafts. Which one is another matter."

Alim looked in a daze. He brushed his finger on the spot on his face where she had touched him, as if confirming that it had actually happened. Then he shut his eyes tightly for a split second and opened them. "Rovan has become Sevari's favourite errand boy, so that means he should have access to the upper levels. They are secure, and you can bet Sevari is either hiding from the shadows there, or directing them. I think this is where we should start the search."

"And you think Sevari would keep the boy with him at a time like this?"

"He is very loyal to the few he trusts. He is... strange."

Already a nervous sweat gathered beneath her suit. Maybe she could just run away now, and nobody would notice. Maybe Alim could just go by himself and bring Rovan and Helverliss out of there. Yes, she would only slow the operation...

"What's the matter? A moment ago you were playful and quivering like a schoolgirl, now you look like death incarnate."

She took a deep breath. "I am terrified of tight spaces."

"Nobody likes them."

"Yes, but I get physically sick from them."

He gave her a sceptical look.

"It's true. All I can think of is the raid shelters. My father's was especially small. He... he said it was because the smaller the hole in the ground, the less chance of the Ehzeri either finding it or destroying it."

"Yet you do it anyway."

She shrugged. "Kind of hard not to. My own interests are bound with the interests of others. Just like The Doctrine, Alim, only I'm applying it to non-Valoii."

"That is..."

"What? Treason? Grounds for execution? Whatever. Let's just get going." She slipped on a pair of gloves and tossed her extra pair to Alim. "Hands are the one thing we need to have traction. Try to let the gears do most of the work."

She grabbed onto one of the horizontal bars that spanned the ring of drive shafts. She swung around and around, then leaped upward to grasp the next one. "Once you get going, you won't be able to stop for long."

Since the machinery did not yet block view of the ground, Capra was able to stave off her panic. But the higher she climbed, the harder it would be to talk herself down from paralysing nerves.

The gears spun at wildly different rates. Under one foot, the gear moved at a reasonable pace, while the shaft above whirled faster than the eye could track.

"Capra..." The voice nagged from below, and it only made her work faster.

A hand slipped, and a gear she hadn't noticed dug into her side. Luckily, the leather held together. "Not now, Alim. We'll have it out later. I promise. You want me to go back, you can earn it."

"I was just going to say that I thought it was admirable."

Another slipped hand, and her foot lodged between two slow moving gears. She struggled to free it and yanked herself up to another driveshaft. "You think what?"

"That you could apply the Doctrine to these foreigners. I don't know that I could do that."

Was he serious? It could be a trick. Appealing to her guilty conscience, her desire to make things right and to help, might be the best way to defeat her.

But something about his tone told her that this wasn't the time for paranoia. "The Doctrine is great, except that it excludes most of the world. Why can't everyone live by it? That's what I figure, anyway."

"I disagree. Why we should feel equal with Yahrein, for example. I would not share a meal with them, much less share the land with them."

A standard Valoii answer, and one that to her was equivalent to the very prejudice implied by Yahrein during the war. There was no point in trying to convince another Valoii that their utopian views should apply to everyone else.

"If this is going to work, we need to stay relaxed and supple and not argue. I'll start us off with something more pleasant." She grunted as she pulled herself onto a large cog and rode it towards another shaft which she wanted to cross. "How are your brothers doing?"

There was a moment of hesitation, but Alim eventually said, "Fine. Koval has been assigned to a new experimental unit. Something involving flying boats."

"And the other one?"

"He left the army last year."

She stepped onto the shaft. It was turning faster than she had anticipated, and she stumbled. Heart thudding and limbs jerking without thought, she recovered and began to tread in the proper rhythm.

Just a few moves behind Capra, Alim struggled on a cog. And below Alim was a mesh of machinery, and no longer could she make out the bottom. Her breaths came short, and she jumped from the shaft just as her head swam with a dizzy panic. She looked above, hoping to find comfort in the tower's immensity, but from here it seemed as though she were locked inside the workings of a child's music box.

Too late to back out now, though. "Remember that one midwinter break where I got you back for that shower prank?"

"What shower prank?"

"Remember, the bottle of soap. Only when I got to it, it wasn't soap."

"Ha. Yes. And I never lived down that walk to my barrack without my clothes."

Laughter was the appropriate response, she knew, but she had just pulled herself in between two very tight gears, and was surrounded by a crown gear at either side. A ticking metal casket.

Only one way to go—through the gears. Gears that only became thicker and more complex the higher she climbed. They ground against her legs and her knees. Already her new technical suit of leather was chafed and worn more than the one she had left behind with the Baron. Now, she pulled herself upward, and this time her arms began to shudder. In the struggling, a knee slammed into the outer part of a crown gear, and it tore a gash through her skin. She hung still for a moment, dazed.

"Are you okay?"

"I'm fine. Just a nick."

"I've had a few already."

"Now you see the wisdom of the tight-fitting leather?"

He made an agreeable grunt. "I would say we are about a fifth of the way to where we need to be."

She went still—as still as one could stand on a rotating gear. It had seemed like an eternity. The heat, the close quarters, couldn't she get just one damned good breath? A fifth. A damned fifth, that's all they had progressed? Her muscles already ached, hair soaked in sweat and oil. In the back of her mouth lingered a bitterness, an oily and metallic taste.

Five more times, it's not that bad, right?

"Capra? What are you doing?"

She couldn't find anything to say. Her legs just kept marking time against the gear, and she tried to breathe away the heaviness setting into her chest.

"You have to keep going. There's a cam here moving closer towards me."

The words sounded as though someone else was hearing them, and she was just a removed observer, simultaneously hovering over the scene yet still chained to a panicking body.

"Capra? What now? Just move aside a little, so I can dodge this cam. The way below has closed up."

Somewhere inside her, the logical side, the trained soldier, cried out against the paralysis. *Are you just going to backwards-walk on the spot for another hour when you could use the same amount of energy to get this over with?*

A breath—a small victory against the panic.

"Capra..."

Grinding metal, whirring gears...

Capra...

She was supposed to be doing something other than walking backwards on the spot inside a cramped machine. Something, something...

"Jorassian! Get your fucking ass out of the way!"

Alim's hollering cut through it all—noise, panic, paralysis—and she grabbed onto the gear above her head. It lifted her out of Alim's way, and she looked down just as the large cam spiralled into where he had just stood.

He wiped his brow and shook his head. "You're going to have to move faster. What were you thinking?"

"I... I wasn't thinking. I told you about my problem. I'm doing my best."

"You can't just run away from this one. You have to focus, if only just this once in your life."

"You bastard."

She leaped onto another shaft. Her balance held, if only because Alim's comments distracted her.

"That's what you do—you talk your way into people's hearts and expect them to pick up your slack."

"It's not—"

"Yes, it is. And when that fails, you hit them."

Up again—if he wanted speed, he could have it. Through a gear, skip an whole shaft and grab onto a cam...

This time, though, she had failed to map out her course. The gear spun her towards the meshing of two gears. These heavy mechanisms wouldn't even flinch if she were crushed between them. She reached frantically to a post above, then flipped around the side of the gear. Her legs and knees knocked into every jagged bit of metal possible, and she skirted around to pull herself on top of the gear that had nearly crushed her.

She felt the panic again. The walls falling in, clockwork death.

"Hurry up, Jorassian. There's nowhere to run this time."

"Alim, shut up. Act like everything is fine. Talk about something else while we climb. Like I was before. Okay?"

"Like what?"

"How much you enjoyed fondling my nether regions. Your brother's cat. Anything."

"I didn't—"

"So you don't find me attractive, then?"

"Yes... wait, no... what kind of question is that?"

All of the times in the communal baths, she had thought he had been looking at her. Maybe he had, but it probably was more plain curiosity than anything of substance.

The banal thoughts distracted her enough that she quickened her rhythm of swinging and squeezing through the machinery.

"I think it's a valid question, so long as my vanity eclipses my panic."

"But I mean... I am sure you have made many men very happy."

"Rather diplomatic."

"What was that?"

"I said it was rather diplomatic. Your answer. Or a polite way of calling me a slut. Maybe both."

"I didn't—"

"Oh, sure you did."

The next clump of machines was a new arrangement, with several gears rotating around the inside of a larger one. If the food tasted as delicious in Blightcross as it did in Prasdim, Capra wouldn't have a chance at making it through.

She thanked the divine for any role it might have in the primitive palates in Blightcross, then paused to grasp the pattern of the contraption's movement.

Just when she was able to predict its rotation, it sped up and tripped another set of machines.

"Damn it, I can't hang here forever."

Alim appeared deep in thought as he negotiated the gear below her. "It sounds like it drives one of the elevators, perhaps."

"Yeah, knowing that sure helps me..." Her arm began to shudder. "So that's why you settled on Jas? Even back then, you thought I was a little too fast for you? She wasn't so innocent, you know."

And his tone drifted into the cold steel shank that had pierced her when they had met on the flying boat. "You know nothing of her, Capra. You insult her with your stupid corrupted memory."

"I've known her longer than you, Alim. Don't forget that."

"She was my wife."

There was a loud clunk and a grating sound. The gears returned to the pattern she had remembered. "Wait two seconds after I go through this thing, and go for it. You don't know when it's going to speed up again."

Once she squeezed through, she returned to Alim's asinine comment. For a moment, she thought about waiting for him to clear the dangerous arrangement, but her vindictive side spoke louder. "She may have been your wife, but I grew up with her. You would shit yourself if I told you about even half of what we did before you entered the picture."

"Jasaf was a soldier, a brave field surgeon, and my wife. Whomever you are talking about is someone else."

"Suit yourself, Alim." If they were at a café or on the street, she would have goaded him into a fistfight. It would be easy. All it would take would be to point out his hypocrisy—the hypocrisy of his blind nationalism, which was supposed to include unity and total equality and breakdown of the traditional mores that had nearly led them to extinction, and his unwillingness to accept that his wife had behaved just as modern as Capra did.

If he were truly unwilling to see his wife as she really had been, Alim would probably be better off in Tamarck, with the king's obsessions about purity and chastity and temperance.

That would be the ultimate insult to him.

She smirked to herself. In her mind, she had beaten him. Uttering the insult was just a formality, and one she knew to keep to herself until the threat of being shredded by spinning jagged metal passed.

It had been a long time since Dannac had gazed with his own damaged eye. He sensed the enemy more than saw them, and if he thought too hard about the vague shapes dancing around the bleak reality of his blindness, he would lose his ability to sense who to kill.

Even then, it was hard.

"The three ahead of me," he said to Vasi. "Are they shadow men?"

The air crackled and he saw little sparks in his limited vision. Sparks from Vasi charging his hand-cannon with *vihs*, and he took this as a confirmation that there was something to attack. He fired, reloaded, and repeated this twice.

"You must still retain some of your family's power," she told him.

He ducked behind an overturned oil barrel. "Why would you say that?"

"Blind men usually have shit accuracy."

"It is luck, nothing more." He dropped a shot into the weapon and loaded the powder. Everyone was fighting everyone, and the deaths far more gruesome than anything that happened in Red Sector.

He gauged this not by his limited sight, but by the rattling screams counterpointing the roar of both engines and the giants. Just now, the wind carried a wisp of smoke across his nose, and luckily this time he did not retch from the stink of burning flesh.

"Tell me what it looks like out there."

"The giants have not moved since that last skirmish we had. And the shadows... the shadows have abandoned their human forms. They are swarming the giants, like corpse flies."

He stood, though it didn't improve his view. "Do you hear the chanting?"

"I have heard it since it started."

The chants wove in and out of his perception. "They know things... what do they know?" He stuffed the hand-cannon into his belt and listened, as though he were standing in a meadow of songbirds.

"What the giants offer is no better than the shadow men."

"But they will undo everything we have done, won't they? Erase our mistakes?"

He felt Vasi's hand clutch his and direct it to his hand-cannon. "This is all you need to concern yourself with at the moment."

She was right, but the chanting rang louder in his mind than Vasi's reasonable advice.

Yes, humanity was the disease, the problem. They needed to...

"They are not just destroying each other, Dannac. They are destroying the city. The giants are not allies. Do not listen to them."

He began to stumble towards one of the hulking dark shapes that he assumed was a fire giant. It made sense. It all made sense now. His religion was wrong, his people were wrong. Everything was not as it should be.

"The giants can return this island to what it once was. I can hear them." He turned to Vasi, and grasped her bony shoulders. "They want to level the city. So the plants can grow again."

"They want us to live in caves."

"Yes!"

"It is the wrong way. Do you think the Blacksmith toils so that we may squander it all by returning to prehistoric idiocy?"

The chant enveloped him, comforted him, reminded him of a purer time. He could only laugh at Vasi's rationalization. He wanted to join the chant, but its exact form eluded him still...

Vasi snatched the hand-cannon from his belt, aimed it over his shoulder. He stood there, half entranced. "What are you doing?"

She squinted and flinched. The weapon hung limply in her hands. Perhaps she was with the shadows, trying to trick him—

The weapon bellowed, and Vasi's hands flailed. There was a thud behind.

Dannac's ears were ringing, and he could no longer hear the chant. "What just happened?" He ripped the hand-cannon away from her.

"I just saved our lives because you were convinced that the giants killing us all was a good thing."

That sounded ridiculous. He obeyed nobody, especially not some occult force. Blightcross may be a wretched city, but he would never agree to join in on its destruction. Yet at the same time, he could not quite remember the last few minutes. He had shot three attackers and...

And fallen victim to the giants' call, like so many crazed people around them. "Perhaps we ought to be fighting against both sides."

"I think you might be on to something."

Dannac sneezed, his nose filled with a rocky odour. Dust, he guessed, from pulverized brick. If only he could truly see what was going on, he could form a real strategy. Merely reacting as he had been was just wasting time and ammunition.

Vasi tapped his arm. "Look, there are still stragglers running around just to avoid being killed by either side."

He shrugged—it wasn't as if he could see them. "I can do little besides fire my cannon until Capra gives me a decent view from above."

"Perhaps it was a mistake to part with your eye."

"I had my reasons."

One of the giants roared, and for those few seconds, the din of battle crumbled under the beast's incredible volume.

"We need to gather those who have not yet been corrupted by either side. I say we bring them all behind the refinery gates to regroup, and plan from there."

He gave a nod and followed her, cannon at the ready.

And now he realized that he had thrown himself into the hands of two women, and cursed to himself accordingly.

CHAPTER SIXTEEN

It might have been a miracle Capra and Alim were still alive and climbing an hour after their last conversation. It would have been so easy for either of them to give a little kick, a little shove, and never have to deal with the other again.

If it weren't for these damned shadow men...

The ticking and grinding, brass and iron, and it seemed as though she would have to squirm through this forever...

After an hour of neither speaking, Alim capitulated. "I never did understand how you got with your terrorist friend."

She said nothing for a while. Then, when the space tightened around her in a jagged knot of metal, Capra took the distraction for what it was. "It was chance. A bar near the border with Flenmar. I was there alone and so was he." A small gear tore through her knuckle. "Son of a bitch!"

"You okay?"

She licked the wound and lurched back into her previous rhythm. "I'm fine."

"So you were in a bar."

"Yes, and there was a raid. I guess the Flens are happy to let Valoii soldiers do what they want. I thought they were after me, Dannac thought they were after him, and we ran into each other on the way out. Been together ever since."

"That sounds rather stupid."

"It's served me well."

"A terrorist."

"Come on. We all know how meaningless that word is. Dannac is a good man."

A good man in a damned shit predicament. Was it really worth gaining back one's sight in exchange for becoming a spy for the Republic?

Now she pulled out the eye. Dannac had not been specific, and it only dawned on her now that this immense machine was something the Republic might be interested in analyzing.

"What are you doing with that?" Alim asked.

She let go of the shaft from which she hung and jogged against a large gear. She then swept the jewel at various angles. "Just a favour for a friend."

"Is that the Ehzeri's eye?"

"Yes."

"What use could it be here?"

"You just never mind about that."

It was tempting to dump it on to him—the idea that he was aiding in a treasonous act and had nothing to say about it, but today marked one of those rare cases in which Capra knew when to keep her mouth shut.

They continued upward. Capra was dizzy and her throat burned from the fumes, but now, since they had only ten more floors to clear, she tried to look forward to climbing, rather than dreading it.

"Some kind of side deal you have, is it? I still can't figure out your angle with the Ehzeri."

"I don't have a clue what you're talking about."

"Come on, I have followed you for six months and picked up most of your activities since you left us. I know you don't do anything for charity, and messing around with that eye at a time like this hardly seems necessary."

"It's a complex situation. An exception."

"What's with the eye, then?"

"Dannac wants a view from high above, so he can better decide how to fight the shadows."

She heard his sceptical chortles as she dodged an inexplicable pendulum. Now it seemed the machine had sprouted its own life and grew for its own sake, like creeping vines of metal.

"So what would the view of this place serve him, eh? Is he a clockwork hobbyist?"

Best not talk. The bastard was too inquisitive for his own good. No wonder the army had sent him to track down deserters. Instead of fighting, he got to dig into his quarry's dirty secrets.

And what exactly had he uncovered about her?

She would definitely have to kill him once this was over.

"Sabotage, espionage... even now, you're doing it, aren't you? Even at a time like this?"

"I said it wasn't like that." *Don't make me tell you about what your wife told me...*

"I'll not be an accessory to treason."

"Then don't."

"Your trial is going to be difficult for me, Capra."

Now she opened her mouth, with her dead friend's secrets begging to leap out and tear up Alim's little pleasant delusions about his married life. And to think she had started to trust the man again. All of his patronizing nonsense had been just that.

"Listen up, Alim. Jas wasn't exactly into—"

"Capra, come back down. The elevator's right here, past this maintenance conduit. There should be a panel in the wall here..." There was a screeching, followed by a snap, and she looked down to find him holding the panel and gesturing into a hole in the wall.

—into the same things as you, friend. She only wanted to shield her family's honour by marrying you...

Luckily for him, finding Vasi's brother and Helverliss was more important than pointing out Alim's delusional marriage. Just as well. The bastard would probably find a way to bring Capra into it. His mind would likely conjure more fantasies than his moral senses could handle, and she'd hate to have to disappoint him. Well, mostly.

He crawled inside first.

"Uh, how are you fitting your shoulders through there?" Her voice wavered, and to her eyes the space looked half the size of what it ought to be.

"Just get in. It won't be very long."

She poked her head in, then retracted it. "I can't."

Alim said nothing and continued to crawl.

Down? No way. Up? It would eventually terminate at some corridor similar to this one. "Alim, wait."

But he didn't.

The callous ass, how could he just ignore her like that?

She put her arms through, then tried again with her head.

Okay, it's not so bad... Controlled breaths, as if she were about to dive under water for a long time. She might as well be—nobody could possibly breathe in that little conduit.

Now Alim's feet disappeared into the darkness, and she began to panic about being left alone. Alone inside this tiny space.

She called out to him once more, and again he did not answer.

The walls scraped against her shoulders. When she lifted her head, it clunked against more stone.

Damn this stalling! How could a person be terribly afraid and paralysed while at the same time knowing how ridiculous the fear really was?

At last, she decided to pretend that she was in fact diving under water, during a nighttime exercise. She had done them before, and it almost felt the same—dark all round, holding one's breath for long periods of time, threats of suffocation— so there was no logical reason for her paralysis.

She pulled herself inside the conduit.

Helverliss watched the boy fondle artifacts and sneer at the abstract paintings. There was something different about him, as if he no longer carried the reverence he once had for Sevari and his order. He almost walked and looked like a younger version of Sevari, perhaps before his traumatic encounters had changed him and tempered his immanent arrogance.

Did that mean that Sevari was dead? Did the child fancy himself the regime's successor?

After a few minutes of his disinterested exploration, Rovan folded his arms and said, "What have you done, Helverliss?"

The boy's voice carried an edge much beyond his years.

"Is it not your bedtime yet, son?"

Rovan turned his back, then spun round and drove his fist into Helverliss' already sore abdomen. Helverliss retched and spat blood, but by now this kind of pain was unremarkable. Rovan still lacked Sevari's precision and understanding of how to inflict the right kind of pain for the right occasion.

"So the shadow beings were fed up with me, eh? They had to send a child to finish their work?"

"They told me about your strange sciences. I saw the books Sevari confiscated, too." Rovan tried to jerk himself into a kind of gangly martial stiffness. "There are fire giants laying waste to my city, and you are the one who called them here. I want it to stop."

"What makes you think I did this? And when did this become your city?"

"I am the Leader. I ask the questions, not the prisoner." The floor rumbled, glass chattered. "They'll destroy everything. Call them off. Do whatever it takes to stop this."

"Again, I say, what makes you think I have this power?"

Rovan slapped him across his jaw. Helverliss could only answer with a laugh.

"Your giants will eventually destroy this tower, and you along with it. Do you want to die, Mr. Helverliss?"

"As a matter of fact, I do."

Rovan blinked. Oh, the ignorance of youth, how the boy must be trying to understand how anyone could invite death...

Give him a few more years of pointless existence, and maybe he would figure it out.

"They warned me about you. Your tricks, your evil philosophies and stupid theories. Thinking men, men who sit around with their thumbs up their asses while people like me go out and make a real difference... and after it all, you don't even care enough for yourself to live?" He kicked Helverliss' shin. "Call off your giants."

"I can't help you, Rovan."

Rovan's miserable frown faded, and he leaned against the wall next to Helverliss. "The shadow men are grateful for what you did, you know."

"I imagine they are. Too bad I meant for them to kill me, and for my death to pull them into oblivion forever."

"You are like them, in the end." Rovan paused, turned his head as though listening. "They want to restructure, to establish order."

So now the shadow men were talking through the boy? Did they think he would be more likely to listen if they approached him indirectly? And through an arrogant teenager, no less?

Rovan continued, despite Helverliss' bored, annoyed demeanour. "Their order will not be chaos, like this one. Nature would be tamed, and especially human nature. Would it not be better to structure our world on *values*, rather than random occurrences? The shadows have values. They exist for their own sake. They are the height of life as we know it... and they offer this same thing to us."

"Big words for an uneducated Ehzeri." And when he braved the soreness and looked up, his heart leapt at the sight of Rovan's featureless eyes—black, glaring orbs.

Rovan's voice changed into a more mature, generic voice: the same as the shadow man who had visited earlier. "This world is unknowable to you. We can make one that is knowable. One you can pick apart and truly understand, instead of discovering new ways to describe your own inability to do so."

Now this was interesting: philosophical debates with the shadow men. Almost interesting enough to put up with living for a while longer. "It's a trick, your offer. You may not be lying to me, but you probably understand that such a world cannot exist with humanity in it. Therefore it may be knowable to me, but I am still unable to know it, since you will eventually kill me in the process."

"We need people to aid us in forming the structure. Would you not help us?"

"Create a shadow world, void of movement? A world that only exists to exalt the existence of yourselves?" He laughed. "It's almost as ridiculous as the world we already have."

"An artist who refuses to create; you really are a failure. No wonder the universities think you are mad."

"Not mad, shadow man, but merely an idiot." His amusement began to wane, and Rovan's stupid face was beginning to grate on his nerves. "Listen, shadow. The fire giants will not relent or go away until both them and your comrades are destroyed at once. Neither side can win, because you are the same entity."

Rovan, or the shadow controlling him, calmly turned away and strode to the exit. "Perhaps the reason you fail is because you refuse to acknowledge what you can really do." And without waiting for a reply, the boy was gone.

Now he began to wonder if his own thoughts had been delusions. Had he or had he not summoned the giants? No, they must have come on their own. They must have appeared in answer to the shadows.

And did it matter? Did he really want to end the destruction?

Blightcross was a cancer upon the world, and had stifled his ideas for decades. Perhaps this was simply justice dispensed by the cosmos.

To Capra, the past few minutes had dragged for an hour. But luckily, ahead lay a faint glimmer of light. She locked her gaze to it, and her vision tunnelled like the very chamber in which she crawled.

How ironic that her tunnelled vision actually comforted her—the less she could actually sense the stone around her, the better. But she still felt afraid. Afraid because she couldn't find, of all people, Alim. Had he already made it through?

That must be the case. She slid along faster now, in the hope that she would find Alim standing in the hallway, where she would beat him senseless for leaving her. It was just like him to toss her into her greatest fear head-first. Now that she thought of it, he had done the same thing a decade ago, at the school's swimming pool, when she had been too hesitant to jump from the diving board.

She still hadn't gotten him back for that.

She reached the point of light and peered below into a hallway. On the floor lay a picture frame, now cracked.

Vague sounds filtered up to her, but she couldn't identify the voices.

And, no Alim.

Slip out just a little more—

There, just turning the corner. Where was he going? And who was the person with him?

Alim walked calmly, and so did the person beside him. They disappeared before she could make any sense of it. She wanted to call out to him, but something in her gut told her not to.

That same something also told her not to count on Alim any longer.

She didn't need a partner anyway. How many times had she breached high-security keeps and vaults alone? Countless times. Granted, there had been no giants trying to burn away a swarm of shadows and destroy everything else in sight, but other than that...

After waiting a few moments to make sure the hall was clear, Capra slid out of the conduit. Except she hadn't put any thought into the maneuver, and tumbled head-first to the floor.

She rolled and recovered, then trotted silently through the corridor. As she began her search, she remembered Dannac's eye, and quickly tied it with the necklace that belonged to her amulet. Dannac could capture his images, and it would stay out of her way.

A few steps down the hallway, she stopped for a moment. It was the mirrors—all along each wall there hung mirrors in flat silver frames. She had found more elaborate pieces in a rundown pub. In the reflection of one, she found the infinity created by the mirror on the wall opposite.

Strange tastes, that Sevari. On one hand, the tower seemed excessive and opulent, but on the other, its stark, functional, and sometimes classical design was the antithesis of the vibrant modern styles she had grown used to on the continent. But it must have had its charm, since Capra spent several seconds staring into that infinity of reflections. Damn, wasting time, and in a mirror, no less. Time to move.

But where to go?

Never mind—this hall only led in one direction.

She startled at a freezing draft across her back. Spun around, ready to kill.

"What the..." she muttered to herself.

Since there appeared to be nothing there, she continued down the corridor. A drop of sweat stung her eye, and she cursed the heat. If only that cold breeze was real.

The mirrors. She couldn't escape them. Every two or three steps, they confronted her with polished clarity. What was their purpose? The other hall was decorated with romantic paintings of wars and revised history. These mirrors made no sense, and the strange feeling of being watched by these frames reminded her of the time she had fallen into Helverliss' painting.

A shriek screamed like nails across glass, and she clapped both hands to her ears. She jammed to a stop and turned around. Still, there was nothing. Nothing but a ringing in her ears, thanks to the deafening screech. Echoes of the unearthly sound raced through her skin as gooseflesh.

That had to be something.

When she turned to leave, the mirror showed something different. A dark female. Capra gasped and jumped back, only to realize that the other mirror showed the same thing.

But it wasn't just a dark female. It was Capra. A negative image, with ruby eyes glowing from some ungodly fire behind them.

They had to be joking. What the hell was this? She was stuck between being sickened by the dark double and intrigued.

She broke through her paralysis and bolted through the hall of mirrors. A pressing urge to blind herself, to not look anywhere near the mirrors. Ghouls, perverted images, all around.

And now out of the mirror.

Standing in the middle of the hall, the dark version of Capra grinned sardonically and played with a knife identical to hers.

The real Capra skidded just shy of the ghoul. The living mirror image made her stomach clench.

"What are you?"

It didn't answer. Instead, it switched the knife between its hands and gestured mockingly. And the encounter became another rip in the universe, another baffling experience, just as Helverliss' painting had made her feel.

Shit, this was probably his own work, or at least a derivative stolen by Sevari. And here she thought that the clock tower was impenetrable because it was full of guards. She could only dream of fighting tired watchmen now.

The ghoul lunged and tackled her. Its only sound was a glassy shriek like before, and the jutting pain between her ears alone nearly disabled her. But when the ghoul stabbed for her throat, Capra caught its arms. She couldn't overpower it, arms shaking against the attacker's strength. The eyes, damned eyes, such a distraction, as if they knew everything about her...

She slipped her knee into the ghoul's hip and pushed it into the wall. Ghouls—how was she supposed to fight an apparition?

Run.

She took off down the hall. There had to be some kind of limitation to the mirrors, some effective range—

Smack. Right into the ghoul, and for a second, she stood, chest touching her opponent's, and stared into its gaze. It couldn't be a person. It was a thing made living, an abomination, and it wanted to kill her.

Goddamn you, Helverliss.

She struck it across the jaw. It grinned, and planted a lazy kick right into her chest, sending her to the floor. It wasted no time in grabbing her by the collar and slamming her against the wall. Capra swallowed a mouthful of blood and slammed her knee into its gut. Its grip loosened some, but she still couldn't rip free.

It screeched at her, and underneath these aural claws Capra heard a whisper. *Stupid selfish slut.*

Capra spat in its face. It licked the bloody mess from its mouth and grinned more.

"You may look like me," Capra said. She then tossed aside her attacker. "But you don't know shit." While the thing lay on the ground, writhing in confusion, she kicked it in the head.

But she could kick and stab all night long. This was one of Helverliss' creations, and it would only fall by some other means. All along the wall next to the mirror, she groped and pressed and tried to think of a way to disable this guardian-ghost.

It was here that she found a diptych between two mirrors. One painting showed a red circle interlocked with a black one, and the companion picture showed a reverse image. It had to mean something. Sevari didn't seem to appreciate decorative art.

Before she could figure it out, the ghoul snatched her legs and yanked them from under her, and her jaw smacked on the floor. Her vision sparkled, and she cursed under her breath.

She twisted free and rushed back to the wall. The ghoul slammed her into it, pressed her face against the stone which surprised her with its warmth. There had to be magic running through the walls.

An icy breath beat on her neck. In the margins of her vision she saw the ghoul's mouth open. Fangs, like a desert viper. She drove her elbow into its rib. Despite the reassuring crack, her attacker answered with hardly a flinch.

The two little paintings—they had to be the key. If only she could reach them, but with her hand pinned and the thing's teeth edging towards her face...

There was no time. Whatever happened was going to happen, and so she cracked her attacker in the ribs once more to buy a few seconds. With the knife she slashed at the canvas, then tore it apart. She groped in the eviscerated picture frame and found a metal knob.

A combination lock.

"You have got to be kidding me. Fuck."

The ghoul's grip tightened. Capra spun the knob at random, but her own scattered heartbeat made it impossible to feel out the clicks and work out the code. Ice against her neck. And claws. The thing had claws. They were now digging into her ribs.

She yelped. Elbowed it again, and it staggered back. Leaped at it, plowed it with her shoulder into one of the mirrors. The next thing she knew, she smacked face-first into the mirror, leaving a greasy streak, and hit the ground.

The ghoul had flown through the other mirror, and was already recovering and ready to resume the fight.

She hitched herself up and dashed to the combination lock. Now more than before, her body's adrenaline scream silenced the finer senses she needed to unlock it. The next best thing—use the knife to unscrew the panel. At least Sevari had skimped on building materials. But what about the ghoul?

An idea knocked into her head like so many cheap shots. It might work. It sounded stupid to her rattled brain, but it was all she had.

She left her mechanical work for the time being and pressed her shoulder against a stone pedestal that sat against the wall. She grunted under its weight and slid it against the mirror. It reached about half-way up the glass. Once satisfied with its placement, she rushed to the ghoul and punched it in the throat. It reeled, and Capra let fly a kick, which sent it again into the far mirror. Just as she thought, the ghoul disappeared into the mirror. A second later, it came out of the one opposite, and tumbled over the pedestal Capra had placed there. She rushed to the dazed ghoul, and with all her strength toppled the pedestal. It fell across the ghoul's chest.

Then came the screeching, unlike any sound it had made before. Her head swam with vertigo, vision sparkled as though from a head injury. She hurried to the lock, began to unscrew the lock's panel. Once this was done, she sawed through a cable with the serrated part of her dagger.

From the walls came a ratchet-clatter, like gears pulling. The mirrors sank into the wall, and shutters clapped over the recesses.

The ghoul stopped writhing on the ground. Capra approached it cautiously.

The fire behind its eyes faded to a flicker.

"See how much better it is to be original?"

The thing vanished.

As if this deranged booby trap weren't enough, footsteps sounded down the hall. There had to be a door in this bloody place, a room, anything. Iron heels boomed and echoed in the cold stone hall, with angry voices bristling with words like "intruder" and "entrails." With the sounds quickly gaining on her, she found a door ajar, and slipped inside. It glided open silently, and she thanked whomever had forgotten to make sure it had closed properly, since it showed no handle on the outside.

The smell—like sulphur and decayed meat. What was this place? There were rows of iron tables, racks of metal implements on wheels, and at the back stood four riveted iron tanks with circular windows and pipes fitted to their caps.

It had to be one of the laboratories Vasi had mentioned. This meant that Rovan should be around, maybe hiding, if he were smart. She crept around the laboratory, taking short breaths through her mouth to avoid the reek. Around each lamp, a haze drifted and shifted, a strange fog.

Louder voices outside. Looking for someone—thumping boots, running soldiers. Damn it all, she should never have given the hand-cannon to Alim.

There was something on the iron table ahead. Not something. Someone.

Capra rushed around the table, but there was nothing she could do. The table included a built-in vise. The person's head was in the vise, the body hanging against the side of the table. She tried not to examine the head too closely, but could not help noticing its warped shape and protruding bones. Despite the bulging eyes and utter terror personified, there was no blood, no visceral reminder of the body's gruesome death. What kind of experiment could require... this? It was barbaric, like something out of the history books in the chapter about backwards medical procedures. Only this was even more depraved. It took her a moment to look away, and this was when her stomach soured and tried to squeeze acid up her gorge, but her will to swallow was too strong.

"Is there anybody here?" It was stupid, but now she shivered with an uneasiness she had never experienced in any of her previous jobs. Then again, this was hardly a cheery break-in on behalf of some rich benefactor. "Rovan? Your sister is worried. I'm going to get you out of here."

At the iron tanks, she peered through the windows of each, but couldn't see anything through the coating of grit. "Rovan? Are you inside one of these things?"

She spun the wheel on one of them and there was a rush of air. She lugged it open.

Nothing.

She tried the next one, though didn't suppose the boy would be so stupid as to ignore an offer of help.

There was someone in the next tank. A man, slumped against the back of it, whose head dripped blood from a perfect hole in his forehead. She recoiled and slammed shut the door. What kind of machine was this?

The pipes led to a smaller, squat tank of iron, which then passed its pipes through a set of crystals, several containers of liquid, and ended in something that resembled a faucet. Obviously it was something involving magic, yet enhanced by Sevari's industrial power.

When she went to leave, the door had sunk into its frame. Only now did she notice that there was no handle. No handle, no studs on the wall, no levers...

The Divine had to be kidding. The joke—only one way out, and it was through the window, assuming she could break it. And then what?

She slammed her fist into the door. Now it was getting ridiculous.

Why am I following these people?

Alim had asked himself this question numerous times, but each time convinced himself that the man in black was leading him to Sevari, so he could take charge of what little troops remained and prove that he alone knew how to bring the city under the rule of order once again.

"The exercise did you good, Alim. Last time I tried to convince you that we only wanted to ensure that you live out your chosen path, your freedom, you ran away and joined the enemy."

"I can't recall what you mean. I was here to find Sevari. To tell him that you and your people should not be welcomed with gunfire. I must get him to shut off his machine..."

Yes—the monstrosity that was laying waste to the shadow beings. Together they could defeat the fire giants, but the machine meant their inevitable defeat.

His new understanding still baffled him. Epiphanies burst into his thoughts—sciences, mystical truths, and all as if he had known them since time immemorial. He understood the power of the shadows, and the savagery of the giants.

Everything that had happened prior had just been falsehood. His alliance with Capra, who he would now take great pleasure in disemboweling, and his idea that ending the great battle was the best course of action, all of it lies just to get him to this point of taking control. Already those falsehoods were dropping from his memory like dead leaves.

The shadow man led him up the stairwell, and they passed several guards. They entered the halls on the museum floor. The shadow man halted in the middle of the hall, some ways from the museum entrance.

"Why are we going here?"

The shadow man spoke in a measured voice. "Mr. Helverliss needs company."

With a hot wind beating her face, Capra's hands clawed at the stone, and she was thankful that Sevari's delusions had driven him to reproduce a classical architecture overflowing with decorative stonework and designs—a few of them perfect handholds. This was a first. She had never before climbed to such a height, and she knew enough to avoid glancing at the ground.

The height tended to deceive a person. Tightrope walkers really didn't do much at all—any person could walk a straight line on the ground. In theory, it would be no different a mile above the city.

In theory.

She did not need to look down to see the giant war machine. It blotted out much of the skyline, and its engine roar dominated the insanity below. She could only wonder what it must be like in the streets, or in the work camp.

The machine fired every five or ten seconds, and its flames constantly licked at the swarm of shadows flitting about its head.

Capra grunted and strained under her own hanging weight. Twice she tried to pull herself over the ledge, and her body gave more noise than strength. In the corner of her view she saw the great hulk of a fire giant collapse. Its legs shook, and it cried out in a keening that Capra would never be able to erase from her memory. And underneath it were several rows of brick town homes, which crumbled underneath the beast's death throes. Brick flew, dust rose to form a pall over the block.

It was the reminder she needed to summon the strength to overcome the ledge. A pressure crushed around her neck, her face flooded with hot blood, and there was a hammering at her temples. Once she hoisted herself onto the ledge, she sat against the wall to recuperate. She couldn't help indulging in a smug grin as she gasped.

There was a window next to her, and once her heart settled, she peered through it. Once again, she found a coating of grease and grit, which she scraped away with her knife like a dirty frost.

Glass cases, paintings on the wall...

There might have been guards inside, but she raised her boot anyway and plowed it through the glass. Finesse and patience? Luxuries.

Once she landed on the soft purple carpet, she readied her knife and prepared to deal with the guards. But the place was quiet and still, as a museum ought to be.

Against the wall she found Helverliss. She rushed to him and began to work at the chains with her picks. "Are you okay?"

He raised his head a little, half-gazed at her with his eyelids sagging over bloodshot eyes. "You? What happened?"

"I came to get you out of here." She leafed through the tools frantically. "Damn it, what kind of locks does that maniac use?"

He made a strange gasp. "You shouldn't be here. You should have left."

Right, he was a downer even on a good day. She shook her head and kept working the locks.

"You look like shit, Capra." He coughed and she heard him spit across the room.

"Thanks."

"You really need to get out."

One of the manacles clicked, and Helverliss' arm dropped from the wall. "Yeah, and you're coming with me. We're going to stop this stupidity Sevari started, and you're going to pay me double for this." She grazed an already chewed-up knuckle against a chain and winced. "Oh yeah, and thanks a lot for designing those creepy mirrors whose reflections try to kill you. Sevari seems to have found a good use for them." She showed him a gash on her arm.

Helverliss fell into a hacking fit. "What?"

"Nearly killed me on the way up here. A double of myself. Only stronger and darker."

"The bastard. I never thought he would even broach such secrets."

"So it really was your invention?" If it weren't for his frail state, she might have slapped him.

Before he could answer, there was another click. Not from unlocking manacles, but one that sounded at the museum's entrance.

"It's over, Capra."

She whirled round. Staring right back at her—Alim's hand-cannon.

"Alim? Help me free him so we can get out of here." She went back to the locks.

"I said it's over. Now turn around."

That fear about him, that feeling crawling in the back of her mind, now appeared justified. She hadn't wanted to fully accept the likelihood as she had watched Alim walk away; the likelihood that she had known deep inside but refused to acknowledge.

"Alim, what did they tell you?"

"They told me the truth."

The hand-cannon hardly fazed her. She drew her knife, advanced slowly.

"They told me that I was a unique human."

"Oh, really?"

"They told me that I ought to be writing our destiny, not blindly following."

She shifted her stance, brandished the knife. It must have weighed a sixteenth of the big weapon Alim held in his jittering hand. "You think Jas would approve?" Bad idea... too late.

Alim growled and now his hand held the cannon with a steeled grip, the barrel straight and levelled to her forehead. "This is why the shadows are superior. They would never have abandoned their rules, their laws, like you had. They are truth. They are exactly what they say they are. If you were more like the shadows, Jas would be alive."

"Don't you know how twisted that sounds?"

"It is perfectly logical. The shadows are the highest form of life possible."

It was getting too strange and circular for her liking. She struck at him with her fist, and he dodged the blow.

Helverliss called out, "Capra, you stubborn idiot, he has a bloody cannon."

But she didn't care. She continued her tentative attacks, all of which missed. It wasn't stupidity. It was that she knew of his weapon's slow reload time. He would not fire his only shot if he were not sure it would disable her, leaving her with little choice but to dog him with attacks vigorous and unrelenting.

"You're not well. Maybe Vasi can help you."

He lashed out with the weapon's handle, and smashed her in the jaw. She reeled and tripped over a low table. Earthenware idols and other items crashed on the floor.

By the time Capra could right herself, there was the cannon again—a circle of black pressed close to her face, an eclipsed sun.

"Now, I have a great duty ahead of me."

"What's that?"

"Bringing down the giants."

She squirmed. "How?"

"With help from your friend. Your friend who wants to die, which makes it necessary for me to find alternate means of adjusting his behaviour." He batted the knife from her hand, then hoisted her to her knees.

Now the cold eclipse rested at the base of her skull, and Alim's body was pressed against her back.

"Alim, this is insane." She fought to filter the fear from her voice. This situation had never been covered by any training, since the weapons hadn't been in use. Would she have any time to react if he fired? Would it kill her instantly?

"Mr. Helverliss, our problem is that Sevari's machine is threatening my people's victory. I want you to tell me how a machine made by man can be so devastating to the shadows, and I want you to tell me how we can stop it."

"Ask Sevari."

"Sevari apparently knows little of its inner workings. And he knows nothing about the nature of the shadow beings, which is the main focus here. Our young leader is still too fond of him to use more advanced techniques for gathering information."

The barrel jabbed into her head harder. "Noro..."

"I would save you, Capra, but I do not even understand what this maniac is asking of me!"

And harder. "I... I think he wants to know how to shut off the war machine."

"It is not merely a machine you can shut off. It only obeys certain members of the Corps. It has a mind, you see. A few friends of mine brought this to my attention after they noticed several of my theories had been adopted by the scientists working for the government. Find these highly secured Corps people, and maybe you'll have a chance at talking the machine out of its orders."

Alim jerked her to her feet. "The shadows have searched everywhere. These special soldiers cannot be found. There must be another way."

"It has a mind, you stupid Valoii. Treat it as one and maybe your shadow friends will find a way to remedy the problem."

The pressure at her neck eased, and she sighed. The hint was vague enough to give them time, yet from the way Alim stared into the distance and whispered to himself, it could be enough to satisfy the shadows.

He began a low, perverse laugh that rippled against her body. Convulsions of a strange pleasure.

"That is all we need. Thank you." He shoved Capra across the room and backed out of the museum, cannon trained on her.

"Alim, wait!"

"It's no use, Capra. He's been taken."

"Then why would he let us live?"

Helverliss groaned and gestured to the chains, and she darted back to his side to release them.

"He let us live because contrary to my assumption, he, or the shadows, were intelligent enough to make use of my nebulous hint. It matters not whether we live or die once they disable Sevari's war machine."

CHAPTER SEVENTEEN

From the brief view he had glimpsed thanks to Capra's climb up the side of the tower, Dannac estimated that their numbers lay between two and three hundred. At the moment, they all cowered behind the fence between the worker's shanty town and the refinery.

"It's as if we do not exist to them," Vasi said, eyes fixed upon the two warring factions.

"It is only a matter of time before one side wins and destroys us." Dannac faced his crowd, most of which accepted him as the grease-streaked regiment's commander. "I have seen images from above. If we all gather—"

Something exploded near the fence, and a tidal wave of dirt soaked them all.

He brushed dirt from his face and said, "If we all gather around the big war-engine, we can better attack the shadow forces."

The crowd murmured.

"They do not appear to agree," Vasi told him.

"Their voices tell me enough." He rested a foot on a busted pallet. "I know you all are sceptical about the machine, but it is our only advantage. It can protect us, equalize the fight. The shadows have superior numbers."

A man holding two hand-cannons spoke. "And what then? How will we take it down and stop the giants and their forces?"

"It will take a balancing act. We will pare down the shadow men's numbers, then switch to the giants to equalize them. We will do this until both forces have been defeated, just like in the legend."

"There are no endless holes to oblivion, no traps this time!" called out another. "How will we bury them like in the legend?"

"This is what we have to deal with. As long as we are careful in how much attention we draw from the giants, we should be able to blend in and destroy them from the inside."

A few in the front brandished halberds and broken pipes and boards bristling with nails, and appeared eager to drop into the fray. Other than that, they were a contingent of tired, blackened faces, and there was much moaning.

Dannac clambered up a pile of brick and twisted fencing. "Look around you. These things don't moan, they don't tire. All they do is destroy. We may be the last chance this city has of surviving." He surveyed the crowd, finding them still rather uninspired. "Most of you are Ehzeri. Most of you would kill for a chance to give your lives in the fight against the Valoii, even though most of you are probably too cowardly to follow through and that is why you are here. But I ask you: is there any difference between these demons and the Valoii? Here is your chance to make up for the way you have turned your backs on the Ehzeri. Fight, damn you. For once in your lives, fight!"

A wave of silence came over the crowd. Could nothing rouse these people into action? It had been wishful thinking, this idea that the leftover people whom neither side wanted could be turned against these demons. Stupid wishful thinking—

All at once, they roared. They bashed together their pipes and boards, hollered the most vile expletives at the giants and shadows, and bared their teeth.

Just as they ought to have.

He waved them through, and the throng flowed out through the gates and breaks in the fence. Vasi shook her head at the display, but Dannac refused to believe that the fight was futile.

"And when we have killed both sides," Vasi said, "they will divide us and set us against each other."

She need not have said it out loud. It was logical, but there always existed the chance that they really could bring down these two forces at once. It may be a ghost of a chance, but Dannac had survived poison gas, phosphorous attacks, and the death-mark of international terrorist, not to mention two years paired with a goat-stubborn Valoii defector. He wasn't about to submit now.

They would put these myths back into their place, and he would dig the holes himself if he had to.

But that was the real problem. They weren't myths at all.

"I still say that we are missing something. Damn, if only I had paid more attention while I had the chance to decipher the painting... Shadows, giants, oblivion... it all ends with darkness. But it didn't. The universe survived, and so did we. So what did I miss?"

He grunted at her.

"You could try words instead of animal noises, you know." Vasi shook her head and prepared to re-charge his cannon. "Part of the reason I was starting to enjoy this place was that the men here do not act like you."

"You are right. But why you would prefer men who are always intoxicated and obsessed with cash money and gambling is beyond me."

"Because they do not treat the women as slaves."

"So sex objects are better than slaves? And they still view themselves as superior, just like back home. There is no difference, really."

She left it at that, and probably for the better. They had their moments of camaraderie, but only against a broader background of mutual annoyance.

Even though it loomed over the refinery grounds, the war-engine's legs stood several city blocks away. Dannac and Vasi dashed across the filthy workers' camp along with the rest of the battalion. So far, most of the volunteers were obeying his directive to avoid returning fire while they made their way to the war-engine's shadow.

This was probably the worst time for him to be bombarded with images from his detached eye. He stopped and brought his hand to his head.

"What's the matter now?"

"The eye."

"You mean..."

He nodded. It was shaky and the angle skewed, but he saw flashes of a bloodied Helverliss. Now he stopped trying to block the images.

"What do you see?"

"Helverliss. In chains. Alim is there too, but he's..." She should have listened to him. He had known all along that Alim could not be trusted, but she just had to give him another chance.

"Alim has turned on Capra."

"Is she okay?"

He shrugged.

"I told you we had to tell Capra about her heritage. It could save her."

"What heritage? It is more dangerous to convince her of a non-existent ability than to leave her to fix her own problem."

"How can you be so callous? After all you two have been through, too."

He resumed his sprint to the war-engine. Vasi kept pace with him, much to his surprise. Now the group began to take position in the streets and alleys surrounding the machine's legs. Clashes broke out, the shadow-corrupted people seeping into the area like a plague.

With Vasi's help, Dannac killed three using the cannon, then led them behind a stack of crates to recuperate.

Vasi was oddly silent.

"What's going on?"

"In the sky, the shadows have made a mad dash for the machine again."

"I thought they had given up on it."

"Well, it appears they have decided to try again."

How he wished to see for himself. Trusting this woman for his sight was degrading. Could he even trust that she knew what she saw?

"The machine keeps fighting them off with its flames. The shadows are already breaking off."

"Good. Now would you recharge my cannon?" When she said nothing after a minute or so, he repeated the question.

"On the side... a man in black climbs the machine."

"Why climb it if he can just fly?"

"Perhaps the machine cannot sense something crawling along its metal body..."

He faced the big blob that he knew was the machine. "You'll have to help me aim." Vasi's enhancement also increased the footprint of the shot, and he was confident that he could pick off the corporeal shadow.

"It's disappeared now, near the head."

"The bloody things have become mechanics, have they?"

"I don't think so..."

The machine then halted. Its cannons fell silent, smoke curled around the thing's arms, and the constant gush of its flame cannons slowed to a trickle of falling sparks. The whine of its engines dropped in pitch, and the sudden change of its sound told him more than the blurred picture.

"They have disabled it?" Now he actually wanted Vasi's opinion.

"It appears so, but I have a bad feeling..."

"What?"

The rest of Dannac's men went still and craned their necks to watch the machine. A wave of murmuring passed through them. It smacked of battlefield confusion, and Dannac knew it was a mistake. He bellowed to them, "Stay on your guard, you fools."

From nearer to the machine a voice said, "It moves again."

"Then get fighting!"

"It is moving, but differently," Vasi said. "I still do not like this."

"Big surprise! There is not much to like about this kind of thing."

The engines bellowed and metal creaked. One of the feet lifted high above their heads. Vasi began to scream incoherently, and she pulled Dannac away from the machine.

"It is moving its cannons. Finding another target."

Damned woman, she made no sense. "Why are we running?"

"Because it is about to—"

The ground shook and there came a metallic crash at their backs. Then screams arose. "What just happened? Vasi, tell me!"

"The machine has stepped on a third of our people."

He gasped and faced the machine. It looked the same as before, and he cursed his near-blindness. He could not discern the bodies belonging to the outcries of pain. "What in the name of..."

"The shadows have taken the machine for their own."

Sevari rubbed his neck and shut his eyes. The knock at the door would not stop, and all Rovan could do was yell, "Go away," every few minutes.

But this time, Rovan pressed the stud and allowed the visitor in. And when Sevari saw Alim standing there, in an overlarge tunic as though he had picked his clothes at random and face covered in grease, he had to stifle his excitement—at last, an ally with whom he could at least commiserate.

"Alim, I am so glad to see you." A quick glance at Rovan, who acted as though Sevari did not exist. He tried to mouth "help" to Alim, but the Valoii showed no reaction. Instead, he spoke to Rovan.

Of all people, Sevari's new friend spoke to Rovan.

"I am here to help," Alim said.

Rovan rolled his eyes and dumped himself from the chair. "Oh yeah? What you got, Valoii?"

Alim gestured to the window. Sevari followed them, and could not shake the feeling of being an ignored child.

"Tell them that the machine has the mind of a person, or one like it."

Rovan stared at Alim, and slowly his mouth curled into a grin. "If it has the mind of a person... it can be persuaded like a person. Turned to our way."

"Exactly."

At once Sevari's head began to hurt even more. The shadows couldn't have found his secret mechanic-soldiers, locked away in the vaults. Only they really knew how the machine worked... how had Alim discovered this?

"Of course," Rovan said, with a chilling maturity. "That is why Section Three needed the bodies. Had I known that, I would have figured it out myself how to defeat your machine."

"Bodies?" Sevari said. "Nobody from Section Three mentioned anything about bodies."

"And how were they supposed to create a bodiless mind? A mind to think for your machine? Did you think they would just create it out of piss and lead?"

"It was supposed to be a working of *vihs*... Are you saying that Section Three was lying to me?"

Rovan began to circle him. "The whole damned refinery lies to you, Till. We'd do anything to keep you from executing us. And Section Three couldn't figure out how to do what you asked, so they found a way around it." His grin was a flash of malice, lopsided with abnormally sharp canines.

It couldn't be true. Rovan was just playing with him.

Even so, Sevari's throat clenched with a sadness and betrayed sourness he hadn't felt since Iermo's assassination.

It couldn't be true. It couldn't be. They didn't need to lie to him, they didn't need to patronize him...

How *insulting*.

"They used human minds? They used my machinery for murder?" He found Rovan's smugness disturbing. "Rovan, was that what they wanted you to do?" Now he felt like the adult again, and that he had failed to protect his protégé from the incompetent cretins he employed. "They wanted you to kill the other workers for them? I thought they were using you for emptying solvent buckets and delivering samples and cleaning up after them, because Spirit knows they don't do it themselves down there..."

"Oh come off it, Till."

"Did you? Did you kill those workers?"

Rovan gave a condescending wave and returned to the window. He shut his eyes for a second, and when he opened them, there stood next to him a shadow being. "It's simple," he told the man in black standing next to him. "Stop trying to destroy it, and find its human mind. It should easily obey us, like half of the idiots out in the streets."

With that, the shadow faded into nothing.

Rovan hopped onto the desk and began to thump his heels against it. "All they told me was that they needed them dead, and that they had only minutes after a person's death to extract what they wanted. They told me nothing more than that."

"You just obeyed them? You killed these people without even knowing why?"

Rovan shrugged. "I was working for you, Till. I wanted what you had. I was playing the game. And it paid well, in the end." He spread his arms and turned in a circle.

Sevari began to feel sick. Is that what they all thought? That he had come into power for something as banal as riches? This tower was for Blightcross, not himself. He lived there because the palace reminded him too much of the old ways, not because of some desire for extravagance.

"This was not what I had meant. I... I was being moved by the worldspirits, not by my own desires. I was moved by history!" He approached Alim. "And you—I thought we understood each other. I do not take betrayal lightly."

Alim's dispassionate face did not change, and he stared through the window, watching the mechanical golem. "This is beyond history, Sevari. It is right. The shadows are total freedom and order. I can finally be everything I knew I was, thanks to them."

"That's preposterous, Alim."

"Call it what you want." Alim gestured to the golem. "Our side is winning, thanks to your incredible innovation."

The corridors hummed in a strange way, and Capra swore that if she ran into another of Helverliss' inventions, she'd just kill him right there. She didn't know where they would go, only that they had to move. *She* needed to move, to feel as though they had any chance of influencing a cosmic battle.

Helverliss, on the other hand, limped behind her. "What is it that you plan on doing? We need to find a way down, not up."

"I have to find Rovan."

Helverliss halted. "Rovan?"

"Do I stutter?"

"What do you want with him?"

She spun round, head askew in a frustrated manner, and said, "I owe it to a friend to rescue him. I need to get him out of here."

As though she had cracked a joke, Helverliss grinned and hacked—she guessed this was a laugh slapped into an outcry of pain by his broken body. "Oh, I bet he's just a sweet little boy who is hiding away from all of the turmoil, waiting to be rescued. Haha."

"What's gotten into you?" Stupid question. His instability had come long before any torture, she guessed.

"Rovan has taken over as the tyrant of Blightcross."

Her mouth gaped. There had to be a mistake. Perhaps Helverliss had finally slipped into a madness beyond repair.

"Yes, I know, it sounds ridiculous but I assure you, Rovan's bravado must have made him the perfect figurehead for the shadows. They do require something of an anchor in our realm, you see."

She watched his face; a face the consistency of tanned leather and tracked with dried blood and creased with tired lines. Something about him told her he was telling the truth.

But she resumed her sweep of the halls anyway, and Helverliss still trailed behind. For one thing, he still could be wrong about Rovan. Also, in the event that Rovan now sat as the shadow beings' leader, it changed nothing in the end. Vasi still wanted to save her brother, and she could find a way to excise the shadows if need be. All Capra need concern herself with was taking him out of the tower.

"Your friends are fighting the shadows? Or are you the only one left?"

"They're fighting."

"You know it won't amount to anything. Deep down, I think you know."

What a fatalistic, broken man. Capra shuddered to think of how short her life would have been were she as doom-obsessed as Helverliss.

"It bothers you because it's true. You know what's going on. You looked into my paintings, and I saw many things about you as a result. You are not half as confident as you appear. You are suffering from a kind of traumatic amnesia."

She made longer, angrier strides. There had to be another way up...

"Just as you ignore me now, so you ignore this trauma, this radical split I sensed. I am linked with my paintings, you know. If I want, I can look into my work and see what it brought out of your unconscious."

Nonsense, and she could only ignore it for the time being. There was a door set into the wall ahead. She nudged it slightly, peered inside: deep blue, cold, and immense. The stairwell.

Four guards stood near the door. It might be easy to take them down, but then again, she was already fatigued, and there would be dozens more on the way up, and they would always retain the advantage of higher ground.

She eased it shut. "I need another way up." To her right, across from the stairwell entrance, stood an ornate set of brass doors and a panel of studs. "If only the damned elevators worked."

"Very interesting, actually."

Now she wanted to slap him. "Look, I know what I did, and yes, it was traumatic, but there's no way I buried any of it. I relive it every night. It would be a godsend to forget."

"I am not speaking of anything recent. Of something that happened at an extremely young age. A death."

She choked for a moment. Not now, not now... "Look, if you're going to intellectualize, you can start by telling me how to stop these shadows. They came from your stupid painting, so you ought to fix it."

"It was a complicated ritual that took days to complete. I was in a trance. I had used a korganum derivative to aid me. I have almost no memory of those days, and I awoke from the feverish work to a completed canvas, swimming with the power of the shadows, yet contained and knowable by even the simplest mind."

She shook her head. "Not good enough." She tried to think of something Vasi might have said about it. Damn—if only she had paid more attention, she'd know what to ask. "Fire giants and shadow men. If the two were left alone, there would be nothing left. What was the real secret to binding and banishing them?"

"Ah. Simple. Humanity."

"What?"

"Mankind was the compromise. Akhli, of course. I had thought this was obvious—that there must be a mediating presence where there are two opposites. Is that really what has been stumping you?" He made a disgusted face.

"No, no. Akhli made a sacrifice. The divine saw this and fixed it all. That's what the texts say."

His tone turned mocking. "Well, you seem to know more about this than I. I will offer no more heretic theories."

Hadn't Vasi said something about duality, when they had found the three circles carved into the ruins? She opened her mouth to mention this, to echo Vasi's sentiments that *two* was the magic number, not three, but there was still the matter of getting Rovan out of the tower. As though the ritual would help to quell her growing impatience, she pressed one of the studs next to the elevator. From the wall came no clunk, no rattle. And yet, she pressed the stud again and again.

"Do you see that hole on the right side of the panel?"

She brushed her finger across it. "Yes."

"I believe it is the mechanism that disengages the building's engines from the elevator system. There should be a key for it."

"How do you know this?"

"I attended a symposium where the inventor of the elevator gave a very long, boring speech about his projects. In the first few versions of this machine, many maintenance men died trying to fix the things when they sporadically began to move, until they finally figured out that they needed a way to fully disengage the machine from the engines during repairs."

She found her miniature glow-torch and twisted on the light. It didn't look like any lock she had seen before. "I don't have time to figure this out."

"Think hard, Capra. Penetrate the mechanism with your mind."

"I really don't have time for this, Helverliss." What an odd thing to say, even for him.

"Really, try it."

So she did, and about all that happened was that she started to yawn. "Time to try my way." With her knife, she began to dig around in the large slot. She felt many odd clicks through the handle, and tried to map out the lock in her mind, as she had done before.

Then something behind the wall slammed, and she jumped back, knife hanging out of the hole. "I think that's it."

"See?"

"It wasn't my mind. It was my random jiggling with the knife."

"Suit yourself."

She left the knife there until the elevator came down, then gingerly pulled it free.

Their ride in the elegant cabin, full of sweeping, plant-like accents in brass and elaborate patterns in a dozen different types of wood veneers, ended a minute later with a loud bang. The cabin shook and seemed to waver for several seconds before coming to a compete stop.

"This should be the floor. Sevari's office is just below the clock face."

And she could hear the ticking, the heartbeat of the tower, muffled and distant above their heads.

Ready to open the door, she brandished the knife, prepared for yet another unfair match. Would she end up fighting the shadows and the giants with that stupid little thing? The thought made her almost as depressed as Helverliss, but then again, the blade hadn't let her down yet.

After wrenching open the door, she peered into the hall. Deserted.

"Maybe you should stay here. You don't look in any shape to confront Sevari and the shadows."

"You don't look fit for it either."

"Just stay here. I'll come out with Rovan, and when I do, I need this thing ready to move to the ground floor. Got it? And start working on a way to stop this. You made this mess, now you're going to fix it."

He nodded, and she headed down the hall without a damned clue as to what she was going to do.

The big iron doors bristled with rivets, and the rose emblem showed proudly on its face. It had to be Sevari's office, and Capra swore that she could sense the corruption spreading from it like a barrel of oil tipped into a pristine pond.

Ear to the door—nothing. Probably too thick. Bursting in through the front door probably wasn't the best idea, but without any alternatives, it seemed she was stuck with it.

The door's frame sported a similar panel to the elevator. She plunged the dagger into it, then jerked it out as she realized that on the other side of the door stood a petulant boy-shadow and a murderous tyrant.

Waiting would only prolong the nervous shock in her gut, and if she waited long enough, her heart might drum itself to death. So she held her breath, and stabbed at the lock, waiting for that strange meshing of gears inside.

And again, the little cams and switches inside tripped its connection to the building's engines, and the door began to crank open.

Sevari startled at the door's sudden movement. Only he possessed the key, and he patted his belt to ensure that it was still there. And it was.

"I didn't say anyone else could come in," Rovan said. He stood and gestured to Alim. "You—take care of it."

And when the door opened, there stood a woman in leather coveralls that sucked against her shape and displayed every curve of her body. Grease spots marked her face, and her hands were black with the same.

Sevari narrowed his eyes. "Where have I seen her before?"

Alim took out his cannon, and aimed it at the woman's head. "I gave you an opportunity to leave, Capra."

So that's who it was—the Valoii deserter. The one with whom Helverliss had allied himself. She was smaller than Sevari had assumed. For some reason, he had pictured the Valoii women as tall, blocky amazons.

And what did she threaten them with? A little knife. It was almost comical.

"Alim, listen to me. You're not thinking straight."

"You ruined my life, Capra. The shadows have given it meaning. You have just tried to make excuses."

Rovan made a frustrated noise. "What does she want already?"

"Rovan?" she said. "Your sister sent me. Your sister, Vasi. Remember her?"

"Oh yeah, sister. How's she doing? I tried to find her. She would have been a better human adviser than Till."

He took offence to this and raised his hand, but Rovan ignored him.

"So my sister has become a traitor, huh? Well, she always was weak, in the end. Her and her stupid *vihs*. Where is she? I'd like her to see what I've been able to do without a single fart's worth of her magic."

Capra edged forward, apparently oblivious to the cannon. "She's worried about you."

"Good for her. Why doesn't she just use her magic to check on me?"

"Rovan, she's down there, fighting against these shadow beings. If you really have been chosen as their leader, you have to call them off."

Rovan hopped over the desk and shoved Alim out of his way. It reminded Sevari of an absurdist comedy theatre. The soldier standing there like a zombie, the only man in the room with any real physical power. The dullard boy making a mockery of his superiors but without irony, and himself, the dictator nobody would acknowledge.

But now he had in this room an ally; the same woman he had wanted imprisoned and made an example of, as a gesture of solidarity with Mizkov.

"My sister is free to join me. If she wants to throw her life away fighting my rule, I can't help that. I'm the brother of the family. She has to listen to me."

"Once you're of age, Rovan. You aren't yet, and you need to listen to your sister."

"Shut up, bitch. If my sister is anything like you, maybe I want her dead."

Now Sevari could no longer stand at the side like a servant. He took Rovan by his shoulders and stared into his eyes with the intensity of a military reprimand. "Now you listen, Rovan. Don't ever say such things again. You will regret them later."

Capra looked about as shocked as Rovan, and Alim simply gazed into nothingness.

"Get your hands off me, Till. It's not like you're one to talk about family values and all that tripe."

"Everything I have done was because I did not know what I had until it was taken from me during the war. Go find your sister, make sure she is safe."

Rovan shoved him aside and approached Capra. Just from the look of her, the cold precision in her eyes, like Alim's but far more lively, she could quarter the kid in half a second with that little knife.

He wished that she would.

"You know what? I'm tired of this. We're all going to the roof. I don't think you two really believe in the power I have."

Capra's stance relaxed somewhat. "Rovan, what are you doing? You don't have to prove anything. Just come with me."

"Shut up and follow me, otherwise I'll just have them kill you."

At last, Capra looked Sevari in the eye, and he noticed a slight glint of understanding. He gave her a shallow nod, though what exactly they were confirming he couldn't tell. That they both recognized the insanity, and probably little else.

CHAPTER EIGHTEEN

Why was she reasoning with a teenager, again? Capra barely contained the urge to bend him over her knee and paddle him, and here she was, following him up the cool grey stairwell. And making eyes with Sevari, as though they were old comrades. Oh the things one can do under the right pressures...

It seemed to her as though some transcendent force had taken their identities and shaken them in a hat. Even the stairwell appeared to be an inverted scheme—cool blue stained glass, calming colours, ignorant of the orange heat permeating the district.

And with that butcher merely a step behind her...

Whispering to her...

"What is your plan, anyway?"

A shiver. "I'm still trying to figure out whether or not I'm supposed to kill you."

Alim's voice boomed at their backs. "No talking."

"Oh let them," Rovan said. "They can't do a damned thing."

They reached the roof, and Rovan stood at the edge, facing the war machine. A group of shadows flitted about them, and Capra tensed, ready to slash at them but knowing fully how pointless it would be.

"All of you watch this."

Capra stepped closer to Sevari, even though it felt wrong. "If you want this city to survive, you'd better tell me just what the shit's going on here."

"Rovan wanted to become rich. He's an arrogant little bastard, and the shadows liked him enough to make him their human leader. He's trying to convince us of the power he knows isn't really his."

"He's going through all this just to convince us?"

"He is a teenaged boy who grew up with nothing. He killed innocent people to get ahead, and he's looking for approval. Somehow I don't think these shadows count as authority figures to him."

She almost tripped. "He killed what?"

"Yes, he did. But I think he's not really cut out for it. He's trying to legitimize it by showing us this display."

Rovan pointed to a tall building. "You think I'm lying? Watch that."

The war machine made a sudden turnaround, and its engines groaned as it lowered an arm. Rovan had a glazed look in his eyes, as though he were in a game or a dream.

There was a boom. Another. Two more. The building began to crumble in a heap of dust and girders.

"What have you just done?" It was time to put the kid into his place.

"They obey me. Even Sevari's big war engine obeys me now. Get it? Can you bring down a building with a mere thought? No."

She nudged Sevari. "Distract Alim for me. I've had enough of this."

Fed up with Rovan's petulance, she came too close to the roof's edge for her liking. It was like watching from the flying boat again, only now she was close to the knots of pipe that stretched from the refinery into the desert. The earth beyond the city was cracked and pipes seemed a perverted sucking of a land that had already been bled for all it was worth. But she knew it was just appearance. There was plenty more fuel buried under the pipes.

And if Rovan were allowed to continue, the city would crumble into the same desolation.

Capra pulled out her necklace, in case Dannac were still alive and in need of a better view. She approached the boy slowly. "You have more than you think, Rovan."

He spun round. "I have the whole district. I know what I have."

"I meant your sister. I think you need to ignore the shadows for a minute and just listen."

Another giant collapsed and took with it two small buildings.

"They tell me you're a coward."

"Consider the source. They can't even do their own dirty work."

Rovan sighed. For a second, the ghost of a scared teenager showed through, but his eyes narrowed again and he crossed his arms. "Don't you like it? Don't you think this power is great?" He looked to Sevari. "It's what everyone wants. I'm the guy who won. I'm the guy who did what everyone dreams of."

"Yes, maybe you are. But you have to think about your sister."

For a moment she watched him for any decent human reactions, until it became clear that he wouldn't show any. Maybe deep inside, real human emotions stirred and butted against the shadow men's corruption. Whether or not she could coax them into the forefront was another matter.

"You don't like killing, I can tell. You thought it was going to be easy, like what you think Sevari did. But it's not, is it?"

He said nothing. The war machine turned again, and its cannons launched a volley at one of the giants. All the while, buildings crumbled in the distance, and strange screams erupted from gangs of shadows in the streets.

"Till was boring. I thought he'd like what I did. The other Valoii only cares about himself." Rovan met her eyes. "Don't you see how big this is? Nobody is paying attention. They're all just fighting and worrying about themselves."

"I see what's going on. I just want to help you. It's impressive, sure, but at what cost?"

"You see? You see what I'm doing? It's big. I've done all this."

She nodded.

The war machine fired again into its opponent, then made its stiff steps towards them. Capra tried not to see it as a living thing, but on the head of the machine, the panels were strangely arranged in a symbolic approximation of a face. Two rectangles for eyes, and a large grate at its mouth that let out puffs of steam every so often.

She gulped. The machine stopped an arm's length from where they stood.

"Those two don't care. Till is so boring now, but I kind of like you." He pointed to the machine. "Get on it."

"What?"

"You're coming with me."

"No."

He grabbed her arm. Her struggling amounted to nothing. The damned shadows—had they given him physical strength, too?

"You want to find my sister, so we're going to."

"Yeah, see what I had in mind was that we'd stop the fighting. You know, so she wouldn't be in danger."

He shoved her towards the edge. Only now did the tower's height hit her, in all its dizzying glory. The vantage point reduced the fight below to groups of tiny insects clashing.

"Close, but my idea is better. We'll find her, and then she'll be safe with us. It'll be great, I think you'll love it here when I'm finished with it. Both of you."

Blightcross was bad enough before all this. She didn't want to think of what it would be like after Rovan's reformation.

He prodded her. She elbowed him in the stomach. "No way."

Rovan's eyes turned black, and he grasped her by the throat. Another voice took over his own. "You will accompany us or die."

She gulped. "Oh yeah?"

Rovan nodded slowly, teeth bared. Capra boiled inside. She wanted to twist off his head and piss down his neck, and all because she knew that right now, she would lose if she resisted.

Even so, she threw a false punch at him, stopping her fist just a finger shy of his face. They exchanged glares for a few seconds before she jumped onto the ladder attached to the side of the machine. Through her hands came the purring of its engines, and she wondered if it wouldn't numb her hands and cause her to fall.

There was a clunk beneath her. Rovan was there, pointing towards the top. She started to climb.

"Hurry up! If you're not into this, I'll just throw you off."

She obeyed, heart racing both from the unsteadiness and from her anger at being subject to a teenager's demands. "Oh, I'm into it all right."

If it weren't a given that the shadows would rescue him in mid-air, she would have kicked him off the stupid machine.

Then again, the machine was the advantage in the battle, the mitigating factor. Rovan had handed it to her. All she needed to do was shut off its engines, and the giants might have a chance at destroying the shadows.

Sevari raised a fist at the retreating machine. His patience was being rewarded—all those hours spent ignoring Rovan's crude remarks and juvenile arrogance, holding back his urge to properly dispense discipline. He had known all along that no amount of help from the shadows could fix the endemic problem of Rovan's flyaway attention span.

"Alim, perhaps you will listen to reason now."

"Rovan will return, and I will be given my ultimate orders."

"Ultimate orders, you say? I can't imagine what that even means." He started towards the staircase. "Come on, old friend. I have some orders for you."

"It is not the order I want."

He skipped stairs on the way down, and Alim's heavy steps echoed behind. "Now that the elevators seem to be engaged again, I can reach a signalling station."

If these shadows thought they had caught the Blightcross Administrative District unawares, they would be delightfully surprised. "Alim, my good man, I know the shadows present the subject with an object of desire. *The* object of desire. The one that nobody will ever achieve. But I think I can offer you an approximation of what they offered to you."

The guards ignored them, and Sevari led Alim back to his office. From there, he called his personal elevator. Once its clunk sounded in the walls, he grinned and mentally thanked History for not abandoning him.

"Where are we going?" Alim asked.

"To my bunker." He fished in his tunic for a small decorative dagger. Once he found it, he pulled the handle apart to reveal a key. He then lifted a nondescript brass plate, set away from the main group of studs, and inserted the key into a secret slot.

"I will not allow you to interfere, Sevari."

"Even if it means taking command of the most elite fighting force ever to grace this world?"

Alim paused. Yes, conflict with the shadows... contradiction would at least stifle Alim's will to act. Even if he never agreed to switch sides, Alim would take time to recover from the fact of Sevari, a mere human, offering the same object of desire as the mystical shadows.

"Listen to me, Alim. This fight is an illusion. Remember the legends? They will both fall in the end."

"There is no Akhli to facilitate this. Without him, there will be a winner, and it will be the shadow men."

"I am Akhli."

Alim's eyes went wide. "Blasphemy!"

Perhaps it was, but one could only fight the transcendent with the transcendent.

"If you are so sure of yourself, why am I still alive, Valoii?"

"The boy still looks up to you. We have strict orders not to harm his friends."

"And Capra is now his friend, is she?"

Alim winced. Another contradiction.

"So, then, your master has taken up friendship with the woman who took everything you loved?"

There was a bang and a jolt. Sevari clapped, and cranked open the elevator.

He loved his office, his little throne room, but deep down he preferred the stark, grey stone and metal of his bunker. It was his cavern, his haven, and it made him smile that finally, he was using it as intended, rather than walking its silent halls alone, imagining what he might do in a crisis.

"Part of this was already here, you see. I just added to it and made it my own. I suspect the shadows missed it because there are traces of metal from the Hex in its outer framework." He waved Alim into the bunker's control room. "You are the first besides myself to see this place. Aside from the crews who built it for me, and, well... the secret died with them."

He took position at a control panel.

Alim appeared even more confused. "Now what are you doing?"

"Preparing to retake the city. You will have complete command of my special unit, and an assured place as an historically necessary implement. I am signalling the sentry in the bunker underneath the armoury. I want him to prepare for your arrival."

"My arrival? I did not agree to anything."

He entered the proper sequence, and stood. "These are not an army of shadow-corrupted oil workers. You will lead them, you will conquer this city for me, and you will cast out whatever influence remains of those damned things, do you hear me?"

Alim grinned—an incongruence that seemed to tear the very fabric of the situation. "I hear you."

Sevari eyed him warily. "Down the hall—the alcove with the red markings around it. There will be a small underground train that will take you to the armoury bunker. There you will meet with my sentinel and take command of my elite unit, of the city's saviour."

There was a pause. Sevari watched Alim's face for signs of scepticism. The moment dragged...

Alim nodded. "Perfect."

Sevari's gut twitched. "This is no ordinary unit. They require special equipment, and tactics. Although, I think your people have used quite similar tactics against the Ehzeri. Go now, Alim. Just into the hall, and you'll find the rail car ready, complete with an honour guard to escort you."

And Alim went without question. With any luck, the lack of shadows in the bunker would weaken him enough.

Sevari eased back into his chair, punched in a few more quick messages to the sentinel manning the signal station below the armoury. He barely flinched when the two hand-cannon shots crashed in the hall outside. Alim's scream relieved him a little—taking out such a wildcard in his operation made it safer, and throwing Alim defenceless into a pack of ravenous lunatics would surely cover Sevari in case officials across the ocean began to wonder why their operative was dead. They couldn't possibly question the cause of death after seeing what the shadows had done to the body.

Anyhow, at least that was one minor issue to strike from his list. There were more important things at hand.

Situation critical. Special Regiment required; all citizens must be neutralized to prevent further corruption. Begin the waking cycle immediately.

By now, Dannac had glimpsed enough of the battle from above to know that his three or four kills every few minutes were slowing them down more than anything.

"This isn't working. We need to retreat and regroup."

Vasi's hand still grasped his wrist, sending a strange tingling through his arm. They flattened themselves against a crumbled wall to catch their breath.

"Look—the armoury," Vasi said. "At the gates... I think there are a few of Sevari's troops there who haven't been taken by the shadow men."

"They have been distracted by the giants..."

"And we'd better regroup around the armoury. The soldiers will provide cover for us."

They both bellowed the new plan as loudly as they could, then bolted along the main road. Along the way there were groups of people giggling and pointing at smouldering buildings and bodies. Others had not given up the initial phase of wild copulation as most had.

"Have you seen any images of Rovan?"

He hesitated. He had seen much of Capra's predicament, and about the only thing he could be sure of was that Rovan was not exactly the innocent little brother Vasi had described. "I have. He is alive."

Lying by omission? Maybe, but Vasi was his sight, and he could not afford to have her distracted by knowing that her brother and Capra were standing atop the machine.

"Is Capra on her way back to us, then?"

He glanced at the blob of movement that, coupled with the commotion he heard, must have been the war-engine stomping towards them. "You could say that."

"I wish I would not have listened to you. I can feel her connection to me. She has power that she could be using..."

"She does not."

If by power, Vasi meant luck, then sure.

Now the gates of the armoury were ahead, and the tall metal scaffolding, now empty, was bent and twisted.

"I can see them—sentries around the wall. They are firing at... everyone."

"Good."

He could make out the general form of the armoury wall, and he saw a vague flutter of motion. "What—"

"The gates are opening. They are giving us sanctuary."

The crowd that had followed him rushed past. "I do not feel good about it."

"Why? They clearly aim to give us shelter in the armoury. It must not be fully taken over by either force..."

They kept running to the gate.

"Everybody back!"

This time a few skidded to a halt and ducked behind rubble. Vasi struggled against him as he forced her behind a chunk of broken masonry.

"Let me go. Why are you doing this? Why are you hiding?"

"Because something is amiss. I will never trust anything that comes out of that armoury. I have too much experience with so-called law to know that it does not suddenly change its character and welcome those in need."

More intermittent images flashed through his mind, beamed from Capra's viewpoint. The eye faced a row of factories, leaving his and Vasi's position at the left margin of the picture. If she would only shift her body a few inches...

It was enough that he could make out a square of men moving towards the open gate.

"Soldiers..."

"Uncorrupted soldiers?"

"I believe so."

"How?"

Sevari must have had them hidden in reserve. Of course he had—what else could all the gloating he had heard refer to? The people here no longer needed Tamarck's protection. Sevari was no liar—Blightcross was a force of its own now.

Vasi beamed with excitement. "I see them—they are marching through the gate."

"How are they armed?"

A pause. "I... I am not sure."

"Lances? Hand-cannons?"

"No."

The view from his jewel offered no details, and he tried to make out the men with his own damaged eyes. All he saw was a single mass of grey moving against a slightly different shade of grey.

Finally, she said, "Black suits of armour. They have... masks. There are tubes in the masks, and they hold strange wands."

"Cannons?"

"No—thinner. On their backs they carry egg-shaped packs."

Screams erupted from near the gate. He gave Vasi a hard nudge.

"I don't know what is going on. There are... it's a mist. A deadly mist."

"Poison? A gas?"

"I... I think so."

Why would Sevari order such an attack? He posed the question out loud, but Vasi said nothing. His cannon was useless. The cloud of gas would just envelop them, and there was no fighting a white version of the shadow men.

"Now, we run."

"What?"

"You heard me. We run and hope that Capra can come up with a way to fix this."

"We can't just run. You of all people—"

"Sevari aims to eradicate any living thing in the city in order to take away the shadow men's ability to fight."

She gasped. "It's insane."

"Yes. But he's right—if everyone dies before the fight is over. The shadows will have a hard time gaining control without footsoldiers to do their bidding."

CHAPTER NINETEEN

At every chance, Capra stole glances at the war machine's many panels. She stood with Rovan on the machine's shoulders, and tried to shuffle towards the head. Each time she sidled over, Rovan would change position and give her a stern look.

Smoke columns reached into the permanent haze-canopy, and the sun glowed a deeper shade of red. Unlike the orderly jets of smoke from the refinery, these plumes slashed the sky at random, and blew into ragged clouds.

Back near the refinery, which now she figured was the shadow men's stronghold, a strange greyness seemed to sap the colour and life from the area.

"Rovan, what are these things really doing to the city?"

"Making it better. And it's not the shadows, but my followers. Me and my people are using the shadows to make the city better, not the other way around."

She let out a frustrated sigh. The way the process of corruption kept changing depending on who she asked reminded her of a popular painting by a famous artist from Prasdim; an illusion that depicted two hands painting each other.

It didn't matter. She had to stop this damned machine. But with Rovan watching, how could she? Damn it all, how could she become the hostage of a teenaged boy?

Capra shuffled over some more, and now her back was against one of the panels. She placed her hands behind her back, and tried to jam it open with the knife. It wasn't as though she needed to be delicate. She just needed to foul the stupid thing.

"Vasi," Rovan said. "Where are you?" A moment later, he nodded. His lips moved, but Capra couldn't make out the words.

The machine wheeled and stomped towards the armoury. She worked faster, and after much jiggling, the plate bent open enough for her to reach into the cavity. All the while, she fixed her gaze on Rovan and made small talk.

Rovan still grinned at his handiwork, his chaos. "We'll pick her up and then maybe you two will lighten up and admit how great this is. You'll love the new city, really."

"Really?"

Instead of answering, he squinted and gazed at a ruined section near the armoury. "No," he said. "What's going on? They're killing us. They're killing them all, the bastards!"

She groped around in the cavity, fingers sliding over round bits of metal and jagged things and braided metal cables. She grabbed anything that might fit between her fingers and pulled, but found nothing delicate enough to snap or dislodge.

She also had to make sure to keep Rovan talking. "Killing what?"

There—something that gave way. A stud. She jammed her finger into it repeatedly. Enough that her fingertip cried out in pain.

"Soldiers. Just like the Valoii." Rovan pressed his hands to his head.

But she barely heard him, since most of her concentration was in her hand, pressing and pulling and scratching.

"They're going to kill her." Rovan flailed his arms towards the armoury.

Like a brood of beetles, a force of hundreds, all in black armour, filled the area within the armoury's walls and flooded out the gate. They spilled through the streets, and engulfed anyone in their way.

With gas, no less. Gas that was not the crude glass canisters she had tossed into countless Ehzeri camps. Gas that did more than cause minor burns and temporary choking.

There was an explosion, and Capra was dazed for a moment before realizing that it was the machine's cannons firing at the soldiers.

She pried open the panel more, and this time stuffed the knife into the cavity. There had to be something important, something the knife could jam or disengage.

"You just going to stand there?"

It took a moment for the words to resonate with her. "Excuse me?"

"Go get my sister. You're the one who wanted to save her, now go get her. Then we can show these sheepfuckers who has the real power."

Was he kidding? Did he have a head injury? Ordering her around like that, as if that would ever work.

She wanted to slap the kid or at least tell him what a little shit he was, but now wasn't the time, especially since he was, after all, corrupted by evil entities. And if Vasi were down there, as Rovan said, among those clouds of gas...

Without thinking, hurried to the ladder, never thinking that she might need the knife she left inside the cavity. The thing began to take slow steps. It shook like mad but she held on, legs swinging under her.

"Better not think about double crossing me, Valoii. I see everything."

Everything except his own stupidity. It was hard to take the kid seriously, even now.

At the machine's hip joint, she halted. The machine was still walking, and there was a complex meshing of machinery she wanted to avoid. The engines blared and their vibration crawled deep inside her body. Eyes shut, tight as her grip on the ladder. Guns blazed above, flames dripped in a hell-rain, some of it skittering across the giant's metal plates, leaving scorched trails.

Her head spun. Ten different acrid vapours floated around her. The machine's foot slammed into the ground, and she lost her grip. She began to slide down the ladder. It ended before she realized what had happened—a shock in her legs, a lack of control, rolling around on the ground, burning hands.

A black form hovered in the distance. A shadow. It sailed towards her, and she flattened against the ground. When the shadow passed, she hauled herself to her feet and sprinted through the alleys. She leaped over bodies, dodged retching citizens whose skin appeared to be flaking off.

"Vasi? Dannac?"

Rhythmic thumping. Boots. Jingling weapons as an accompaniment, almost like chimes. She darted behind a derelict carriage. The sound edged closer, beating in time like the gears of the clock tower.

The soldiers looked nothing like any soldier she knew. They wore all black—something she couldn't grasp, given the temperatures of the area. It looked like leather but it wasn't. Their masks looked like hideous bug heads. As they passed, she heard a chilling, hollow wheeze and hiss emit from the men. It was their breathing.

They marched with an unnatural stiffness; a precision even her countrymen couldn't match.

As she scrambled to find Vasi and Dannac, the war machine threw out a grating sound. Its arm jolted still halfway through its own movement. Was it breaking down after only hours of life?

It could be... hopefully it was the knife jabbing into various parts as the thing moved.

But before she could feel optimistic about the little victory, a wave of coughing overcame her. She went to her knees, eyes flooding. Damned poison...

"Capra?"

It was a hoarse voice, familiar. She tried to answer, but only retched. The surrounding chaos bled into a mass of spilled colour, under a curtain of hot tears.

"It's her. Come on, we need to get her some air."

It was Vasi and Dannac. The scene around her darkened, and she lost all control of her muscles, before all she knew was darkness.

The sound of her friends' voices. Distant rumbling. Her first action: rubbing her arms, rubbing out the crawling itch racing through her flesh.

She sat up. Both comrades were perched on rubble, watching her intently.

Vasi handed her a ripped handkerchief. "Rovan, where is he?"

Capra rubbed the crud from her eyes. "He's on the machine. He's controlling them."

"What?"

"The shadows chose him as their human... governor. He thought I'd come down, get you, and bring you to him. He wants us all to just relax and enjoy his new city." She spat in an attempt to rid her mouth of the chemical taste. "Why am I alive, anyway?"

"I purged the poison from you."

"Just not from my mouth."

They both displayed an incredulous look. Somehow, it reminded her that she had Dannac's eye, so she detached it from her necklace and gave it to him.

"So you just left my brother with that... abomination?"

"It's actually pretty interesting, Vasi." Then she remembered that Ehzeri hated machines.

There was a click as Dannac snapped the jewel into his forehead. "The machine is crawling with shadow men now. It had started to fire randomly, but it is back to its old self."

"You mean... they're fixing it?"

He gave her a blank look.

"I tried to sabotage it. I had thought it was starting to break down, but... damn it. What's going on down here, anyway?"

"I had organized most of the non-aligned people, and we were going to regroup around the armoury. Sevari's troops have wiped out our resistance."

"What?" But she needed no explanation. Sevari was the kind of man who could see the logic in destroying everything in order to save it. And the part that scared her? It was easy to see how practical the solution was.

"What they don't realize," Vasi said, "is that when the shadow men run out of humans to take, they will just take lower forms of life. Plants, animals, insects. This is crazy, it is not a solution at all."

Muffled voices called out all around them. Retching, coughing, pleading.

"The poison soldiers." She had nearly died from their gas once before, and didn't want to tempt fate with a second opportunity.

She crept through the wreckage. A few blocks away, the war machine lumbered and righted its askew weaponry. Its metal no longer gleamed and shone. Now it showed a darker, dull finish, and parts of it sported gashes and scorch marks.

Vasi caught up to her. "Rovan is still up there. We have to get him down."

"I'd love to, but how? And you're forgetting that he's the shadow men's leader now. What are you going to do once we save him?" She glared at the war engine. "I spoke with Helverliss. He thought it to be obvious that your missing piece is humanity itself. He says there had to be... oh what was it he said... a mediator involved in the opposing forces, if they are not to completely nullify everything."

Vasi blinked and became a motionless idol. "That's it... the damned circles. Even our Ehzeri family knots showed the answer. Three powers, not two. But it's not what you think."

"Dannac, what do you—" Capra whirled to face him, but he wasn't there. "Dannac? Where did you go?" She then spotted him sprinting away.

"I've got something to take care of. I'll meet you later!"

"But—"

"See you at the book shop... later."

There was a note of uncertainty in his voice—one Capra was sure she'd never heard. But he'd disappeared into the smoke, and all she could do was take his word.

Vasi gasped and gazed to the sky. The sun now was barely a sliver on the horizon, and the machine's flame guns bathed its torso in an orange glow. Behind it, the refinery's smokestacks glowed in a similar fire. Despite the creeping darkness, Capra made out streams of shadows gathering around the machine.

"They're retreating?" Was it because of Sevari's troops?

"Regrouping, not retreating." Now Vasi looked at her with an intensity she had never seen out of the woman. "Capra, things are desperate. You need to know something."

"What?"

"You are Ehzeri."

Capra's heart clunked at Vasi's words, like random junk tossed into gearwork. "That doesn't make sense."

"Don't think about it. There's no time to think or explain. You have my family amulet, you have Ehzeri features, and you showed aptitude."

Capra touched her face, ignorant of the grease and dirt she was spreading along her cheek. The face, her face, was not Ehzeri. Capra Jorassian was a prime example of a common Valoii woman, ignoring her capital offence. "Why are you telling me this?"

"Because now that I have a family member, one with *vihs-draaf*, we have another option. We can alter... we can call upon a powerful force. Without it causing mass devastation."

"Whoa, this is crazy. Look—I have olive skin, standard Valoii hazel eyes, and look at my damned nose."

"You have just described a typical Ehzeri. You have just described the typical citizen of the Bhagovan Republic. There is really not so much difference... except in beliefs and priorities."

Vasi pulled on the chain around her neck. On the necklace hung an amulet identical to Capra's.

So someone way back in Capra's family had come across the same artisan, probably during the war. It meant nothing. They were wasting time with this nonsense, and just to make things that much better, Dannac had vanished.

She resumed her cautious jaunt through the rubble, peered behind broken walls and bits of twisted furniture.

"Capra, listen to me. If you can't accept that you are the enemy you were sworn to destroy, just listen to this. You can access the same power I have. If we do it together, it can multiply by a factor of hundreds. I know how to do certain things. Certain things only done on the battlefield. Things I haven't been proud of, but with your help, might work for the better."

It was too much. Magic, of all things. No, it wasn't something she could deal with at the moment.

"I am going to start a working, and I want you to play along. What I'm going to do is channel aspects of both these creatures. I now understand the painting. Helverliss forgot to account for the archons."

Capra skidded to a halt. "Archons? What do they have to do with it? They came way before anything to do with Akhli."

Vasi shook her head. "Akhli *was* an archon. This is what we've all been missing. The archons are the mitigating factor. They are the mediator between the two forces. Helverliss thought it was humanity, but he was wrong. Archons are what keep them in line. Humanity is just a... just an aberration of perception. The human is a void, a gaze, nothing really... the archons were created as a necessity when the other two primordial forces came into being. Three circles, they must all touch each other, else all will cease to be."

"I don't understand."

"I am going to imbue us both with the essence of the fire giants and the shadow men. Then we will combine our efforts to... become an archon. A true archon, one who knows its place. I could just allow the archon my family imbued me with to take over, but without your help, I would be a mindless destroyer no different to the fire giants."

"How? What good is that? And how can I turn this archon of yours into a helpful one? I don't know what you're asking of me."

"Would you trust me?"

"But Dannac—"

Vasi took her hand. "Stop. When you feel sick during thunderstorms, when you feel this uneasiness you cannot get rid of through exertion or sex or whatever it is you did to deal with it—these are all symptoms of pent-up *vihs*. You have to accept what I mean to do, and allow your threads to work with mine. It is family... this is how we do things. You may think you are Valoii, but the connection is there." There was a hint of guilt in her voice.

It was stupid, but if she could make up for her crimes against the Ehzeri, she would try it.

And it just might help to defeat the machine. The chances were better that Capra would defeat the damned jumble of engines with a clothesline and a stick, but it was technically possible.

Normally, smoke was nothing Dannac's eye couldn't penetrate. But every few steps, something would warp in his view. The sudden changes made him dizzy, and he would duck into an alley, breathing heavily, clutching the hand-cannon. Something wasn't right. Nothing was right in Blightcross, but in this case—

The hand-cannon fell from his hands, and his arm jerked behind him. The attacker whirled him round and slammed his face into the bricks.

"Hello, old friend."

A familiar voice. Yet he still saw no hands, no person, restraining him.

"Just a cordial reminder, Dannac." The attacker's form materialized. "We made your sight, we know how to counter it."

"Yaz."

"Good man."

"I was looking for you."

Yaz released him, though his weapon was still trained on Dannac's chest.

Dannac could not express in words the gratitude he felt about regaining his sight. But the last person he wanted to see on such an occasion was Yaz. There he stood, and even with his inhuman sight, Dannac could not mistake the man's thin mouth and trimmed beard.

"You're lucky I didn't kill you when you pulled me aside, Yaz." He wasn't a fool—Yaz could have, and always will be able to, kill him. But he couldn't bring himself to admit it openly.

"I didn't want to complicate things by speaking to you in front of those women you've been consorting with. Now, about your eye. Did you get what I want?"

There was no way to know for sure, but he could only assume that Capra had done her best to expose the gem to the clock tower's inner workings and secure areas.

Yaz rubbed together his slender hands. "Chemical weapons troops, gigantic walking machines... Sevari has surprised me. If I can get even a glimpse of what he's done for my government, I'll be taken care of for life." He brought out a small metal sphere. "This is the remote device I threatened you with." He handed it to Dannac. "As a show of good faith."

Dannac ran his fingers along the smooth, cold metal. "Good faith?"

"Of course, I will have to take you in to extract the images from your mind. It is a painless process, so don't worry. All that is needed is for our surgeons to apply a special beam of light to the eye, and it will reflect back the images from your mind."

"Then take the eye and leave me alone."

Yaz flashed an unnaturally patient smile. "The eye must be in your head during the process. How else would we extract the images from your mind? The whole mechanism is integrated into your brain, you see."

Dannac stuffed the sphere into his pocket.

"Now, another thing I'll need from you, and this is all in good faith, remember, is your Valoii friend. When we escape from here, it will be under somewhat vague pretences, all right? I don't care what it is. Say you paid me for transport, whatever. After she is comfortable, we'll drug her, and before you know it we'll be in the Republic drinking to another victory over Mizkov."

Capra. Assuming she survived whatever it was she planned to do, could he really turn her in?

Did he really think he had a choice?

"In case you forgot, dear friend, you have no choice."

"I could kill you."

"That would be dishonourable."

"It would. But that does not mean I cannot do it."

"But you won't, because you know that there are a thousand agents just like me, and we are a petty bureaucracy. We hold grudges, Dannac. Big grudges. The next agent might destroy your remaining family, or the entire village you came from. They are quite creative."

Dannac had done worse, and more than once. One sure thing—he was no good to anyone dead.

"You are sure your government needs a Valoii soldier to interrogate?"

"Oh yes. They usually die long before we get close enough to capture."

He sighed and checked his cannon. "Let me find her."

"Work, Capra. That's all you have to do, work hard."

It didn't make sense. None of it did—not Vasi's strange instructions, and not the way it seemed as though every moment until now had been a dream. The sensations were colours nobody had ever glimpsed, a kind of sight nobody had ever possessed, a silent voice demanding of her things about which she knew nothing.

The world around her faded and flattened against itself, a false backdrop. Now when she gazed around the darkness, the shadows and the giants both shone like fiery beacons. There were six giants left, and they all were stomping towards the war machine.

She began to understand that this distant power pressing through her was what Vasi needed, and that she could pull more through if she concentrated, like opening a tap.

"How much of this do you need?"

Vasi gazed into the distance with flaming orange eyes. "As much as you can pull from the structure."

"And what's this going to do for us?"

"Give us the ability to fight them in the only way possible."

All of this effort, this strange concentration, this half-existence in some negative realm, and Vasi wasn't even preparing a final blast of holy fire that would solve everything in a flash?

A breath later, there was a flash, but not of holy cleansing fire. It was a flash of stopped time, a moment captured, a thought suspended.

Capra could no longer make out the giants or the shadows. The world around them was buttressed by a frame of blue streaks. She reeled in a thrall. Any word, idea, or symbol she tried to think of to integrate the experience fell through the metal grating that was her awareness, like trying to scoop water with a fork.

And in another flash, Vasi sent a tendril of blue cord shooting from her forehead. There was no time to even question it before the cord pierced Capra between her eyes. She reeled, stumbled, clutched her head as if a spike of *something* buried itself deep inside. Her skin crawled and tightened and her body cried out in a flurry of aches, but she stayed frozen in place. She had to trust Vasi, or there wasn't any point in trying to fight these primordial forces.

A burning raced through her body. Vasi had disappeared, and when Capra's mind began to clear, she realized that she was no longer Capra. Her body was strange. A tail flicked behind her, and the contracting muscles rippled up her back.

As soon as it had happened, Capra once again found herself kneeling amid smoking rubble and calamitous cannon fire.

She saw the shadows as orange flame, the same as what the giants had become in her mind's eye. Now there hung in her mind a kind of kinship, an understanding with them. She felt the power of the giants, their ravaging urges, their dislike of calm rationality, and the shadow men's calculating individualism and desire for their own way. A kind of strength flowed through her, and an impulse to destroy the giants along with their sworn enemy.

It was a bloodlust.

She began to search for Vasi, until a voice inside answered her.

I am right here, inside you. Kill them while you can! We can only hold this form for so long...

This form? She looked at her hands. The veins throbbed and her fingers seemed longer than usual, and the skin darker.

The part of her that had resisted the transformation became horrified at being combined with another person in this one strange body, but exerted no influence.

Everything is as it should be. This is not the same as before... we will only kill the shadows... only the shadows...

It was time to get back to work, and so she dashed through the ruins, towards the war machine. The speed, the power, so new, almost intoxicating. An equal footing with these monsters from primordial times.

An instinct drove her to leap into the air, and she unfurled a set of wings, began to beat them as though she had always known them. The feeling of hot wind rushing at her face, the thrill of gliding across the city... and a deep burning, almost painful. A death drive.

She twisted and twirled, laughed with a strange glee. Any anxiety about the world had been destroyed; she was no longer capable of it. She descended on the machine—her only desire, her only goal.

The machine twitched as soon as she landed on one of its arms. The panels became a fountain of orange—the new, true appearance of the shadows, and they slithered out from the metal to block her. She grabbed the first one and bit into its neck. It shrieked and fell into a heap, dripping down the war engine's arm. Evidently, this form was capable of physically interacting with the shadows.

And it worked both ways. One shadow wrapped its limbs around her back. She clawed and bit at the strange substance. Three more joined in and began to snap and flail their limbs like whips, and each lash bit into her new body—*their* new body—with the bite of a flaming razor.

"What are you?" asked one of the shadow men. "This is not right."

She kicked out at the one, knocked it over the edge, but another moved into his place. "It reeks of humanity, but it fights. It sees and touches us..."

Another slash across her chest, ripping what remained of her leather. She wanted to talk with the creatures, yet a strange urge choked her. It was Vasi.

There is no reasoning with them.

Kill them.

Kill them all.

One of the shadow men turned its limb into a spear and lunged at her. She tossed the shadow from her back, but cannon fire shook the machine, and she stumbled. The spear pierced her shoulder. It drew no blood, and she felt a foreign, shocking sensation. It was not rending muscle and breaking bone, but a deeper hurt, as though they had stabbed into the centre of her mind.

She snapped the shadow man's limb over her knee, then tackled him. During the struggle, the machine's arm swivelled again, causing her to slide towards the elbow joint. With the shadow under her, she slammed against the machine's upper arm. She bit into the thing's neck. Despite that the act horrified her, she let the shadow's substance flow into her mouth and into her, and in seconds it ceased its shrieking.

Standing on the machine's shoulders was a familiar figure. Rovan. All around him shadows skulked and darted, and his eyes glowed as if the departed Blightcross sun had taken refuge inside the boy's head.

Now she spoke: "Rovan? It's me."

"Another of Sevari's tricks?"

He won't recognize us, Vasi. He is too far gone...

"Rovan, please. We want to help you."

"I have all the help I need." Rovan then gave a rude gesture and stepped behind his cohorts.

She tensed her long, clawed fingers and leaped into the air, wings unfurled. The district was a giant oven filled with plenty of currents, and she soared towards the machine's head. Whether Vasi approved or not, her new instinct urged her to attack Rovan.

She met two shadows in mid-air, and ravaged both in quick succession. Once she landed on the shoulder, Rovan stared back at her from the opposite end. She ignored the lingering pain from her wound and loped across the machine's back. A shadow tried to spear her with a sharp limb, but she caught it, stared into its nonexistent face. Her mouth watered, and she shivered from a thrill that horrified and excited her.

After drinking this one, Capra's appetite deepened, and only Rovan would satisfy it. After that, she would feed on the giants, which now surrounded the war machine. Their flames licked the machine, though the only thing that seemed vulnerable to their attacks were the shadows hiding within the thing's panels.

One of the fire giants must have understood this: it held back its fire and instead rushed the machine head-on, tough head-armour bristling with spines. Its collision sent the machine reeling. The shock made her lose her footing, and her clawed feet screeched against iron as she tried to keep from falling. But she couldn't stop, and sailed over the edge to the ground. Two shadow men took the opportunity to pounce while she was dazed and falling.

But her wings launched her up again, high above the city. She dove straight for Rovan. The shadows pursuing her no longer mattered—already her appetite was bored with the commonplace, and Rovan was something new.

The machine shook and bucked, both from the giants' attacks and its constant cannon fire. Capra left her wings unfurled, and bared the teeth she now understood to be far longer than usual.

Rovan glanced behind him, then widened his stance, as if finally accepting that he could not escape. "Some kind of animal? A freak?"

"We are neither. Please, I don't know if I can stop this... you have to surrender."

Capra sensed Vasi's unwillingness to let Rovan die.

But she had said to kill them all.

She didn't wait for Rovan to babble, and leaped at him. The boy would fall easily—

Except that he caught her in mid-air with a single hand, and grinned maniacally as he slammed her into the machine's head. She snapped at him with her teeth, but he dodged and forced her as though she were a sack of flour.

"The shadows tell me you are all of us combined. That explains how weak you really are. You have the fire giants' weakness. We are perfection." Rovan smashed her with several punches. The boy's blows pounded twice as much rending pain through her as the shadows had, and she scared herself with otherworldly outcries of pain—a shriek not unlike the shadows' own death screams.

Three shadow men joined in and flayed her with their almost liquid limbs. Before long, she realized the futility of struggling. Instead, she reached around the machine's head, blindly as she had before, to search for some control to upset.

You cannot kill him, Capra.

I must.

There has to be another way.

There is no time.

It was easy for Vasi to protest—she didn't seem to possess the physical connection to the body that included feeling its strange version of pain.

Rovan ceased his attack. "Just like last time, only now the world will see how weak you really are. Akhli was a trickster, a fool, and it was only dumb luck that made him succeed. He was not the apex of life."

A strange change in vocal tone and vocabulary—it must be the shadows speaking.

With her claws she tore open the head panels and plunged her claws inside. The machine jolted again, and Rovan's grip loosened.

A grating sound rose above the din of engines and fighting. Gears grinding, a chain reaction of fouling. She hoped.

Rovan pulled back his hand dramatically. Capra fought against the things holding her, while still clawing at the metal innards at her back. Even in this strange, winged form, Capra couldn't avoid Rovan's savage attack—he nailed his fist into her with such force that his hand lodged inside her chest.

The un-assimilated aspect in her mind was horrified. As his hand pulled at her very being with a surgeon's precision, she saw no blood. But her movements and fighting slowed, and her once-hard limbs softened and dangled in her captors' hands, and more inhuman screeches came from within and horrified her.

All she could do was allow Vasi to come through and try reasoning with the boy. "Rovan, it's me—your sister."

"Lies. My sister must be dead, and all thanks to you and everyone else who can't accept my rule."

"She is not dead, she is here, inside this being! You have to listen to me. Stop this."

Rovan pulled out his hand, and Capra cried out against the savage pain. Her strength poured from the wound in the colour of the Sparkling Sea, staining her leather blue and leaving bright tracks down her leg.

There was a clunk behind her, and the metal under their feet jolted and groaned. Engines bellowed, and everyone standing on the thing's shoulders slipped and stumbled. With little strength left, Capra knew she was headed for a fall. On her way towards the edge of the machine's back, she grabbed Rovan's leg.

As they fell together, she twisted to dominate him. Shadows darted around but kept clear of them, likely after having realized that Capra could destroy them.

A heartbeat later, they hit the ground.

CHAPTER TWENTY

When Capra opened her eyes, her mind overflowed with images from her time unconscious—how long had it been? The air still thrummed with clattering metal and inhuman screams.

The images—pits in the ground, a violent clash underground, smoke and steam, blue sky above.

Winged people, catastrophic thunderstorms shaking the earth.

"It's awake."

Capra slammed back into the world of ruin and blackness. People gathered around her—Ehzeri, Naartlanders, even a few men sporting the silly flat-top hairstyle of Tamarck. Something told her they were not exactly normal. It could have been their bulging, unblinking eyes. Or it could have been a kind of filth that went beyond the unavoidable grit in Blightcross.

They were hunched like animals and they moved with abruptness and caution.

"What is it?" asked one of them.

"It's human."

"No, it isn't."

Someone prodded her with a stick. She gnashed her teeth and brought herself to her knees, slipping on the pile of rocks. Now the memories became clearer, and she realized that yes, she was an archon at the moment, along with Vasi buried somewhere within the strange form.

"Is it one of us?"

A wizened woman clambered onto the pile, stared Capra straight in the eye. "It is not. But they want us to recuperate it. It must be changed or killed. It is dangerous."

These people acted much different to those who were taken by the shadows. They appeared fearful and base, while the shadows' corruption was more depraved and sophisticated. The shadow-infested people worked for a kind of gratification, while these people, the disciples of the fire giants, almost seemed subservient to some unseen power.

The old woman reached into her rags and brought out a glass jar. It held a thick, clear liquid. "Drink it, demon!"

Capra shook her head.

"The venom of our masters is an elixir. It will heal you."

She reached out to accept it, but a spike of instinct paralysed her arm. "It will kill me."

With that, the woman splashed the liquid at her. It burned across Capra's chest, made a white steam that reeked of sulphur. She hissed at the dumbstruck crowd and clawed at them.

Leave them, they cannot harm us. We must find Rovan.

Rovan, of course. She leaped into the air, still reeling from the burn and the great fall, and she could not reconcile her not-quite flesh body with the fact that it still was material, substantial, and subject to injury.

Once in the air, she saw Rovan gliding above the sand, a shadow at either side holding him. They flew towards the desert beyond the refinery. The war machine was retreating away from the city.

The giants lumbered on in pursuit. Behind Capra, at the heart of the city where they once concentrated like schools of fish, there were no shadows. They must be following the war machine. At the very least, the town might be spared more damage. The machine fired incessantly from every flame gun and cannon still working. Sparks gushed from its arm joints when they moved, and many of its engines coughed as it tried to correct its aim.

If the machine is destroyed, Rovan will have no more shadows to surround him.

Capra knew what Vasi was thinking, and she hoped it was true. She also hoped that at the end of this, she would not be left with any of these killing instincts. This archon she had become was capable of being controlled, but she couldn't bear to think of what carnage would come if this force were set free without a mind to tame it.

And what about the giants? Was she in any position to fight them, assuming she could destroy the shadows and their machine?

It could have been her reservations about ripping Rovan's heart from his chest, but she now decided that with all of the shadows concentrated in the machine, she'd best leave the boy for now and attack it.

She dived at the war engine. Its panels may be resistant to attack, but up close, rivets could be broken and screws undone. She had already come close to disabling it twice.

This would be the last time.

Cripple the thing once and for all. Set off what remained of its ammunition. The ensuing explosion would destroy the shadow men.

A voice sounded near her head. Next to her, in mid air, was a man in black. A shadow in human form.

"You are a catastrophe, Capra. Look at you. A contradiction."

"That is how you see it. You are out of date, Sir. Obsolete."

"Opposites cannot reconcile."

"They are the same thing, shadow."

"Join us."

"I already have, in the most profound way possible."

She did not recognize the words or thoughts as her own. Only Vasi could dialogue with a ghost.

She folded back her wings and slashed a streak across the sky on her dive towards her target. Wind and strange joy, this freedom coupled with a drive she couldn't escape.

There it was, so close, and there, at its midsection—a scorched patch of armour. All she needed to do was reach in and pull out some cog or wheel or cable.

The flame gun spat just as she came in to land. The fire caught her right side, and her wing became a torch. She spiralled downward. The pain reminded her of the phosphorus burn she had suffered, only this time, it might kill her.

She slammed into the sand at the thing's feet. Numbness overcame her body—*their* body.

The deep drive to destroy both sides continued to gnaw at her, to nag and push, but could she continue?

Cold metal touched her leg. A section of buried pipeline, and it ran for who knows how far. If the shadows' war engine fired and missed the giants it aimed to kill, and it likely would, the whole city might explode when the attacks ignited the pipeline.

She rolled off her charred wing and staggered upright. A giant iron leg was right next to her, and she dug her claws into it and began to climb, panting and wincing through a tide of pain.

It was a paradox. A supernatural body that was also flesh and vulnerable. A desire to destroy divorced of any meaning. Vasi was right—this creature they had become was a synthesis of the two forces. A reconciliation.

Like she had scaled the clock tower, she scaled the armoured beast, only this time with raw power and claws rather than finesse. Every reach with her right arm became a symphony of hurt. Her hands vibrated, left a trail of blue blood behind. A few more pulls and she would be able to crawl along its hip joint.

A shadow seeped out of the metal. She grabbed it with her free hand and tore into its neck with her mouth, drank its dark substance.

And when she arrived at the hip area, she went straight to the broken section. Her hand darted to the cavity, but just before it touched the mechanisms within, a film of the shadow men's orange form blocked her. She clawed at the cavity frantically with the same result—the shadow men had reinforced the armour with the very stuff of their existence.

Faced with such an impasse, and her own depleted energy, she was at a loss. She shrieked in frustration—an act that felt strange and foreign.

She attacked the metal with her teeth. The gnashing and snapping pierced the membrane of shadow, and there was a deep groan from within the contraption. Sharp metal raked her face as she went further, tearing the remaining armour with her claws and continuing to rip at the machine's entrails with her teeth.

In answer, it began to shake and whine. Her claws pierced it enough for her to hang on. More sparks rained down from the arms, which now dropped and twitched. Torn hoses threw oil and fuel into her face, and broken pipes shot scalding steam.

She was almost too distracted to notice the giants encircling the machine. One enemy at a time, and this one was still standing. Where was its gunpowder and flame essence?

It veered awkwardly, sending Capra's legs swinging as she tore into it. Sparks and iron grindings showered her.

Then its torso shuddered with volleys of cannon fire. The shots exploded into the sand and enveloped the area in a dust storm. It fired salvo after salvo into the desert, and its aim seemed completely random now.

The gash in the metal beast was such that she could kick into it, and she used the last of her strength to bust rods and linkages. Each blow jarred her with the shock of kicking a stone wall. An explosion sounded in the distance—secondary to the cannon shots themselves. An oil well?

And the guns fell silent. The engines idled, creaks and screaming metal dwindled to squeaking.

But there was still a profound shaking. The thing swayed and stumbled. Below, the sand began to shift into a stone-dry whirlpool. The sound of a river cutting through a valley. A sense of something very wrong—

or is this right?

—and she leaped off the machine, despite that she could barely fly with a half-scorched wing. She sailed for a few seconds, skimmed over the writhing ground, and could not help skidding across the sand when her momentum died.

In the distance, the ground coughed gasps of black smoke. The burning oil wells, ignited by the machine's haphazard cannon fire, seemed to belch in concert with the spasms Capra felt underneath her.

The sand flowed against her, towards where the sinking had begun at the feet of the war engine. She pawed at the mountain of sand pushing her back the way she had come.

Her wings beat madly, but the rush knocked her over before she could fly. The wave carried her into the widening hole.

The damned cannons and well explosions must have caused earthquakes.

And the entire desert seemed littered with sinkholes.

Pipelines buckled, and the black blood of Blightcross spurted into the air, until the sand devoured and silenced the geysers.

Capra clenched her jaw and jammed shut her eyes against the onslaught. It was only an attempt to make her end more comfortable. Even Vasi's conscience did not try to convince her that survival was likely.

There was plenty of company—this hole was the size of a small village, and swallowed equipment, roughneck camps, and of course, the shadows and their commandeered war machine. At least she had succeeded in that...

There was a drop. No longer did she roll and suffocate. Below was pure black, and the world was collapsing into this abyss. She twisted and flailed, her thoughts bouncing between joy and utter horror. The size of the hole struck her like a mace to the head—she couldn't comprehend the blackness swallowing the desert, as though the world were imploding into the infinity of the night sky.

She was resigned. That is, until the war machine fell past her, flailing and chugging as though it might affect its own fate. Rovan still hung on, and for the first time, Capra knew that he was genuinely scared.

You have to!

She came out of her daze and spread her wings. At first, she careened to the left, but remembered to compensate for the damaged right wing. She scooped Rovan from the falling machine and pulled into a nearly vertical climb, face broad against the moonlight. During her ascent, she passed two fire giants falling to their inevitable deaths in the pit. The earth's rumbling still echoed in the great hole.

Once she passed through the opening, back into the smoky desert air, she beat her wings in a frenzy. The screams of giants permeated the skies, chilling cries that pierced through Capra's exhaustion and pain, made her shudder with revulsion.

Already, the form made of both herself and Vasi began to disintegrate—Capra felt a strange rending sensation, as though from a torture apparatus. In her wings, back, legs, it was too much to continue. She tumbled to the ground, Rovan still in her arms.

Just before they hit the dust-lined street on the outskirts of the city, Capra fell into her own black abyss.

It couldn't be, yet Dannac knew that the two women bleeding on deserted paving stones were his companions. He relaxed his grip on the cannon, bent to check Capra's injuries. Whatever she had done, it had worked: he had watched with his own enhanced eye the explosions in the well, the sinkhole that swallowed both the shadow men and their war engine and the remaining fire giants.

What had she done? What had the strange, silvery light been that he had glimpsed shooting from the hole?

He listened for her breath, felt her pulse. Both were strong. He checked Vasi, and she was also alive.

Now it hit him why exactly he had come to find them.

There was no escaping Yaz or his successors. He should have let himself die on the battlefield, never have gotten involved with the Republic's spies. Sure, they helped his people when convenient, but it was all manipulation.

And now, he had no choice.

CHAPTER TWENTY ONE

There were two colours: the blue of sky unstained by industry or the smoky breath of war, and the reddish-brown of the land. When Capra looked at her hand, it appeared drained of any colour, as though she were an apparition. The tents stood as still as boulders, despite the wind that tossed dirt into Capra's face and whipped around her hair.

"Hello?" There had to be an Ehzeri around. "Hello? Anyone?"

Only when nobody answered did she realize that the wind lashing her made no sound either. As she walked, the experience became a series of disjointed flashes, like the sparks of visibility in a thunderstorm.

In the next instant, she clutched a crossbow. In the other hand sat the deceptive weight of a phosphorus grenade.

She wandered among the empty tents. Inside one she found a charred corpse. In the next, a steaming bowl of rice, and vacant place-settings on the rug. And in another, she saw herself.

A version of herself in twin braids and a cropped cotton top. Around her navel were traditional Ehzeri tattoos. On her neck was... nothing. No military brand.

Capra stared at this version of herself, watched her write on a scroll. She crept closer, the other continuing to write away without a single break in her motions. Her scratching made no sound. Only Capra's own heart drummed, the rest of the world going on in this dead silence.

She wanted to touch her double's face. She dropped to her knees in front of the girl. Still, no sound, no indication of noticing Capra's presence.

A wave of grief overcame her, and she tried to blink away the stinging in her eyes. She wept, and the phosphorus grenade flipped from her hand, rolled on the carpet as silently as a Valoii assassin's knife drawn across an Ehzeri militant's throat.

The grenade's detonation made no sound, either.

A muffled voice demanded something, but she couldn't make out what. She winced and hauled herself upright. The sky was red, and the air slightly cooler. There was an eerie quiet about the city.

A black form darkened the sky in front of her. Her eyes focused and she saw that it was one of Sevari's men, fitted with a strange mask and outfit.

"I said, are you capable of walking, Valoii?"

She took his extended hand and stood. "What... happened?"

"Temblors. All across the oilfields. They've been known to be unstable, and it seems they cracked at just the right time. Saved the city, they did."

She vaguely remembered tearing out the war machine's guts of metal cable and cogs, and the ensuing explosions. "But how... how did I do it?"

The soldier ignored her strange question and led her into the street. There were groups of bruised and burned people huddling around carriages. People sprinted across the square to meet the open arms of friends once thought to be among the dead.

Something didn't make sense.

A bulge in her tattered leather. She reached into the pocket and grasped a hard object. She nearly dropped it when she realized that the object was Dannac's eye.

A heaviness pounded her chest, and she ran away from the soldier, screaming Dannac's name. She screamed at every group of the reunited, and the only responses were the kind of tolerant stares meant for raving trauma victims.

But it was no use. Dannac had left. That was why she now held his eye in her palm. It was clear to her why he had planted his eye on her person and left. She was his insurance—the keeper of the images his Republic allies wanted.

So he had chosen to run, rather than hand it over. Why did he care? Ruining an ally of Tamarck and Mizkov was his reason for living, yet he had withheld the eye from them. It made no sense.

There was no use in trying to understand. Clearly she didn't know Dannac as well as she had assumed. There would be time to sort it out, after the aches healed and things made sense again.

She hopped into one of the Corps wagons, despite that only days earlier, these same soldiers were under orders to kill her. It didn't matter now. Sevari could jail her forever, for all she cared at the moment. One of the haggard citizens passed around a gunnysack of rations, but Capra waved them away. Fatigued, yes, but without any appetite whatsoever.

Even the rumbling of this wagon's engine stirred blurry impressions of the war machine. The strange existence as an angel made flesh. Vasi.

She, or they, or *it*, had slammed into the ground. That much she remembered.

It wasn't enough. A missing piece gnawed at her. Where was Vasi?

Just thinking of Vasi kicked her into a hazy recollection.

The shock of splitting into her own body. Vasi lying in the street. Rovan on the ground, chest rising and falling, eyes glaring with the collective madness of the defeated shadows.

They couldn't still think they had a chance, could they? There he had been, gleaming with a maniacal grin, reaching towards Capra with his bloodied hand.

She had barely been able to stand. She crawled over to him, clutched his bloody head in her arms.

It was automatic. The pressure across his throat, the locking position of her arms—the economy of death as outlined by Valoii training doctrine. The shadows would only return if she let this last one remain in their world.

"Vasi, I'm sorry." She used the last of her strength to clench harder, to hopefully put him out of his misery quickly.

And that was all she could remember.

"They say that almost half of the population followed those damned things into the hole," one of the passengers said.

"Did you see the silver light pass out of the hole?" asked another.

Thus began a round of speculation. Capra wasn't interested. It could have been her, it could have been an exploding machine component.

She knew she was no angel, and nothing could convince her otherwise. Not even if God himself fitted her with the commonplace golden pike and wings of the archons.

The wagon passed a tent painted with a rudimentary blue emblem displayed by surgeons. There were mostly Ehzeri standing around it. The wagon stopped for a few passengers who wanted medical attention.

Just below the wagon, a young woman bent over a boy. His face was bruised and black, and—

Rovan.

The girl looked up at the morning sun with glistening eyes and a look of abject guilt. Vasi.

A surgeon, or at least a young man who acted like one, came to Rovan's side. Capra wanted to jump off the wagon and explain or apologize or console—anything—but she did not.

"He won't wake," Vasi told the surgeon.

Oh, Vasi, he's dead.

The surgeon performed a quick examination. Why would he bother?

"I'm sorry. All of his functions seem to be intact, but he must have suffered a profound damage to his mind."

Alive? She hadn't even killed him properly?

The surgeon stood, and scanned the crowd. "I am afraid he may not recover. If you mean to keep him alive, he will need constant treatment." He appeared to be hiding a scowl, likely at the prospect of an Ehzeri having to deal with the financial burden of such a patient. He shuffled to the next casualty, went on as though the previous one had never existed.

Maybe she would see Vasi again in the future, but for now she couldn't face her. There were questions that she wasn't sure she wanted answered.

Questions such as how Capra could enter a *vihs* working complex enough to bind two people into a single form with no experience or hereditary ability, or what Vasi's wild claims had really meant.

Ultimately, she decided that she didn't care. It was over, and she still had to figure out a way to stem the flow of Valoii soldiers sent to kill her. The gods had interfered in her life, the very ones she didn't care to acknowledge, and as far as she was concerned, they could damned well keep trying, for all the difference they had made.

Just as she'd finished the thought, she startled at the sight of the unmistakable tattoo of a Valoii soldier. The man's naked upper body was a canvas of inflamed skin, scored and burned, on which the Valoii characters remained undamaged, almost defiant. Supine, lifeless, eyes replaced with sheer blackness...

Alim?

She stood and peered round the others packed against her. "Alim!" she called. By the time she thought to hop out, a group of nearby city workers had already loaded Alim and other corpses into a vehicle.

He wanted to kill you. Don't forget that. And he sure wouldn't be feeling sad about leaving your body behind if he had to, so stop thinking you're a monster for letting him be taken away to some industrial crematorium.

The wagon let her off near Orvis Dunes, and she walked the deserted street that had seemed like such an oasis in this industrial hell only days before. A few of the interesting shops and apartments had caved in, but there still stood Helverliss' bookshop. The block of buildings sat in its grimy, half-restored colonial glory as though its historical nature had shielded it from this momentary diversion of insanity.

It amazed her to smell fresh brewing shalep, and she moved her tired legs faster. The closer she came to the café, the more she heard strange sounds: baritone thumping, a strange keening, and chords of some radical harmony.

She entered the café to find it brimming with the same people she had met here before, and there was a combo playing on the little stage. The bass player smoked a cheroot as he played, and the violinist still bled from a gash on his head. The harmony they played had no pleasing centre of tonality, yet it seemed fitting.

The man at the counter didn't ask for money when she approached the counter and waved randomly at the chalkboard. He just gave her a mug and a pastry, and she sat among the other residents of Orvis Dunes, listening to the strange music, while the city around them smoldered.

All of the patrons, including Capra, gazed at the entrance each time someone new straggled in. But this time, she nearly spat out her drink.

Limping along, smoking a cheroot, was Helverliss. At his side, Irea braced him. He nodded and collapsed into a seat across from Capra, while Irea went to the counter.

"How the hell..."

He showed a sliver of a grin. "I wasn't going to just sit and wait for you."

"I'm sorry. Things happened and I wasn't able to retrieve you."

"Don't worry about it. As luck would have it, Irea had escaped and found me. But by the time we made it out of the tower, nobody really cared about us prisoners."

She leaned back and rested her boot on the table. Something in her wanted to kill him for creating the painting. Maybe the thought was a remnant of the archon creature, or just a bad mood. Nevertheless, she flashed him a smile and told him how they had defeated the chaos. He slammed his fist into the table when she reached the part about the archon. "Of course. How could I be so stupid? An archon is... well, the missing piece. The ring that completes the knot. The aberrations that arise when one is taken out are..."

"Quite fatal, I imagine."

"Which is why your friend was not at heart a real archon. Why she was flawed, why she was only suited to destroy... the Ehzeri didn't know how to properly construct these things."

She shrugged.

"Humanity was never a mediator. The human subject is what happens when the knot is complete. Imbalances cause delusions and chaos..." And despite the bloody wounds, his livid complexion, and his frail voice, he seemed full of life again. "This will give me much to think about."

She stole one of his cheroots. It had been a while since she'd last tried smoking. "All I care about is that I survived being turned into an archon."

"About that."

"Hm?"

"Well, I had already begun to work on a theory relating to psychoanalysis. One involving *vihs* in people such as yourself. Since you claim to not be an Ehzeri, there might be some other explanation for your ability to use the power in concert with Vasi."

She let her foot drop from the table and leaned in close.

"The traumatic event you witnessed at a very young age caused you to empathize with the Ehzeri in a profound, subconscious way."

"What?"

He turned away to cough. The man should be in a surgery, not a café. "Vasi was mistaken. I am sure that with further investigation, I would find that you were not actually Ehzeri, but that your subconscious was able to access their characteristics as a result of the extreme fear you felt. A child's mind cannot comprehend brutality, and so your ability may be an infantile complex meant to deal with how you witnessed someone murdering those people. I did not glean the details of the memory from the painting, but..."

"I'd rather not know right now."

"But this could be a groundbreaking case study. Do you want to live on believing in some far-fetched tale of misplaced heritage?"

She exhaled through her nose, the smoke tingling and jabbing her senses awake. "I'm more concerned with my payment."

For a long time he said nothing and stared at her. Probably trying to work his strange theories around her. But what if he were right?

Did it even matter? It was something she would have to figure out later. There were far too many thoughts in her mind whose voices eclipsed any curiosity about why she had been able to do the impossible.

At last, Helverliss sighed and squished his cheroot into the ashtray. "You didn't exactly return my painting."

She gave him a cold stare. "I think I did far better than that, Noro. That painting was a mistake."

"What of your friend?"

"Dannac's gone. Personal issues."

For a long time he said nothing. He stood with his hands in his pockets, which, Capra noticed, were empty.

"Noro?"

Helverliss met her eyes. "They looted my shop. I had thought my savings to be safe, but clearly the shadows gave the mob some way to... I don't know. Perhaps they read my mind."

Capra's throat tightened. She leaned forward, rested her forehead on her hands. The hair draping across her face reeked of sulphur, oil, and blood. "Of course," she mumbled through her hands. "Noro?"

"Ehm. What?"

"I hope you die in a fire or something before I'm rested enough to kill you myself."

"I'm fairly weak. You probably still could."

"I'm pretending that I couldn't for your own good."

"Ah. Denial. Probably the most useful coping mechanism we have. 'I know very well, but nevertheless...'"

Capra paused, swept the hair out of her eyes, took a deep breath. "Maybe I'll stay here for a while, see what kind of work I can get. Everyone's probably broke on the continent anyway, right?"

Helverliss clapped and cheered. "That's my girl! Well, as long as you're staying... I wonder if you could make me a small loan?"

THE END

AUTHOR BIOGRAPHY

C. A. Lang is a product of Nelson, British Columbia, and it shows. While meandering through the natural health industry in everything from editing to personal training to sales, he frittered away nearly a decade writing widely, all the while nurturing an unhealthy affair with no less than six guitars. Growing up around Victorian architecture likely had something to do with his appreciation of steampunk, although we're not quite sure why he felt the need to ditch the steam engines and go all internal-combustion on the genre. He has settled in Kelowna, B.C., where sometimes he can be found abusing a gigantic jazz guitar in public, hanging around certain wineries, and running obscene distances just to atone for it all.

CPSIA information can be obtained at www.ICGtesting.com
Printed in the USA
LVOW110058130612

285811LV00001B/8/P

9 780987 82482